Excessive Entanglement

Excessive Entanglement

First Edition

Copyright © 2012 Nick d'Arbeloff

ISBN: 1-4793-5225-X
ISBN-13: 9781479352258

Excessive Entanglement

Nick d'Arbeloff

In its 1971 ruling on Lemon v. Kurtzman, the Supreme Court outlined a three-part test for determining if a government action violates the First Amendment's separation of church and state: The court ruled that, first, the government action must have a secular purpose; second, its primary purpose must not be to inhibit or to advance religion; and third, the action must not precipitate "excessive entanglement" between government and religion. This decision, known as the Lemon test, is now the standard by which government actions are judged for First Amendment compliance.

I.

Devlin McGregor stared at the screen in front of him. He had been contemplating the numbers and readings for what seemed like an eternity—or two. Yet still his brain was rejecting the obvious conclusion. He was scared—of being wrong or of being right, he wasn't entirely sure.

He got up, stretched, and walked to the coffeepot. He chose the cleanest of four unwashed mugs, poured a half-cup of burnt coffee, took a sip, and returned to his desk. And stared again.

Something must be improperly calibrated.

Once again, for what must have been the tenth time, Devlin looked at the instruments and ran through their configuration, checking off each setting like a pilot before a flight. Nothing amiss. To the best of his knowledge, everything as it should be.

The data must be correct.

2.

The early morning sun penetrated the trees in Providence Park, giving the yellows and reds of the changing leaves a glowing luminescence.

Suzanne took a deep breath, inhaling autumn as she gently pushed the baby carriage along the path.

This was her favorite part of the day. There was enjoyment in the frenetic, unpredictable, high-speed blur that was her workday, but she cherished this little 15-minute sliver of relaxation and contemplation.

A jogger passed, nodding in silent greeting; two squirrels screeched at one another in a nearby tree. The sound of falling acorns had been a relative constant for the past couple of weeks.

Her baby stirred, spasmodically shaking his tiny fists before settling back down into quiet slumber. She reached down and gently repositioned the blanket around his shoulders. She stared into her son's peaceful face; the love she felt for him was overwhelming. She wished that she could just stop time, suspending the rush of civilization so that she could immerse herself in nothing but his life, his needs, and his rapidly growing awareness of his surroundings.

But that was not an option. She looked at her watch: time to head back. She gently tilted the carriage, pivoted counterclockwise, and headed left down a path towards her home. By this time, the baby's nanny would have already arrived, and would be preparing bottles for the day ahead.

She came to the edge of the park, exited and came to a stop at the crosswalk. The sight and sounds of morning traffic caused her blood pressure to begin its slow steady rise from a state of relaxation to what would be the day's first peak of tension as she read emails before departing for work. She was adept at controlling the pressure, and better than most at maintaining outward calm—she had to be, but serving within the administration made it nearly impossible to claim any semblance of true inner tranquility.

The light changed and she crossed, then took a side street which led to another where she lived. She passed a parked car in which two men sat; the driver reading a newspaper, the other a book.

She closed her eyes for a moment, absorbing the sun's first warming rays into her Fairfax, Virginia neighborhood. A dappled pattern of elongated tree shadows played on the townhouses to her left as she walked.

At last coming to her own street off to the right, she smoothly lowered the front wheels of the carriage from the sidewalk to the pavement, then the rear, and proceeded across.

As always, as Suzanne approached her house, her brain began to churn with ruminations of the tasks and projects that would demand her attention over the course of the day. She hadn't noticed that the car with the two men had pulled silently out into the street behind her, until the hybrid engine switched from electricity to fuel and accelerated. Her thoughts of work vanished in an instant, replaced at first by a burst of confusion; *what is this idiot doing?*

But within a fraction of a second, thought itself was supplanted by raw adrenaline and instinctual self-preservation. As she broke into a run, the car bore down on her with unmistakable intent.

For the last half second, time stood still. Her fate seemingly inescapable, her brain formed a dense stream of emotions and thoughts: mourning the loss of motherhood, the sacrifice of career, never seeing her son walk or grow into a young man, the little boy's irresponsible father taking custody. All of this congested as one overflowing mass within her consciousness until, at the last possible moment, Suzanne refocused her energies and lunged forward. Simultaneously, the car strangely swerved left, the passenger-side mirror missing her right hip by no more than an inch or two.

She pulled up, heart racing, confused but overwhelmed by the realization that both she and her little boy were alive and safe. She turned to see the car that had come so close to ending her life, but saw only a taillight disappear as it turned left and out of sight.

She looked down on her son, who was—incredibly—still sleeping. Suzanne reached a hand into the carriage to adjust his blanket, but pulled it back, suddenly feeling a sharp pain in her side like the sting of a wasp. She looked down and spastically brushed the insect away. Another sharp pain erupted in her chest as she noticed that on the street by her feet was not an insect at all but some kind of tiny dart.

As her vision started to blur and her brain and muscles relinquished control of her body, she released her grasp on the stroller and fell helplessly to the pavement.

The carriage started to roll forward, very slowly at first, then gathered momentum as it accelerated down the street. Suzanne tried to reach out, but could not; as she fought desperately to keep her eyes open and trained on the speeding stroller, she felt the last of her body's energy fade away. The carriage slammed into the side of a parked truck, its rear wheels lifting a foot off the ground upon impact. The baby was thrown forward, but the buckled safety straps held firm; his forward motion was arrested, and he was thrown back down, deeper into the carriage. No sound emanated from the half-enclosed cocoon for one or two seconds, but then erupted in force.

The now sunlit neighborhood woke to the sound of a baby screaming with fear, panic, and confused rage, while its mother lay in a twisted heap nearby.

Suzanne Ortega, Deputy Director of White House Communications, was dead.

3.

Devlin McGregor walked down the polished hallway toward the frosted glass doors of the facility's executive conference room. He was accompanied by his boss, a jolly, heavyset NASA veteran named Pete Michaels.

Devlin had worked for Pete for a little more than eleven years, or roughly half his career at NASA. Pete had been a great boss. He'd supported Devlin from the start, steering him onto projects where Devlin's natural abilities could flourish.

Up ahead, Devlin watched as two suited members of NASA's top echelon opened the doors and entered. He was nervous. Pete knew it.

"Keep in mind, Devlin: these people are no smarter than you, but they do know the game. When they challenge your assertions, it's not personal. They're just trying to cover their bureaucratic butts, and make damn sure they don't get everyone all worked up over nothing."

"I know, I know. Thanks Pete. I appreciate all the help you've given me in getting ready for this."

"Hey, my butt's on the line too, you know."

Pete grinned at Devlin as he grabbed the gleaming stainless steel handle and swung the half-inch-thick glass door open, then gestured for Devlin to enter.

30 years earlier, as a freshman at Harvard, Devlin had initially believed that everyone around him was at least three times smarter than he—a bumpkin from Garretsville, Ohio. He had held back in class, afraid that his parochial, small-town upbringing would cause his class contributions to be off-key and subject to ridicule. However, as he listened to others, he began to realize that his classmates had no particular lock on insight, and that his own thoughts seemed more logical, better arranged than those of his peers. It wasn't long before he emerged from his shell and became one of the stronger participants in most of his classes; his grades followed suit.

This self-confidence had stayed with him. Though not often called upon to deliver presentations to NASA management, he was well-prepared, and—despite some anxiety—was actually looking forward to it.

The meeting was going well. Devlin had presented his methods, and was now moving through his preliminary data.

"As you can see here," Devlin gestured to one of two visuals of the newly discovered planet on the large screen, "2033 DA$_{16}$ has a circumference of 29,887 miles, roughly 20% larger than Earth, while the rotational speed at the equator is remarkably close to ours, at 1,195 mph. This means that the length of a day on the planet is approximately 25 hours."

Devlin moved on to a new set of images. "Now, the planet's orbit around its sun is fairly slow; one year is 528 earth days. Since the planet's axial tilt is only 17.8%, versus 23.4% for earth, the seasons should be less pronounced."

"Mr. McGregor, what do we know regarding water coverage on 2033 DA$_{16}$?" asked a rotund, well-dressed man seated at the table, as he gently ran his thumb and middle finger around the perimeter of his meticulously groomed Vandyke beard.

"Our data doesn't give us a precise figure at this point, but we're estimating that land and ice cap comprises 40% of the planet's surface. However, one feature of the planet I find quite interesting," Devlin noted, "is the configuration of land mass. While our current technology does not give us an exact picture, we believe there are more than 15 separate continents fairly evenly distributed across the planet."

Devlin drew a deep breath, brought up two final images, and prepared to announce the finding for which the group had been assembled. Devlin pointed to one of the images.

"On the left is a chart showing the atmospheric make-up of Earth: 79% nitrogen, 20% oxygen. On the right is the atmospheric make-up of 2033 DA$_{16}$: approximately 75% nitrogen, 23% oxygen."

Devlin looked at Pete, then at the group of executives, making eye contact with each. As he'd expected, his nervousness had abated, and he'd quickly found himself enjoying the event. *And now the finale.*

"Unless further analysis undermines the data collected thus far, it appears that the planet would support life as we know it, and is therefore fully habitable by human beings."

One of the executives shook his head in wonder, then spoke up.

"Amazing, truly amazing. Mr. McGregor, as the discoverer of this planet, have you given thought to what it might be named?"

"I have."

Interpreting this softball question as indication that the meeting was drawing to a successful close, Devlin paused for effect.

"I would like to call it Cerulea."

"Cerulea," the man repeated slowly, rolling the name over in his brain. "And why is that?"

"Well, it's quite simply the most beautiful bright blue sphere that I've ever seen."

4.

An aide knocked twice, heard a muffled invitation to enter, then opened the door and stuck his head in.

"Madam President, we'll be touching down in about 15 minutes."

"Got it. Thanks, Jay."

The aide departed, closing the door behind him. President Virginia Belknap looked out the window of her cabin, her mind elsewhere, then back down at the half-finished eulogy on her desk.

She stared at the words, holding her forehead with thumb and forefinger. Suzanne's death seemed such a tragic waste. The Virginia police, working with the FBI, had concluded that the cause of death was cardiac failure brought on almost instantaneously by the injection of Batrachotoxin R, one of the most lethal and fastest-acting poisons on the planet—derived from the secretions of a certain species of frog found in Central and South America. It had entered her bloodstream via a microdart, an increasingly common projectile munition developed by the CIA but now widely used by hunters and animal control professionals for killing or subduing large mammals. They'd also noted that, with no witnesses—and no murder weapon, the likelihood of finding the perpetrator was extremely low.

The President sighed deeply. Suzanne had been an incredibly loyal and capable member of her staff—and a friend. Perhaps because of that, she wanted to transcend the usual platitudes, and say something a little more meaningful, but it wasn't coming to her. She thought of the many times the two of them had worked together on finding just the right phrase for an important speech, and smiled at the irony. Then, thinking this over, it occurred to her that she knew exactly what to say; she picked up her pen and began to write.

After filling up several pages, she felt the whine of the jet engines give way to the other-worldly, high-pitched hum of the electric lift fans as the aircraft prepared to land. The President took a final sheet of paper and wrote one last sentence. She re-read the final few paragraphs, then looked at her watch; they would be right on time.

Although Suzanne's family was honored to have her speak at the funeral, the President was also keenly aware that her presence could be a logistical nightmare, making such events far less intimate than they might be otherwise. But Suzanne Ortega had been one of her top speech writers for more than three years.

And even though it meant that she would miss the final press conference of the OAS summit meeting in Caracas, it was unquestionably the right thing to do.

Besides, the absence of the U.S. President would shift the limelight to some of the lesser known leaders of the Organization of American States. As a result, they'd be forced to make some firm commitments on the summit's key initiatives before a world audience. The issues involved were age-old, but the relative importance of each had changed considerably.

Terrorism, an unpleasant and accepted constant in daily life, was no longer confined to Islamic fundamentalists. It had become an inefficient and inappropriate means to an end for a sizable number of both religious and secular organizations, including racist groups, eco-terrorists, drug cartels, and opponents of ever-increasing globalization.

But the threat from terrorism had met with substantial competition. With increasing frequency, it was eclipsed by the perils of nature. Natural disasters were tragically common; global warming—in combination with a growing human population approaching eight billion—was generating tremendous stress on the planet's ecosystems and natural resources. Just one such disaster typically took far more lives than most terrorist acts put together.

Terrorism was also overshadowed on occasion by disease. The century had already witnessed one devastating pandemic, in addition to several localized epidemics. Despite the world's growing knowledge regarding contagion and containment, shorter winters and longer summers had allowed many previously unthreatening pathogens to propagate across wide areas of the globe.

The aircraft came to a rest on a field adjacent to a cemetery on the southern edge of Suzanne's hometown of Red Cloud, Nebraska. The President grabbed her suit jacket from a hanger behind her desk and put it on; she folded the eulogy and placed it in an inside pocket. Through the window she could see her Secret Service team assembling to escort her to the graveside service.

Arriving directly at her destination still took some getting used to. Air Force One, the huge 797 that had been the President's primary means of long distance travel for her first two years in office, had been relegated to overseas flights and relabeled Air Force Bravo.

Its replacement, known as Air Force Alpha, was designed for vertical take-off and landing and was capable of traveling roughly twice the speed of sound. Its technical name was the SB-3 FanJet. The plane was equipped with two large jet turbines for supersonic travel, but converted this power to electricity for take off and landing, driving 12 large-diameter lift fans located in the wings and under-body of the fuselage. The technology had been developed by Sonic Blue Aerospace, a start-up company out of Pasadena whose founder had helped to engineer the Joint Strike Fighter, the military's primary workhorse for over 20 years.

While the aircraft offered only marginally more interior space than the huge Lockheed VH-71 marine helicopters that used to ferry the President to Camp David and local venues, its tremendous speed, combined with its VTOL capability, meant that she could walk out of the Oval Office and be virtually anywhere in North America in under three hours.

There were no crowds to greet her on this occasion; she walked singly down a set of steps and onto the field. The President shivered slightly—less from temperature than from the cold and lonely realization that this event marked the death of a close colleague and friend who she would never see again. With Secret Service agents on all sides, President Belknap proceeded toward the gravesite.

5.

Chief of Staff Roger Tucker entered the Oval Office a few minutes before 2 pm. He sat on the far sofa in front of the fireplace. He always chose this position; he could see both doors as people entered and, during boring meetings, of which there were many, he could look out the window and daydream a bit.

He was reviewing some briefing papers on his tablet for his 4 o'clock when President Belknap entered. He stood instinctively without immediately pulling his eyes from the report.

"Hey Roger. Coffee?" she asked, walking over to a sideboard.

"Madam President. Please." He placed his tablet on the sofa, and walked over to where the President was pouring two cups of coffee. She handed one to him. "So how was the funeral?" he asked.

"It was quite touching, actually." She paused, reflecting on the event earlier that morning. "I've got to say, the plains of Nebraska somehow add a desolate poignancy to a funeral service." Then, as if wrapping up the event for long-term storage, she added crisply: "Very sad."

"I'll bet," Roger offered. He'd been fairly close to Suzanne as well, but they'd decided that both of them attending the service would be too much—not to mention inefficient.

Ginny Belknap leaned against her desk, sipped her coffee, and changed the subject. "So. What's this all about. A new planet?"

"Yes, Ma'am. But, if I'm not mistaken, there's a little more to it. Cheryl didn't offer much detail, but it was clear that there's something special about the discovery."

"How so?"

"Not entirely sure. She was somewhat cryptic when I pressed her, and said she'd rather explain in person. She's bringing the discoverer along with her."

At this point in his career, Roger was fairly unflappable, and hardly prone to excitement. But after one fairly uneventful year into the President's second term, he'd found himself intrigued by Cheryl's call.

He'd served Ginny Belknap for 5 years. Initially, when the President-elect had approached him during her transition, Roger had tried to convince her out of it, reasoning that the appointment of a gay chief of staff would start her administration off on the wrong foot.

She, however, dismissed the concern as old-fashioned, and wouldn't be denied. Over half a decade, they'd dealt with natural disasters, economic crises, raging conflicts in developing countries—a colorful assortment of cataclysmic events. It was widely held in Washington that they made a formidable team. Although, despite the President's willingness to pour him a cup of coffee now and then, he held no illusion as to who was the boss. It was her steady intellect and diplomatic talents that had made the difference—as they worked to convert problems into political success.

The President's secretary knocked, and then opened the side door.

"Madam President, Cheryl Wald and Devlin McGregor are here."

"Thanks, Mary. Show them in."

The President glanced at the daily schedule on her desk, and quickly consumed a few pertinent facts regarding McGregor's background.

Cheryl Wald and Devlin entered the Oval Office. Cheryl was a tall woman with short hair and sharp features. She wore a non-descript olive suit, but somehow made it look like the latest thing. She was smart and incredibly competent; Ginny Belknap had appointed her NASA Administrator mid-way through her first term; though they had not had ample occasion to interact, Ginny liked her a great deal.

"Cheryl, great to see you."

"Likewise, Madam President. Roger; how are you?"

"Good, Cheryl. Please..."

He gestured to the sofas. Since Roger's tablet occupied the center cushion of one, Cheryl and Devlin walked to the other with its back to the door. They all remained standing.

Cheryl Wald introduced Devlin McGregor; they exchanged salutary nods. The practice of shaking hands had been banned during the pandemic earlier in the century. It was well-documented that the practice had been the single greatest contributor to the spread of the disease. Intended as a temporary measure, health officials urged all people in all nations to continue utilizing an alternative greeting, even after the pandemic subsided, and most did. The handshake was now fairly rare—reserved for special occasions and ceremonial greetings.

"I believe we overlapped years ago at Harvard," the President said warmly to Devlin. "You graduated in '07, is that right?"

"Yes, Ma'am, that's correct."

"I was class of '05—although my guess is, given your academic focus, we probably didn't have many professors in common."

"I would guess you're right, Madam President." Devlin thought of several clever ways to elaborate on this simpleminded response, but—as with so many visitors to this office, the words had not arrived in time, and he remained silent.

President Belknap smoothed the skirt of her suit with one hand as she took a seat in the elegantly upholstered Queen Anne chair between the sofas, and crossed her legs. They all took a seat as well.

"Devlin has been deeply involved in planetary analysis, using data from the Darwin and Cash telescopes," Cheryl began.

She went on to explain the basics of the discovery, then turned it over to Devlin to draw the final conclusions. When the short briefing was complete, the President leaned back in her chair.

"I'll be damned," the President exclaimed. "Mr. McGregor, this is an incredible discovery; one that will have a huge impact on how we look at the universe—and at ourselves, for a long time to come."

"Madam President," Cheryl interjected, "there's something else you should know."

The President and Roger Tucker both turned and offered their attention.

"It's possible that this news will have an even greater impact than you think. Before the decision was made to pull the plug on the manned Mars mission, NASA engineers and other scientific organizations had been aggressively exploring different techniques for accelerated space travel.

"The most obvious candidates were nuclear and antimatter," she explained. "At first blush, it looked like antimatter was the most viable, but containment proved elusive. Ultimately, the team settled on nuclear-powered ion beam technology, which would have required nearly three months of travel time for a thirty-day stay on the red planet.

"However, two other concepts were also explored—both far more ambitious," Cheryl continued, "the Alcubierre SEC drive and the Heim gravity engine. While many in the scientific community believed both of these designs to have impassable limitations, there were others who were determined to see them through."

Cheryl paused, then looked directly at the President. "About two years ago, scientists at the Defense Advanced Research Projects Agency, working in conjunction with the Max Planck Institute for Gravitational Physics, successfully demonstrated a working prototype of the Alcubierre drive. NASA scientists are in the process of confirming the results, but it's believed that the breakthrough is real. In typical DoD fashion, all of this is strictly classified."

"I'm sorry Cheryl, but I'm not exactly sure what you're telling us," Roger said haltingly.

"Let me put it this way," Cheryl explained. "The planet that Devlin has discovered is roughly 27 light years from Earth. Using ion beam technology, it would take nearly 100 thousand years to get there. Using a ship equipped with an Alcubierre drive, it would take less than 15."

"You mean 15 thousand," Roger clarified.

"No. I mean just 15," Cheryl said firmly. "Perhaps a little too far for a round-trip mission, but certainly close enough for a one-way journey."

There was silence.

After 5 years together, Ginny Belknap and Roger Tucker had developed an ability to communicate their thoughts to each other without speaking. As they held each other's glance for just a brief moment, they shared their mutual reaction to what they'd just heard: this news could change the path of their next three years together considerably.

In fact, as they returned their eyes to their guests, both suspected that the thought they'd just shared might be significantly understated.

6.

The damn thing was jammed. Belechenko pushed upwards with all his strength but it wouldn't budge.

Maybe I'm too old for this shit, he thought to himself.

He carefully pulled a small cloth from a toolkit and wiped the large bolt one more time with lubricant, then put it back, precisely. This time, he gave the wrench a hard clockwise shove, then reapplied heavy counterclockwise pressure. He strained hard; he could feel the beads of sweat forming on his forehead.

He thought he sensed some movement, and maintained strong pressure on the wrench. Ever so slowly, the bolt started to give. As he continued to push hard on the wrench, he felt 45 minutes of frustration give way to satisfaction.

Belechenko removed the wrench and placed it into its designated clip in the toolkit. The bolt now loose, he removed it by hand, making slow, practiced turns, and placed it into a pouch in the kit. He snapped the pouch closed with the bolt inside.

He rotated the cover plate aside, and at long last looked upon his quarry: a small circuit board roughly 2 inches square. He very delicately moved the board from side to side until it was free of its connector, then placed it in a specially designed slot in the toolkit. He pulled out the new component, put it in place, and began the process of resealing the cover plate.

The task complete, all tools and parts in their proper place, he drew a deep breath and looked up. The stars were mesmerizing; a maze of bright piercing white lights in an ocean of absolute black. He held the vision for a few seconds, allowing his mind to float free of his responsibilities and simply revel in the majesty and mystery of it all.

Breaking his trance, he looked down at the clock on his sleeve; 55 minutes of oxygen left. *Not bad,* he thought, and started inching along the hand and footrails toward the Space Station's secondary hatch.

Commander Vladimir Belechenko was 49 years old. Like so many of his peers, he had, from a very young age, dreamed of being a cosmonaut. But he never could have imagined what that meant or what lay beyond his first trip into space at the ripe age of 24.

For nearly two and a half decades, he had been integrally involved in maintaining and expanding the International Space Station. For the last seven years, he had served as the ISS Commander, overseeing all aspects of its scientific mission.

His rise within ISS organization had been rapid, but it had not been all that easy. He had had to work very hard, and devote an unreasonable amount of his life's energy to the cause. This devotion had consequences. Unmarried, no children, and a social life that was practically non-existent.

He felt a sudden rush of acute sadness as he entered the interlock. This trip and mission should have been assigned to a younger astronaut, but he had reserved it for himself. After years of Earth-bound administrative duties, he had longed for a simple maintenance mission in space. It felt wonderful to be intensely and completely focused on a task as simple as the removal of a bolt, and he would miss it terribly. He'd be back on Earth in less than 48 hours, and this would probably be his last spacewalk—possibly his last trip to space.

7.

As Belechenko closed the final hatch on the other side of the interlock, and gently pushed off and floated into the command capsule, one of his crewmates looked up from her monitor.

"Commander, it seems you have a message from the U.S. President."

"The President of the United States? What does it say?"

"Very little. Only that you are requested to contact her on a secure channel at your earliest convenience."

She handed Commander Belechenko a printout of the message which included a special access code for the communication.

"Understood. Thank you."

Not a common occurrence. He couldn't even imagine what would cause President Belknap to contact him directly. They had chatted once or twice at various ISS ceremonies, and seemed to "click" as they say in America, but standard protocol would have any message from the President pass through and be delivered by the chief of NASA.

Anxious to know what it was all about, he quickly moved through a checklist as he studied several monitors in the command capsule. It appeared that there were no alert conditions requiring his attention, so he notified his crewmate that he would be in his quarters and departed.

The personal living modules attached to the ISS were relatively new. They had been added as an assortment of non-astronauts had begun visiting the Station, and it had become at times awkward for all those aboard to share the central sleeping areas. The module Belechenko inhabited for his 4-day stay was sparse; essentially a large cylinder about 10 feet long and eight feet wide. There was a sleep harness, facilities for relieving himself, several small storage lockers, a cramped workstation with a communications link, and—every astronaut's favorite feature—a "bulletin board" that used air suction to display photos and drawings that children might send to their mother or father in space. Belechenko had a posted a picture of his parents, and a beautiful drawing of some kind of insect sent to him the day before by his four-year-old niece.

He wedged himself into the workstation, and logged onto the videophone in his quarters. Ordinarily, the system would establish a default connection with

ISS headquarters in Houston, but he cancelled the connection and manually entered the access code he'd been given.

He heard a voice with no video: "Commander Belechenko, this is the White House operator. Please stand by for the President. You may have to wait for several minutes. Would that be all right?"

"Yes. That would be fine."

"Thank you for your patience, Commander."

Belechenko looked at his watch. If he calculated correctly, it should be just before 7 pm in Washington.

As Commander of the ISS, there had been any number of moments when he felt the full weight of his position, and was incredibly proud to be the leader of such a magnificent, multicultural effort. There were other times, however, when major initiatives were late, or things simply didn't work as they should, and he felt like a failure, a mediocre manager who had clearly risen to his level of incompetence.

As he sat there, waiting for the President of the United States to come on the line, it occurred to him that this could easily be one or the other. He had absolutely no idea which.

After a minute and a half, the White House operator announced that the President would be with him shortly. A few seconds later, the video feed was activated, and he was face to face with Virginia Belknap. She spoke first.

"Hello, Commander, it's good to see you again." She smiled with what appeared to be a genuine affection. He liked this woman, and returned the smile, but it didn't make him any less nervous.

"Good evening, Madam President. Good to see you as well. How may I be of service?"

She ignored his question: "So, I understand you wanted one last hurrah up there. Is it as fulfilling as you'd hoped?"

He relaxed a little as he spoke. "Oh, it's nice to get away once in a while, and worry about the mechanical, rather than the political health of this place. Yes, I'd say it has been fulfilling."

"Well, I'm jealous. I suppose joining the White House maintenance crew for a few days might be a nice respite, but somehow I doubt I'd get away with it."

They both laughed gently. There was a brief pause.

"Commander, I have some news that I'd like to share with you, and a proposition."

Belechenko's nervousness slipped away entirely, replaced by intrigue.

"I think the English expression is—'I'm all ears.'"

8.

The fire roared noisily, feasting on the gigantic birch and oak logs in the eight-foot hearth. There was a loud pop as a glowing, walnut-sized coal ricocheted off the protective screen and landed harmlessly on the ornate, blue and gold Italian tile.

The two men continued their conversation, seated in large wingback chairs upholstered in thick, rich leather—each holding a glass of 50-year old cognac.

"I don't give a shit!" exclaimed one of the men, leaning toward his guest. "And don't talk to me about risk. I've spent my life bathed in risk—it's why I am where I am!" he barked emphatically, gesturing to the opulence of the room without taking his eyes off those of the other man. Then, calming down: "Look, I derive no pleasure from that woman's death, but the stakes here demand action. If the second half of this plan succeeds, our ability to control the process will be heightened considerably."

"All I'm saying," the other began haltingly, "is that, while I fully understand the benefits of moving forward, I also know that it'll further increase the odds of discovery. And if we ever got caught, it'd be game over; end of story."

"First off," said the other carefully and coldly, rising from his chair. "Let's get one thing very fucking clear: there is no 'we' here. If you succeed in getting someone inside, then *you* succeeded; if you fail, then *you* failed." He looked the other man in the eye and pointed for emphasis, his index finger extending from his grip on the snifter. The smooth, caramel-colored liquid swirled inside the glass. "Is there any confusion on that?"

"No, sir." He had worked for this man for the better part of three decades; yet still, his use of "sir" prevailed. It was both out of respect and sheer intimidation; somehow, he had never managed to climb up onto the plateau of first-name familiarity.

The man standing was bluntly handsome, with a chiseled face and thick black hair, which was gelled straight back. He was of average height, dressed in a charcoal grey cashmere turtleneck and jeans. Although the vaulted ceiling, made of dark mahogany specifically selected from a tree farm in Brazil, rose 30 feet or more over their heads, he still appeared to his guest as a giant.

The man in cashmere took several steps towards the hearth, and stood with his back to the room, staring at the fire. Once again, he dropped back to a more reasoned tone: "Having someone on the inside will be invaluable. Without it, we'd be no better off than all the assholes and incompetents who are starting to throw their hats in the ring." He turned slowly towards his guest, and ended the discussion as he had on so many previous occasions; "I need you to do this for me, Doug."

The man seated looked up at his boss, and replied almost without free will: "I'll make it happen; you can count on it."

"Good. And Doug," the other said sternly, locking eyes with his guest. "As always, let's keep this operation small and discreet."

"Yes sir."

However, as he accepted the assignment, Doug realized that "as always" was not what it used to be. At an earlier point in time, his assignments required him to bend a rule or two but rarely to break the law. Now, virtually every assignment was illegal; some, in fact, were capital crimes.

But he was in way too deep to dwell on it; He said that he would get it done, and that was that.

9.

The day of the public announcement was a brilliant October day: crisp, sharp, full of the optimism inspired by cloudless, deep blue skies.

Senate majority leader Jack Wily felt a surge of confidence and patriotism as his car quietly entered the West Wing's entryway. This would be a momentous effort, one that would unite and align the people of America—and the world—behind a powerful, compelling goal. The moon shot launched in the 20th century would pale in comparison. Even the manned mission to Mars, abandoned in 2026, was dwarfed by this challenge. This would be bigger, bolder, with an overwhelming impact on the human race. He felt a little flush as his mind soared with a hundred derivative thoughts.

The car door opened and he got out, buttoned his suit coat, and took his briefcase from the driver. He had come to this place many times in the past seven years; he had spent countless hours in dozens of meetings—many quite tedious and unpleasant. Nonetheless, every once in a while as he passed the U.S. marines on duty and entered the foyer, he got goose bumps. This was one such time.

The President was standing as Wily was ushered into the Oval Office; she was reading what he assumed was her prepared speech for the morning's event.

"Madam President."

"Jack, come on in. Hey, I think your team's done a terrific job here. I'm very pleased that the leadership on both sides of the aisle is fully bought-in before we go public with this thing."

"Thank you, ma'am; we've certainly worked a lot of late nights to get everything in place."

Roger Tucker entered from a side door, nodded at the President, then greeted Jack.

"Shall we?" he asked, efficiently gesturing to a door which led to the Garden. The President grabbed her coat from off a side chair and slipped it on, and the three of them walked to the door, which was immediately opened by a guard standing outside. Roger and Jack stood by the door waiting for the President to exit, then followed her out onto the colonnade.

President Belknap turned to Roger as she pulled her shirt cuffs free of her sleeves.

"Roger, before we announce this thing to the world, have we gotten final word from Belechenko?"

"Just this morning," Roger grinned. "And he's good to go. In fact, we're scheduling a press conference for you and the new Mission Commander early next week."

"Excellent."

Ginny Belknap was a good president, and she knew it. While no one could yet point to any specific grand achievement of her administration, she had upheld the office honorably, been respected worldwide as an honest and capable statesman, and clearly proved that—as the second woman to hold the office—gender held no advantage over executive competence.

They made their way to the Rose Garden, and the President strode up to the podium. Surrounding the assembly were vibrant rows of red, orange and white chrysanthemums; standing guard on the perimeter were Horse Chestnut trees and Willow Oaks proudly displaying their fall foliage. The Gardens at the White house occupied land originally purchased by George Washington from a local tobacco planter—but it was not until 1961 that it became an outdoor site for white House ceremonies at the direction of John F. Kennedy.

Since the White House was still interviewing final candidates to replace Suzanne Ortega, Ginny had written her speech herself. As such, she knew it well, and could pay much less attention to the two glass screens of the teleprompter on her left and right. She focused instead on the horde of reporters seated before her. Her eyes moved across the crowd; she saw hungry faces waiting for some scrap of news to quell their insatiable appetites.

The White House had done an excellent job of keeping this announcement quiet, and she smiled slightly thinking that the feast she was about to offer would take the media weeks, perhaps even months, to digest.

10.

President Belknap had grown up in Rochester, Vermont, in a simple but comfortable farmhouse on a rural dirt road just off Route 100—a winding, two-lane highway that runs pretty much the length of the state.

Her father had taught English Literature at Green Mountain Academy, a respected private school in Waitsfield, about 20 miles north. While this was not an especially high-paying job, one of the benefits of her father's tenure was that she and her two younger brothers all attended the school for free.

Her mother was a social worker, and spent most days visiting local families, and serving as a conduit to ensure that those in need understood and benefited from all of the services that the state provided.

Her parents' influence, along with a top notch education which also included degrees from Harvard and Georgetown's School of Foreign Service, had given her a thoughtful perspective on the world and its machinations.

That perspective had played an important role in how she viewed this new planet's discovery.

The President cleared her throat and began to speak:

"Many hundreds of thousands of years ago, our ancient ancestors began a slow steady migration out of Africa to the Middle East, Europe, and eventually to all parts of the globe. As new civilizations germinated and evolved, each region developed a separate and unique culture. Some of these societies were aggressive, militaristic. Others were agrarian and passive. Today, there remain distinct cultural differences between continents and between nations. While we cherish the world's diversity, we also know that many of the problems we face are the result of cultural conflict and the propensity of some cultures to visit aggression on their neighbors.

"The civilized world as we know it was not architected. It was born of circumstance, shaped by events: catastrophes, pandemics, wars, Great Experiments. In short, the current state of our global community is less the result of design than of chaos theory.

"The same could be said of our relationship to the planet. The growth of our species and the pace of human development have forced us to radically alter our surroundings to meet critical needs. Vast, complex ecosystems, of critical importance to planetary health, have been decimated—before we truly understood their importance.

"Let me pose a question to you, and to all of the citizens of this planet: What if we could start over? Knowing what we know, with the hindsight of history giving us the lift to rise above past mistakes, and technology providing the means to avoid past catastrophes and failed strategies, could we do better?

"If we had a blank slate, a tabula rasa, a new planet on which to build a new global community, would humankind be capable of making great leaps forward? Could we possibly create a world in which war, famine, poverty, bigotry and inequality were absent? In which men and women could enjoy life, liberty and the pursuit of happiness without sacrificing each other's welfare or the environment?

"Ladies and gentleman, I believe the answer to these questions is yes. And I am incredibly excited to tell you this afternoon that mankind has been offered just such an opportunity..."

As the President spelled out the existence and implications of Devlin McGregor's discovery, and of the decision to pursue a one-way journey to the planet—a colonization, you could almost feel the eyes of the world population upon her.

"Many in America believe that our Constitution represents a near-perfect framework for the governance of mankind. I am, of course, somewhat biased in my belief that it's among the very best. But the truth is that there are many, many nations with innovative and forward-thinking mechanisms for managing a range of different rights and freedoms, just as there are new and clever models for structuring and positioning the basic building blocks of government.

"As we begin to wrestle with the technological challenge of reaching this new world, we must also look at all the different systems employed on Earth—including those dealing with education, agriculture, jurisprudence, energy and environmental management, and face the daunting task of designing how this new world will operate.

"By anyone's estimate, this will be a Herculean task; one that must fall upon all of our shoulders. Toward that end, I will be seeking the assistance of the United Nations in forming a Mission Council, a global body comprised of experts from all across the globe..."

Cerulea's discovery had demanded a grand vision for how the people of Earth must respond, and this President was not the least bit shy in obliging.

II.

The world's reaction was immediate.

By the time President Belknap left the Rose Garden and re-entered the Oval Office, four heads of state had already made their way through the White House switchboard, and the internet was starting to swarm with news stories and commentary on the announcement.

Within one hour, all major media outlets had developed a full color graphic for their video, print, and electronic coverage. By evening, virtually every news source on the face of the Earth was focusing on the announcement and speculating on all aspects of the trip to Cerulea. This, of course, despite the fact that there was very little news to actually report.

Overall, however, for those interested in learning more about space and astronomy, there was plenty of good material.

◖◗

In the year 2033, there was never any difficulty in finding information on a given topic; the issue was simply deciding which source to tap. In fact, now that instant translation technology had become quite robust, the number of available sources had increased by several orders of magnitude.

The line between print and television had long ago blurred and then vanished altogether as the whole idea of scheduled broadcasts became antiquated and downright silly. While there were news organizations that focused their limited resources on either print or video, or on a specific geography or news topic—such as world news or entertainment or sports—the larger outfits had no choice but to offer it all. Among these were the minor players, the major players, and the titans.

In the United States, this latter category was a small club, consisting primarily of the *U.S. Times* and the *American Standard*. The *Times* was a construct of the New York Times Company, while the *Standard* was 15-year-old brand developed by the News Corporation.

It was well understood that the *Times* leaned towards the progressive and the *Standard* towards the conservative, but since both organizations sought to garner a greater share of the other's audience, they generally did their best to walk the center line. It was only when news events were partisan in nature that each tended to drift towards their political corner.

Both organizations culled news reports, interviews, images and video from literally thousands of contributors—ranging from actual reporters to bloggers to bystanders in the right place at the right time. Editors then shaped this cacophony into polished news products for a range of formats; anything from digital newspapers to websites to passive news shows to packaged feeds for specific devices.

Ironically, in an age when technology made news available almost as it happened, the newspaper was still one of the mainstays of the business. However, the whole concept had evolved considerably—transformed by what was called electronic ink technology. As the cost of producing the physical newspaper had skyrocketed, conversion to an electronic format had been seen as the only economically viable option for both the publisher and its customers. Most households had one or more large, foldable broadsheets; these were as thin as paper, but were actually electronic displays which offered the latest news stories and features at any given point in time.

Like a newspaper, the reader could browse and scan the headlines for stories that might be of interest. But unlike its paper counterpart, it allowed the reader to zoom in, connect to related stories, and view multiple photographs, video clips and even—when appropriate—live reports. In a sense, major news organizations viewed the newspaper as the pre-eminent delivery vehicle, since it now combined all available formats, and served as the ultimate amalgam of classic reporting and real time internet news feeds.

The President's announcement forced both the *Times* and the *Standard* to see whether, among the rising mountain of available material, they could find some actual substance with which to populate their pages.

12.

While the vast majority of those following the announcement were swept up in the excitement of it all, digesting endless ruminations on the technical feasibility of such a journey; there were some who regarded the announcement through a very different lens.

On the day following the President's speech, an editorial appeared in the *Standard*, written by a man named Randall Reese—President of a group which called itself Americans for Moral Truth.

Reese began his piece by sharing in the enthusiasm, but quickly focused on his concerns:

The President's announcement of a new, habitable planet called Cerulea, and an ambitious plan to mount a manned mission, captures our imaginations and puts forth a bold and exhilarating vision for Mankind's next great journey.

However, let us not allow the technical hurdles to consume our thinking as we prepare for the mission. What the President has outlined is nothing short of the perpetuation of the human species; the colonization of an entirely new world. This is not a responsibility to be taken lightly.

Since this new civilization will sprout from the efforts and sensibilities of the men and women we send on this one-way expedition, a number of questions should be carefully considered:

Just what kind of society do we wish to create in our collective image? What values do we believe would best serve Mankind's first colony? How do we go about selecting the right individuals for this great cause? And, most important, who will be the architects of Cerulean culture? What laws will govern its growing populace? What guiding principles will instruct the beliefs of the Cerulean people?

For too long, the faithful on this planet have watched as God has been removed from too many aspects of daily life—all in the name of compromise and diversity. Now, our Creator has challenged us to help him establish a new Garden of Eden; to guide an entire civilization toward the Kingdom of Heaven and salvation. How we answer this challenge will determine whether we have truly learned from His guidance, and whether we deserve His love and grace.

I pray for President Belknap and others involved in this adventure to have the wisdom to address these issues judiciously. Surely, all of us want to be proud of what may become

Mankind's first offspring. I call on all those who understand the importance of this quest to contemplate these questions deeply, and work hard to find the right path forward.
May God bless Cerulea.
Randall Reese
Waukesha, WI

This Op-Ed piece was not widely read; in fact, it only appeared in the top layer of editorials for a small demographic among *Standard* subscribers. Other readers would have had to either select it from a list or drill down behind other Mission related commentary.

And, at first glance, it didn't seem a cause for concern. Although America was still very much a nation of faith, the salve of time had cooled the fervent activism of the religious right considerably; allowing a number of issues—so contentious at the turn of the century—to subside in the national consciousness.

Nonetheless, a dutiful aide in the White House, whose job it was to filter the daily deluge for items of interest, thought the editorial significant, and included it in the President's daily briefing package.

13.

R oger Tucker leaned back in his chair.
"Devlin, although I'm not sure I'm going to be capable of understanding the answer, how is it possible for us to know that the atmosphere on Cerulea will support human life?"

Devlin smiled. "Well, it would probably take me all day to explain the science behind it. But I think I can offer you a conceptual summary."

"All right; let's hear it."

"Using telescope spectroscopy, we can easily measure the chemical makeup of extrasolar planetary atmospheres—"

Roger waved a hand, laughing. "Forget I asked."

Roger, Devlin, and Commander Belechenko were sitting in the Cabinet Room, down the hall from the Oval Office. There were large diagrams and various charts spread out on the oval mahogany conference table, along with a couple of half-eaten pizzas and several cans of diet soda.

Outside the four sets of large French doors, each capped by a half-round window and adorned with crimson wool damask draperies, the skies were gray, and leaves were beginning to fall from the trees as a blustery October breeze dislodged them from their summer perch.

Ordinarily, meetings in the Cabinet Room were guided by precise protocol, with every member of the cabinet occupying a specific chair in accordance with the date their cabinet-level department was established. However, at this meeting the three men followed no protocol whatsoever, simply huddling at one end of the table—this being the only room available at the time.

Devlin refused to let Roger off the hook. "No, bear with me," he insisted. "When a planet travels in front of another, we have the opportunity to see how light is filtered through the nearer planet's atmosphere. Using a measurement technique called spectrometry, we can actually see the distinct signatures of different chemicals and gasses."

"Okay, I think I get it." Roger thought for a moment. "And this planet is 27 light years from Earth?"

"Yes, give or take."

"Translate that for me."

"You mean, into miles?" Devlin asked.

"Please."

"Well, one light year is about 5.9 trillion miles. To put it into perspective, the distance between Earth and the sun is just 93 million miles; between Earth and Mars is anywhere from 35 million to 234 million, depending on their orbital positions. So, at 158 trillion miles from Earth, traveling to Cerulea is equivalent to traveling to Mars and back—at its farthest point—over 12 thousand times."

"Holy shit. And you're telling me, at that distance, we can determine the size, rotation speed, and approximate landmass? How?"

Devlin grinned. "Well, the science here is so basic yet so ingenious, it's hard to believe."

"Try me."

"The problem with viewing distant planets is usually not the telescope's ability to magnify; it's the interference from ambient light—typically generated by a planet's sun or other nearby stars. So, earlier in the century, the idea was put forth to essentially build a pinhole camera in space."

"A pinhole camera?" Roger asked incredulously. "Like the things we all made in high school?"

"Exactly," Devlin confirmed. "The concept involved a powerful infrared telescope which focused on distant planets by looking through a small hole in a giant starshade floating in front of it in space."

"Wait a minute," Roger interrupted. "You're saying that there's a telescope up there which is the equivalent of me holding a piece of cardboard in front of my face with a pinhole in it?"

"Yup. It's called the New Worlds Imager—also known as the Cash Telescope, first proposed by Webster Cash of the University of Colorado in 2004. The telescope is, of course, quite complex—but at the same time brilliantly simple: the starshade, roughly the size of a football field with a 30-foot hole in it, eliminates all extraneous light, so that the telescope can get a much clearer view of the planet itself.

"Right now, the Cash Telescope can determine planet size, orbit and rotational speeds—even give a rudimentary picture of landmass, oceans and weather. In time, as technology evolves, it may be able to provide much more detailed images of a planet's surface; but we've got a ways to go yet."

Roger looked at Devlin for several seconds with a cocked smile. "I must say, Devlin, I'm intrigued and amazed. So is there anything about Cerulea that seems out of the ordinary?"

"The fact that it is so similar to Earth is probably its most extraordinary characteristic." Devlin then thought for a moment. "Actually, one thing I found curious was the high level of magnetite in Cerulea's atmosphere," Devlin noted.

And what does that mean?"

"Not a lot. But it means that there is probably a large amount of iron ore within the planet," Devlin offered. "Which means there's probably a large amount of metals, including gold and platinum."

"That is interesting," Roger mused. "Though I'm guessing it'll take a while before gold or platinum is of any interest to a nascent Cerulean society."

"Don't be so sure," said Devlin. "As soon as there's any manufacturing of electronic devices, there'll be a strong need for gold—just as it's in high demand here on Earth."

"Gentlemen," Belechenko politely interjected, "shall we move on to the science behind what's going to get us there?" The ship's technology was supposed to have been the focus of their meeting.

"Good idea commander," Devlin remarked cheerfully. He then launched into a lengthy, fairly technical explanation as to how the ship was actually capable of moving so quickly through space.

Roger tried hard to follow along. "So what you're telling me is that, in order to achieve these speeds, this thing actually warps space? On the one hand, it's absolutely incredible. On the other, it seems a little, I don't know, cliché."

"True. But it's worth noting that much of what you see in well-written science fiction is, in fact, based on someone's educated guess of where things might be headed," Devlin replied. "Anyway, to answer your question, the Alcubierre SEC drive does indeed warp space. The acronym stands for 'space expansion-contraction'; the drive simultaneously collapses space in front of the ship and creates space behind it. In doing so, it can overcome what has always been seen as a fundamental speed limit and achieve 'FTL,' or faster-than-light travel."

"It is not unlike a surfing pool like you see at your amusement parks," added Commander Belechenko, "where there is a large wave being constantly generated behind you. Only in this case the wave is made up of space, not water, and it is literally creating light-years of distance between the ship and its point of departure. Meanwhile, in front of the ship, it contracts space, which reduces the distance to the target destination."

Devlin picked up the thread. "As this occurs, the spaceship sits in what's called a 'warp bubble.' Even though it is traveling at FTL speeds, it is actually stationary within its bubble, so the entire crew experiences no acceleration or deceleration."

Roger shook his head in amazement. "Okay, I think I understand. So why isn't this thing called a 'warp drive'?"

Devlin laughed. "You know, it was. But when the DoD got a hold of it, they must have decided that they needed a different name to be taken seriously, so the Alcubierre warp drive became the Alcubierre SEC drive."

"The whole idea was first conceived by a guy named Miguel Alcubierre, a Mexican theoretical physicist, in 1994. Einstein's general theory of relativity suggested that the surface of space-time could actually be curved by matter, and Alcubierre, after first successfully describing the necessary gravitational field mathematically, concluded that his warp drive was, in fact, possible—provided that science could eventually harness what's known as 'exotic matter,' or matter with negative energy density. For a long time, this was seen as one of several fundamental problems with Alcubierre's theories.

"Then, starting in 2025, there was an incredible series of scientific breakthroughs, which ultimately led to the successful attainment of exotic matter. Still, the building of a working prototype shocked all of us. It still seemed that an actual test was a very long way off."

Roger looked at both men quizzically. Once again, he knew he would never fully comprehend what Devlin and Belechenko were saying, but he understood the concepts. And he knew that to strive for a deeper understanding would not be a good use of his time.

Roger had been raised in Germany, Saudi Arabia, Japan, South Korea, and Nebraska; an army brat. As a child, he'd become very adept at assimilating into new cultures, in large part by learning just enough about a large number of topics to properly navigate a new environment. This skill had served him extremely well as White House Chief of Staff.

"At FTL speeds, would the crew age more slowly?" Roger finally asked.

Belechenko smiled. "Very good question, Mr. Tucker, but I'm afraid not."

Devlin jumped back in. "The passage of time inside the warp bubble would be no different than outside. If the journey took 14 years in Earth time, then the crew would age exactly 14 years."

"This is, of course, why we are planning a one-way journey; it is also one of the reasons the ship must be so large," Belechenko explained. "There must be two generations on board; one with the training and expertise to guide the ship and successfully execute the journey, and another to establish the colony and form the foundation of a new civilization. Training of younger crew members during the voyage will be of critical importance. Upon arrival, it will be necessary to have a substantial number of young men and women in their late teens and early twenties. These crew members will be small children at launch."

"Wouldn't it make more sense to send an unmanned probe to the planet first?" Roger asked.

"Another good question," Belechenko replied. "Yes; ideally, we would prefer to send a probe, so that we could learn more about the planet in advance. However, we've estimated that the cost of sending such a craft would be well over half of what it will cost for a manned mission, so economically, the benefit is relatively minor. In addition, since it would take 14 years for us to send a message to the probe, and for the probe to send data back to us, and we expect that an unmanned craft would most likely require additional guidance before reaching the planet, it might well take 56 or even 84 years before we got our answers."

Roger looked at Belechenko. "Interesting. So you're saying that a manned expedition will have to navigate some unknowns before reaching the planet?"

"Yes, most definitely" Belechenko confirmed. "Devlin's data allows us to be quite certain that the planet is habitable, and we will equip the ship with all appropriate technology to reach the planet and establish a surface colony. However, there will no doubt be more than a few issues which the officers and crew will have to resolve."

"For example? Roger prompted.

"Well, for one thing, we will not have a detailed picture of the planet's land-masses until the craft reaches Cerulea's solar system. The crew will be responsible for mapping the planet and choosing an optimal site."

There was a moment of silence as Roger took this in. "Commander, do you honestly believe that people will sign up for this mission if we don't even know where they're going to land?"

Belechenko and Devlin both smiled and exchanged a knowing glance. "Actually, Mr. Tucker," Belechenko responded, "I think we will be overwhelmed with applicants clamoring to go on the mission."

"What makes you say that?" Roger asked.

"Well for one thing," offered Devlin, "just look at the success Virgin Galactic has achieved; they're now ferrying over 35 thousand people a year up to their space hotels and back."

"But those people are signing up for a four day vacation—Cerulea is forever!"

"Yes, but for many young men and women—even couples with families—it's also the ultimate human adventure. It's irresistible," Devlin insisted.

"Bear in mind," Belechenko added. "There have been past expeditions with what I would say are far greater risks, and far greater unknowns. We have an excellent idea of what the ship will encounter. Your own Lewis and Clark—or even Christopher Columbus, for that matter—had far less understanding of what they'd be forced to confront."

"I suppose that's true," Roger reflected. "So, just how big will the ship need to be?"

"We've still got a lot of work to do, but we are estimating that the full crew complement will be in the neighborhood of one thousand at launch, including children. Over the course of the journey, new births will bring this to approximately 1800." Belechenko noticed the look of surprise on Roger's face. "I know that sounds very large, but remember that the ship will launch from space--not from Earth." Belechenko noted. "All of our existing space-based resources, such as the ISS, the L5 Spaceport, and the Lunar Extraction Facility built for the aborted mission to Mars will all come into play. It could be said that we've already built the factory; now all we need to do is retool and build a new ship.

"The one catch is that we will have to move quickly. There is a launch window in just over four years wherein the planets in our solar system and those in Cerulea's at the time of arrival will be in an optimum position. If we miss this opportunity, it could add up to five years to the mission, since we would then have to use traditional propulsion to navigate around various planets."

"And you're confident that you can build it in time to hit the window?" asked Roger tentatively.

Belechenko paused briefly before answering, allowing Devlin to fill the void.

"Piece of cake," Devlin said smiling.

14.

Georges Ventine walked out of his apartment and headed west up Rue d'Uzes. It was late afternoon. He had grabbed a sweater on his way out the door, and as he started to walk, he swung it over his shoulders and loosely tied off the sleeves in front of his chest. It was a gorgeous, golden afternoon, but the temperature was dropping, and he knew it would be cool on his way home.

The streets of Paris were crowded with the quiet shuffling of rush hour traffic. In 2024, France had become the first nation to outlaw gas-powered cars from its streets. Although various types of trucks and other vehicles still used fossil fuels, all passenger cars were now hybrids of some sort, often incorporating electric motors in combination with biodiesel or ethanol engines. By 2030, all developed countries had followed suit; there were now over 1 billion cars buzzing around on the planet—more than double the number of vehicles in the year 2000.

Georges jumped out into the street as he crossed Rue Montmartre, casually zigzagging between crawling vehicles. He headed south for a bit then took a right on Rue St. Marc.

He was on his way to meet his fiancé, and noted that he'd be early. Ever since he'd proposed one month prior, he'd made a special effort to be more thoughtful, which included being on time. This was somewhat new to him. He wasn't inconsiderate, but after three and a half years with Martine, they had started to take each other for granted—with him the greater transgressor. He wanted to change that.

He walked three blocks, headed south on Rue Favart, and came out on Rue de Gramont.

Georges was 34 years old, and one of France's foremost authorities on agricultural genetic engineering. He currently led a research team of over 35 scientists, backed by the Swiss firm Syngenta and Monsanto in the US.

Raised in Paris, he had moved to the States to earn a PhD from Auburn University in Alabama. Thereafter, Georges Ventine had wasted no time establishing himself in the field. Just 2 years after graduation, he had won the prestigious Wolf Prize in Agriculture for discovering a gene that allowed corn to be grown on arid farmland in Africa without the need for irrigation. His discovery was a sensation and, while much of Europe's antipathy toward genetically modified foods had faded following the six-year blight that began in 2021, it was often said that Ventine's discovery was the final blow to GMO resistance on the Continent.

And Ventine's star continued to rise; it had recently been rumored in Le Monde that he was on a short list to replace Adrien Renais as the French Agriculture Minister.

Ventine took it all in stride; in fact, he wasn't as enamored as he thought he'd be of running a research center—let alone a government ministry. He didn't mind the workload, but the pressure to produce new products had significantly constrained his team's scientific creativity. Every once in a while, he would fantasize about living with Martine on a sprawling farm somewhere in France, starting a family, and just tinkering in his own lab without the distractions that came with renown and organizational responsibility.

As he rounded the corner onto Rue de Quatre Septembre, he could see the green and white awning of the Café de la Paix—his destination—about four blocks ahead.

His wristphone began to vibrate. He looked at the identification of the caller on the screen, furrowed his brow, tentatively stepped into a small vestibule on his right, and answered the call.

"Bonjour, Georges Ventine."

"Mr. Ventine, this is the White House calling; please stand by for a call from Roger Tucker."

Ventine, like virtually every working professional in the developed world, wore on his wrist a powerful computer that served as telephone, messaging device, administrative assistant, and filing cabinet. He also wore a small ear bud at all times, similar in size to a turn-of-the-century hearing aide, which contained both speaker and microphone.

As he waited, Ventine immediately had two thoughts: First, though he was skeptical of the caller id at first glance, the call was not entirely a surprise. He had a feeling that he might be asked to consult on the Cerulea project, and suddenly found his mild ambiguity at the prospect giving way to excitement. His second thought was a small pang of doubt as to whether he could really add value to such an important mission. However, this rare hiccup in self-confidence faded quickly.

"Bonjour, Monsieur Ventine. This is Roger Tucker, Chief of Staff to President Virginia Belknap."

Ventine appreciated the proper salutation and pronunciation, and the fact that this gentleman didn't simply assume that he knew who the US Chief of Staff was—though, of course, he did.

"Bonjour, Monsieur Tucker. How may I help you?"

"Please, call me Roger. Monsieur Ventine, I am calling on behalf of the President and the Cerulea mission. We believe your expertise could be extremely valuable to the project, and—if you're interested—we'd like you to come speak with us about the possibility of your involvement."

Ventine, who was known by all his colleagues for his calm and steady nature, suddenly found his heart beating rapidly in his chest and his mouth a little dry. He was very impressed by Tucker's humility—a rarity among Americans and something he was not expecting. He was suddenly overwhelmed by a burning desire to be a contributor to this grand effort. His thoughts raced ahead; realizing that he might have to give up his current position; his brain immediately accepted the compromise and started to romanticize the notion of burning the midnight oil as just another member of a world-class research team.

"Mons- Roger, I think I would like very much to discuss with you how I might be of service. Can you tell me a little bit more about how you see the agricultural component taking shape?"

There was a slight pause on the line.

"Um, well, Monsieur Ventine, we were kind of hoping that you could tell us how to shape it..."

After a brief discussion in which Roger made clear the role they wanted to discuss with him, Ventine bid goodbye and terminated the call. However, he continued chatting with his wrist device until he'd successfully rearranged his now-changed schedule and requested appropriate travel arrangements. A young woman walked by, wearing a bright yellow sundress and pushing a baby stroller; she thought nothing of a man standing in a doorway barking commands to a computer.

Once finished, Ventine stepped out onto the sidewalk and walked at an accelerated pace. His world was now very different than it had been 10 minutes ago. As he entered Place de l'Opera and spied Martine at a table near the back, he realized he was late. Farmhouses and children were now the last thing on his mind.

15.

Cynthia Fossett looked down 14 stories onto Pearl Street from her office at the Second Circuit Court of Appeals, then looked uptown at the expanse of Manhattan Island.

She was anxious.

She was expecting a call any day now regarding a new job, and she was incredibly conflicted as to whether it was the right path for her. At the same time, she was worried that the call might not come at all, which caused anxiety of a different sort.

18 years earlier, with a fresh JD from Fordham, Cynthia Fossett had clerked for Supreme Court Justice Elaine Stewart. At the age of 24, she was exposed daily to some of the most far-reaching and important legal issues facing the nation and, indirectly, the world. It was heady stuff, and made all the more rewarding by Justice Stewart herself. Never had Cynthia known a smarter, more thoughtful, and more insightful individual—or a better boss.

Justice Stewart recognized Cynthia's potential, and thought it important that she get some experience with a private firm. Justice Stewart helped Cynthia land a job with the prestigious Brown, Bradford & Poag in New York City.

Then, after just 7 years at the firm, Cynthia was offered a judgeship in lower Manhattan, and she took it. She was at the top of her game, and her colleagues thought her crazy. But it was exactly what she wanted.

The appointment to the federal bench came three years after that.

Her wristphone beeped quietly, and she activated the call.

"Judge Fossett, this is the White House calling; please stand by for a call from Roger Tucker."

This was it. The call she'd been dreading—and eagerly anticipating.

Two weeks earlier, Supreme Court Justice Charles Maynard had experienced a heart attack. His third in as many years. While the doctors had said it was fairly mild, and that they expected a full recovery, it was widely believed that he would resign. He was 83. Cynthia knew the White House was putting together a short list for his replacement, and it had been speculated by a host of pundits that she would be at or near the top of the list.

"Judge Fossett, this is Roger Tucker, White House Chief of Staff to President Belknap. I believe we met several years back when you were first confirmed."

"Yes, Mr. Tucker, I remember well."

"I'm guessing that you might have been expecting this call."

"Well, Mr. Tucker, let's just say that it doesn't come as a complete surprise."

"Well, I don't mean to be coy, but what I have to say may do just that."

"I'm listening."

"Judge Fosset, should Justice Maynard choose to resign, we have decided not to nominate you for the SJC."

"Oh. I see."

Cynthia's heart sank. Although she was terrified that the nomination process, the move back to Washington, and the demands of the Supreme Court would rip her comfortable life to shreds, she also wanted the job desperately.

"Mr. Tucker, I nonetheless want to thank you for calling. I'm honored that—"

"Please, hold on a sec. We've actually got something else in mind. It concerns the mission to Cerulea."

"Oh. I see."

"As you're probably aware, we're assembling a team of individuals to lead each component of the mission, and we'd like to have you draft the blueprint for Cerulea's justice system."

Cynthia was dumbfounded. Like everyone else in the civilized world, she was following the mission's progress, but she had never given the first thought to the possibility that they would seek out someone with her background to play a role.

There was a rather long period of silence as Roger waited for a response and Cynthia's mind raced. The possibilities here were overwhelming. In a matter of several seconds, her brain had somehow traveled from a position of terrible disappointment to hesitancy and doubt to one of pure enthusiasm and certainty.

"Please understand; we're not asking for an immediate response. In fact, I just wanted to see if we could arrange for you to come talk with—"

"I accept. I would be honored to join the Cerulean team."

This time Roger was taken aback, and required a moment to recover.

"I'm... that's... that's terrific. The President will be extremely pleased...."

They agreed to a meeting in Washington in two days time. Cynthia looked at her wrist to make sure the connection had been terminated, took a deep breath, and placed her head in her hands, reeling from the fact that she'd just reconfigured her entire life in the course of a two-minute phone call.

16.

R andall Reese was furious.
        He had not worked his entire life to instill a sense of morality in the culture of his country only to see it go up in flames—or up into space—overnight.

As he watched the nightly news and read the daily papers, and followed the progress of the mission, he found himself increasingly angry at what he knew to be a backwards and dangerous blueprint for humanity's next great chapter.

President Belknap, her homosexual chief of staff, and their band of social scientists had only given transparent lip service to civilization's most important principle, and it left him seething with outrage. They had ignored the appeals of a large percentage of the American public, and he was simply unwilling to let things stand. The mission's current social and moral trajectory was unacceptable, and he would act.

Reese was the founder and President of Americans for Moral Truth, a growing organization based on the precept that America and the world would only progress as a civilization when it directly acknowledged that God is the centerpiece of mankind's existence; it will only advance when it sees and serves this Truth. The question rattling around in the back of his mind was just how far he was prepared to go to bring about this eventuality.

He had grown up in a strict yet stable household in Waukesha, Wisconsin. Though his childhood had been uneventful, it had been honest—and secure. Reese never got into trouble, never snuck out, never really enjoyed adventures of any kind. Never had sex until his mid-twenties.

Of all this, Reese was extremely proud; he firmly believed that his upbringing and lifestyle had bred in him an integrity that was all too rare in American society.

His family had not been particularly religious. They had gone to church most Sundays, and said grace before dinner, but it wasn't until Reese reached his 30th year that he truly discovered—truly began to cherish—the Bible.

He had been married for 5 years, and he and his wife Sylvia were about to have their first child. It had been a normal pregnancy, but with one month to go before the due date, Sylvia became quite sick. The doctors were baffled; his wife was running a high temperature, and couldn't hold food down. After a week with no diagnosis, the situation looked grim. Sylvia was delirious, and Reese was near the brink. One night in the hospital, at his wife's bedside, unable to sleep, he had picked up a Bible and began reading—and praying. Something came over him and, while nurses and doctors came and went, Reese kept to his verse; 12 hours passed, 24 hours, 36. The hospital staff started getting as concerned about the husband as they were about the mother. Finally, after 48 hours of non-stop Bible prayer, and nearly three days without sleep, the nurse forced Reese out of his near-trance to tell him that his wife's fever had broken, and the baby's heartbeat appeared normal.

Sylvia gave birth two weeks later to a perfectly healthy baby boy. From that day forward, Reese saw life in a new light. To say that he'd been born again, or found Jesus, seemed a cliché. Reese had simply communicated with God, and God had listened. Never again would he take God for granted, and never again would he sit idly by while others behaved in a way that negated or ignored God's miracles.

Life was sacred, and Reese would fight to see that this truth was acknowledged by all. He knew deep in his being that God's presence was a critical cornerstone not only of America's but of mankind's existence. Whether in government, in schools, or in the workplace, His power, His grace, and His love should never be forsaken.

It was early Wednesday morning. Reese had just finished breakfast and was reading an article in the *Standard* reporting on the mission's education plan.

For weeks, both the *Standard* and the *Times* had cluttered their front pages with the machinations of the Mission Council, and he couldn't take it any longer.

The Council was the governing body for the mission, architected by the United Nations Security Council, and—not surprisingly—structured in a similar fashion.

Reese walked into his study, sat down at his desk, picked up the phone, and called his old friend, Joe Condon.

Joe was a lobbyist in Washington, and had spent his life working many of the same issues as Reese—but from a decidedly different angle. To Joe, the end always justified the means, and Reese had always been uncomfortable with this approach. Nonetheless, Joe had tried very hard to get Reese more directly involved in his anti-mission efforts.

"Good morning Randall."

"Morning, Joe. Listen, I was wondering if you could brief me on what your group has planned for this week."

Reese was crossing a line, and he knew it. He had made his decision quickly, but not spontaneously. In his heart, he was absolutely confident that this was the only appropriate course of action.

"Well, the event has grown nicely. We are now expecting about 80 thousand, give or take."

"That has grown. Last we spoke I think it was roughly half that."

"Well, Max Caulfield's public statements last week served as a real catalyst. And here's the best news: he's agreed to speak at the rally."

"Caulfield? Speaking at Saturday's event?"

"Yes indeed. Got the call yesterday afternoon. His deputy chief of staff informed me that the Senator has decided to take a much more active role in opposing Belknap's committee. We'll be making an announcement early this afternoon."

In Reese's mind, Caulfield's participation gave aggressive activism true legitimacy. He looked out the window of his study and watched as a bird landed on a statue of the Virgin Mary in his backyard.

His rising anger over the past month had suddenly metamorphosed into pure energy. "Joe, what would you say if I were to indicate my willingness to join the rally as well?"

"You know what I'd say: fantastic! We would be overjoyed."

"All right. I'm in. But there are some particulars I'd like to discuss before anything is public."

Reese hit a few keys on the keyboard in front of him and brought up his schedule.

"Could we meet tomorrow afternoon at around 2 pm; your office?"

"Randall, for you, I will clear the entire afternoon..."

17.

The announcement of Cerulea and the mission to reach it had given the Belknap administration a second honeymoon.

The press had closely covered all of the key appointments related to the mission: Vladimir Belechenko as Mission Commander; Gerhardt Schmidt as Chief Engineer, Georges Ventine as Head of Agriculture and Biosystems, Jiro Kawamoto as Head of Energy and Environmental Planning. In fact, the world had eaten it all up with a spoon.

Since America was footing most of the bill for the mission, it was widely expected that President Belknap would simply insert Americans into most of the key positions. Once again, she confounded expectations, and received substantial praise for the team she was assembling.

That is, until she announced that Cynthia Fossett would spearhead the planning for Cerulea's legal system. As an Appeals Court judge, she had presided over a number of highly controversial cases, and conservative leaders took one look at those that contested their beliefs and balked. Since Fossett would be leading the team which crafted the new planet's constitution, she was pivotal; the new planet's social behavior and evolution would depend on the fruits of her efforts.

Within the core of the conservative base, the appointment had hit a nerve. Nonetheless, Ginny prided herself on being able to disarm the activist elements of both the Progressives and the Conservatives. She believed in the Council's choice, and it was her sincere hope that she could once again prevail in convincing key conservative leaders that Judge Fossett could admirably serve both sides of the aisle.

18.

"Madam President, I am not a student of political science. In fact, I've spent my life fairly far removed—both mentally and physically—from the goings-on of mainstream society. So please help me to understand; how has the world come to find itself in this situation?" Belechenko asked ingenuously.

"Well, the roots of this thing go way, way back to the early 1900s," Ginny replied. "And perhaps back even farther to the birth of this country."

President Belknap and Commander Belechenko were having a drink in the Vermeil room at the White House. The room was darkly lit; they were seated across from each other with a blazing fire in the fireplace between them. The Mission Council—over which the President presided as Chairman—had just completed an exhaustive review of the mission schedule and had reviewed the status of each major component of the project. The good news was that the leadership team they had put in place appeared to be making excellent progress. Most of the key milestones were on track, and the morale and overall dynamic of the various teams seemed to be extremely healthy. The bad news was that, despite the obvious competence of the team, there was increasing unrest from religious conservatives regarding the team's make-up and perceived ideological bent.

Of most concern was the belief that the mission team—and ultimately the society that would evolve on Cerulea, would be far too secular, and that generations of Cerulean humans would grow up without any appreciation for their God, or for the core values that served as the foundation of a healthy civilization.

What had initially been random, disconnected protests and editorials now looked to be more of a coordinated effort. News reports of those publicly opposing the mission's direction were at one time sporadic; they were now more frequent, and suggested that some of these events had been well-planned.

Belechenko was fully capable of ignoring the protests. He had certainly developed an immunity over the years to all of the political maneuverings surrounding the International Space Station. However, this was different. His role was more prominent, and this mission was just as much a political adventure as it was scientific. He realized that, whether he wanted to or not, it was his responsibility to better understand the underpinnings of the debate.

The Commander leaned back in his wingback chair, and took a strong sip of whiskey from the heavy lead crystal glass. The ice cubes rattled as he removed the glass from his lips. The whiskey tasted strong and smooth; his body shuddered as it processed the spirits.

He was intensely handsome. He had an athletic build made strong and muscular through a youthful addiction to soccer, and a smile that could melt a Siberian glacier. He had aged extremely well; his electric blue eyes grew deeper as he grew wiser, and the tips of grey on his short-cropped hair gave him a highly distinguished demeanor.

"Please, say more," Belechenko urged. "When you say that this issue dates back to the birth of your United States, what do you mean?"

"Well, there has for a long time been a heated debate as to what role religion played in the establishment of America. I'm sure you're aware that the country was founded by people who felt they had been persecuted for their religious beliefs in England."

"Yes, of course," Belechenko replied.

"Well, the progressives would tell you that, because of this, it's very clear that the founding fathers—a sacred group of wise men, according to our cultural lore—believed that true religious freedom, and the separation of church and state, was a critical cornerstone of the republic."

"That sounds logical," Belechenko noted. "Is this not documented?"

"Yes and no. In the first amendment, the Constitution clearly states that the government will not make laws regarding either the establishment or the free exercise of religion. However, many believe—In fact, the majority of Americans believe—that the term 'separation of church and state' is taken from the constitution, and therefore is solidly embedded in our legal system. In truth, it appears nowhere in the Constitution or the Bill of Rights, or in any state document, for that matter."

"Then what is its origin?" Belechenko inquired. He watched as the President took a sip of her vodka & soda, then held the glass in her lap.

Ginny was an elegant woman; a redhead with piercing green eyes and a dramatic widows peak. Though no one had ever described her as striking in her earlier years, she had developed very beautiful features: accentuated cheekbones, a graceful neck, broad shoulders, and an attractive figure.

"The term was actually pulled from what has come to be called the Danbury Letter—a letter Thomas Jefferson wrote when he was President to a group of Baptists in Danbury Connecticut who were concerned about religious liberty in their state. In it he quotes the first amendment, stating that the government will "'make no law respecting an establishment of religion, or prohibiting the free exercise thereof,'" he then continues 'thus building a wall of separation between church and State.'"

"So religious conservatives do not accept this as evidence that government and religion should be kept apart?" Belechenko asked.

"No, the conservatives would essentially say the opposite," Ginny replied. "They hold that there is ample evidence that the founding fathers believed that their power to form this nation, along with their power to govern such a nation, was derived directly from God. Therefore, rigid separation of church and state is totally inconsistent with the founding fathers' intentions.

"In fact, religious conservatives make the case that one of the primary objectives of the First Amendment was the very opposite of what the Progressives make of it today. They see it as expressly stating that government should not impede or interfere with the free practice of religion. In other words, separation of church and state in our society is intended not to eliminate religion from public debate, but to ensure that all of our varied religious beliefs and traditions can be shared, debated and properly supported—including, of course, by the government itself."

"I always thought that the U.S. government did its best to steer clear of religious issues. This is not true?"

"Not by a long shot. Our history is riddled with examples of government getting entangled with religion. Here's one small example: do you have any money on you?"

"I.. yes, I think so."

"Let's have a look."

Belechenko reached over and placed his glass down on the solid, mahogany table to his right, then leaned toward the fireplace, reached into his right back pocket, and produced a thin, folded set of bills.

"Okay, now open a bill for me."

"Which one?" asked Belechenko. "I have some ones, a five and some twenties."

"It doesn't matter. Any one will do." Ginny got up from her seat, and, carrying her drink, crossed in front of the fire and sat on the left armrest of the Commander's chair.

Belechenko pulled the outer bill, a twenty, from the stack. Ginny noticed that he had organized the bills by denomination: twenties on the outside, then the five, with the ones on the inside. All the bills were also right side up, facing the same direction. She remembered, with an inward smile, her father's habit of doing the same thing. Belechenko placed the others next to his drink, and opened a twenty dollar bill. He looked at the face of the bill.

"Okay, what am I supposed to see?" He asked.

"Turn it over," Ginny said as she leaned over to look at the bill he was holding. Belechenko could smell her subtle, but very distinct perfume.

Ginny pointed to the center of the note. "There, above the White House." "'In God We Trust.'" read Belechenko. "Hmm; I don't think I've ever noticed." He paused for a minute, their shoulders nearly touching as they examined the money. He inhaled quietly and deeply through his nose. "And this is on other bills as well?" Belechenko asked, turning to look at President Belknap, their faces now unnaturally close.

Ginny held his eyes for a moment before breaking eye contact and getting up to return to her seat. "It's the same on the one, the five, and every other piece of U.S. currency, including all of our coins."

"Interesting, but not exactly concrete proof of your founding fathers' intentions," Belechenko noted, somehow wishing that there'd been more for the two of them to look at on the twenty dollar bill.

"No. In fact, the words were first introduced just after the civil war, then placed on all currency in the 1950s during the cold war with the Soviet Union. However, it is one illustration as to how religion, and the notion of God watching over the nation, is prevalent within our society. Many would say that this idea of the United States as a country chosen and blessed by God is the reason for our success; others, of course, claim that it's simply an example of our perceived arrogance."

Belechenko was fascinated by the discussion, and by the President's in-depth knowledge of the subject. He was equally entranced by Virginia Belknap herself. This was not a sudden realization. Since they'd first met, he had always looked upon President Belknap as an incredibly smart, engaging, and, well, sexy woman. He tried to expunge the thought from his mind, believing such feelings toward the President of the United States to be quite inappropriate, but he was unsuccessful.

She turned her eyes from the fire to look at him, and he realized he'd been staring—for perhaps longer than he'd intended. Taking another sip of his drink, he broke the silence with a question: "And Madam President, what do you believe?"

This time she was staring. "Commander, do you think it's possible, at least when we're alone, that you could call me Ginny? The Madam President thing starts to wear on me after a while."

Belechenko swallowed the sip of whiskey in his mouth and paused, a little dumbstruck. "Madame President, I don't think that would be--"

"Sure it would," she interrupted. "You're the Supreme Commander of the mission to Cerulea, and you report to the Mission Council, a global body. Can't world figures address each other as friends?"

"I suppose I could try."

They held each other's eyes for a moment. "I'd appreciate it," Ginny said firmly. Feeling she'd been a bit too forward, she quickly reverted to the subject at hand. "So what do I believe, you ask? Well, I think what the founding fathers believed is a topic for unlimited debate, and I'm not certain it's the central issue."

"What is the central issue, in your view?"

"Well, if the whole point here is to ensure freedom to practice the religion of your choice, then it seems to me that government involvement is not such a terrific idea."

"Why not?"

"Because it's much too slippery a slope. Conceptually, it makes perfect, logical sense to me for the government to support—and perhaps even to encourage—the practice of various and diverse religions; in fact, governmental encouragement of spirituality in all its forms could in many ways be of tremendous benefit to our society. However, the problem arises when concept meets reality."

"Meaning what?"

"Well, if government supports the practice of religion, it is going to have to be incredibly skilled at making absolutely sure that it never promotes one religion over another—or, for that matter, promotes religion over atheism, since that too is a form of religious belief. The bottom line is that the government is incredibly bad at anything requiring such a skillful balance." She thought for a moment. "No, it's worse than that: the government is simply incapable of walking that fine line, so my belief is that they should simply stay out of it."

"And yet, the mission team is forced to achieve this balance, yes?" Belechenko leaned forward and gestured with his hand. "I agree that it is inappropriate to advocate one form of religion for Cerulea, but isn't it imperative that religion be a part of this new society?"

"I would say it's imperative that all inhabitants of Cerulea have complete freedom to believe and practice what they choose. Therefore, the only responsibilities of the Mission Council are to ensure that the crew is properly diverse, that it represents people of different races, religions, sexual orientation, economic standing, and that everyone has complete access to all of the religious teachings of their faith, and that they're given complete freedom to practice that faith."

Belechenko smiled broadly, his eyes twinkling in the firelight. Clearly his mind had let go of the discussion, and Ginny wondered where his mind had drifted. Reflexively smiling back at him, she asked "What are you thinking?"

"I find your intellect intoxicating, Ginny." She blushed but held his gaze, and somewhere in the back of her mind realized a barrier had just been crossed.

19.

The protesters marched down 17th Street to Pennsylvania Avenue and began to amass in front of the White House.

They had gathered earlier in the morning at Farragut Square to organize themselves, distribute signs, and set ground rules.

God save Cerulea. Planet of the damned. Save mankind: Impeach Belknap. Perpetuate our species and our values.

Roger walked to the window of his West Wing office and watched the protesters in the distance

He then turned his head back to a large screen nestle within a bookcase on one wall of his office for close-ups and audio.

Roger's office was down the hall from the President's, and looked north while the Oval Office looked south. It was bright and well-lit, fairly orderly, and welcoming. There were a number of books pulled from their shelves and stacked on various surfaces; some of which had been left open. Roger didn't have a lot of free time to read, but he did in his youth, and would often pull down books, looking for ideas for a speech, or insights into the machinations of political life.

President Belknap knocked once on his open door as she entered.

"Madam President."

"Roger, do you have a minute to discuss Friday's meeting?"

"Of course."

Ginny turned to the screen. Neither of them spoke for a few moments as they listened to an on-air reporter on location describing the protest:

"The protesters have made it clear that they disagree strongly with the President's approach to the mission. Specifically, they believe that those chosen to manage certain aspects of the mission are highly partisan and do not represent the nation's values.

"Randall Reese, of Americans for Moral Truth, spoke this morning at a rally on the steps of the Capital..."

The station cut to a clip of that morning's event.

"It is clear to me," bellowed Reese to a gaggle of reporters and a sizable crowd behind them, "that this administration has no right to highjack a mission of this importance, and hold it hostage to the values of a minority of Americans. We must make it clear to all involved that the colonization of Cerulea represents a critical step in mankind's evolution, and that a new civilization on a distant planet, based on a rudderless value system, would not be a step forward, but a painful and tragic step backward."

"Mute," Roger commanded; the audio coming from the screen fell silent.

"So much for our second honeymoon," Roger mused.

"Oh, I think that reaction by Reese and his crew is to be expected," said Ginny. "In fact, I thought that we'd have heard from them sooner."

"What's frustrating is that global surveys indicate overwhelming approval of our approach to the mission, Roger noted. "My worry is that Reese and others like him could present a real obstacle to the Mission—or even force us to reconfigure the Mission Council."

"Unlikely, but anything's possible," Ginny responded. "Why don't you ask the folks in Communications to formulate a strategy for keeping Reese at bay? At the very least, we can make sure that the voices that support us are just as loud."

"I will do just that," Roger confirmed, tapping the action item into his tablet.

"Good. So, with regard to the Friday meeting, I want you to work with Belechenko to establish some clear priorities..."

They discussed the Mission Council meeting, formulated a rough agenda, and outlined some goals for each of the major subcommittees. As the President left his office, Roger hit a button on his wristphone and instructed his electronic assistant to organize a meeting with Belechenko and some members of his staff that afternoon.

He looked out his window and suddenly saw police lights in the distance, and a whirl of activity. He turned back to the screen, and saw chaos. He reactivated the sound. President Belknap, who had been alerted to the situation as she'd left Roger's office, returned abruptly and sat on the edge of his desk. They both watched in disbelief.

It was mayhem.

Police had arrived and seemed to be forcing themselves in between what were obviously two opposing camps. There appeared to be broken bottles on the street. An ambulance was visible and the EMTs were placing a woman with a cut on her forehead into the rear of the vehicle.

Both sides were shouting at each other and waving signs and fists. Another five or so officers joined the melee and they seemed to tip the balance. The two sides were increasingly isolated, and slowly but surely, the heat of the moment began to dissipate.

"Roger, go back," Ginny commanded. "I want to see what caused this."

Wearing a wireless pointing device on the middle finger on his right hand, Roger made several almost imperceptible hand motions; the screen responded and the scene jumped back in time.

"Further back," she asked.

Roger went back further, until the scene was of a relatively docile protest, with fifty or fewer protesters chanting and holding signs.

Suddenly, the camera panned and a small group of people stepped in between the camera and the protesters, and started shouting back. More joined, some with signs of their own, and the confrontation grew more intense. A policeman with outstretched arms started asking both sides to step back.

At that moment, behind the officer's back, a man ran forward, raised a bottle he was holding in his hand, and hit one of the original protesters--a woman--over the head. She raised her hand to her forehead; blood began dripping down her hand and face.

Roger and Ginny recoiled as they watched. In a flash, additional police could be seen entering the fray, adding more muscle to the task of separating the two groups. Three or four of the protesters lifted the bleeding woman and started carrying her away from the crowd. EMTs came to their assistance, and placed her on a gurney.

Roger realized they were back to where they'd left off; he commanded the screen to pause.

He turned to the President, and they looked at one another for a moment in silence.

"I'm not sure what to make of that; it's hard to believe," Roger said, breaking the silence. "It all happened so incredibly fast."

"Unbelievably fast," Ginny agreed, shaking her head.

Roger began taking some notes. "You don't need to say it. I'll double the security for the dinner on Thursday and for Friday's meeting. And," he paused, looking at her once again, "I'll move that discussion with the Communications team up a little higher on the priority list."

Ginny slid off the desk and walked toward the door.

"Do you think we should set up a meeting with Reese?" Roger asked.

Ginny turned and gave it some thought. "No, not yet."

She turned to leave, then paused. "Roger, I'd like to review our statement on this before it gets distributed."

"Will do." Roger watched her walk out and resumed his note-taking.

He stopped after a minute, and looked back at the screen. He put his pen down, swiveled in his chair, and switched over to a summary of breaking news stories to see who had already picked up the incident, then switched back to video.

Any differences that once separated televisions and computers were fading from society's collective memory.

As he watched the aftermath, he again paused the picture and turned his head to the side, contemplating some question that had just occurred to him. He went back to where the shouting started and began to watch the entire scene once more.

20.

"Johnny Walker Black, neat," said Condon.

"And you sir?" the waiter asked.

"Cranberry juice and soda," Reese replied.

"Very good, gentleman. Back in a minute." The waiter nodded, and headed off to the bar.

Randall Reese and Joe Condon sat in a well-appointed booth; the crisp, white tablecloth punctuated by elegant, cut crystal water glasses, heavy, polished flatware and a single fresh-cut orchid in a small vase. As they resumed their conversation, a man walked up to them from over Condon's shoulder and greeted Reese.

"Randall, good to see you again; I thought you gave a hell of speech at the rally."

Reese edged out from his seat; they bowed their heads to one another. "Thank you, Senator. I just hope I'm not joining this battle too late."

The Senator smiled in response to the question, "Oh, to the contrary; I think our troops just picked up some badly needed momentum," he said, winking subtly, his southern charm ever-present.

"Senator Caulfield, do you know Joe Condon?" Reese gestured to Condon, who started to slide out of the booth.

"I believe we've met. How are you, Joe?" They bowed their heads as Condon stood.

"Good, Senator, thanks. Nice to see you again." Despite Condon's role in helping to organize the recent event, he had never directly interacted with Caulfield, but he felt there was no reason to point that out. Besides, this meant that their next meeting, in the senator's mind at least, would now be their third, which meant that Condon could practically claim him as a friend.

"We were just discussing troop movements and forward logistics," Reese joked, extending the metaphor. "Care to join us?"

The Senator chuckled. "No, I think I'm most valuable in civilian clothes-- but thank you for the offer." He winked again.

"Understood," said Reese, knowing that this was the end of the exchange. "Great seeing you."

"Good luck and Godspeed," Caulfield said, nodding to both of them as he turned and headed for the exit.

They were at the Old Ebbitt Grill, a venerable dining establishment, roughly half a block from the White House. It had been in existence since the 1850s, and was a well-known watering hole for politicians and Capitol Hill staffers. The restaurant had been a favorite of such figures as Ulysses Grant and Teddy Roosevelt.

The décor was Victorian, with mahogany beams overhead, antique gas lamps, and bars of thick marble with brass accents. On the wall were a number of paintings depicting various historic Washington scenes, along with several mounted big game trophies supposedly shot by T Rex himself.

They settled back into their booth. The waiter arrived and efficiently delivered their drinks.

"To the battle," Condon said, raising his scotch.

Reese raised his glass in return: "Here's to it."

They both took a sip and placed their glasses in front of them. Reese pulled the swizzle stick out of his juice, put one end to his lips and drew a breath to clear remaining drops from the straw. He then began absent-mindedly turning it in the fingers of his right hand, tapping one end then the other on the table cloth in front of him.

"Is this war winnable?" Reese finally asked, looking at Condon as he continued the metaphor. "I'm not a veteran of this type of warfare."

"Oh, I think you know more about these tactics than you let on," Condon replied, refusing to let Reese play the innocent. "But, to answer your question-- yes."

The press was starting to fall in line. The protest had become front-page news, and seemed to be staying there. Not because the protest message itself was particularly newsworthy, but as a result of how badly the protesters had apparently been treated by the pro-Belknap contingent. To the whole world, it clearly appeared as if those defending the Mission Council were distinctly intolerant of opposing views. In turn, opposition was growing.

Reese put the straw down next to his glass and leaned forward. "Let's walk through our strategy from thirty thousand feet."

Condon took a deep breath. "All right," he said patiently. Condon was a big man, just over six feet and about 225 pounds. While he'd put some excess weight on his torso over the years, his size was mostly brawn. A linebacker in his college days at Texas A&M, Condon had climbed the ladder of success as a lobbyist not through intellect, but through brute force and determination. He was canny, but mostly he was doggedly persistent, and he always kept his focus.

As the two men had begun working together, Condon had at first been intimidated by Reese's sharp mind, his intuitive sense for shaping a message, and his extremely loyal following. As time went on, however, he'd begun to realize that there was a lot that Reese needed to learn.

The waiter arrived and took their order. After he'd departed, Reese looked at Condon and spoke: "If I understand it, the goal of these protests is to soften up the electorate for the general election next summer, correct?"

"Exactly right," said Condon. He took a heavy sip of his scotch and leaned in. "If we can get Belknap and the Mission Council on the defensive, we should be able to push the President's global approval rating below 60 percent, and her domestic rating below fifty. That'll give Butler a path to victory over the progressive challenger."

"Got it. I understand all that. My question is this: By the time Butler—or whoever it turns out to be—"

"It'll be Butler, Randall, take my word for it," Condon interjected.

"Okay. By the time Butler takes office, the mission will be a fast-moving train. It's not at all clear to me how we stop it."

"Easy," said Condon. He drew another deep breath and spoke softly but firmly. "Assuming we gain control of the Senate—and I think we will—we launch an eleventh hour barrage of legislation, swap out some of the key Council leaders and crew officers, and replace them with our own people."

"Joe," Reese said sharply, clearly frustrated, "I know that's the goal, but I don't understand how you intend to simply 'swap out' mission staff. The Mission Council is a global body, and it's chaired by the President; no one on the Council or the crew is just going step down. And even if they did, the US can't simply appoint replacements. We will have to abide by the Council bylaws."

"You raised two issues. Let me address the last one first," Condon replied. "While the US Congress can't appoint replacements on its own, it certainly can use its leverage. This country is financing over fifty percent of the mission; we can certainly play hardball with regard to who should fill open slots."

"Now as for the first issue," he continued, "are you sure you want to know how we might open up some slots on the Council and crew?"

The two men looked at each other across the table for several seconds. Reese's mind raced; he realized he was on the edge of yet another threshold he wasn't sure he was prepared to cross. Not knowing meant plausibility of denial--but it also meant he'd be getting himself involved with his eyes shut, and that scared him.

Just as he opened his mouth to speak, the waiter arrived with their salads.

21.

Mike Victor zeroed in on one of the faces from the news clip that Roger Tucker had sent down. He copied and pasted it into a search engine to see if he could get a positive identification. This was always an iffy proposition. While the ability to match facial photographs in a database was now fairly straightforward technology, there were still a lot of false positives—and total misses. Of the twenty-three faces that he was able to pull off the video thus far, only four had found a positive match.

Mike had worked in the White House intelligence lab for just over four years. He was incredibly patient, incredibly thorough, and painstakingly honest. He was known by everyone from the President on down as a straight shooter who would never draw a conclusion if the data didn't support it.

Roger Tucker entered the lab. "Mike, how goes it?"

"Not bad, Roger. But not great. I've got a few IDs, but I don't think any surprises."

"How about the bottle incident?"

"Well, not at all conclusive, but I'll let you be the judge. Take a look."

He turned in his chair from one workstation to another. Wearing a pointing device a little larger and more complicated than Roger's, he made several small gestures with his hand, and soon had a close-up of the man hitting the woman with the bottle on-screen.

"So, let me take you through this." As Victor subtly tapped his middle finger and thumb together, the video advanced, frame by frame. "If you look closely, right... here, you can see the bottle actually breaking."

"Okay, what can you tell me?" Roger inquired.

"Well, again, not much, but there's a few things here that don't seem right." Victor paused, once again advancing the video by a few frames, then reversing it.

"Like what?" Roger asked.

"Well, here's the issue. It looks like your basic beer bottle, right?"

"Right," Roger agreed.

"The problem is that the average beer bottle is a fairly solid object, so there are two things we should be seeing here that we aren't." Victor paused again.

"Go on," Roger encouraged.

"Right. First off, if you ask me, the bottle breaks a bit too easily. See right here? Second, the woman's head barely moves on impact."

"Okay, so what does this tell us?" Roger asked, hoping for a conclusion.

"Right now, nothing." Victor leaned back in his chair.

"What do you mean, nothing?" Roger's raised his voice. "Are you implying that it may have been a fake bottle or something?"

"Maybe, but there are probably a dozen possible explanations—a Hollywood bottle is only one of them."

"Okay, Okay. What else you got?"

Victor moved the video forward a couple of seconds. "Right here, as we see the Woman raise her hand to her forehead, we also see blood start dripping down the woman's face and hand—like we'd expect it to."

"Anything seem amiss here?"

"No, probably not. But there is one more thing. There are a few frames a little further on that seemed strange."

"Strange how?"

Victor advanced the video further. "Here we go. As the other protesters take hold of her to carry her away, she pulls her hand away from her forehead for just a second or two. Right... there. See?"

"I see. So what?"

"Well, there's no gash. There should be at least a black line where the blood is leaving the wound."

"Well, I'll be damned." Roger squinted at the screen.

"Once again, though, it doesn't tell us much. If she'd been pressing hard enough with her hand, she could have closed the wound temporarily."

Roger shook his head, smiling. "Mike, I've got to admire your restraint. What's the next step?"

"I'll send it to the computer forensic lab and let the big boys take a look. They've got better equipment, and can simulate force of impact far better than I. If this was staged, they'll be able to tell us.

"I'll also try and get my hands on the EMTs' report to see if that tells us anything."

"How long will all that take?"

"Probably a day or two."

"Okay, great work Mike. Thanks. Keep me posted."

"Will do." Victor swiveled around to the other workstation as Mike headed for the door. "Oh, Roger, one more thing."

"What?"

"One the faces I identified belongs to one of the guys confronting the protesters."

"Do we know who he is?"

"Not by name, but it's clear that the very same guy was in a news clip of a large rally several months back in Milwaukee."

"What rally?" Roger asked.

"Oh, I have it here somewhere." Victor fumbled through a stack of open windows on his screens. "Here it is. Looks like the rally was for a group called 'Americans for Moral Truth'"

Roger stared at Mike Victor, momentarily speechless. After a few seconds, he spoke. "Mike, can you do me a favor and put all of this in a preliminary report? No conclusions, of course, just a summary of the data."

"Sure, no problem."

"And can you get it to me this afternoon?" Roger pleaded

Mike looked at his watch and bit his lower lip. "Hmmm. How about if I got it to you sometime this evening?"

Roger smiled. "That's fine. Thanks. And tell CFL to analyze this stuff immediately. If at all possible, I want their findings by day's end tomorrow. If you need help on my end to expedite it, just call my office for the authorization."

Roger walked quickly out of the lab.

22.

The budget session had come to a close. President Belknap leaned back in her chair.

"Thank you everyone."

Almost in unison, all those around the table said "thank you, Madam President" as they gathered their things, stood up and left the room.

Roger Tucker sat across the table and remained seated. As the last of the meeting participants departed, and the door closed behind them, Roger spoke.

"I've got some news on Tuesday's protest," Roger opened.

"Oh? What have you learned?"

"Well, as I'd suspected, it appears that the incident at the protest was staged. The bottle was made of breakaway glass—plastic resin, actually, the same stuff used in movies. And, of course, there was no cut, no actual blood. It was theatre for the cameras, plain and simple."

Ginny stared at Roger, then turned and shook her head in frustration. "How do you intend to handle it?" she asked finally.

"Well, I've briefed several reporters on what we've got—Including Jerry Sinclair of the *Times*, and I think they'll pursue it. However, unless they can find out who's ultimately behind it, I don't think the story will have any staying power. And, unfortunately, the incident seems to have had its desired effect; the religious right's opposition to the mission is getting louder."

"Great." Ginny noted sarcastically. She looked up and stared at the ceiling, seemingly lost in thought.

It had been a tough couple of weeks. The day following the protest had been brutal. The media was all over the incident, and the video clip was being watched on hundreds of websites by a believing and horrified public. While no one in her administration was thought to have had any connection whatsoever to the supposed perpetrator, it still seemed to put everyone in the West Wing on the defensive, and created a massive fire drill that was only just now subsiding.

Then, to make matters worse, the next day a wealthy businessman named Derek Butler had announced his candidacy for the White House, promising to work diligently to "mend the moral fabric of society" and to "reinforce the spiritual foundation of the human race"; the latter a not-too-veiled threat to assail the Mission Council once elected.

After a few seconds, she furrowed her brow and leaned forward. "Roger, you don't suppose the protest and Butler's announcement have anything to do with one another."

Roger held her stare for a moment before answering. "Well, I can't say the thought hadn't crossed my mind. But frankly, I don't think so.

"Nonetheless," he continued, "that doesn't stop me from thinking that the guy is clearly a wolf in sheep's clothing. All his talk about a centrist, bipartisan administration is pure posturing. I just don't understand why the media—and even the progressive pundits—are ignoring the fact that there are more than a few well-known hard-core Christian conservatives on his campaign payroll."

"True," said President Belknap. "But we also know that there some high-profile progressives as well."

"That's smoke and mirrors. The problem is that Butler's background is all but hidden from the eyes of the voting public. Oh, his resume's plain for all to see. A decorated marine, MBA, division manager of ExxonMobil at the age of thirty, wunderkind CEO of Diametrix, blah blah blah. But his political views are completely masked. It would seem as if, never in his entire career, before his run for the White House, had he ever given a political speech or been forced to take a stand on a single political issue."

"I think it's for that very reason that many on both sides of the political divide have responded so well to his announcement," the President noted. "In fact, as the mission to Cerulea has taken shape, and I've come under fire for taking what many see as a progressive stance on various aspects of the colonization effort, some interesting percentage of the voting public has been looking for an outlet for their doubts and concerns—and Butler's candidacy fits the bill quite nicely. To many, I'm sure I seem downright radical next to his steadfast middle-of-the-road policies and pronouncements."

Roger seemed to consider the President's words, then looked at her with a fresh thought. "Has it occurred to you how well the Butler campaign responds to all of our announcements? They always seem to have incredibly well-formed reactions and statements available for the press within minutes of any White House or mission-related event."

"No doubt about it; they're very sharp—right on top of it," the President replied.

"Boy, I'll say," Roger mused.

Ginny leaned back in her chair and sighed. Truth be told, since she wasn't up for reelection this time around, she didn't pay it much attention. For the first time, she could enjoy the office without that gnawing distraction. In fact, she had already begun to contemplate how history might treat her.

The presidency had been a wonderful experience, and regardless who was next, she knew that her stewardship had been perceived as consistently positive by a majority of Americans and the world populace. Her approval ratings had never dropped below 55% at home, and had stayed well above 60% across the globe. She was now engaged in a calling that, if successful, would put her firmly in the history books next to one of the greatest achievements of humankind. Thinking selfishly, her legacy was safe.

But more often than not, her style was not to think selfishly.

She broke away from her reverie and offered a Roger a final thought: "I wouldn't lose a lot of sleep over it," Ginny concluded. "They do seem to know what they're doing, but once a progressive candidate emerges, things are going to get a whole lot more complicated. Give it time."

"I guess you're right," noted Roger, "it's always easier to have your act together in the beginning."

He leaned forward to collect his papers off the table.

23.

Condon heard the car before he could see it. Though the engine was nearly silent, he had learned to identify the sound of tires displacing pebbles and small rocks on the long dirt road into his property.

He leaned forward in his rattan rocking chair, folded his newspaper back to original form, and placed it on a small slate-topped table next to a large mug of black coffee. He stood up, took his coffee, and walked along the gleaming grey farmer's porch. He came to the top of the steps and leaned against one of the large, cream-colored pillars that framed the entrance to his ranch house.

He held his hand just above his eyes to shield them from the morning sun, and watched as the sleek, out-of-place sports car came around the bend in the drive out by the East pasture, and kicked up a torrent of dust.

The sky was cloudless, and the day was warm and getting warmer. Condon looked over at the large, oversized copper-faced thermometer mounted to a window-frame to his right. Eighty-three degrees. *It'll break a hundred before noon* he thought, looking back as the machine pulled up in front of the house.

Condon had done well for himself. He was one of the higher-paid lobbyists in Washington. While not among the super rich, which in America was now a fairly large club, Condon was more than comfortable. After dedicating himself to his business for nearly two decades, he had decided a few years back to begin enjoying the fruits of his labor, and he and his wife had purchased and fully restored an old ranch house from the 1800s.

He loved it. It brought him home—back to Texas, and it had brought his family back into his life after too long a hiatus. But it hadn't taken him long to realize he wanted more. While he'd been a successful lobbyist, he never gained the type of respect and power that he thought he deserved. Before he wrapped up his Washington career, he wanted his political wisdom and instincts to be acknowledged in a larger, more public setting. And if he pulled this off, he would have his hour upon the stage.

As he greeted his guest, and gestured him up onto the porch, he wondered whether asking him to meet here at the ranch was such a good idea. The visitor was clearly not the ranch type, and worse, he seemed to violate the peaceful, rural atmosphere that defined the place. Condon suddenly felt a little nervous.

"Coffee? Iced tea?" Condon asked as he gestured for his young visitor to take a seat in the chair opposite the one he'd occupied moments earlier. He noticed that the man was chewing gum—a habit Condon thought repugnant.

"Iced tea would be great. Thanks."

Condon walked over to a side table, poured a glass of iced tea, and returned, handing it to his seated guest.

The young man had been referred to Condon by an old colleague who had just taken a position with the Butler campaign. He'd told Condon that the kid had recently left the army under questionable circumstances, but that he was clever, apparently competent, and willing.

"Thanks for coming," Condon said firmly, taking a seat as well. "I think you probably know something about service to God and country, and I don't think I can remember a time when such service was so badly needed."

"I quite agree."

There was a pause as both men looked out on the pasture, and listened to the chirps and buzzing of birds and insects in the rising morning heat.

"So I've obviously studied up on your background," Condon said, breaking the short silence, "but what we're asking of you is rather extraordinary. Do you have any issues with the plan?"

"None at all—seems like a slam dunk" the guest said, grinning and working his gum at the same time.

Condon's nervousness increased; though he'd dealt with many unsavory characters in his life, this one was in a higher bracket. He didn't like this man at all. But of course, he hadn't expected to.

24.

Jim Stanton, along with the other members of the crew, had become an instant celebrity. The world knew his name, and was rapidly learning all about his upbringing, the intricacies of his role and responsibilities as Mission Captain, and, of course, his love life.

People Magazine and all the other entertainment news outlets had already done countless stories on him, which meant that, increasingly, each incremental story bordered either on mindless minutiae or simply manufactured gossip.

Jim couldn't care less. While fame was new to him—and somewhat exhilarating, he was a very intense and focused individual whose dedication to the task at hand truly eclipsed all other concerns.

He dutifully attended the press events, and was fairly adept at working the room when called upon to do so. Nonetheless, he found it strangely unfulfilling. From the moment he was selected, Jim spent the bulk of his day and night at the Space Center working the myriad details of the mission. What private time he had outside of the job, he guarded carefully.

His girlfriend was similarly dedicated. Stacy Tillinger was a doctor, a pediatrician, at a hospital just three miles from the Space Center. But from the crack of dawn to very late at night, that distance might as well have been 300 miles or more. Nonetheless, Jim and Stacy did their best to spend some quality time together every night before grabbing a few hours of sleep apiece. Sometimes they'd grab a late bite to eat at an all night café; sometimes they'd simply chat over a glass of wine at one or the other's apartment.

And, with increasing frequency, there was romance. In fact, before the mission had entered their lives, what existed between them could have been described as an average sex life—complete with lengthy stretches of neglect owing to their frenetic schedules and frequent end-of-day exhaustion.

But as the mission had started to take shape—and despite the fact that their lives had become even more complicated and overloaded—their late-night activities had been infused with an explosive passion. At first this change in their relationship seemed to have come out of the blue—a mysterious and exciting new force which electrified their physical chemistry. However, they were both intelligent, analytical human beings, and it didn't take long for them to understand and acknowledge the source of this carnal phenomenon: In the not-too-distant future, Jim would be leaving on a one-way mission to a distant world, and would never see Stacy—or Planet Earth—again.

◎◎

Jim passed through the security gate on Saturn Lane, took a right on Second Street, and parked his car in the main lot. As crew captain, he had access to a lot much closer to Mission Control, but he preferred to park with everyone else.

He grabbed his tablet and some briefing books out of the back seat and stuffed them in his backpack. He then locked his car and began the long walk to his office. He had never measured the distance, but he guessed it was in the neighborhood of a half mile of connecting walkways.

In all, the Johnson Space Center, 25 miles south of downtown Houston, was made up of roughly 100 buildings spread across a campus covering 1620 acres.

Like most of the people he worked with, Jim was in excellent physical condition. He was about six feet two inches, with short-cropped brown hair and large brown eyes. His long legs allowed him an impressive stride, and he made it a point to attain and hold a fast, rhythmic pace as he moved from place to place within the Center. His profession demanded that he dedicate time to working out, but he found that, by applying his heart and muscles throughout the day, he could maintain—or even exceed—his fitness targets with workouts that were 25 percent shorter than his peers. And given his schedule, every minute counted.

As he passed Building Z, Jim caught sight of Najid Malik, a crewmate who he knew to be on his way to the same meeting.

"Morning Naj!" Jim said cheerfully.

"Morning Cap!" came the response.

Jim smiled. He was not a big believer in titles and formality, but he truly enjoyed Naj's use of this moniker. Although Jim's position demanded some distance between himself and the crew, he and Naj had become friends.

"So, are you on your way to Ventine's presentation?"

"I am indeed. Actually, I'm looking forward to it. As we move toward launch, my ignorance as to how we're going to feed ourselves on this journey is starting to bother me."

Jim chuckled. "I hear you. I've done my reading on the subject, but I agree—I'm pleased to finally get a look at the big picture."

"Have you met this guy?" Naj asked.

"A number of times; very impressive. Very smart. After you hear his plan, I think you'll feel relieved that our gastronomic fate is in his capable hands."

They continued walking and talking about various issues, as they made their way to Building A-1. Naj had been spending much of his time recently focused on operational procedures immediately pre and post launch.

"So how goes the effort to solve our acceleration problem?" Jim asked.

"Well, I've been working with the launch engineering team on a timeline," Naj reported, "and our belief is that the migration from launch to K-1 will last approximately three hours. After ten hours, we should be at K-12; and if all goes according to plan, we'll achieve an operating speed of K-35 in hour 22. We'll then hold that speed for two days until we reach open space and can activate the SEC drive."

Since the ship would be launching from a standing start in space, at a point equidistant from the earth and moon, there was no reason for a dramatic acceleration at launch. To the contrary, it would be dangerous. Instead, the craft would slowly begin to crawl from its space-dock, then gradually add thrust as the crew moved through a comprehensive post-launch checklist to ensure that the all systems were performing within specification.

'K' referred to kilometers per second; so K-35 meant 35 kilometers per second, or roughly 75 thousand miles per hour. The theoretical limit of the spaceship's ion engines was K-46—just shy of 100 thousand miles per hour. This whole calculation was a frustrating addition to Jim's worries. While everyone knew the ship would have to have another form of propulsion other than the SEC drive, it was never envisioned that it would have to achieve these speeds or cover such large distances. However, after a number of scientific organizations expressed strong concern over the activation of the Alcubierre SEC drive within proximity to Earth, the team had had no choice but to engineer this capability.

"And what does that timeline imply with regard to crew movements and lockdown?" Jim inquired.

"Oh, I think impact on crew movement will be minimal. We've designed the curve so that at no point will any crew member experience more than 1.3 Gs."

"And lockdown?" Jim asked, referring to the need to have absolutely all objects within the craft securely stored to minimize damage.

"We've got some more testing to do, but we believe that we can stand down from a lockdown after 12 hours or so."

"That sounds encouraging."

They walked into the entrance of Building H, and headed down the long, polished corridor toward the conference room.

25.

Roughly twenty senior crew members and research leads were already in the room when Jim and Naj entered; some grabbing coffee and food from a generous breakfast spread at the back of the room; others were seated, chatting.

Naj headed toward the coffee, and Jim looked for a place to settle in. Just as he mentally selected a seat on the far side of the table and started heading over, he heard a familiar voice:

"Jim!"

Jim turned, and smiled.

"Come sit by me; we can chat a bit before things get started."

Jim began walking toward the seat where the man was gesturing.

"Commander Belechenko, good to see you. I didn't know you'd be here today." They nodded to one another in greeting, and Jim put his materials on the table.

"Well, I hadn't planned on it, but was in the neighborhood, had some extra time, so I thought I'd listen in."

Jim knew this couldn't possibly be true. He had gotten to know Commander Belechenko fairly well, and the man rarely, if ever, did anything at all that was not 100 percent deliberate. Nonetheless, he didn't pursue it.

"Well, I'm actually glad you're here. There's a quick issue I wanted to work with you regarding the WPS. I read the spec and had some concerns with the back-up modules."

The two men sat down at the large, oak conference table, and were quickly deep in conversation. The WPS, or water processing system, was a fairly complicated piece of engineering, and affected just about every facet of the ship's operation. Its completion remained one the top threats to the launch schedule.

After several minutes of discussion, they came to a resolution as to next steps. Jim took some notes to capture several of his commander's key suggestions.

"Thanks, Commander, I'll set up a meeting for later this week with the WPS engineering lead to work through this. Would you care to join that discussion?"

"I have full confidence that the two of you will identify the correct approach. Just copy me on the final plan."

As the Commander finished his sentence, Georges Ventine entered the conference room with a stack of materials under his arm and placed them at the head of the table. He was of average height, but had thick dark hair to his shoulders, large, thoughtful brown eyes, and an athletic build.

Ventine looked up and grinned broadly as he noticed Stanton and Commander Belechenko, and immediately approached.

"Gentlemen," he said, in his velvety French accent, and placed a hand on each of their shoulders.

"The man of the hour!" exclaimed the Commander. "I'm very much looking forward to your presentation this morning."

"I am glad one of us is," Ventine countered.

The three men chatted and laughed for a couple of minutes, until Ventine looked at his watch and realized that the meeting was set to begin.

He walked to the head of the table, and casually asked everyone to be seated.

"Can anyone tell me how much oxygen a healthy adult human being consumes in one day?" Ventine asked loudly, hoping to quiet the chatter and get everyone focused.

At least a dozen hands went up. Ventine pointed to a young woman halfway down the table on his right.

"A human being will process roughly 1.8 pounds of oxygen in one 24-hour day," the woman offered.

"Exactly right," Ventine confirmed. "Now, does anyone know how much oxygen is produced each day by a normal, adult tree?" Ventine inquired. Four hands shot up. Ventine smiled. "Is there anyone who is not on my team who might know the answer?" The room laughed, and no one raised their hand. Ventine looked around the room, then settled his eyes on Commander Belechenko and Jim Stanton.

Deciding not to pick on Jim, he chose his boss instead. "Commander, care to hazard a guess?"

Belechenko smiled and leaned forward, more than willing to play the game. "I think I recall that it's just over half a pound per day."

Ventine pointed at the Commander. "Correct—an average of point seven pounds, to be precise. So how many trees would be required to service one human crew member?"

"Would these be deciduous trees?" Belechenko asked.

"Ahhh. Very smart man, yes?" Ventine asked the room, as everyone laughed. "This is why he is our boss, yes?" And laughter again.

"Actually, Commander, they are deciduous, but we have recently discovered a way to trick them into replacing their leaves as they shed them. In other words, there is no winter, only spring, summer and fall—all mixed into a continuum."

"Very impressive," the Commander noted, "then I would say, to be safe, you'd need three trees for every human." He leaned back, sensing his part in the play had concluded.

"So, at a bare minimum," Ventine said, hitting a button on the remote on the table in front of him and turning to view the screen behind him, "to support a crew of 1800 men, women and children in a closed environment, we would need 5500 trees.

"However, we will instead have close to 45 thousand trees, living in four separate atriums, each representing a separate and distinct ecosystem. This is important because, if trees in one atrium develop a disease of any kind, it is critical that it not be allowed to spread.

"We will compress and store excess oxygen, ultimately to be used for our transport shuttles once we reach the planet.

"Now, trees are good for much more than oxygen; a healthy percentage of each atrium will be fruit or nut trees..."

∾∾

Jim was riveted. While he had read much of what Ventine was telling him in briefing papers, somehow Georges' style and delivery made it come to life, and as happened on occasion, he found himself becoming incredibly excited about the mission to come. He had been to the ISS several times, but never had he, or any astronaut, been on board a ship of this magnitude.

He wondered if Ventine was envious of the crew, or whether he preferred to remain Earth-bound. It struck Jim that very few of the Mission Council's functional leaders would actually be making the journey. Commander Belechenko, Cynthia Fossett, Georges Ventine—even the guy who discovered the planet, Devlin McGregor—would all be remaining behind, while he and Naj and the rest of the officers and crew got to experience the most incredible adventure in human history.

Ventine was now discussing food growth and storage: "...we will, of course, freeze-dry much of the food we grow—especially the fruit. While on Earth this process consumes large amounts of energy, in space it consumes very little. This is because space itself is, in effect, a very efficient freeze-dryer..."

Jim thought ahead to daily life aboard the ship. He always felt both exhilaration and anxiety as he envisioned himself captaining the craft. While he reveled in the incredible opportunity, he occasionally felt sick to his stomach when contemplating the burdens of leadership.

He forced such thoughts out of his brain, and redoubled his focus on Ventine's presentation.

26.

"Judge Fossett, perhaps you could begin by describing the task in front of you, and giving me a rough outline of how you plan to approach it."

The interview had been Roger's idea. He thought that, by exposing the workings of Cynthia's team to the general public, it might allay some fears regarding Cerulea's eventual constitution. Cynthia wasn't so sure.

Although she'd had her fair share of experience with the press, the whole thing still made her rather nervous. The two of them were in Cynthia's temporary office in an old building off of McPherson Square, across from the Import/Export Bank. The windows looked as if they hadn't been cleaned in years, and the radiator hissed quietly—clearly a holdover from the previous century, but overall it was warm and comfortable.

The *Times* reporter was in his late twenties; he was on the heavy side, with thinning brown hair. Cynthia judged him to be smart and capable, but she had no idea how much—or how little—he knew when it came to constitutional law.

"Describe the task," Cynthia repeated, thinking it over. "Well, for starters, it's terrifying." They both laughed. *At times, to the point of near paralysis,* she thought to herself.

In fact, during the first month or two, there were many mornings when all she wanted was to curl up under the blankets and hide from the responsibility. It was only by ignoring the magnitude of the effort, and focusing on the day's to-do list, that she could eventually calm herself sufficiently to get out of bed and carry on.

"As you may be aware, we've put together a world-class team of legal scholars, lawyers and judges to help us establish the set of laws and principles that will govern Cerulea, she began. And as I said, it's an overwhelming responsibility. However, it's important to note that we are not creating the legal framework for Cerulea, so much as we are assembling it."

"Please, go on," the reporter urged.

"Well, our initial focus has been on documenting the key similarities and differences between all of the world's democratic constitutions. There are a large number of basic principles that, due to their prevalence among civilized nations here on Earth, will obviously form the bedrock of the new planet's civilization."

"Such as?"

"Oh, such as the three branches of government, a bicameral legislature, pro-visions for a common defense—"

"Defense against what?" The reporter interjected.

Cynthia smiled. "That's a good question; one to which I certainly do not know the answer. I'm sure, however, that all would agree that the Cerulean colony should institutionalize its right to defend itself."

"What other principles?" The reporter inquired.

"Well, there's an evident need to include things like equal rights, freedom of speech, freedom of assembly, freedom of religion, the right to due process."

"In other words, the standard ingredients of a democracy," the reporter said, stating the obvious as he peeled one page off the yellow legal pad in front of her and continued his note-taking on a clean sheet.

"Yes," Cynthia said poignantly, "but, in this era of technological sophistica-tion, it's important to note that we very much wish to avoid creating a pure democ-racy."

"Excuse me?" The reporter asked, sensing something newsworthy. "You mean to say that you don't intend Cerulea to be a democracy?"

"Yes, of course we intend Cerulea to be a democracy, but not a pure democ-racy." Cynthia replied emphatically. "Many people believe that our country is a pure democracy, but it very clearly is not. In fact, the framers of our constitution worked diligently to see that it wasn't."

"But I thought—"

"You thought as many do in America," Cynthia continued. "The United States is a republic, very carefully crafted with various checks and balances to ensure that all individual rights are protected. A pure democracy is one where majority rules. Period. Many historians and scholars have likened this to a 'mob-ocracy,' or a society in which a mob, no matter how misguided in its views or preju-dices, can do literally whatever it wants."

"I'm not sure I understand," the reporter said, staring. His pen dormant in his hand.

"Rest assured," Cynthia explained, "this is an incredibly common misper-ception." She was extremely pleased to have caught her inquisitor up in this issue; it was her hope that, by explaining some of the basic principles of modern govern-ments, the interview could be less a witch hunt for "gotchas" on sensitive wedge issues, and more of an honest exploration into the basic issues her team was work-ing to address.

They faced one another across a small oval table in front of her desk. The afternoon sun had begun to flood the table with glare; she got up from her chair and crossed to the window.

Cynthia was slight—about five feet three inches, but her intellect was apparent in her face. She had wide brown eyes and long brown hair which she almost always wore pulled back neatly in a bun. She dressed sharply and was a consummate professional.

"Do you live in the city, or a suburb?" Cynthia asked, as she closed the blind.

"I live on Connecticut Avenue—In the city. But I grew up in a small town in Illinois," the reporter replied.

"Okay then. In many small towns, government is often by town meeting. Was that the case in your town growing up?"

"Yes. I think my parents attended every one."

"Well, that's an example of pure democracy," Cynthia remarked, returning to her seat. "Unlike the federal government or the state of Illinois, where representatives are elected to decide major issues, town meetings permit a majority of citizens in attendance to decide major issues directly." Cynthia was gratified to see the reporter resume his note-taking. "Now, were it not for the U.S. and state constitutions, the majority attending a town meeting could, in effect, act as a tyranny, passing any laws they wished—perhaps to outlaw persons of a certain race or characteristic, or to tax only those who'd inhabited the town for a certain number of years or less."

"So how do you avoid such tyranny on Cerulea?" the reporter asked.

"By mimicking the structure of successful republics—using a representative form of government, and ensuring that multiple branches create natural checks and balances on one another. Bear in mind, this may be easier said than done. Given today's technology, it would be very easy for the people of a state or nation—or planet, for that matter—to vote daily and directly on a wide range of issues that affect their lives."

"Do you envision that there will be any features of the Cerulean government that are not currently in use on this planet?"

"Good question," Cynthia noted, but it was one she had anticipated. "The short answer is—not many. The longer answer is more complicated."

"How so?"

"Well, in America—and in other republics—one fear is that all branches of government may, at some point in time, all align under a common majority. Once that happens, the minority has very little protection."

"But isn't that the will of the people?"

"No. It's simply the will of the majority. To paraphrase Jefferson: The concentration of legislative, executive and judiciary power in the same hands is precisely the definition of despotic government."

"Could you explain?"

"Sure. Let's first look at how things might work in a pure, or direct democracy," Cynthia began. "Hypothetically, let's assume that all major issues—including, even, the passage of major spending programs—are decided by the electorate through electronic voting over the internet. Now, let's pick an issue..."

"How about gun control?" The reporter suggested.

"All right. People worry that I'm an unabashed progressive, so I'll play along; we'll focus our fictional scenario on the right to bear arms."

In fact, in a gun control case earlier in her career, the plaintiff—the City of New York—had argued that population density demanded a reduction in the number of firearms, offering data from a seven-year study correlating violent crime, population growth and weapons availability. Cynthia had sided with the plaintiff. The Big Apple now boasted nearly 10 million inhabitants, up 25 percent since the turn of the century. The crime rate had risen steadily and, with expanded self-defense and "deadly force" laws now on the books, vigilantism had become a persistent problem. If gun ownership wasn't tightly monitored & controlled, it was easy to see how further rise in crime could precipitate a full-fledged guerilla war between criminals and citizens.

It was because of such rulings that her appointment to a federal judgeship on the Second Circuit Court of Appeals had not come as easily as her previous career advancements. She was one of three nominees sent to congress in President Belknap's first year in office, and the conservatives rode into session in full battle dress.

The first day of hearings, they attacked her background voraciously. Of all of the nominees up for consideration, she became the poster child of the conservative effort to paint Belknap as dangerously out of step with the mainstream.

At first, it appeared that it had worked; the administration did not have the votes for confirmation. But President Belknap played the game differently from many of her predecessors. She and Roger Tucker worked out a backroom deal with the conservatives whereby, for as long as she held the office of President, the opposition would get to choose one nominee for every 3 that Belknap put before congress. The only conditions were that each side's candidates had to be chosen from lists that had been drawn up and approved in advance, and that, with regard to Supreme Court appointments, all bets were off. She was handing them 25 percent of the judgeships that would be awarded during her administration—but in return, she was all but removing the issue from the table, while guaranteeing that she would keep the judicial branch properly staffed with well-qualified men and women—albeit 25 percent less progressive than many in her administration might have thought ideal.

The arrangement was fairly groundbreaking, and Cynthia was confirmed.

Cynthia watched as the reporter finished writing in his notebook, and looked up. She then continued with her hypothetical scenario.

"To set the stage, let's say that a very popular and powerful national figure has endured a tragic event involving a firearm—a son or daughter is killed in a senseless shooting. The tragedy is a huge news story, and there is a tremendous outpouring of support and sympathy from the public. A centrist senator—the senate here being a body that only crafts legislation so that the public may vote on it—drafts a bill that would outlaw all firearms. Then, in an emotional whirlwind, despite strong resistance from the gun lobby and gun owners, the electorate passes the bill. So, by the emotional whim of the majority, it's now illegal to own a gun."

"But if this is the will of the people -"

"The will of the majority," Cynthia corrected the reporter. "The public may have, by a razor thin margin, temporarily sided with the view that guns should be illegal. Very nearly half the country may well believe that outlawing firearms is a rotten idea, but they have no recourse. Thus, for whatever reason, a slight majority could make any number of rapid-fire, ill-informed decisions, and the minority would have to go along—regardless of whether the decisions made any sense at all. This is the whole purpose of a republic, or representative democracy. The representatives we elect are expected to study issues in a way the public does not and, through careful debate, arrive at conclusions that are in the best interest of the country as a whole, not just the majority."

"Understood," said the reporter. " But you're obviously not planning such a direct democracy for Cerulea, so how is the example relevant?"

"Well," Cynthia replied, "let's now assume that the same thing occurs within our current system."

"It never would," the reporter insisted.

"No?" Cynthia asked. "Let's assume that the national figure is a powerful senator, and with a large and vocal portion of the public behind him, he succeeds in getting his fellow senators to pass the bill. Then the House of Representatives passes the bill with a veto-proof margin. O.K. I know—mighty unlikely, but not impossible. So, it's now illegal to own a gun. Despite our carefully crafted republic, the majority just trashed the second amendment."

"But wouldn't it then go to the courts?" The reporter asked.

"It certainly would," Cynthia responded. "And it's assumed that the courts would strike down the law as unconstitutional. However, let's stretch this scenario further and allow that, after several successive terms of progressive administrations, the Supreme Court also holds a progressive majority. They uphold the new legislation."

"Okay, but that's how our system works, isn't it? The voting public elected the president and the legislature, and they, in turn, appointed members to the Supreme Court. If that's the will of the people -"

"Once again, the will of the majority," interrupted Cynthia.

"But if all three branches of government came to the well-thought-out conclusion that guns should, in fact, be illegal, isn't that an example of the government acting in the best interests of the people?"

"Perhaps," said Cynthia. "Remember, I'm supposed to be the unabashed
progressive; so I think I'll steer clear of a direct answer on that one. The point I'm
trying to make here, however, becomes crystal clear if you insert other issues in
lieu of guns."

"Such as?"

"Well, let's say that the same groundswell of support in all branches of government passed legislation that, say, allowed the government to tap any citizen's
private communications at will? Or to prohibit the practice of a specific religion?
Or that protection for National Parks and all protected lands be removed in favor
of development? Or that law enforcement no longer needed to abide by due process—they could hold anyone without charging them, or torture them to gain
information, or simply deport anyone they perceived as a threat?"

"With all due respect, Judge Fossett, some of those examples would require
overturning the Bill of Rights, which seems truly unlikely."

"Does it?" Cynthia inquired. "The Bill of Rights is made up of amendments,
which can—and have—been repealed. In modern history, fear has trumped logic
and common sense on many occasions. If the government and the public perceive
a serious enough threat to the country, I think it's entirely possible that you could
have a temporary majority who would go along with just about anything. And the
worst outcome, of course, would be the granting of special powers to one or more
bodies of government. Once this happens, the majority has essentially given the
government the right to bypass the entire system, and the minority—even though
it represents nearly half the population, will have lost the fundamental rights that
the founding fathers so wisely gave to them."

"I guess that's happened a few times in history as well," the reporter conceded.

"Indeed it has."

There was silence as the reporter took some notes. Eventually, he looked
up. "Judge Fossett, there has been much speculation by many conservatives that
you and your team will take steps to further limit the role of religion in the Cerulean constitution. Randall Reese, among others, has said publicly that this is unacceptable, and that he'll do everything in his power to oppose it. Can you talk about
how you plan to address the church and state issue?"

There it was. All the other questions and discussion had been just a warm-
up for this one. Cynthia drew a deep breath.

"Boy, this is a tricky one," Cynthia began. "As you know, the first amendment states that 'Congress shall make no law respecting an establishment of religion, or prohibiting the free exercise thereof.'

"Many have argued that this language does not forbid the federal government from allowing the establishment of religion in a public setting. Rather, they maintain, it forbids Congress to make any laws on the subject, or to interfere with someone's desire to practice their religion of choice.

"It is further argued that the separation of church and state is actually an interpretation of the Constitution based upon Jefferson's later writings, and not an inherent principle of the document itself. In fact, some would say it's based on a misinterpretation of his views.

"However, if we combine what appear to be the founding fathers' intentions with stare decisis—the maxim that courts should abide by precedent and established law, then throw in some modern-day common sense, I think the right path forward becomes pretty clear."

The reporter looked her straight in the eye, pen at the ready. "Please continue," he said without emotion. Cynthia thought she sensed a slight change in the reporter's demeanor, and briefly wondered might have caused it. Nonetheless, she continued.

"First, it should be acknowledged that during our nation's history, numerous clauses within the Constitution have been interpreted as the judiciary has sought to resolve a long list of legal issues. Many of these interpretations have had much less to go on than the issue concerning church and state.

"Let's begin with the framers. While Jefferson's Danbury Letter is often looked at as the lynchpin of the separation argument, it should be noted that many other founding fathers were vocal on this issue.

"George Washington and John Adams both noted their belief that America was not founded on the Christian religion. James Madison at one point stated clearly that the appropriation of funds for the use and support of religion is contrary to the Constitution.

"As for established law, there have been over a dozen Supreme Court decisions over the last two centuries which reinforce the notion that the government must maintain absolute neutrality in all religious matters.

"In 1971, in its decision on Lemon v. Kurtzman, the court actually outlined a three-part test for determining if a government action violates the First Amendment: The court ruled that, first, the government action must have a secular purpose; second, its primary purpose must not be to inhibit or to advance religion; and third, the action must not precipitate 'excessive entanglement' between government and religion.

"This three-pronged test was later used to decide Edwards v. Aguillard, a 1987 case contesting a Louisiana law which prohibited the teaching of the theory of evolution in the public schools unless that instruction was accompanied by the teaching of creation science.

"The Court held that the Louisiana law was not enacted to further a clear secular purpose, that the primary effect of the law was, in fact, to advance the religious viewpoint that a 'supernatural being created humankind,' and that the law significantly entangled the interests of church and state by seeking 'the symbolic and financial support of government to achieve a religious purpose.'"

Cynthia knew that these precedents were critical to her team's position, and to the public's perception of the Constitution they would eventually unveil. She felt it imperative that the reporter properly grasp their importance.

"Are you with me so far?" she politely asked her guest, who had been busily scribbling notes throughout.

"I am." He kept his eyes on his pad as he wrote. "Judge Fossett, how do you regard the Lemon v. Kurtzman decision? Specifically, do you agree with the test as articulated by Chief Justice Burger?"

Cynthia felt her stomach sink. She had not mentioned Burger, and it was suddenly clear that the reporter not only understood her argument, but also that his relative naïveté during the earlier portion of their discussion was at least partially an act. Her feeling of control drained away.

"Judge Fossett?" The reporter looked up. Cynthia spoke carefully but deliberately.

"I have a great deal of respect for the decision; I think that Chief Justice Burger's detailed opinion was long overdue. Which, I guess, brings us to the application of common sense."

Cynthia reflected back on the speech her mentor had given her years before when they were working a separation case. She stood and walked across the room, regaining some confidence as she offered her final thoughts.

"As we were all taught in grade school, this country was founded by people who were escaping religious persecution in their homeland. They saw America as a place where they could exercise their beliefs without governmental intrusion or pressure.

"What's more, our country has always held freedom of thought and expression as one of its most important values. I think virtually all citizens would agree that, without such freedom, the United States would literally lose its identity.

"So I ask, then: How is it possible that we could tolerate our government supporting any activity that advocates one religion over another? How could we possibly allow for tax-paying citizens to feel religious intimidation in a classroom or government building—paid for with their taxes?

"I can certainly appreciate the ridiculous extent to which political correctness is taken in this country, but I think it's a small price to pay for a society in which people from different cultures with wildly differing belief systems can live together comfortably.

"So," Cynthia stated firmly, "I think it's safe to say that the Cerulean constitution will take the separation of church and state very, very seriously."

Cynthia looked at her watch, and noted that they'd gone way over the allotted time for the interview. She'd also begun to suspect that the reporter's aims might be less than objective. "I think that's about all the time I've got today; did we cover everything you were after?" Cynthia asked.

"Most definitely," the reporter replied. "This was... incredibly helpful." They bowed their heads to one another, and the reporter gathered his notes and his coat, as Cynthia moved back to her desk.

"Thanks for coming."

"Thank you, Judge Fossett."

The reporter left her office, and Cynthia began absentmindedly scrolling through email messages as she wondered whether she'd just helped to quell the nation's growing unease, or simply shoveled more fuel on the fire.

27.

The convoy of 17 flatbed trucks passed through the gate and pulled out onto Old Gentilly Road heading west. They would loop around and get on Interstate 10, and ride it all the way to Houston, a journey of about 350 miles.

The trucks were carrying several key modules of the spacecraft that had recently cleared final test. Included were containment and irrigation systems for the craft's bio-oxygenation systems—what many mission staff simply referred to as the "greenhouse units." They had originally been engineered and manufactured at the Italian Space Agency's Alenia Aerospazio factory in Turin. From there, they'd been transported via two giant Antonov AN-755 cargo planes to Lockheed Martin's Michoud Operations facility in Louisiana for staging. One month prior, they had cleared final test as Georges Ventine and his team went through an exhaustive systems check, simulating every error condition and possible mishap imaginable. With the exception of a few bugs that had taken them several extra days to resolve, the units had pretty much passed with flying colors. Once the tests were complete, Lockheed engineers and ship crew members partially disassembled the units and carefully loaded them onto flatbeds for transport to Mission Control.

Once at Mission Control, they would be reassembled, retested, and disassembled once again—In part to ensure system integrity, and in part to give the crew further practice in putting all the pieces together. The next step was to get them on a shuttle for transport up to the actual ship in spacedock where they would be assembled and tested one last time.

They were scheduled to depart Earth for the spacedock in two months, on what would be the 27th shuttle flight serving the ship.

The trucks crossed under route 47 and continued down Almonaster Boulevard, passing a cemetery and Read Boulevard on their right.

In the passenger seat of the lead truck was a man named Jean-Pierre Moreault. He had worked for Georges Ventine in Paris, and had joined the team a month or two after Ventine had signed on to lead the agricultural engineering effort for the mission. Georges trusted Jean-Pierre implicitly, and had asked him to ride along with the equipment on its final leg to Mission Control. Next to Jean-Pierre was Mike McKenna, who'd been driving a truck for Lockheed Martin for over 25 years.

Jean-Pierre watched as they passed the tail end of a freight train running parallel to the road in the other direction. He leaned back, took a deep breath, and settled in for what he'd been told would be a six or seven hour ride.

The convoy took a right turn on Jourdan Road, crossing the railroad tracks and then passing under Interstate 10. Up ahead, Jean-Pierre saw a man up the road with a gas can in his hand. Jean-Pierre looked further and saw an old station wagon pulled over onto the shoulder of Route 90 just before it crossed Jourdan.

As they passed the man, Jean-Pierre waved and the man waved back.

"Not sure where that guy's going," Mike said from the driver's seat.

"What do you mean?" Jean-Pierre asked.

"I think the nearest gas station is over by the airport—in the opposite direction."

Jean-Pierre looked in his large side-view mirror, then across at Mike. "He'll figure it out eventually."

The line of trucks moved along. As Mike started to turn the truck right onto Route 90, Jean-Pierre looked again in the side mirror at the row of trucks behind them. As he returned his gaze to the road in front of them, his brain abruptly signaled an alarm. He quickly looked back in the mirror, but their truck had already made the turn, so he no longer had a mirror view of the convoy. He leaned his head out the window to have a look back, but was checked by his seat belt. He jammed his hands down to the buckle and fumbled it free.

"What the hell are you doing?" Mike asked.

"I saw something," Jean-Pierre said as he thrust his head out the window. In truth, he was not sure of what he saw, or why he'd suddenly felt something was wrong. His heart was beating rapidly.

He looked back and saw that three trucks had made the turn onto Route 90 and four were still on Jourdan Road. He looked at the station wagon on the shoulder, nestled in the curve of the convoy, and then back down Jourdan to see if he could find the guy with the gas can. His eyes locked on the man, who was now a considerable distance up the road, but no longer walking. He was standing still and facing the intersection and his car. The gas can was on the ground at his side, and he was holding something in his hands.

Jean-Pierre's heart sank into his stomach. He pulled his head back into the truck and furiously grabbed for the door handle. He pulled the lever, and pushed the door open.

"Jean-Pierre, for chris'sakes, get your ass back in the truck!" Mike hollered as Jean Pierre stepped down onto the running board and jumped.

It was too late.

As Jean-Pierre was about to land on his feet, the blast reversed his direction in mid-air and sent him flying up over the truck, over the road, and into the culvert on the other side.

Several trucks on each end of the convoy were knocked over onto their sides from the concussion, and sent skidding across the road. The two trucks closest to the station wagon were ripped apart by the explosion, with truck parts, tires, and their fully tested, canvas-covered greenhouse units literally blown to bits.

❀❀

Jean-Pierre regained consciousness fairly quickly, and tried to use his arms to get up. His left arm sent daggers of pain back to his shoulder. Clearly broken. He rolled onto his right side and managed to lift himself with his good arm to a sitting position. Every square inch of his body felt bruised, including his brain, which was barely functioning under the rhythmic pounding of a splitting headache. He cupped his broken arm in front of him with his right hand and, very slowly, worked himself up onto his feet.

As he climbed up the embankment onto Route 90, his eyes widened in horror as he took in the scene.

Where the station wagon had been was now a huge crater about 30 feet across. Moving out from the crater was what seemed like one huge, sprawling, twisted mass of metal and wreckage. There were several fires burning, pouring black smoke up into the cloudless sky. People were yelling to each other, as several drivers hurriedly tried to pull the injured away from the flames. Jean-Pierre watched as two men pulled another across Jourdan Road and into the grass beyond. The injured man was screaming all the while, and it was clear to see why. Exactly half his face was blackened and shriveled from direct exposure to the explosion. His shirt was gone, and his right arm was missing; nothing more than a short, blackened stump protruding from his shoulder.

As Jean-Pierre walked into the wreckage, looking frantically for some way he could be useful, he saw another driver's leg sticking out from under one of the large steel plates that comprised the greenhouse flooring. Jean-Pierre knew immediately he was dead. He'd been directly involved in the design of those plates; each one weighed over a ton.

A man approached him and asked him a question. Jean-Pierre looked the man in the eye and stared for a moment. The man appeared to repeat whatever he'd said. Jean Pierre yelled back: "I didn't hear you," but suddenly realized he could barely hear his own voice.

Suddenly there was another, much smaller explosion, and the two men instinctively crouched. They both turned to see the truck that had been second in line behind Jean-Pierre's burst into flames. The fire raced along the road where a stream of oil had leaked from the truck's engine. For the first time since he'd seen the wreckage, Jean-Pierre suddenly felt the piercing pain of his broken arm.

The man next to him yelled something else, gently grabbed Jean-Pierre's good arm, and led him across the street. As they took their first step down the embankment toward several other injured men lying in the grass, flashing lights in the distance off to his left caught Jean-Pierre's attention; an ambulance and two police cars were speeding down Jourdan Road toward the scene.

28.

For a world voraciously consuming all news related to the Mission, the convoy explosion was a funereal feast.

Within hours of the blast, news outlets were ablaze with related articles, footage and commentary, offering details on the method and materials used by the saboteur, in-depth descriptions of the destroyed greenhouse units, and endless conjecture on what impact the event might have on the Mission as a whole.

The vast majority of those expressing their opinions were incensed. One letter, which appeared in the top layer of the *Times'* editorial section, condemned those responsible, as well as their "sophomoric and knee-jerk reliance on acts of terrorism to communicate their opposition." It went on to note that, "in an open society such as ours, it strains credulity to think that anyone might honestly believe that violence of this nature could possibly further their cause."

A letter to the editor appearing one layer down in the *Standard*, however, looked at the convoy catastrophe in a slightly different light: "The loss of life cannot be condoned, but the fact remains: the Cerulean colonization effort is on the wrong track. If the Mission Council refuses to listen to the voices of the faithful, then perhaps the faithful must find a way to amplify their collective voice."

Although the public expression of such sentiments was not a common occurrence, every instance encouraged others to cross the line between silent and active opposition to the mission. As time passed, each such letter was just a little less out of the ordinary than the last.

29.

"Commander," the President said squarely, "how did this happen?"
"Madame President, this I do not know. We followed every protocol to the letter. No one outside of the mission knew of the transport date, and we made sure that there were numerous decoy transfers of equipment not related to the mission which both preceded and followed this event."

"Commander," Roger interjected, "you'll excuse me if I don't find myself shocked to hear of a leak. In our business, it's a fact of life." There was a slight irritation in his voice. It had been less than 24 hours since the explosion; Roger had gotten very little sleep, and had so far had a rotten day. It hadn't helped that the article on Cynthia Fossett had appeared in this morning's *Times*—adding yet one more heavy ball for him to juggle over the next day or two. Roger was seated in his customary spot in the Oval Office, across from the Commander and the mission's Chief Engineer, Gerhardt Schmidt. To his right was President Belknap.

"Mr. Tucker," responded Belechenko, "with all due respect, I am not in your business, but I have successfully managed operations of this sort many times quite effectively. The ISS never once experienced a single mishap during two decades of development."

"The International Space Station was never as controversial as this mission."

"Perhaps, but I should tell you that whoever leaked this did so with up-to-the-minute information," stated the Commander.

"How so?" asked Ginny.

"In addition to the decoys, we also had four separate routes for the convoy—the final route was chosen only 30 minutes prior to departure."

Roger and the President looked at one another, once again engaging in a brief, wordless conversation on the significance of the Commander's revelation.

"Commander, do you have any ideas as to who might have passed on the information?" Ginny asked.

"At this time, I do not."

Ginny drew a deep breath and exhaled. "Well, I think that we will have to proceed on the assumption that movements of this sort will be compromised. Given that fact, Commander, tell us your plans with regard to security changes from here on in."

"Madam President," Belechenko began, "we are moving hundreds of thousands of tons of equipment from all over the globe to mission control in Houston and the Baikonur Cosmodrome in Leninsk. I have, of course, already asked our chief of security to revise our security strategy. However, I want to be clear: providing any guarantee against such—"

"Guarantee?" Roger interrupted, "those trucks in Louisiana were sitting ducks!"

"Mr. Tucker, I can assure you that--"

"Assure me of what, Commander?" Roger interrupted again, clearly annoyed that he was going to have to spend the next several days mired in the reaction to this event.

"Enough." President Belknap said firmly. "We are going to focus here on today's problem—not yesterday's. Now, Commander, please finish."

"Madam President. Mr. Tucker. I acknowledge that, in the absence of secrecy, the security around our trucks yesterday was insufficient. While I think it will be difficult—both logistically and from a cost standpoint—to provide physical security to all future truck deliveries, we will do our very best. As I said, I have asked the security team to draw up a revised plan for review by the Mission Council."

"And when might we expect a draft?" The President inquired.

"Within 48 hours. Will that suffice?" Belechenko asked, looking first at the President, then at Roger.

"Yes, I think that will be fine," the President stated. "Roger: would it be helpful if you had bullet points--or at least a rough outline of the revised plan by end-of-day?"

"That would be incredibly helpful." Roger said cooperatively, feeling somewhat sheepish that he had acted out. "Would that be possible Commander?"

"I'm sure it would, Mr. Tucker," Belechenko said warmly.

"Okay, the next question is how this will affect our schedule," Ginny remarked, pleased to be moving the discussion forward.

Belechenko deferred to Schmidt. "Gerhardt, what is your team's time estimate for replacing the lost greenhouse units?"

"Well, from a time perspective, we believe that the impact will be fairly significant," Schmidt replied. "Bringing our spares up to specification will take eight weeks or so. Then add another three weeks for final test and transport. Since the bio-oxygenation systems represent critical path, we can't schedule much other work in the interim. Total schedule hit should be ten weeks at a minimum. However, I believe the bigger issue is cost. These systems were already 25 billion over budget. Building new spare units will probably add another 10 billion to that."

The President sighed. "Well, I was preparing to present the Mission Council with a new budget request of 150 billion; I can certainly add this to it. The U.S. Congress is on the hook for half of it, and I think we've got more than enough votes. Once we sign on, I'd be surprised if all other countries don't fall in line. Frankly, however, I'm not as worried about getting more funds as I am about ensuring everyone that this won't happen again. A few more such delays and suddenly we could be six months behind."

"And at risk of missing our launch window," Gerhardt Schmidt added.

"Gerhardt, I assume you'll be giving the Council a revised project schedule this week to reflect the delay?" The President asked.

"Of course, Madam President," Gerhardt confirmed.

"Okay," said the President, rising from her chair. "Gerhardt, thank you for joining us this morning."

"My pleasure, Madam President." They nodded farewell to one another. Roger and Belechenko likewise rose and bowed slightly to Schmidt. As he exited the Oval Office, the President, Roger and Belechenko once again took their seats.

"Next item," said the President. "The article in this morning's *Times*. I think we all felt that it might make sense to give Cynthia some public exposure, but I'm nervous nonetheless. Roger, what's your take on the reaction thus far?"

"I think it's too early to tell. On the one hand, the article is very straightforward, and seems to do a good job of demystifying the challenge faced by Judge Fossett and her team. As I'm sure you recall, I had suggested this interview; I believe, on balance, she comes across as very thoughtful, very eloquent, very fair."

"And on the other hand?" The President asked.

"While most readers will respond positively, the article may inflame the hard-core conservative opposition."

"Why would that be?" Belechenko asked.

"Well," Roger began, "We knew going in that the conservatives mistrust Judge Fossett based on several of her past rulings, and her comments in the article do not in any way allay their fears. Ironically, I think they'll be worried that Cynthia's comments on minority rights will make it harder for them to use majority pressure to influence the process. But most significant, they will most likely view her comments on church and state as all but precluding the involvement of religion in the activities of Cerulean government. And most inflammatory, I'm guessing, will be her use of 'common sense' in deciding the issue."

"How do the numbers look?" Ginny asked.

"Right now," said Roger, "61 percent of the public supports the Mission Council and the activities of Judge Fossett, while 34 percent oppose. All in all, still a healthy margin—but it's important to remember that just six months ago it was 72 percent to 25."

"When will we have new numbers?" the President inquired.

"We'll take a snapshot this afternoon, and then again in two days time. Although I personally believe that the strategy of making Judge Fossett more conspicuous is a good one, it also carries some risk." Roger noted. "Even while the public may warm to her, the opposition may get louder at the same time. The goal is to create a better understanding of the mission in the public's mind, without giving the opposition too much ammunition. But either way, it will be a bit polarizing."

"I understand that," Ginny said, "and I agree—hiding her behind a veil of obscurity is simply the wrong way to play it. Please forward the numbers as soon as you have them."

"Will do." Roger stated.

"Right. That's it. Thank you both," Ginny said, rising and walking back to her desk. Behind her, she heard both Roger and Belechenko offer the obligatory and somewhat annoying "Thank you, Madam President" as they walked to the door.

Just before they exited, Ginny turned. "Oh, Commander—" both Roger and Belechenko stopped and turned to face her, "I wanted to ask if you have time later today to prepare for the Mission Council meeting; say six pm?"

"Certainly, Ma'am. I will see you at six," Belechenko replied.

"Great, thanks." She turned back to her desk. The Commander walked out and Roger paused for a second looking at Ginny's back, before he exited as well.

Roger knew the President better than most—If not better than anyone, and as he headed off to his next meeting, he wondered whether he'd just seen a twinkling in her eye that he'd never seen before.

30.

The sabotage of the Mission convoy in Louisiana remained unsolved.
Predictably, a number of conspiracy theories were unfolding. One suggested that it was the work of ecoterrorists who wanted to halt what they saw as the contamination of another planet. Another hypothesized that it had been perpetrated by one or more religious groups objecting to the progressive nature of the mission. And another proposed that the saboteurs had been hired by a rival contractor who'd lost out on the construction contract.

Everyone, it seemed, had an opinion. In addition to the internet's obsession with the topic, it was also the talk of every town. No matter where you were—Paris, Prague, Buenos Aires or Beijing—people argued endlessly over who was behind the explosion, whether there would be more attacks, what it meant for the mission, how the Council should respond. Terrorist acts were by no means uncommon; in fact, most developed nations had learned to accept them as a natural outgrowth of civilization—like industrial accidents or epidemics. But the Mission to Cerulea had so captured the public imagination that this relatively minor incident took on abnormal importance.

Unfortunately, progress in investigating the incident—which usually prolonged a story as evidence and leads trickled in—was simply not forthcoming. The station wagon which carried the explosives was untraceable; it appeared to have been put together using junkyard parts from over a dozen different states, while any part that might have carried an identification number had been filed down. The explosives themselves were made from ammonium nitrate, a very common chemical fertilizer available from thousands of suppliers nationwide. The only lead in the case, which quickly hit a dead end, were the car's Virginia license plates; it turned out they'd been stolen from pick-up truck registered to small-town lawyer from Pembroke, Virginia—over two years prior.

Despite the best efforts of the FBI, which by this point in time were fairly proficient, the incident looked as if it might go unpunished.

31.

Roger Tucker looked at his watch. 10:45. The first presentation had run only fifteen minutes late. *Not bad*, he thought, but he was anxious to get on with it; if possible, he wanted to be back at the White House for a noon meeting.

Though Roger was not an official member of the Mission Council, he had come to the meeting at the request of the President to hear a presentation delivered by Nombeko Nseki, in charge of growth planning and population management. She and her team had put together their preliminary plan for bringing a sufficient number of humans and selected animal species to adequately seed the new planet with life—assuming, of course, that Cerulea wasn't crowded with life of some kind already.

The idea was for Roger to get a sense of just how incendiary the plan might be once it hit the press, then figure out in advance how best to deal with it.

The meeting was being held in what had been designated as Mission headquarters, a sleek, angular, mirrored glass office building overlooking the Potomac in Alexandria, Virginia.

Roger was sitting off to one side, at one of a dozen glass-topped tables set up in a classroom configuration. Each table had 5 stations, incorporating an interactive touchscreen on which an attendee could review meeting information, zero in on elements of an ongoing presentation, and take notes or ask questions using a screen stylus. Simultaneous translation of all materials was available to anyone wishing to view a presentation of background materials in their native language

He had arrived early and had actually learned a fair amount from the first presentation, given by Jiro Kawamoto, summarizing the energy strategy for the new planet.

Kawamoto had made one thing clear: there was no magic solution to Cerulea's energy needs. Instead, an array of technologies would be employed as needed and as appropriate.

This was not a huge departure from the energy situation on Earth. Around the globe, private money had poured into new and innovative renewable energy projects; while some of these had been financial disasters, others offered more than interesting returns. On a regional basis, countries were starting to make much smarter decisions regarding which technologies best suited a given geography. In and around the Pacific Rim, geothermal plants were pevalent and productive;

in arid climates, the use of increasingly efficient solar power had exploded; and offshore wind power, exploiting technologies used in the deployment of oil platforms, was beginning to provide a substantive percentage of energy required for coastal cities.

Kawamoto had stressed that such "energy opportunism" would be the goal on Cerulea as well, and that any non-renewable source of energy—as well as nuclear—would only be considered as a last resort, and only on a temporary basis.

As Roger had listened to the presentation, he found himself envious of the Mission Council's ability to work from a blank slate. In the current world, where he lived, pulling civilization away from fossil fuels was slow-going; great progress had been made, but it still required tremendous effort to work the politics and move the gears of global policy.

Sure, there was a great deal of investment in renewable energy projects, and the world had managed to bring its greenhouse gas emissions well below turn of the century levels. But ambitious targets across the globe had fallen short—the industries, companies and politicians that benefited from traditional fossil fuel production stubbornly obstructed the most aggressive carbon reduction policies and initiatives. And as the increasingly affluent peoples of China and India sought to emulate the lifestyles of their U.S. brethren with larger houses, air conditioning and modern appliances, energy demand had soared—from 10 terawatts at the turn of the century to 28 terawatts in 2030.

"Peak oil," the point in time when the world reached its highest level of oil production, had come and gone in 2012. But the development of new oil resources—usually shale or oil sands, was still pursued with a vengeance. Worse, coal was still mined in ever larger quantities. While it was abundant and inexpensive, it was also the dirtiest of all available options. The key to so called "clean coal" technology—underground storage of a coal plant's CO_2 emissions, or sequestration—had shown promise and had provided the industry with political air cover for decades, but had yet to make any sizable dent in the overall footprint of the coal industry.

Filling in for rising demand was nuclear. Following the French model, nuclear plants in the United States began to proliferate at a tremendous pace beginning in the early 2020s. Needless to say, this was the cause of much consternation. In the U.S., the waste storage issue was finally resolved in 2018 with the commissioning of Yucca Mountain as the nation's primary storage site. Other countries followed the United States, and nuclear power's growth was now on par with renewables.

☙❧

After a short break following Kawamoto's talk, Nseki at last took the podium, and began moving through her presentation. Roger was impatient.

Finally, he said to himself as all screens displayed a visual labeled "population metrics," *what I came to hear.*

She obviously had been told of his presence, because as she started in on the data, she glanced directly at Roger.

"The number of humans required to build a genetically healthy population is actually much lower than many might expect—in the neighborhood of 160 people, equally split between men and women."

There were a few murmurs from her audience at the relatively small number of humans required. "For the record, numerous scientists have postulated that the Continent of North America was initially populated by roughly 70 humanoids who came across the Bering land bridge from Siberia."

Nseki moved on to another visual. "However, if we consider basic events that might impact successful propagation, the need for contingency planning increases the figure substantially.

"Therefore, in addition to a starting crew of one thousand, we are proposing an on-board reserve of 4,000 frozen embryos. Preliminary investigation indicates that we could build this reserve fairly easily by simply gathering existing stock from fertility clinics around the world.

"Unless circumstances demanded otherwise, these embryos would not be used at all during the voyage. Instead, they would be harvested gradually over time as the new colony is established and begins to grow."

Roger drew a deep breath. This was exactly what he wanted to hear. Small numbers, no new donors required specifically for the Mission, and—most important—no destruction of embryos. It was surprising that this issue had remained sensitive for so long, especially given the fact that society had long ago decided that trading healthy embryos for medical breakthroughs was an acceptable sacrifice. Nonetheless, with opposition to the Mission from religious conservatives seemingly on the rise, it was only logical to understand how much fuel was being added to the fire.

As if sensing his relief, and wanting to make sure it was not premature, Nseki continued. "It's important to note that genetic screening will be crucial, here. Any harmful recessive traits in the early Cerulean population could have a devastating impact on the colony's ability to thrive. Given what we anticipate will be limited healthcare resources during the first decade, it will be imperative that we take whatever steps we can to ensure that all crew members—and all embryos—are as genetically healthy as possible."

Roger smiled; genetic screening wouldn't cause a fuss. *Hell, the U.S. military's been doing it for years*, he thought to himself.

She went on to describe the storage techniques that would be employed on board the spacecraft, then spoke at some length regarding population management on Cerulea.

"One of the primary metrics when discussing population management is the total fertility rate, or TFR, of females within a population," Nseki explained. "The TFR represents the average number of offspring that each female will produce in her lifetime. There will be times when growth of the colony will be desired for survival and critical mass—and a TFR of 3 to 4 may be optimum; and other times when zero growth will be important. On Earth, zero population growth typically equates to a TFR of approximately 2.1; on Cerulea, we are estimating that, initially, it will equate to a slightly higher TFR of 2.3 due to a higher mortality rate, then gradually come down over time.

"Of course, the TFR of Cerulean females will not be in any way regulated or bound by Cerulean law," Nseki assured her audience. "However, birth rates can and will be influenced by economic incentives. These will primarily be in the form of taxes on a family's energy and resource footprint; families with more than two children might pay a slight premium, which could then be scaled from moderate to more aggressive as inhabited areas reach a point of saturation."

Nseki offered a number of graphs indicating the estimated growth of the Cerulean population, and outlined a conceptual plan for migrating the growing population to other geographies. Eventually, she moved on to a new topic.

"Now, while it is unclear at this juncture what types of organisms might exist on this new planet, we will be prepared to carefully introduce and build sustainable populations of several animal species, if appropriate.

"Since there is no existing source, obtaining the embryos for these species will require substantially more work..."

Roger was fascinated by Nseki's material, but looking at the clock on his wristphone, he realized he could still make his noon luncheon, and thus decided to skip this section of the presentation.

He quietly grabbed his briefcase and jacket, and headed out.

32.

Nombeko Nseki concluded her presentation at 12:30, and the Mission Council meeting broke for lunch.

Devlin McGregor, who had been appointed by President Belknap to the symbolic post of Mission Advisor, rose from his seat and quickly scanned the gathering. After a moment, he saw who he was after, and walked quickly across the room.

Devlin approached his target. "Judge Fossett? I'm Devlin McGregor."

"Good heavens, Mr. McGregor, I certainly know who you are. None of us would be here if it wasn't for you! It's very nice to actually meet you."

"Likewise, I was wondering if you had lunch plans. I—I thought perhaps we could talk for a bit."

"Oh, um," Cynthia paused. She had intended to spend the hour working in her office, but decided it could wait. "I'd like that," she said finally.

"Great." They headed down the corridor to the cafeteria, grabbed sandwiches and chose a quiet table at the far corner of the room.

"So Devlin, I've read a great deal about your discovery, of course, but I don't remember reading anything about you. How long have you been at NASA?"

"Coming up on a quarter of a century."

"Wow. That's impressive. And I understand you recently won the National Medal of Science. Congratulations!"

"Thank you," Devlin said shyly.

"So what do you make of this grand adventure?"

"Well, for starters, it's a dream come true. To make a discovery of this type, then to win the Science medal, and then be allowed to remain involved in the expedition is kind of mind-boggling. I still have to pinch myself a few times a day just to make sure it's all real."

"I know what you mean--I find myself in the same position. But it also hits me just as often how much effort it's going to take to pull it off and do it right."

"Well," said Devlin, changing tone, "that's kind of what I wanted to speak with you about. Maybe it's silly, but I feel somewhat protective of this new planet."

"I don't blame you. You're the discoverer."

"Not because of that per se. It's more that, well, it's as if I've told the world about this wonderful new untouched oasis, and I'm now scared to death were going to ruin it as we have this planet."

Cynthia laughed, then leaned in and, touching his arm, said earnestly, "Devlin, it appears you and I are birds of a feather."

"Well, I'm very glad to hear you say that. It baffles me how we've allowed the world population to climb to over eight and a half billion people, when in the year 2000, as I started my career at NASA, a population of six billion was already straining our resources.

"You know, when I was a boy, the notion of wilderness was more than a concept. The Amazon Basin, huge swaths of Africa, even our own National Park system offered a real glimpse of nature without mankind's footprint all over it. Today, there is truly no such thing. By placing man's needs above everything else, we have steadily consumed everything that was most beautiful on this planet, and I'm terrified the same thing will happen to Cerulea."

Cynthia sighed deeply. "There's a wonderful quote from a book my father gave me when I was young: "If people destroy something replaceable made by mankind, they are called vandals; if they destroy something irreplaceable made by God, they are called developers.""

"I believe that's Joseph Krutch, is that right?"

"Yes, that's exactly right! Holy cow, Devlin, it's refreshing—and a little scary—to come across someone who's as rabid on these issues as I am."

"Well, sometimes I just can't understand why we are such a minority." Devlin slumped back in his chair, seized by momentary despair. Recovering his resolve, Devlin leaned forward. "So Cynthia, here's the problem as I see it. If we've allowed ourselves to overwhelm this planet, what can we do to ensure that Cerulea won't meet the same fate?"

It was Cynthia's turn for reflection. She stared at her half-eaten sandwich, then looked up with apologetic eyes. "It's complicated, Devlin. The problem is that, in order to gain acceptance for Cerulea's constitution, we have to appease many different constituents.

"If we tried to implement some type of hard limit on Cerulea's population, with all that might imply, we would inevitably infuriate a lot of people; there's a good chance that those countries sponsoring this mission—including our own—would shut off our funding, thus ending the mission. As it is, I think that even a tax to incent lower birth rates will be fairly controversial."

"Frankly, Cynthia, hard limits are fine by me. When President Belknap first announced the discovery of Cerulea and the plan to launch a manned mission, she talked about creating a new world where humanity's progress would not necessitate sacrificing the environment. Well, if we aren't even going to aim for that goal, then we shouldn't aim at all!" Devlin pounded the table, causing their plates and silverware to rattle.

Cynthia and Devlin looked at each other in silence. She could see the intensity in his face, the tightness of his muscles.

She suddenly had the frightening realization that she and her team were following a path of compromise, rather than pursuing what they, like Devlin, truly believed to be the best course for the Cerulean colony.

She leaned back in her chair, holding Devlin's gaze. "You're right Devlin. You're absolutely right."

Ever since her appointment, she'd been in fear of going too far, of angering the opposition. She now saw clearly that, in fact, she wasn't going far enough—not by half.

33.

Belechenko raised his arm and used the sleeve of his t-shirt to wipe the sweat from his brow; Jim Stanton's pace was faster than he was used to.

The two of them left from the Space Center 20 minutes ago, and had already jogged several miles. They had just reached a path that ran along Clear Lake, a large inlet off Galveston Bay.

"So, Commander, why aren't you coming with us on this voyage? I would think that someone with your experience would be chomping at the bit for this kind of adventure."

"Oh Jim, I guess, like so many things, it's a question of timing."

"Meaning what? If you don't mind me asking."

"I don't mind at all. I think if I was your age, I would look at the opportunity very differently; I would still have over half of my life ahead of me once the ship reached Cerulea." He paused, allowing himself to catch his breath. "At the same time, if I was your age, I doubt very much that I would have been offered the chance to serve as Mission Commander."

"I see your point." They jogged for a while in silence.

"Do you suppose Georges Ventine and the other functional leaders feel the same way?" Stanton asked.

"I'm not sure. I do know that none us will be making the journey, and I'm guessing that age and career have something to do with it." A flock of seagulls were making a racket on the beach off to their right. One of them took off from the surf with a fish in its beak; three others took flight and chased it.

"All of us were asked to serve the mission as a result of our accomplishments here on Earth," Belechenko continued. "In other words, we've built a career here—whereas, at your age, you were chosen primarily for your potential."

"That makes sense," Stanton remarked thoughtfully.

"So tell me, Jim, how is crew selection proceeding?" Belechenko decided that, given the extra effort required to jog and talk, he'd prefer to ask rather than answer questions for a while.

"A little slower than I'd like, but we're making progress," Stanton replied. "Choosing astronauts has been fairly straightforward; most of them have been through a similar battery of tests over the years, so it's very easy to do an apples to apples comparison. It's the civilians that take time."

"How so?" asked Belechenko. As they jogged, their strides had fallen into a common rhythm, which seemed to lessen the amount of energy required to maintain the pace.

"Well, for one thing, we've received roughly 10-15 times the number of applications we were expecting, so the preliminary review process was brutal."

"Are you getting applications in accordance with the diversity spec drafted by the Council?"

"Mostly, yes. Plenty to choose from with regard to both genders, and a good pool of young families—both with and without children, including a fair number of same-sex couples."

"How about nationality and religious diversity? Any issues?"

"A few. For some reason, we've had only a handful of applicants from South America—and so far, none at all from Argentina."

"Why do you suppose that is?" Belechenko asked, looking down at his jogging watch; unless he wanted to push his normal workout, they should turn back soon.

"I couldn't say, but we've sent a small team down there to recruit. The same with the Yoruba religion—no qualified applicants so far, but we're working it."

Belechenko turned to Stanton with a quizzical expression. "Did you say Yoruba?"

"Yes; didn't you read the Council's spec?" Stanton grinned. "The Yoruba dominated west Africa before European colonialism and the trans-Atlantic slave trade. The culture and religion are, I believe, still a major influence in Nigeria and several other African nations. Anyway, the plan calls for one Yoruba couple."

"Fascinating," Belechenko remarked. "So let me ask you the reverse of the question you asked me earlier: why do you suppose all these people are willing to give up their life on Earth for the great unknown?"

"Great unknown? Are you kidding me? We know that it's a gorgeous planet, not unlike our own, and that they won't have to share it with eight billion other humans! What else do they need to know?"

They both laughed. The truth was that they probably knew as much or more about Cerulea as was known about the moon before Apollo 11. Multiple scientists using several different methodologies had confirmed and reconfirmed Devlin's data; but the lack of detailed images created an aura of mystery and adventure around the Mission. This would not be resolved until they reached the outer edges of Cerulea's solar system and could at last survey the planet's surface. And, of course, the scariest question of all: while the odds of the planet being inhabited by billions of humans was a long shot, whether there was life—or intelligent life—on the planet would not be known until they reached orbit.

"I think that many of the people expressing interest," Stanton reflected more seriously, "are, quite simply, thrill seekers. In virtually every interview I've conducted or observed, the applicant will say that they find the opportunity to inhabit a new world is impossible to resist."

Belechenko looked once again at his watch. "We should head back, Jim."

"No problem, Commander." They both slowed and pivoted, then began jogging back the way they'd come.

"How many of the civilian adults are scientists—or backyard astronomers?"

"I see what you're getting at, but only a few are in it for the science. Most just find the idea of colonizing a new planet thrilling. I certainly do!"

"Do these people know that it'll take 15 years for them to get a message to their friends back home—and another 15 to get a reply?"

Jim laughed again. "Well, it's not exactly what our interviewers lead with; but rest assured, everyone will know all the hard facts before they sign on the dotted line."

They jogged without talking for a mile or so. Finally Stanton, who had obviously given the last topic some thought, broke the silence. "My guess is that, once we send out confirmations to the folks we eventually select, there'll be a few who back away once the enormity of the thing hits them."

"Let's hope it's just a few," Belechenko offered.

34.

The glass shattered as it hit the tile floor.

"Damn it!" exclaimed Randall Reese, expressing his frustration in an uncharacteristic outburst.

He walked to the pantry off the kitchen, opened a cupboard, and grabbed a broom and dustpan. He walked back to the sink, put the dustpan on the counter, and began sweeping up the broken glass.

He shook his head as he worked the broom, his mind angry at his actions but also fixated on what he'd just read.

"Dad, is everything okay?" Reese's son entered the kitchen, having heard his father swearing. Jake was 19 years of age, a sophomore at Loyola University in downtown Chicago, and home on break.

"Jake, could you give me a hand?" He said to his son, nodding to the dustpan.

"Sure. What happened?"

"I dropped a glass, what does it look like?" Reese snapped. "I'm sorry, not your fault. I was reading something that angered me, dropped the glass, and over-reacted. Please forgive me."

Jake shrugged, grabbed the dustpan, and knelt down near the small pile of glass that his father had corralled with his broom. Reese began sweeping glass into the dustpan.

Jake stood up with the now full dustpan, eyed the newspaper sitting on the counter, then walked over to a cupboard under the sink, opened it, and dumped the glass into the trash.

He walked back to the counter. His father took the dustpan from his hand, and headed to the pantry to put broom and dustpan away. Jake picked up the paper and scanned the headlines. "What got you going this time, Dad?" Jake asked as his father returned from putting the boom away.

"Oh, it's mission-related, as usual," Reese said gesturing to the article on the bottom of the front page. "I'm just incredulous that this president could be so insensitive as to appoint an atheist to draft the constitution for this new planet. What truly infuriates me is that Fossett has the gall to admit in that interview that she's using her own 'common sense' to guide her efforts."

Jake was well aware of his father's mistrust of President Belknap and intense dislike of Cynthia Fossett. In fact, he was growing tired of his father's tirades on the subject of Cerulea. Jake quickly skimmed the article, and turned to his Dad: "It seems to me that she's being fairly methodical. I don't understand what's so offensive."

Jake was smart, well-spoken and fairly well read. While he'd worshipped his father when growing up, parroting any of his opinions or statements as if they were gospel, Jake had become much more independent since he'd left his catholic high school and headed off to college. Overall, while he still shared his father's general outlook, he did not share his vehemence, and wouldn't think twice about challenging his Dad when he felt he was taking an issue too far.

"Jake, let me ask you one simple question," Reese said calmly, leaning against the counter. "Do you think it would be appropriate if children on this new planet were raised without any religious encouragement?"

"I don't know the answer to that, Dad. I'm grateful for having been raised to appreciate God; it means a lot to me. And I guess I'd feel a little sorry for any kid who wasn't. So, yeah, it probably wouldn't be appropriate if kids on Cerulea missed out on all that. But, well..." Jake paused.

"But what," Reese encouraged.

"Okay, don't get mad, but some of my friends think that we—our family— are way over the line. They think that, like, your public statements are just an attempt to make sure that the mission reflects your beliefs. I don't know. One of my teachers said that forcing one set of beliefs over another is actually worse than encouraging no beliefs at all."

"Which teacher said this to you, son?" Reese asked carefully.

"Dad, that doesn't matter," Jake responded dismissively.

"Well, what do you think?"

"I'm not sure. I'm pretty certain that God will remain a pretty important presence in my life as I get older, and that the beliefs you and Mom have instilled in me are good ones. Whether they're the only ones, or whether they should be taught to every child, that's, like, a fairly tough question to answer."

"But don't you think that, if you'd never been exposed to the church and Jesus Christ in school, you would never have had the opportunity to adopt the right beliefs and values?"

Jake opened a cupboard, grabbed a box of dry cereal, and leaned back against the counter thinking over his father's question as he shoved a handful into his mouth. Outside, a cloud moved in front of the sun, and the light in the kitchen darkened.

"I think I might have answered that differently a couple of years ago," he began, mouth half full. "Lots of my friends went to regular public high schools, and, like, never received any religious education whatsoever. In fact, some of them are reading the bible for the first time as part of their bib lit class. Yet, if you ask me, these are pretty cool people, who seem to have their head screwed on straight."

Jake paused, munching on another handful of cereal. "I guess what I'm trying to say is that, well, it doesn't seem that a lack of religion in their lives caused them much harm."

"Jake, the church has given you direction; it's given you a heightened sense of right and wrong; it's given you, in large part, your ability to look at issues like this philosophically. How can you say it's not important?"

"Dad, listen to me. I do think it's important—to me. But what I'm trying to say is that the church may not be the only way to get there. You remember Michael Barnes, who lived across from me freshman year?"

"Vaguely. What about him?"

"Well, he was one of the nicest, most thoughtful guys I ever met. I think I probably learned a lot more about values and virtue from him than he did from me. And, like, I don't think he'd ever been to church in his life. He told me once that, at his middle school in Seattle, his entire class voted voluntarily to strike 'under God' from the pledge of allegiance because he and all his classmates felt it wasn't appropriate."

"And what do you think about that, Jake?"

"Dad, it doesn't matter what I think!" Jake replied, clearly frustrated. "The guy is totally centered—he knows who he is and has as much or more direction than I do!" Jake gestured to the newspaper. "I don't know why you let yourself get so out of joint over this stuff! I don't see why you can't let people find their own way sometimes..."

"I'll tell you why!" Reese shot back, getting a bit heated, "because if the world were left in the hands of people like Judge Fossett, it would rapidly evolve into a moral cesspool, that's why! Cerulea represents the perpetuation of mankind, the first opportunity for the human race to take the lessons learned from our life on this planet and apply them to a whole new chapter of our evolution! And I will not sit idly by while an atheist president and her band of godless advisors rob mankind's next great step forward of its moral compass!"

Jake was practically yelling: "Dad, get off it! Are you saying that the only way to instill the right values in a society is through Jesus Christ?"

"Yes, Jake that's exactly what I'm saying! And I'm awfully surprised to hear you so casually dismiss the importance of the Lord!"

"Dad, you really don't get it, do you?"

"Don't you dare tell me what I do and don't get!" Reese roared. There was dead silence as he locked eyes with his son. After a few seconds, it was broken by the sound of a car horn.

Jake broke eye contact, looked quickly out the window and walked toward the door, grabbing his knapsack off the counter as he went. "Whatever, Dad. That's my ride. I'm outta here—should be back later tonight."

Jake went out and slammed the door behind him.

Reese walked to the window and watched as his son got into his friend's car and they drove away.

His face was hot and he could feel his temples pounding.

35.

Ginny leaned back in her chair and looked at her watch. She breathed deeply and continued reading the report in her hand. She'd read the same paragraph now at least three or four times, and was retaining little. There was a lot on her mind.

Roger entered the Oval and tapped his watch. "They're ready for you."

The President stood, walked around to the front of her desk and grabbed her blazer off the back of a chair. "Well, I guess I'm ready for them." She pulled her sleeves from each cuff, and left the office with Roger.

Ginny had given literally dozens of press conferences over the past seven plus years, but she never felt fully relaxed heading into one—and this was no exception.

Truth be told, once she started taking questions, and developed a rhythm, she actually enjoyed them. But she also knew that, if caught off guard, she could say things that caused her and her staff to scramble for days—sometimes weeks.

"Did we hear back from our friends in China regarding the budget?" Ginny asked.

"As a matter of fact, yes," said Roger. "They have approved the incremental outlay, and will be announcing it shortly."

"Think they'd mind if I beat them to it?" Ginny asked, as they approached the Brady Press Room.

"I think that's fine—just don't commit them or mention any specifics, and I'll work it as soon as we're done. Just remember, that's only for 5 billion. My guess is you're going to have to pay them a visit to negotiate the rest."

"I had planned on it."

"Different topic: did you get a look at Reese's latest editorial that I placed in this morning's briefing package?"

"I glanced at it. Why?"

"My guess is it'll come up at least once today. How do you plan on handling it?"

"Delicately, as usual. It seems that Cynthia's interview was well-received overall; I'm not going to give Reese additional limelight by furthering the feud. "

A guard swung open the door to the press room, and Ginny heard the familiar warning from her press secretary: "Ladies and gentlemen, the President of the United States."

Roger pulled off to the side and stood with his back to the side wall, as the President stepped up onto the dais and nestled in behind the podium.

"Good afternoon." The President paused as she adjusted the microphone and placed her tablet on the podium in front of her. "As you all know, this press conference will focus exclusively on the Mission to Cerulea. I have no opening statement today, so let's jump in with questions."

She looked out at the crush of reporters, cameras and cables. She pointed at a short, disheveled gentleman about 3 rows back on the right. "Jim, why don't you start us off."

"Madame President, how do you respond to criticism that last month's attack on the mission convoy in Louisiana was the direct result of poorly planned security? And what are the Council's plans with regard to increasing security around future transports?"

"Jim, as you know, there are limitless resources that could be applied to securing every facet of this mission. If we wish to secure every single activity, both our budget and our schedule would be extended by an order of magnitude. Nonetheless, I think in this case the critics have a point; security was simply not what it should have been, and I take full responsibility. All major components being shipped from the Michoud Operations facility and elsewhere should have a more robust security strategy with sufficient resources applied. I have instructed Commander Belechenko to develop and implement an appropriate strategy before any more components are transported."

The President turned and focused on a tall woman in a dark blue suit in the back of the room. "Molly."

"Madame President, what do you estimate will be the total financial impact to the mission from the explosion?"

"Well, the replacement cost of the units destroyed in the explosion is approximately ten billion dollars. However, we anticipate that added security will require additional funds as well. Once Commander Belechenko's team has those numbers, we will release them.

"Zeke."

"Madame President, in a recent interview, Judge Fossett was quoted as saying that our system of government is vulnerable to rule by mobocracy, and that one of her goals is to ensure that the Cerulean Justice system is not a democracy. Do you agree with Judge Fossett? And does this imply that Cerulea will not follow our own system of majority rule?"

The President smiled slightly, knowing that this question was a minefield; her answer would be carefully dissected and studied for its implications and possible inconsistencies.

"Zeke, I think there's a couple of different concepts tied up in your question. Let me see if I can untangle this and explain. If I remember correctly, Cynthia referred to Jefferson's 'Notes on the State of Virginia.' In that essay, he noted that concentrating all the powers of government--legislative, executive, and judiciary—is, and I quote, 'precisely the definition of despotic government.'

"Now, as I'm sure you're all well aware, our system of government is not, strictly speaking, a democracy; it is a republic—or republican democracy. The point here is simple," she continued. "Our republic is structured so as to ensure that our representative government respects and carefully considers the views of all citizens—not just those of the majority. In this fashion, we limit the extent to which 'mob rule' can impose its views on the rest of the population.

"And Cerulea's constitution, I believe, will contain those same safeguards. So, in effect, Judge Fossett merely explained how Cerulea will mimic our system—not how it will differ in any substantive way.

"If memory serves, Alexander Hamilton was unequivocal on this issue in a speech urging the ratification of the Constitution. Let me see if I can pull it from memory: He was challenging the perception that pure democracy was the optimal form of government, noting that 'the ancient democracies in which the people themselves deliberated never possessed one good feature of government. Their very character was tyranny.'"

Ginny realized that her penchant for the academic occasionally left her audience confused. She quickly sought a different approach.

"There's a more modern saying that is, perhaps, more succinct: 'Pure democracy is two wolves and a sheep deciding what's for lunch.'"

The room of reporters laughed.

"Michelle."

"Senator Max Caulfield has stated his belief that you and Judge Fossett have 'high-jacked' the mission, and that the world deserves more balanced representation on the Mission Council. How do you respond?"

This question pissed Ginny off, but she remained outwardly calm. How could she have high-jacked the mission when it was her administration that had gotten it off the ground in the first place? What's more, the effort required to assemble the Mission Council had been exhaustive. She had bent over backwards in her attempts to populate the team with leaders from many different nations and with a true cross-section of world views.

The president drew a deep breath and responded. "As most of you know, the process by which we researched and recruited members of the Mission Council was above-board and fairly comprehensive in scope. We have representatives from all seven continents, and from virtually all industrialized nations. In fact, I would say that we have done a fairly good job of ensuring that the Council can't be high-jacked by one particular interest group or another. And judging by some poll numbers I saw last week, I would say Americans—and much of the world population—would agree.

"Gretchen."

"Madame President, the mission to Cerulea is already almost 20% over budget, and some are estimating that costs will increase further as we near the launch date. Do you believe that the nations supporting the mission will be forthcoming with additional funds, or will the United States be forced to bear the burden of this cost increase?"

"Gretchen, budgeting for a mission of this sort is an art, not a science. It should come as little surprise, then, that we will be forced to find—and fund—solutions to unforeseen challenges as we move toward launch.

"The U.S. will indeed be asked to help shoulder these increased costs, but we will do so only at established levels. In fact, I've received word just today that China is in the final stages of deliberation on a new funding measure which will cover the cost increase incurred thus far. As the second largest contributor to the Mission, this is an important milestone. Other mission partners are going through similar processes. Overall, I do not expect financial commitment to be a significant issue.

"Sally."

"Several members of the Mission Council are planning trips to the L5 spaceport to review mission progress. Do you have any intent to make such a trip and, if so, will you transfer powers to the Vice President in accordance with the 25th amendment?"

The room laughed again. "At this time, I have no immediate plans to travel to L5. However, if I were to do so, I would not expect to be incapacitated by the journey, so I don't think a transfer of powers is relevant here.

"Blake."

"Derek Butler has said that, if elected, he would seek to pass legislation which gave the United States voting rights over all aspects of the mission in direct accordance with our financial support. Do you agree with Butler and would you support such legislation?"

"No, I do not agree with Derek Butler on Mission voting rights and I certainly would not support any such legislation. The voting rights of the Mission

Council participants were established via treaty. Our Congress may pass legislation urging that we take actions counter to the terms of this treaty, but Congress most certainly cannot, under any circumstances, make unilateral changes to Council bylaws.

"Furthermore, the cooperation of nations across the globe is an essential ingredient of mission success. The United States does not own Cerulea, and therefore I do not think that a display of U.S. hegemony here is in any way appropriate. In fact, I would argue that it would be counter-productive to mission success.

"Greg."

"Madame President, the following is a quote from an editorial by Randall Reese in this morning's *American Standard*: "Judge Fossett's use of what she deems to be "common sense" in determining the role of religion in Cerulean society is a complete betrayal of American and world history, and a blasphemous denial of mankind's spirituality. The Mission Council should immediately replace Fossett with someone who has a better knowledge of constitutional law, and a greater appreciation for Our Creator." How do you respond to Mr. Reese, and will the Mission Council take up the issue of replacing Judge Fossett?"

Ginny knew it was coming, but somehow allowed the question to generate within her a potent mix of anger and exhaustion. It was suddenly crystal clear that such assaults on the mission were not occasional distractions, they were here to stay. It was obvious that, from here on out, some portion of her day—her life— would now be consumed by war room strategy sessions in a never-ending effort to counteract anti-mission rhetoric.

She calmly regained her resolve and responded forcefully:

"I read the entirety of the *Times* article, as I'm sure many of you did as well. Judge Fossett was quite forthcoming in detailing how legal precedents would guide her team's efforts. Do I believe that her use of 'common sense' was inappropriate? No, I do not. After one has looked at all the data relevant to a given issue or pending decision, common sense born of experience is how any competent professional blends inputs to form a conclusion.

"This country has consistently upheld the separation of church and state, and for good reason. While we are all free to pursue religion and spirituality as we see fit, governmental involvement would inevitably favor or endorse one path over another. If, hypothetically, the government did get involved, and by chance endorsed the teaching of Buddhism or Islam in our public schools instead of Christianity, I'm sure Mr. Reese would be equally upset—perhaps to the point where he himself would argue for the removal of government from our schools.

"Cynthia Fossett is not betraying history; quite the opposite—she is respecting it, and while the Mission Council has bylaws and procedures for adding or removing appointed personnel, I have no inclination whatsoever to suggest or explore the replacement of Judge Fossett."

As she concluded her response and looked for another reporter to call on, it occurred to Ginny that she had just completely contradicted her comment to Roger before taking the podium.

36.

"I think they're more than a little suspect" the senator offered quickly with his sharp southern twang, "he's a damn Yankee and a self-declared centrist at a point in time when this country and this whole goddamn planet needs a candidate with backbone and real moral fortitude! Someone who understands what's truly important to me and all of the other god-fearing Americans in this state and across this nation!"

Senator Caulfield leaned forward from his seat on the sofa, downed his last sip of coffee, replaced the cup in its saucer, and leaned back again.

There was silence.

The candidate's campaign manager and an assistant sat in overstuffed chairs, facing the Senator. They were in the Presidential Suite at the Four Seasons overlooking mid-town Atlanta. Max Caulfield had grown up in Buckhead, near Chastain Park, roughly ten minutes north.

The Suite and its view were both fairly obvious ploys. Caulfield knew that Derek Butler's near-limitless financial resources would be invaluable as the campaign heated up. This little reminder was hardly subtle, but to a veteran of five senate campaigns, it was nonetheless effective. And the view—well, the view was a cheap shot, but Caulfield had to admit that it was a clever cheap shot.

His reticence to publicly support Butler at this early date was not surprising—it was simply too early to be picking horses, and it was clear to all that such a weighty endorsement would not be made quickly, and it would not be made without a fair amount of horse-trading. But then, there was that view of mid-town.

"More coffee, senator?"

"I'd like that. Thank you, Liz."

Liz got up from her seat, took Caulfield's cup and walked to the sideboard for a refill. His use of her name was a good indication that his anger was, she hoped, short-lived. She knew the game, knew that pre-election posturing demanded that he remain aloof. Still, she chided herself for having asked him what his constituents thought of Butler at this point in the campaign.

Perhaps it was good for him to get it off his chest, she thought as she placed the cup of black coffee in front of the senator.

"So I understand you grew up not far from here," she said, sitting back down.

"I did indeed," the senator said, taking a sip of his coffee. "I was…"

The door to the suite opened and Derek Butler, preceded and followed by several campaign aides, blew into the room like a tornado.

One aide immediately went to a desk in a corner of the suite, another to the bathroom, another to the coffee station. Butler, however, calmly and intently locked eyes with the Senator and approached. Caulfield slowly stood up from his seat.

"Senator Caulfield, it is great to see you again," Butler said, shaking the senator's hand firmly. "I am incredibly pleased that you could carve out some time to come and see me today."

"Not at all, Mr. Butler. Since you seem to be emerging as an important player in next year's election, I rather think it's my duty to make time for you."

"Please." Butler gestured the senator back onto the couch. His campaign manager had gone to retrieve her bag as her boss entered the suite. As she approached, Butler looked at her and was about to speak when she cut him off-- "got it covered. Call me when you're ready and we'll head to the event." She quickly and efficiently rounded up the other staffers in the suite and herded them out into the hall, closing the door behind her.

"She seems very capable," Caulfield said as Butler took the seat Liz had occupied moments earlier.

"I believe she is," Butler replied. "So far, so good." There was a brief pause. "Can I get you anything..."

"No, I'm all set," the Senator said firmly.

"So I wish I could spend more time in your hometown," Butler began, "but I'm afraid we're on to the next stop first thing tomorrow morning."

"That's a shame. Next time we're both in Atlanta, why don't you pay me a visit at Gum Creek?"

"I'd like that. Your farm is in South Georgia, in Tifton, is that correct? I believe it was once owned by the great grandson of Charlie "whippoorwill" Crockett."

"True on both counts. I like a man who does his homework."

They both chuckled. Caulfield took another sip of his coffee and leaned back into the sofa, cup in hand. "So what would you like to talk about today?" He asked openly but a little disingenuously. He of course knew damn well what Butler was after, but wanted to see him squirm a bit.

"Well, senator, I won't beat around the bush. I would very much like you to consider backing my bid for the presidency."

So much for squirming, Caulfield mused. Butler continued: "I know it's early, and I know that the likes of Max Caulfield is not about to make such a decision lightly, but, well, I wanted to begin the process, and start to get an understanding of what's important to you, where you agree and disagree with my positions, and frankly, whether I've got a snowball's chance in hell here or not."

Caulfield looked at Butler and smiled broadly.

"I certainly admire your candor, Mr. Butler."

"Please, it's Derek."

"Well, Derek, I'll do my best to be equally candid. It is awfully early, and I don't intend to make a decision anytime soon, but I have no problem whatsoever in some frank discussion along the way."

The senator took another sip of coffee. "Tell me, I've gotten the impression from your stump speeches that you don't entirely agree with the president regarding the mission to Cerulea, but I don't think you've outlined exactly how you might play it differently. Can you tell me what you got in mind?"

"We haven't wasted much time here, have we senator?" Butler responded.

"I would say not," said Caulfield, still expecting Butler's answer to his question.

Butler held eye contact, his mind calculating how much he was willing to trust the Senator with information to which only a handful of campaign insiders were privy. He decided to throw a few chips on the table. "I think it's safe to say that I'm not a big fan of the Mission Council," Butler offered. "Overall, I think the expedition might be better served if there were a few more centrists involved."

Both men knew the meaning of the word centrist in this context. The senator leaned forward and entered the game. "As I think you well know, I fully agree with you on this issue. The question, of course, is tactics. How might a Butler administration make that happen?"

Butler doubled his bet. "Well, for instance, if some key members of the council were to step down for any reason, we would work very hard to select and install appropriate replacements."

Caulfield leaned back and narrowed his eyes, carefully considering Butler's implication. While he welcomed a man with a bias for action, he was not expecting to cover so much ground in this brief visit. But he liked what he heard. He liked it very much.

He carefully squared the pot. "Interesting. Well if, by chance, there was some attrition on the Council, I would be very pleased to help you fill the gaps."

The two men looked at each other in silence, subtle smiles on both their faces.

After several seconds, Butler got up from his chair and grabbed a bottle of water from the sideboard. He walked past the red marble fireplace and across the thick oriental carpet and stood looking out the window, his back to the couch. The suite was lavish, and larger than Caulfield's DC apartment; *the guy seems right at home here* Caulfield thought to himself. He heard the plastic seal break as Butler removed the cap and took a long drink.

"My investment firm has taken a long hard look at the Atlantic Station expansion project," Butler said, looking out at mid-town Atlanta and the site of the most ambitious campaign promise of Caulfield's 30-year political career—a promise that was in desperate need of financing.

The senator rose from the couch, surprised once again by the candidate's brazen manner. He slowly walked over and joined Butler at the window, not entirely sure what was coming next. Butler turned to his guest and ended the suspense. "We think it has solid potential, Senator."

The two men smiled at one another; Butler extended his hand and they shook hands. "Please," said Caulfield, "call me Max."

37.

Roger Tucker looked at the display on his wristphone, noting the incoming call from Cynthia Fossett. He turned his head back to a document on his screen, and then in a flurry of keystrokes, completed the sentence he'd been working.

He leaned back in his desk chair, touched a button on his wrist, and swiveled to face the window.

"Cynthia, how are you?"

"I'm great Roger; swamped, but doing well. How about you?"

"Roughly the same. What can I do for you?"

"Well, I got your email last night with some poll results, and I wanted to make sure that I understand what I'm looking at."

Roger laughed. "Seems too good to be true, huh?"

"It sure does. Perhaps you could give me your take on what it all means."

"Be happy to." Roger clasped his hands behind his head as he leaned back in his chair. "Essentially, what the data is telling us is that 62 percent of Americans and 71 percent of those around the globe believe that your efforts to create a constitution for Cerulea are on the right track."

"This is all in response to the Times interview?" Cynthia asked.

"Partially. The numbers were pretty strong before the interview, but that piece clearly caused a bump."

"So all this time, while I've been afraid of speaking up for fear of angering conservatives, it turns out that the world actually supports my approach?"

"I would say the world strongly supports your approach. Now, there's also a slight rise in those who disapprove of your approach—mostly in the U.S., but I'd say it's insignificant; nothing at all to worry about."

"Wow. I've got to tell you it's all fairly liberating. I feel as if I've been tiptoeing around trying not to make any noise for months and months, and then all of a sudden I'm praised for speaking out."

Roger smiled. Here was an incredibly accomplished woman—yet with little sense of the workings of Washington. "You should feel very proud of yourself and your team," Roger said encouragingly. "You're doing a great job, and people like what they hear. We'll arrange to have you speak up more often."

"I'd like that, Roger, I'd like that a lot. Thanks for your help."

"Not at all. Anytime, Cynthia."

After her lunch discussion with Devlin McGregor, Cynthia had been wrestling with her conscience. As she ended the call with Roger, the wrestling match was over; her conscience had emerged victorious.

38.

Vladimir Belechenko uncorked what looked to be a very expensive bottle of red wine and filled each of two glasses on the kitchen table.

He put the bottle down and cupped his hands. He was nervous. He had never been in the residence, and it felt a little awkward. No, more than awkward, it somehow felt illegal—as if by just being there he was doing something wrong and inappropriate.

He walked over to the window above the sink and looked out at the ellipse, and beyond it, the Washington Monument. A flock of Canadian geese flew into view, heading Southeast in a V formation. Belechenko watched as their silhouettes passed over the World War II Memorial in the fading light then veered out of sight somewhere over the Tidal Basin.

Ginny had gone to change. She had been over an hour late, leaving him to wait outside the Oval Office until she finally returned from a meeting and together they'd proceeded up to the residence.

All that waiting had made him more nervous and now he was waiting again. Anxiety was not a particularly familiar feeling for the Commander. Over the course of his life and career, he had consistently been able to maintain a steady head and hand when circumstances caused others to fall apart.

He turned and studied two photographs on the wall by the window. One was a picture of Ginny's two grown daughters, arm in arm, at what looked like a formal party of some sort. The other was obviously a family photo taken when the children were quite young. They were outside under a tree on a sunny summer day; Ginny's ex-husband stood behind his three girls.

"Some wine, Vladimir?" Belechenko's heart skipped a beat, surprised by the president's voice. He turned to Ginny as she offered him his glass. She looked incredible. She was wearing a belted black turtleneck sweater and jeans; he had never seen her with her hair down--both figuratively and literally--and she looked—well, to Vladimir Belechenko, she looked absolutely gorgeous.

He took the glass and they silently raised their glasses in salute, and each took a sip. The wine was wonderfully smooth and full; Belechenko could feel much of his previous anxiety melting away; he felt comfortable in Ginny's company.

"You look very nice," he managed to say, wondering why he felt it necessary to employ such an understatement.

"Thank you. It's not often I get to socialize in something other than the buttoned-up uniform of a female chief executive," she said, smiling.

"Well, here's to many more such opportunities," he said, smiling broadly. They both took another sip of wine.

"So, I've got a confession." Ginny put her wine glass down on the table and opened the fridge. "I had the kitchen stocked with ingredients, but had nothing prepared. I thought it might be nice to cook for a change."

She pulled some fresh vegetables and some other items out of the refrigerator and put them on the counter.

"Care to lend a hand?"

"I'd like nothing more," Belechenko replied. She handed him a knife, a bell pepper, and a cutting board.

As he went to work slicing the pepper, he asked Ginny about her family. "So tell me, were your daughters with you when you were in the state department?"

"Oh no, they came later," Ginny replied, pouring some olive oil into a pan. "I met my husband during my last assignment, in Brussels. Somehow I convinced him to move back to Vermont with me, and that's where our daughters were born."

"So how did you go from Vermont to Washington?"

"That's a long story."

"I'd like to hear it," Belechenko urged.

"Well, after the girls entered elementary school, I began teaching political science at the University of Vermont. It was great; I often think I could have been very happy as a college professor. But it was short-lived.

"After a couple of years, I was encouraged to run for a seat in the House of Representatives against this total idiot of an incumbent."

"That must have helped your chances," Belechenko remarked.

"I wish it had; I lost the race. But I caught the bug, and four years later won a seat in the Senate."

"So your family remained in Vermont?"

"They did, and that was very hard on me. But my husband was terrific; he was a doting father to the girls, and I flew home as often as I could, and called every night. You know, I have no regrets; it was where I wanted to be, but it was not without a cost."

Belechenko looked up from the cutting board, inviting Ginny to continue.

"Overall, I'd have to say that my daughters and I stayed pretty close; it was my marriage that suffered. I had developed an entirely separate life in Washington which didn't include him, and when the girls finally left for college, there was this huge chasm between us. He didn't want to move to Washington, so for quite a few years we maintained a long-distance marriage; he was traveling a fair amount anyway, consulting for several multi-nationals.

"Then, just as my husband came to the conclusion that he wanted to separate, the progressive frontrunner in the '28 presidential race imploded in a financial scandal, and I was urged to run in his place. My husband's reaction was amazingly selfless; he shelved the separation, and offered to go the distance.

"Ironically, the campaign brought our whole family closer than we'd been in many, many years. The girls were terrific campaigners; I think they had a ball. And my husband was a brick through the whole affair. He'd be there when events called for it, and would do his own thing when they didn't.

"For two years he remained the loyal soldier. But we still saw very little of each other, and Washington really wasn't his thing; mid-way through my first term, he told me that he wanted out. It was sad, but it was the best thing for both of us."

Ginny smiled recollecting. "Boy, I remember the uproar among the White House staff; they were scared to death that the divorce would stop our agenda in its tracks."

"Did it?" asked Belechenko.

"No, it really didn't. I was very proud of the American people; this was a very honest and straightforward split between the two of us, and I think that's the way it was received."

Ginny unwrapped a package that she'd taken from the refrigerator, and placed two pieces of fish into the pan; they crackled in the hot oil.

"Anyway, that's the story. What about you? Were you ever married?"

Belechenko smiled.

"What?" Ginny smiled back involuntarily.

"Well, no, I've never been married—in the traditional sense of the word," Belechenko explained. "But my brother used to say that my commitment to a bucket of bolts orbiting the Earth was stronger than his marriage would ever be."

They both laughed, and moved on to other topics.

39.

Derek Butler handed some papers back to one of his aides and bounded up a set of steps to the stage.

He had been working an issue on the fly during a long-winded introduction by Elmer Hogan, the mayor of Fremont, California, and had just received a signal that the mayor's oration was at last winding down.

The Butler campaign was in high gear. This day alone, the candidate had already spoken at a pancake breakfast in Decatur, Illinois, a packed VFW hall in Peoria, and a high school in Silverton, Colorado.

Butler was good at virtually all aspects of the process. He was excellent at strategy, and, given his corporate background, he was an able and clear-headed manager. He was a gifted speaker. He could also be very personable, and connected well with the electorate at small gatherings—though it was felt by some that he was a little too good at connecting. A recent editorial had sardonically quipped that "one secret to Butler's success is clearly his sincerity; his ability to turn it on or off at will puts him in an excellent position to round up votes in the coffee shops and living rooms of small town America."

Not a lot was known about Butler other than the impressive entries on his resume. He was born in Armonk, New York, but spent the bulk of his childhood in Overland Park, Kansas. His father had been a call center manager at Sprint; his mother a call center representative. He'd been the star of his high school football team, but an injury in the fall of his senior year put the brakes on his college ball career—and any potential scholarship that might have gone along with it. So he'd decided to join the Marines and get his degree while exploring the world. Through the Corps' SOCMAR program, he studied at a number of different colleges as his assignments moved him from place to place.

After the marines, Butler grabbed an MBA from Michigan and began a rapid ascent to the upper echelon of the business world. He rocketed upwards at ExxonMobil, promoted to head all European operations at the age of thirty-one. Eventually, he was brought in as chief operating officer of the Diametrix conglomerate, and assumed the CEO slot two years later after his predecessor's untimely death of a heart attack.

Under his guidance, the company grew tenfold, and Butler amassed a fortune, ultimately landing himself in the top fifty of the Forbes 400 richest people on the planet.

But his celebrated background revealed almost nothing about his views on the political issues of the day. These were his to disclose as he saw fit, with virtually no need to square his beliefs with past statements or political actions. There simply weren't any. A candidate's dream come true.

Butler took the stage and waved to the adoring crowd of over five thousand. His rallies had been growing steadily, as was every important metric of the campaign. He was wearing a crisp, white, Brooks Brothers button-down shirt with sleeves neatly rolled up just below the elbow, dark grey flannel trousers, and black Berluti loafers—which ran somewhere north of two thousand dollars a pair.

He grinned, whitened teeth gleaming in the mid-day sun, and played the usual pointing game to fans he supposedly knew in the first couple of rows, then asked for quiet and began to speak.

His stump speech was still in its formative stage, but he was quickly learning what issues hit the mark and which appeared to veer off to the left or right.

In an age when the world was being asked to sacrifice more and more in order to protect the planet's increasingly fragile natural resources, one of Butler's favorite topics was the importance of putting human needs over everything else.

"I ask you," he paused for effect, "why is it that, with millions of people starving in this world, we insist on vigorously protecting huge tracts of land in Africa, South America, and our own United States, when this land could be used for agriculture and the development of housing, schools, and hospitals?

"Why is it that innovation, the engine of our global society's success, is dangerously constricted by regulations which lessen productivity, impair progress, and threaten our ability to better serve humanity?

"In Genesis 1:26, God said 'Let us make man in our image, after our likeness: and let them have dominion over the fish of the sea, and over the fowl of the air, and over the cattle, and over all the earth, and over every creeping thing that creepeth upon the earth.' So I ask you: when we have the ability, the technology, the drive, the imagination to solve some of the greatest problems facing mankind, why is it that we must subordinate the needs of desperate men, women and children to those of plants and animals?

"Why must humanity sacrifice its well being for the sake of lesser species?"

The crowd erupted after each question, becoming slowly hypnotized by the rhythm of his speech. While many of his detractors believed that Butler's campaign themes were simply a thinly veiled ploy to let free enterprise do what it wished, he would not be put in a box quite so easily. By consistently invoking the poor and downtrodden, he successfully persuaded many to see him as a progressive champion of human dignity, fighting for the disadvantaged.

Another favorite topic of Butler's stump speech was, of course, the mission to Cerulea. Fully aware that the mission had captivated the world's imagination, his objective was to support the expedition with lofty rhetoric, yet at the same time send clear signals to those objecting to the Mission Council's approach that he was on their side.

"If you elect me to be your president, which I very much hope you do," he paused, and grinned broadly as the audience erupted yet again with wild applause. "I will do my very best to see that the mission meets with your approval. I want all of you to be extremely proud not just of man's incredible achievement in perpetuating our species to a new planet, but proud as well of Cerulean society as the offspring of our own. I want you to be proud that a new world—a new civilization will grow from infancy to adulthood with the same moral foundation and soaring dreams, beliefs and values as its parent.

"And if you, the American people, as the primary benefactors of this great enterprise, find yourselves concerned that your future progeny is in any way misaligned with your beliefs, then I will be not be shy in taking the necessary action."

Butler knew that this message was difficult for the crowd to digest as he delivered it from the stage. However, he and his staff were well aware that, as it found its way into newspapers, web sites and video, where the nation could better parse and analyze its meaning, it would provide substantial comfort to a critical demographic.

40.

They had just finished cleaning up. While Ginny made some coffee, Belechenko dialed up some music—Tchaikovsky's Serenade for Strings.

He sat down on the couch and briefly closed his eyes, listening. He knew the piece by heart; it seemed to wrap itself around his contented state like a warm blanket. Eventually, Ginny walked over and placed a cup of hot coffee in front of Belechenko, then sat down next to him.

"Thank you, Ginny. I had such a wonderful time with you tonight," Belechenko gushed, intentionally avoiding understatement.

"I must say, I'd almost forgotten what it's like to have a nice quiet dinner, and I certainly can't remember when I last laughed so much," she replied.

Their eyes met for what seemed like a very long time. Finally, Belechenko broke off and looked at his watch. He had not lied—dinner was wonderful. It had been a long time since he'd shared a romantic evening with a woman, and he'd enjoyed it thoroughly. More than that; he was pretty certain that he was falling in love with Ginny, and it scared him. In part because he had no idea where the whole thing might lead; where it could lead; where she would allow it to go. Although he'd felt absolutely no tension or awkwardness whatsoever all through dinner, suddenly he felt anxious again, and thought it might be best if he took his leave before he found himself unable to keep his hands off the President of United States.

"I really should get back. Tomorrow we begin an exhaustive three-day review of project plans for each major module of the ship, and I should get a good night's sleep."

Ginny continued staring at Belechenko, narrowing her eyes as if attempting to see more deeply into what was going on inside his head. She said nothing, and let the silence linger. They had easily avoided talking shop for most of the evening, and she was not going to let the night end with both of them resuming their official roles and engaging in "mission-speak."

He turned and put his hands on his knees to raise himself from the couch.

"Vlad," she said quickly.

He turned to her but before he could speak she leaned over, put her arms gently behind his neck and pressed her lips to his.

He felt a shudder pass from his shoulders down to his toes; once again, his anxiety vanished. He leaned back and put his arms around her waist. Their kiss deepened as Ginny pushed him back so that she was now lying on top of him. Belechenko tightened his embrace and Ginny responded by combing his hair gently with the fingers of her right hand.

Finally, their lips parted and Ginny propped herself up on an elbow. "Now, what was it you were saying about your schedule tomorrow?" she asked playfully.

Vladimir Belechenko grinned. "Oh, just that I've got a couple of meetings tomorrow, but nothing too important."

"Good, because other than a morning call with the President of China, a speech in Miami at noon, and dinner in New York with the U.N. Secretary General, I've got a pretty light day as well."

Belechenko blushed. "Well, then, I guess the evening is still young."

Ginny smiled, as a strand of her hair fell down against Belechenko's cheek. He reached up and brushed it away, then pulled her head toward him for another kiss.

41.

R andall Reese rotated a pencil nervously on the pad of paper in front of him. First tapping the pad with the eraser, then the tip, then the eraser, then the tip.

He had spent the day in the offices of The Condon Group, Joe Condon's lobbying firm in Washington.

Joe's firm had been quite successful over the years, as had the multitude of other lobbying firms in and around K Street. Lobbying was big business, and getting bigger. Often called the "the Fourth Branch of government," billings for Washington firms now totaled more than $38 billion, up from just over $2 billion at the turn of the century. Then, as now, this equated to roughly double the amount given to candidates through campaign contributions. In Washington, the ratio of lobbyists to legislators in the federal government was now a little over 20 to 1. In some states, it was approaching 30 to 1.

Reese and Condon had been planning the agenda for a massive demonstration on the mall to take place in just 30 days' time, and were now discussing turnout. Billed as the "March for Mankind," their network of organizers was optimistically projecting a crowd of nearly a million people.

But they were far from overconfident. In fact, they were quite worried. A huge turnout could be a tremendous boon to their efforts, but a weak one could kill them. And they both knew it.

The public's opinion of the mission and how it was managed had, for months on end, garnered very high marks in both the US and abroad. However, regularly scheduled and well choreographed protest rallies, along with Butler's candidacy, had dramatically accelerated the public's questioning of the mission. While those in opposition remained a minority, it was clear that the minority was hardening, and that there were some small cracks that they should be able to widen with the right strategy.

"I think we've got a strong base in place and growing nicely," Condon offered. "But to tip the scales, we really need to appeal to a much broader section of the public. As always, the question is how to throw red meat to the base and gently catalyze the middle without offending everyone else."

Reese put the pencil down and turned in his chair toward Condon. "I don't know. You're the political expert, but I've observed over the years that, as often as not, it is the fervor of the base itself that brings in the middle, not some bifurcated strategy that seeks to feed each constituent."

"Don't sell yourself short as a political expert, Randall," Condon said with a laugh. "I think you're right; in many cases, the base can be the catalyst—but not always. It has so much to do with the mood of the center. Sometimes it's a volcano ready to blow; sometimes it's cold, solid rock."

There was a brief silence as both men paused to think.

"Sometimes it needs a trigger," Reese said pensively. Then, looking up: "Maybe I'm stating the obvious, Joe, but we need an event, a gaff, a transgression on the part of Belknap or the council; something that will give us a hook with which to really galvanize those on the edge and get them involved in the march."

"Easier said than done," Condon griped. "Provoking Belknap is damn near impossible. She's one of the best diplomats I've ever seen. You can't force her to put her foot in her mouth—in seven years as President, I don't think those two body parts have ever met."

"She's not the only possibility," Reese mused. "Fossett could probably do the trick."

Condon considered the idea. "Be careful, Randall, we sure as hell don't want to turn the woman into a celebrity."

Reese ignored the comment, lost in thought. "We both know full well that Fossett's as liberal as they come. She may have scored a few points with her New York Times interview, but I'll bet that, if unmasked, a wide swath of the public would recoil at her extremism. The question is how to draw her out." He turned to Condon, "Joe, do we know anyone over at Counterpoint?"

"Sure, I used to work with Mike Murphy, the producer, back in my days as a Hill staffer. But he's straight up; there's no amount of money that would get him to do our bidding."

Counterpoint was one of the longest running and most highly respected shows on television. Initially, it had begun as just another two-bit, right versus left mud-wrestling match, with little regard for serious exploration of real issues. But over time, the show's creators rose above the fray and did something very clever. They adopted a true debate format, with strict guidelines. There was a panel of respected judges who would intervene if a guest on the show broke the rules. For instance, if a majority of the panel perceived that the guest was not actually answering the question that had been asked, they could activate a red light and literally shut them up on the spot.

"I don't think we would need him to do anything improper. All we'd want him to do is listen to a great idea for a debate, then do what he does best."

Condon was not fully convinced. "What have you got in mind?"

"Very simple," said Reese, the idea gelling in his mind. "A straightforward debate on the pros and cons of the Cerulean Constitution."

"And the debaters?" Condon asked.

"Reese versus Fossett."

"Hmmmm. You might have something there," Condon mused. "You know, that might be helpful in other ways as well. If we could get her to cross the line, it might also add authenticity to the—"

"Joe!" Reese snapped. "For the last time, leave me the hell out of it!"

Condon shook his head and smirked, muttering something under his breath. "I'll give Mike a call first thing in the morning."

42.

The CEV had just reached escape velocity. At eleven point two kilometers per second, or 25 thousand miles per hour, the USS Integrity, a third generation Crew Exploration Vehicle, was now traveling just fast enough to break free of Earth's gravity.

Jim Stanton's mind was a mass of confused emotions, shifting restlessly on a foundation of very little sleep.

He was exhilarated that construction was now well underway. His four-week mission would be to oversee the completion and testing of the ship's water processing system, and would be the first time he and all of the ship's officers would be working together in space.

Over the past several months, he had started to feel less awkward in his role as captain, and no longer felt quite as clumsy trying to navigate each day in what felt like gigantic shoes. In fact, there were now times when they seemed to fit fairly well—though these moments were not as common as he'd have liked.

However, just as he was beginning to think he might make a good Captain, he was nearly knocked unconscious by a decision of the Mission Council: it had been proposed that he, Jim Stanton, assume the initial governorship of the Cerulean Colony.

The council's logic made sense. It was felt that, after a 14-year mission with him as Captain, the entire ship would regard him as their natural leader. And it was not envisioned that his gubernatorial career would last very long. After one year on Cerulea—equivalent to roughly 528 Earth days—there would be an election for which Jim would be ineligible. Under the Council's plan, he would also have strong leaders in place for each major function of the initial Cerulean government.

Nonetheless, this new development had Jim's head spinning at twice its normal speed.

But this wasn't all. Wrapping itself around all of these thoughts and anxieties was one more: Stacy. Leaving her this time had been one of the most difficult and emotional events of his life. Of course he'd be back in less than a month, but his departure on this trip was somehow different from those of the past two years. This one said, incontrovertibly, *I will soon leave this planet forever—without you.*

There were nights, lying in bed in Stacy's arms, when he literally fantasized about having some accident that would prevent him from participating in the mission. Nothing too serious; just something serious enough from which he could recover and live a long happy life with Stacy.

They had very openly discussed his impending and final departure, but it never helped; neither seemed to achieve any kind of acceptance. It was going to happen; it was going to rip both of them up inside, and that was that.

Early on, he'd simply assumed that Stacy would join the mission. But she was reluctant. First it was her parents—both aging and in need of her assistance and support. Then it was her mild asthma—something they both knew was more excuse than anything else. Over time, however, Stacy slowly came around; her cold feet warmed considerably, and, finally, she made up her mind to join the crew. In fact, she actually began looking forward to the testing and training regimen required of all prospective crew members.

It hadn't lasted a week; her first battery of tests revealed that she carried the gene for cystic fibrosis. Stem cell research, accelerated by the passage of legislation allowing the use of fertility clinic embryos in 2010, had enabled a cure for a number of diseases such as diabetes, several forms of cancer, and muscular dystrophy. However, while tremendous leaps forward had been made in treating numerous other diseases and conditions, including cystic fibrosis, the rules for admission to the crew were quite strict: if an applicant carried a gene for a non-curable disease, they were disqualified, without exception.

Jim drew a deep breath and watched the CEV commander prepare the craft for separation from its Ares booster. Forcing his brain to shift gears, turning his back on his doubts and anxieties, he thought about the technology of the ship he would command versus that of the archaic workboat that was taking him into space. Talk about inefficient; the booster, along with the required propellant, weighed over ten times the actual weight of the CEV service module.

All of a sudden the tremendous shaking ceased, the view through the main viewshield went from a blur to solid black, and Jim could see the Moon in the distance. The clarity was amazing. Entering space was like suddenly putting on glasses with the perfect prescription, after living your entire life oblivious that such vision even existed.

Through his suit's earphones, he heard the communication with mission control:

"Booster is clear. Activating side thrusters for eight seconds."

"Roger that, *Integrity*."

"Mission control, we have achieved proper trajectory."

"We confirm that, *Integrity*. Proceed."

"Activating forward thrusters for thirty-two seconds."

"Roger."

Jim felt the acceleration push him back against his seat. The feeling of entering space while strapped in was a strange sensation; while your body remains fixed in place, you literally feel your bones and internal organs start to float inside your body in the absence of gravity. The acceleration provided the sensation that gravity had briefly returned.

"Mission control, acceleration is complete. We are on course for L5."

"We confirm that. Enjoy the flight, *Integrity*. We will recon at 0130."

"Roger that, mission control. *Integrity* out."

Jim looked down at the gauges on the wrist of his suit. All parameters normal. He looked back out the viewshield and smiled.

As he eyed the small, glinting speck that was the L5 spaceport, he felt an overwhelming zeal for this mission and all that was to come.

He was in space and on his way to his ship, and he was exactly where he most wanted to be.

43.

Roger watched through the window as Air Force Alpha touched down on the South lawn landing pad. A moment earlier, he'd heard the distinct sound of the lift fans activating at altitude.

Roger and Jeff Wheeler, Deputy White House Communications Director, were in the Oval Office awaiting the President's arrival. They were working on President Belknap's eighth—and final—state of the union address.

Jeff Wheeler was a relatively new arrival. He'd been brought in to replace Suzanne Ortega, whose death had left a large pair of shoes to fill. Suzanne had known the President's style intimately, taking Ginny's ideas and putting them into sentences that were almost indistinguishable from what she might have written on her own.

Wheeler had planned communication strategy and messaging for some of the world's largest publicly held corporations, and was a master at nuance and threading the needle when delicate issues called for precise treatment. As the President's state of the union speech took shape, Roger and the President were quite impressed with his abilities.

But choosing Wheeler had not been a given. The White House was leaning in a different direction when a couple of big contributors to the President's earlier reelection campaign had unexpectedly suggested him, then pushed hard to have the White House give him due consideration.

The President entered through the side door from the colonnade. Their meeting was scheduled for nine-thirty am; she was a few minutes early.

"Good morning Madam President," Roger and Wheeler offered, standing automatically.

"Good morning gentlemen." She handed her gloves, coat and scarf to an aide, who exited the oval as Ginny walked over to her desk to grab a file and her tablet.

"How was the breakfast in Chicago?" Roger inquired.

"Productive," Ginny replied. "There're a few follow-up items, but we can work them this afternoon. Now," she said, taking a seat, "tell me where we are with the speech."

Roger looked at Wheeler and nodded for him to take the lead.

"Well, Madam President, I think you'll be pleased with the latest draft," Wheeler opened. "You should have a copy on your tablet. As you requested, we've greatly expanded the section on economic progress, and re-wrote the section on foreign policy achievements. We also added several paragraphs on the mission schedule and funding."

There was silence as Ginny reviewed the new draft, using rapid thumb-strokes to page through and manipulate the document.

"I like this..." she said, eyes glued to the screen. "Good, I see you incorporated the sentences I sent you last night." More thumbstrokes as she looked over other sections. "On the economy, let's make sure we spend more time outlining the results of the first term tax overhaul; remember, a lot of this may seem like old news, but it's our last chance to summarize what we've been up to for the past seven years."

Wheeler took note of everything she said, taking notes all the while. The three of them then went on to discuss the section on new proposals, making several changes as they went.

Ginny felt more relaxed about this State-of-the-Union than those over the past several years. This one was not about bold new initiatives; it was first and foremost a summary of all that she and her team had accomplished. On the one hand, this felt a little bit like a cop-out; she couldn't simply give up with 11 months left in her presidency. On the other, she couldn't pass up the last opportunity she would have to fully impress upon the nation and the world how they should view her legacy. In short, she was simply doing what every second term president had done before her.

After about twenty minutes of additional discussion on various aspects of the draft, President Belknap put the tablet down on the table in front of her and looked at Wheeler. "Let's shoot to review these changes on Monday at the latest."

"Yes, Madam President."

She then turned to Roger. "What else do you have for me?"

"Let's see. We've moved up your trade agreement meeting with the Indian ambassador to this afternoon, and I've scheduled a dinner this evening with the senate leadership to review the new mission budget request."

"What's your take on how they'll play it?" Ginny asked.

"I think they'll give it a green light without much hesitation," Roger replied. "We've still got incredible support, and they know it."

"All right. What else?"

"That's it."

All three stood up. Ginny headed back to her desk and heard the obligatory "Thank you Madam President" behind her. She raised a hand in acknowledgement.

"Actually, there is one more thing," Roger said, stopping at the door. Wheeler, who was following Roger, stopped as well.

Ginny turned.

"Jeff and I decided that it makes sense to get Cynthia Fossett some more exposure. We've scheduled her on Counterpoint for a debate with Randall Reese."

The President pursed her lips. "When?"

"One week from tomorrow."

"You think she's ready for that?"

"I do, but we're hedging our bet. We've asked her to participate in several prep sessions beforehand."

The President leaned against her desk and crossed her arms. "Roger, was this our idea or someone else's?"

"It was initiated by a call from Counterpoint. Why do you ask?"

"You don't think this is in any way a set-up?"

Wheeler interjected: "I don't, Madam President. I've known the producer, Mike Murphy, for several years; he's not one to play favorites. And I think Cynthia will do a great job."

Roger added: "Before confirming, I even went back and reviewed her senate hearings for the second circuit—I think she's got a real knack for this stuff."

"Okay, if you think she can handle it, go ahead. However, if you have any doubts after the first prep session, kill it—or at least postpone it. I don't want to stir up a hornets' nest before that speech."

"Understood. Thank you Madam President," Roger confirmed.

Roger and Jeff Wheeler turned and left the Oval Office. Ginny stood for a moment, staring at the door they'd closed behind them. The idea of Cynthia debating Randall Reese struck her as a high-risk gambit. Then again, perhaps she was making a mountain out of a molehill. Cynthia would do a good job, and—if nothing else—it was a debate that the public had a right to hear.

44.

The two men looked up through the mist. The leaves on the trees were a lush, dark green, and plump with moisture. The drizzle made the air tangible; the smell and feel of warm rain and wet soil smothered their senses.

They walked along a row of trees, then stopped. One of them knelt down on one knee and brushed the soil and mulch off a green cover plate. He put two fingers into the holes of the plate and jerked upwards, removing the plate and setting it aside.

"Voila!" exclaimed Georges Ventine. "This gauge is reading roughly 83 PSI, so the problem must be between this junction and the control room."

Jim Stanton said nothing. He was looking at the gauge and stroking his chin, thinking. "That could be," he finally offered, "or it's possible that the pressure build-up behind the mist atomizers is simply a little higher than specification. Which, of course, may not be a problem at all; I think we'd all far prefer the water pressure be a little too high rather than too low."

"Okay," Ventine said. He replaced the plate and gave it a shove with both hands to reseat it firmly. "The only way to know for sure is to take a look at the last console before the water returns to the filtration and recirculation pumps."

The two walked down the modestly graded bank and hopped down onto a stone-covered path which wound its way through the man-made forest. They were now three days into the testing of the WPC, and were miraculously ahead of schedule. Although there were a few issues and irregularities, all in all Stanton, Ventine and the entire WPC team were very pleased that the system seemed to be coming on-line with minimal hiccups.

As they continued walking through the trees toward the pumphouse, a voice came through both men's earpieces. "Attention all crew: docking and attachment of the aft SEC drive module will occur in two minutes. Be advised that slight tremors and echoes are anticipated."

Stanton and Ventine stopped and looked at each other; both felt a chill ripple through their body.

"Well, Captain," Ventine said softly. "It looks like your ship will soon be ready to fly!"

"Our ship, Georges," Stanton returned, "and don't forget it. I don't want you thinking that your ass isn't on the line right next to mine."

Ventine chuckled. "Right behind yours, Jim. Besides, you won't be getting much help from me once this bird leaves orbit."

They walked down to the console and checked the gauges, and were about to make some adjustments as the final announcement came through: "Docking will occur in ten seconds. Eight. Six. Five, four, three, two, one." The entire ship shuddered slightly, and for a few seconds thereafter they could hear the omnipresent echo of metal on metal contact resonating through the ship's skeleton.

Jim Stanton waited silently for a few more anxious seconds. Finally: "Attention all crew; warp module attachment is complete." Stanton and Ventine could hear cheering in the background as the announcement was made. Jim extended his hand, and Ventine shook it firmly in celebration.

While it would be two months before the forward warp module was attached, and then nearly a year of testing before the ship could even attempt FTL, the *ESS Humanity* was now one major step closer to launch.

45.

The door of the warehouse slammed behind him. Condon removed his sunglasses and let his eyes adjust to the dim light, while his lungs fought to process air laden with dust.

This had not been a pleasant journey. He had followed all of the instructions he'd been given: walking north from his office on K Street all the way to DuPont Circle, grabbing the red line south, transferring to the orange line and heading east to Smithsonian station, then doubling back and heading west all the way to the end of the line at Vienna/Fairfax. After that, he'd walked southeast through a maze of suburban neighborhoods, finally reaching the back of the warehouse just off Hunters Branch Road.

It had taken him nearly three hours door to door. The cloak and dagger routine—complete with sunglasses and hat—all seemed over the top, but he was more than willing to follow the rules if it ensured that this sordid world he was now visiting would never collide with his own.

He heard a sound off to his right, and saw a man approaching. *What the hell am I doing here?* Condon asked himself. *Are my foolish ambitions really worth all this?* As his eyes finally adjusted, he saw that the man was wearing a polo shirt and khakis, and looked like a casually-dressed businessman, though this didn't stop Condon's hands from sweating or his heart from racing.

"Mr. Condon, right on time."

Joe Condon just nodded, too nervous to speak.

"You can call me Doug." Condon nodded again, hoping the man wouldn't notice the tension trapped in his head and limbs.

"Follow me," the other man said firmly, and walked across to a side door which he held open for his guest.

Condon entered the small room and saw the back of another man looking down at a large diagram on a folding table. As the man turned, Condon recognized him at once from their previous meeting.

"Hey Joe, how ya doin'?" The man patted Condon on the shoulder, then stood smiling as his jaw busily worked his gum.

"I'm just fine, Donny, and you?" Condon couldn't have cared less.

"Terrific," Donny grinned back. Condon couldn't stand this man.

"Any trouble getting here?" Doug asked, closing the door behind him and approaching the table.

"No. You're directions were, um, just fine."

"Any issues with colleagues or anyone recognizing you along the way?" Doug was polite but it was clear that this had been the meaning of his previous question.

"No. Absolutely not," stammered Condon. "At least, not that I could see. I followed your instructions to the letter."

"Good. Well then, let's dig in." Doug gestured to the diagram. "What you see here, Mr. Condon, is a map of the Washington Mall. The first thing we need from you is an overview of where things will be placed. Let's start with the stage."

Joe gave the men a thorough briefing on the layout of the event. They both asked pointed questions, and Condon responded with specific answers. They then turned to a discussion of the crowd.

"If this event approaches a million people, then I would guess the crowd boundary would extend back to about here," Doug noted, pointing to an area back around 14th street, in front of the Washington Monument. "But crowd density will depend a great deal on other factors, including weather, the quality of your sound system, and even the temperament of the protesters. What else can you tell us about who might be where? Are you expecting certain groups to arrive early or late?"

Joe Condon had not given these issues much prior thought but he answered as best he could.

"You gonna have an area up front for VIPs?" asked Donny.

"Yes we will, though it won't be large. No more than about a hundred people total."

"Okay. Now the 64 thousand dollar question," said Doug. "Where will the press be located?"

"Our plans call for the main press station to be here," Condon pointed, "directly in front of the stage. The VIPs will be on either side. We'll also allow several cameras on each side of the stage."

"The press down front gonna be on a platform or somethin'?" Donny asked, leaning in to look more closely at the diagram.

"Um, I don't think so, why?" Asked Condon.

"Well, if you can put them up a few feet, it would be helpful," Doug explained. "Although it'll block people directly behind them, it's important that the bulk of cameras have the ability to turn around and have a direct view of the crowd."

"Oh, I see," said Condon. "Then I'll make sure that we add a platform."

"Good. Now, last but not least, let's talk timing. Did you bring the speaking schedule for the event?"

"Yes." Condon reached into the inside pocket of his suitcoat and pulled out several copies of the agenda that he and Reese had completed several days earlier. "Here you go." He handed a copy to both men and kept one for himself.

"It's possible that the event will get delayed or even cancelled after our work is done, so the question is this: who's the last speaker that you want to be heard without interruption?" Doug asked.

Condon and Reese had not thought about it quite this way when they'd drafted the schedule. He looked down at the list in a bit of a panic, having no idea where the interruption should occur. Several moments passed as Condon ran through ten different scenarios in his mind.

"Joe!" Donny finally barked. "Let's go, pal. We're burning daylight here!"

Condon looked at Donny, then at Doug. "The last speaker will be Max Caulfield," he said definitively.

Condon swallowed hard, and felt his palms start to sweat again.

His anxiety was now obvious; Doug tried to offer some reassurance: "Don't worry about a thing, Joe. You're doing the right thing—this is the very best strategy for getting the country's attention."

God, I hope so, thought Condon.

46.

"We've got one minute, folks. Let's begin clearing the stage!" Mike Murphy shouted. "Mr. Reese, Ms. Fossett, good luck."

Cynthia looked across at Randall Reese as the two of them received last minute make-up. She knew Reese had a great deal more experience with events of this sort, but she was ready.

The last several days had been a whirlwind. Once the media had been alerted to the upcoming debate, the event became the buzz of every news outlet on the planet. Copies of the draft constitution were made available to the public, and were now being downloaded at a frantic pace. Counterpoint was expecting one of their biggest live audiences since they'd adopted the debate format ten years prior. Overall viewership—both live and in the 3 days following the debate as the show was streamed to computers and media devices worldwide—was expected to approach 320 million people.

And the prep sessions had been grueling. Cynthia had been forced to think through and articulate positions for over 45 separate issues, in anticipation of possible questions from the panel.

Jeff Wheeler had been her savior. He had served as the stand-in for Reese during numerous mock debates leading up to the actual event. Wheeler threw himself at the task, and proved to be an articulate and aggressive adversary. While Roger Tucker and others had urged her to moderate her responses, Wheeler's eloquent attacks during debate practice led her to believe that she had to fight fire with fire; otherwise, she feared that she would appear wavering and dispassionate. In the end, while it had been incredibly hard work, she felt confident that she was ready to defend not some watered-down, middle-of-the-road viewpoint, but the specific rationale of her legal team. She was very proud of that—as was Devlin McGregor.

She had asked if Devlin could sit in on the prep sessions and, while he'd been a silent observer, he'd been an outspoken and invaluable advisor during late night phone calls and over early morning coffee. In fact, Devlin was seated in the front row of the studio audience, and was one of the few people she could actually see from the podium, before the bright stage lights washed out the remainder of the crowd.

The stage was cleared, and a young woman counted down and cued the moderator. They were live.

"Good evening and welcome to Counterpoint. I'm your host Kim Mayer, and our guests tonight are Randall Reese, founder and President of Americans for Moral Truth; and Cynthia Fossett, senior member of the Cerulean Mission Council and a former judge on the Second Circuit court of appeals. Our topic of debate this evening will be the constitution for the Cerulean colony. Currently in draft form..."

Randall Reese was extremely nervous. While he'd been praised throughout his career as an excellent public speaker, he had never felt truly relaxed in front of the microphone or the camera. It wasn't that he worried about what to say; somehow—thank God—his brain seemed to produce the right words when the moment called for it. It was something deeper inside, a stagefright that came from the center of his being, entered his bloodstream, and made him feel as if he'd had a sudden onset of the flu—complete with muscle aches and chills. While over the years he'd become adept at hiding his fears and symptoms, tonight he felt especially vulnerable, knowing the stakes and the size of the audience evaluating his performance.

Nonetheless, here he was, and—he reminded himself—it had been his idea to be here. He too had prepared for the event, but less formally than Cynthia. He had spent a great deal of time on his own, studying quietly in his office at home. For Randall Reese, it wasn't about strong responses on dozens of issues; he felt it was much more important that he forcefully present the big picture. He wanted those watching to walk away reflecting on the importance of God in the lives of all humans, and the need to weave faith and prayer into Cerulean life. If he achieved this, regardless whether he won on any specific issue, Reese would consider the debate a victory. At the same time, he knew the game, and fully understood that, in order for his vision to prevail, it would be critical to undermine the public's confidence in Fossett—and Belknap's Mission Council as a whole.

After Kim Mayer had finished her introduction and reviewed the rules of debate, there was a brief silence. On Counterpoint, there was no applause allowed. If it occurred once, the audience was warned. If it occurred a second time, there would be a five minute recess during which the audience would be removed. This had only happened three times in ten years.

There were no opening or closing statements. In addition, since the guests on Counterpoint were usually not candidates within a campaign, they were not asked questions directly; instead, they were simply asked to offer their views on a given topic.

"We will begin tonight with the rights of the minority within a republic, a subject that has received a great deal of attention of late. The current draft of the

Cerulean constitution takes several new paths on this issue that differ substantially from our own constitution.

"Specifically, the draft states that, in order for any bill to be passed into law by the legislature, one house of congress must pass it by a margin greater than a simple majority; it must be approved by either a three fifths majority of the senate or a two thirds majority of the House of Representatives.

"It also states that every member of the House of Representatives will be limited to one four-year term, with half of all House legislators ending their term every two years.

"In addition, the draft mandates that the president be elected by greater than fifty percent of the voting public, and that every citizen eligible to vote is required to vote.

"I would like to ask both of you to comment on how you believe these measures will or will not benefit the Cerulean people.

"Mr. Reese, you will begin; you have three minutes."

Randall Reese straightened himself behind the podium, and nodded to the host.

"Thank you Kim, and good evening to America and the world.

"Let me begin by saying that the protection of the minority within the United States was carefully engineered by our founding fathers, and remains a hallmark of our success as a nation.

"Over the course of our history, I believe that the U.S. Constitution has allowed our government to be fairly agile in responding to the needs and circumstances of our people. In short, we have been adept at walking the line between our need to protect the minority, and our country's need to progress and evolve. It is my firm belief that the added provisions that Ms. Fossett has inserted into the Cerulean constitution would severely limit a new and fragile society's ability to respond to its people's needs. Furthermore, and perhaps most important, I greatly fear that these new constitutional edicts would, in fact, jeopardize the rights of the majority.

"With regard to congressmen serving a single term, and a presidential candidate requiring upwards of fifty percent of the vote to prevail, I'm concerned that these constraints will add cumbersome burdens and delays to our democratic process. However, such concerns are minor as compared to those over the need for a supermajority to pass legislation.

"This is a very high hurdle, and it worries me that a minority of legislators could easily hold back vital new laws when a preponderance of congress and the people favor them.

"I think it will come as no surprise when I tell you that, like most American citizens, I am a man of faith. As such, it is particularly disturbing to me that, time and time again, the minority in this country has stymied the majority on issues related to spirituality and religion.

"My greatest fear is that a determined minority of Ceruleans will, at the expense of the majority, rid this new society of what it should hold most precious: its faith in God—the creator of Earth, the creator of mankind, and the creator of Cerulea."

As Reese finished his response, he felt a mild improvement in his symptoms. But the sound of applause, which normally hastened his recovery, was completely absent. Kim Mayer stepped in to fill the void.

"Thank you, Mr. Reese.

"Judge Fossett, you now have three minutes to offer your thoughts."

"Thank you, Kim."

Cynthia brought her eyes up from the show's host to look directly at the camera. The lack of applause made the auditorium eerily quiet. She could hear a few people shifting in their seats, and distinctly heard one person cough several times.

"I think the best way to offer my thoughts on these statutes is to offer some insight on why they were written into the Cerulean constitution in the first place."

Cynthia paused, her pulse pounding in her temples. She reminded herself to obey one of the essential rules she'd learned earlier in her career when giving speeches—*allow space between thoughts and sentences; what seems like an awkwardly long pause to me is a welcome respite to the audience.*

"Let me begin with the need for either a three fifths majority in the senate or two thirds majority in the house.

"When the executive branch and one or both houses of congress belong to the same political party, a dynamic often develops wherein the party in power moves to pass a sizable body of legislation over the strenuous objections of those in other parties.

"The problem here, as we've observed many times over, is that legislators in the majority are under tremendous pressure to serve the interests not of their constituents, but rather those of the majority itself. In other words, the intimidation felt by majority legislators leads them, as a group, to advocate laws and statutory changes that they would not necessarily support as individual lawmakers, and the citizenry suffers as a result.

"For the record, the solution to this problem has been around for a very long time. The ability to block a slight majority from passing legislation has been in use since the 1850s; it is commonly known as the filibuster. In 1917, during the administration of Woodrow Wilson, the filibuster was converted from a legislative tactic to a more formalized procedure, with the passage of Rule 22. This allowed the senate to end a filibuster with a two thirds majority vote, a device known as 'cloture.' In 1975, believing that the two thirds majority was too high a bar, the senate reduced it to three fifths, or 60 out of 100 senators. More recently, this device was threatened with extinction when Conservatives exercised what had become known as the 'nuclear option.' This sought to eliminate the filibuster by amending the rules of the Senate through a questionable parliamentary procedure. However, as we all know, the ensuing Constitutional crisis caused the effort to backfire; the 'nuclear option' has not been used since, and Rule 22 remains firmly in place.

"On Cerulea, the intent is simply to incorporate Rule 22 into the Constitution, mandating that either the Cerulean senate have 60 votes to pass a bill, or that the House has a two thirds majority to compensate for the lack of a three fifths majority in the Senate. The point is simply to force bipartisan cooperation within the Congress, and lessen the ability of a slight majority to bully the minority.

"It could be said that the Cerulean constitution, as drafted, is less restrictive than our own. In the United States congress, a bill goes down to certain defeat if the senate cannot end a filibuster by invoking cloture. In the Cerulean congress, the house of the people can save such a bill from defeat and pass it into law if a supermajority believes it's the right thing to do."

Cynthia paused again, and took a deep breath. She could feel her self-confidence increasing, knowing that her words were shaping themselves into well-formed sentences.

"With the time remaining, let me quickly address the other two provisions.

"Limiting a member of the Cerulean House of Representatives to a single four year term is less about the rights of the minority than it is about true representational government. For starters, it's worth noting that the average length of service of congressmen in our own House of Representatives has risen dramatically over the past two centuries. On the heels of the civil war, the average tenure was just over one two-year term; by the middle of the twentieth century, it was four and a half terms, or 9 years; at the beginning of this century it was five and a half terms, and currently the average is over 6 terms.

"The intent of our founding fathers was that the House of Representatives be 'of the people'; that members of the House be elected to represent the people and problems of their district. Today, with the average member in office for over twelve years, the focus of the House is little different from that of the Senate. On Cerulea, the objective is to return the House to what it was intended to be: a group of citizen legislators, each with a fresh, first-hand impression of the problems facing the people of their town or region.

"The requirement that the election of the president garner fifty percent or more of the votes is actually to protect the majority—not the minority. Perhaps an example would help here: Let's assume that three political parties offered three different candidates, and that two of these were strong, capable and qualified leaders, while the third was a fringe candidate advocating radical policies which discriminated against a large percentage of the populace. I don't think it's difficult for any of us to envision a situation where the two strong candidates split the mainstream vote, allowing the fringe candidate to emerge victorious.

"This is clearly a case where the majority must be protected from the minority. By mandating more than fifty percent, the cerulean constitution ensures that the people will not be led astray by a candidate who was supported by a minority of the electorate. While this will necessitate that election organizers plan on the possibility of a runoff election, we believe this is a small price to pay for ensuring that only a majority may appoint the government's highest leader."

Cynthia saw the yellow light illuminate next to the camera lens, and knew that she had to quicken her pace in order finish without being cut off by the moderator.

"As for mandatory voting for every eligible citizen, there are now nearly fifty countries with such laws in place—up from roughly 35 countries at the beginning of this century. It is not a new concept; Australia began compulsory voting in 1924, Belgium in 1892. While some decry this obligation as a limitation on our freedoms, research has shown it to have a sizable educational benefit as people pay more attention to the issues at stake, and—last and perhaps most important—it eliminates the distortions that aggressive get-out-the-vote campaigns have on the electoral process."

"Thank you, Ms. Fossett." Kim Mayer jumped in behind Cynthia's last sentence, at the exact close of the ten second grace period. Each speaker was only allowed two such overtimes in the course of the debate.

Cynthia breathed a sigh of relief. Her strategy was to explain, as simply as possible, the logic behind the Cerulean Constitution, and she felt that, thus far, she was right on track.

She looked down and saw Devlin giving her an enthusiastic thumbs up.

47.

Derek Butler laughed.

He sat casually on the edge of the couch. Outside, the lake lay motionless, devoid of any movement—in direct contrast to the human drama taking place on the large, wall-mounted screen in front of him.

Butler was watching the debate with several campaign staffers and a loyal aide he'd known for many, many years. He looked out the gigantic picture window of his Virginia mansion, and ruminated on the scene before him and the things which lay ahead.

He leaned his body back against the pillows and imagined himself as the director of a grand production. The people in this room were stagehands at his command; the vista outside simply one of the many beautiful backdrops he might select for any given scene; even the people appearing before him on the television were, in ways very few understood, actors following a script that he had, in large part, authored.

He knew that the months ahead would not be easy; there would be many new scenes requiring artful direction, and there would be several as yet unnamed actors who would have to be cajoled into their proper roles. Nonetheless, the show was progressing on schedule, and Butler was confident that it would have a long, successful run.

48.

"Our next topic," Kim Mayer announced, "will be one that has generated conflict since our nation was founded over 250 years ago: the separation of church and state.

"The Cerulean Constitution contains little ambiguity on the subject, stating quite specifically that the government or any government-funded entity or organization is prohibited from employing any religious symbolism or engaging in any religious activity."

Cynthia took a sip of water, and mentally prepared to re-enter the ring.

"Ms. Fossett, per our standard debate format, you will lead off on this round. You have three minutes."

"Thank you, Kim.

"James Madison, founding father and fourth President of the United States, wrote the following in 1811: 'The appropriation of funds of the United States for the use and support of religious societies is contrary to the article of the Constitution which declares that "Congress shall make no law respecting a religious establishment."'

"Thomas Jefferson echoed these sentiments, stating that 'religion is a matter which lies solely between Man & his God.'

"While many believe that the establishment clause in the U.S. Constitution is open to interpretation, it's clear that some awfully important architects of this nation were in strong agreement as to how the issue should be settled.

"And frankly, given the extent to which our country cherishes freedom, and given the resources we expend fighting wars to free people of other nations whose ability to speak their minds is in jeopardy, it amazes me that this remains a contentious issue in our society.

"To myriad legal scholars, the defense of separation is straightforward: every school, every government building, every city park, every government program is paid for by the taxes of the citizenry. If that citizenry comprises people of many faiths, and includes those who do not recognize or acknowledge God at all, then it is simply inappropriate for the government to advocate or support one faith over another—or even to advocate faith itself.

"Our freedoms, guaranteed by the constitution, allow us to practice our religion of choice. Our freedoms allow us to organize and promote our religion of

choice through private organizations. The only constraint—the only constraint—
our nation places upon our religious freedom is that the government is not allowed
to make the choice for us. Many scholars would hold that this isn't only appropriate, it is critical if we are to preserve the freedoms upon which this nation was
based.

"Furthermore, when the Cerulean colony is established, it is anticipated
that it will have approximately 1800 citizens. This is a very small number. So small
that Ceruleans holding one set of beliefs may easily find themselves, in the course
of daily life, influenced or even pressured by those who hold another. This is both
unavoidable and, to some degree, natural.

"What would be unnatural—and an offense to people who had traveled for
nearly fifteen years to arrive on Cerulea—is for the fledgling government of this
new state to act in a manner that even appears in any way biased toward the viewpoint of a certain group of its citizens.

"For these reasons, the team of constitutional lawyers who are drafting the
Cerulean constitution unanimously concluded that a more vigorous clause delin-
eating the separation of church and state was required."

Cynthia held the camera's gaze for a moment before looking at the host and
nodding slightly to indicate she was finished with her response.

"Thank you, Ms. Fossett. Mr. Reese, you now have three minutes."

Ralph Reese tried his best to remain outwardly calm, but inside he was
fuming. He had said to himself several times over as the debate approached that
he would not let himself react to anything Fossett said, and would instead focus
on delivering his own message, but at this moment he was finding that resolution
extremely difficult to fulfill.

That she could stand there and offer up atheism as a form of religion, and as
a justification for boldly refusing to provide any religious support to the citizens
of mankind's first extraterrestrial colony, absolutely enraged him.

Before opening his mouth to speak, he drew a deep breath in a futile attempt
to steady his nerves.

"In his 1789 inaugural address, President George Washington said 'the pro-
pitious smiles of heaven can never be expected on a nation which disregards the
eternal rules of order and right which heaven itself has ordained.'

"In Chapter 13 of Romans, St. Paul is more explicit: 'For there is no power
but of God: the powers that be are ordained of God.'

"In short, government derives its moral authority from God. The moral
truths that God offers us must serve as the foundation for human society—
whether that society is on Earth or on Cerulea. Without these truths as a moral
compass, those who make up a government would literally be afloat on an ocean of

ambiguity, justifying their actions in accordance with personal desire rather than in accordance with what God has taught us to be right.

"James Madison, despite what Ms. Fossett would have you believe, understood this perfectly. He said, and I quote, 'we have staked the future of all of our political institutions upon the capacity of mankind for self-government; upon the capacity of each and all of us to govern ourselves, to control ourselves, to sustain ourselves according to the Ten Commandments of God.'

"And though I doubt that my words tonight will resolve this issue, let it be known to all listening to this debate that the words 'separation of church and state' appear nowhere in our constitution. This phrase was used by Jefferson as he sought to assure a group of Baptists that the government was not on the verge of declaring a national religion.

"Jefferson had actually borrowed the wall of separation metaphor from the writings of Roger Williams, a prominent Baptist preacher and the founder of the Providence colony, who described the tragic consequences should 'the wilderness'—the outside world—penetrate the wall that protected the 'garden of the church.' Thus, the wall of which Jefferson spoke was very specifically to ensure that the state did not harm the church, not the other way around."

Randall Reese's words cut like a machete—each one crisply slicing the air that lay between him and his audience. He was angry, but his emotion was controlled and focused; his sentences fervent, but carefully constructed. He was absolutely determined not to allow his emotions to dominate his delivery; yet he was also determined to forcefully insert into every listener's brain the realization that this woman was out of touch, and that her way of thinking represented a danger to what would clearly be one of the most important chapters in human history.

"Allowing the church to influence the government—and the people as a whole—is critical if we do not wish to see humanity devolve into selfishness and corruption. Again I quote George Washington, the father of our nation and its first president: 'Of all the dispositions and habits which lead to a political prosperity, religion and morality are indispensable supports.'

"It is interesting to note that most Americans somehow fail to understand that our U.S. Constitution was founded on religious principles. In fact, the Bible serves as the source for many of the most fundamental tenets of our current form of government. Perhaps most important might be the three branches of government themselves: judicial, legislative, and executive. This governmental structure was derived directly from Isaiah 33:22: 'For the Lord is our judge, the Lord is our lawgiver, the Lord is our king.' Other examples abound.

"It is not a coincidence that the constitutions of all fifty states directly acknowledge God. Or that the Declaration of Independence references God and the Creator. Or that every unit of U.S. currency carries the words 'In God we trust'—which also happens to be our national motto.

"In short, an overwhelming majority of the world's population believes in God, and look to a Supreme Being for guidance in their lives. This is what centers the human race. It is what gives each of us a purpose on this Earth.

"I find it reprehensible that we would deliberately seek to perpetuate mankind on a distant planet without directly assisting the citizens of this new world in their natural quest to connect with their Creator."

Reese turned to Cynthia, his eyes glistening with conviction.

"Ms. Fossett, I believe your team's lack of religious awareness will endanger the spiritual health of Ceruleans. In fact, if you and your Godless cohorts do not rethink your approach to Cerulean law, I greatly fear that the ability of mankind to survive on this new planet will be threatened."

A large orange light illuminated behind Randall Reese, indicating that five or more of the nine-member panel overseeing the event had found this last comment to constitute a personal attack—something strictly out of bounds according to the rules of Counterpoint debate.

49.

"**H**oly shit, where'd that come from?"

Roger Tucker had reentered the Roosevelt Room of the West Wing moments earlier in time to catch Randall Reese's scathing condemnation.

He was standing with his arms crossed, between a sofa on which President Belknap and Jeff Wheeler sat, and an armchair which held Vladimir Belechenko.

Belechenko smiled at Roger then turned his head back to the television. "I'm not sure, but I think that Cynthia just got a break."

"Don't be so certain," President Belknap offered. "Reese is no fool. To assume that his last comment was an inadvertent outburst would be naïve."

"But he has broken the rules, and now looks rather silly," Belechenko countered.

"To us? Yes, he looks silly." Ginny confirmed. "But to those who might share his beliefs, he may well look like a hero."

Tucker looked at Jeff Wheeler. "Jeff, what do you think?"

"Well..." Wheeler began thoughtfully. "I'd say that Cynthia--"

"Shhh." The President raised a hand. "If you don't mind, I want to hear Cynthia's response."

The room fell silent as all eyes and ears focused on the monitor.

50.

Cynthia was shocked. She stared at Reese as he took a long drink from the glass of water on his podium; while she was well aware going in that he opposed her efforts, she was somehow not prepared for the incredible depth of hostility he obviously felt for her personally.

"Mr. Reese, our panel has concluded that your last comment impugned your debate opponent," Kim Mayer said sternly. "As you know, we insist that all comments and responses deal only with the topic presented.

"As a result, Ms. Fossett will be given a one minute rebuttal. Per the rules of this forum, any additional personal statements will bring your participation in this debate to an end.

"Ms. Fossett, please proceed."

Cynthia felt flustered, realizing that the attention of all watching would now be sharpened. She intentionally took her time.

"Thank you.

"I think it's important to point out that my 'cohorts'—the legal team assembling the Cerulean Constitution—are a diverse group." She paused and took a quick sip of water, not out of thirst, but to further cement her lock on the audience—a courtroom trick she picked up from watching litigators during her days in private practice.

"The group includes three Christians, two Hindus, three Muslims, and a Buddhist. Some of us are devout, others less so. All of us, however, have a deep and abiding respect for how the framework we craft will positively or negatively affect the rights of Cerulean citizens.

"As Mr. Reese noted when quoting St. Paul, each of us, as humans, may well derive our powers and personal strength from God. However, within a republican democracy, governmental authority is most certainly not derived from God. Within a republican democracy, government derives its power and authority solely from the people.

"Were this not the case, then we would still be living in an age of Monarchs: a time when leaders were supposedly anointed by God, were not bound by laws, and the freedom to follow one's own faith was virtually non-existent."

Cynthia paused again. She looked directly at Reese.

"In fact, any substantive review of history would clearly tell us that religious tolerance is weakest in those societies where church and state intermix. It is only in those countries where separation is enforced that such tolerance is strong and consistent.

"Therefore, if we intend Cerulea to be a society of one single religion, with one single set of beliefs and one single set of practices, then merging church and state might make great sense.

"However, the world's intent and desire is for Cerulea to be every bit as diverse as this planet. As such, separation is an absolute necessity.

"Let me end by stating that, while I do not contest James Madison's belief in a higher being, his stance on separation was unequivocal. As he entered his 70s, half a decade after completing two terms as President, he wrote that "Religion and government will both exist in greater purity, the less they are mixed together.""

Following Cynthia's response, Kim Mayer called for a five minute intermission, during which Cynthia and Randall Reese were allowed to return to their dressing rooms.

Cynthia used roughly half the time reviewing notes on other issues, the other half for some quiet breathing exercises.

Reese spent his minutes in silent prayer.

51.

With both participants back at their podiums, Kim Mayer brought the debate back on-line.

"We now move on to a section of the Cerulean draft constitution that will most likely prove no less controversial: the environment. Constitutional protection of the environment is, of course, not new; France first adopted their Charter for the Environment in 2003, and since that time over a dozen countries have followed suit.

"The draft Constitution goes farther than what we've seen to date, however, stipulating that the preservation of the environment should be considered an equal priority to the advancement of humanity.

"Clearly, this will have a tremendous impact on Cerulean life, and will cause societal evolution to behave in very different ways than is the case here on planet Earth. Perhaps nowhere more so than with regard to procreation, given the draft Constitution's declaration that public policies must support sustainable population growth, and must not unduly cause harm to the environment or to other species.

"Mr. Reese, you have three minutes to offer your thoughts on this aspect of the draft Constitution. Go ahead."

"Thank you." Reese turned to Cynthia. "Let me begin by offering my apologies for any personal statements made in my last response."

Cynthia nodded her acceptance, yet was quite sure that, were it not for Counterpoint rules, an apology would never have entered his mind.

"The primary issue here," Reese began, "is the manner in which this section of the draft Constitution characterizes mankind in the context of his environment and other species.

"In the Bible, the Creator makes it clear that man is to have dominion over the Earth. Yet the Cerulean Constitution essentially places mankind at the same level as plants and animals.

"If mankind is to progress, it is imperative that humans be given the resources they need to grow and develop. Surely, we do not wish to tell a fledgling Cerulean population that they must go hungry so that the environment is preserved.

"As Cerulean society builds schools for the children, houses for its people, factories to make the goods required for survival, I do not believe it appropriate to insist that, at the same time, Cerulean government ensure that no plants or animals are harmed in the process.

"What strikes me as beyond inappropriate; what I see as an abomination of all that mankind represents, is the notion that mankind must somehow limit its numbers as if we were some herd of beasts!

"It is not lost on me nor do I believe it is lost on anyone listening that 'sustainable population growth' is nothing more than a thinly veiled call for government sanctioned birth control, abortions, and limits on offspring.

"In Genesis, God commanded man to 'Be fruitful and multiply, and fill the earth and subdue it'"

Reese looked over at Cynthia.

"I'm sorry if you--" He stopped himself and looked back at the camera. "I'm sorry if there are those who do not appreciate and hold sacred the giving of life. Bringing a child into this world—or any other—is unquestionably a blessing from God. I find it very sad that there are now many communities—even entire nations—that are lacking in energy and hope because of a declining birth rate. Children are a gift that refresh society; to limit such a gift would have tragic consequences for our spiritual well-being.

"If government is to limit the number of children we may have, is it not then directly interfering with one of the most important liberties of all? Is not our inalienable right to the pursuit of happiness circumvented when we are told that we may no longer give birth?

"And what of the inalienable right of any child whose life is taken away by a society that allows the intentional termination of a pregnancy?"

Reese took a drink and paused. He then drew a deep breath and began softly, challenging the audience to listen more closely to his words.

"I'm afraid that the Cerulea that this Constitution would foster is not a place I would want to live. The freedom to build a family; the freedom to feed my family, to provide a life of comfort for my family. These are freedoms which all of us should cherish.

"If Ceruleans are to be constrained in their pursuits; if they are to be held back in their efforts to build a happy life for themselves and their families; if the potential of man is to be checked by concern for plants and animals, then I would suggest that perhaps the placement of humans on Cerulea is not a goal to which we should aspire."

Reese stared into the camera, seeking to ensure that this last protestation be indelibly imprinted into the consciousness of all those watching. The stage was momentarily quiet; two well-lit islands of conviction, surrounded by a dark shroud of evolving public opinion.

Kim Mayer broke the silence. "Ms. Fossett, you now have three minutes to offer your thoughts."

Cynthia was incredulous. *The gall of this man!* she thought to herself, furious at the notion that the mission should be cancelled because her team had not come up with a Constitution that Randall Reese and his band of extremists found acceptable. The statement, aside from being a tactical cheap shot, was, to Cynthia, proof of Reese's pure, unbridled arrogance.

She let the clock tick down and stared at him, wanting very much to make him noticeably uncomfortable before she offered her response. He looked over once, saw her gaze, then looked away quickly.

"Ms. Fossett?" Kim Mayer implored.

Cynthia calmly turned and looked into the lens.

"I am not a Biblical scholar, but I am quite familiar with Genesis.

"When God asked the male and female he had just created to 'be fruitful and multiply,' I don't recall him saying 'until you have completely exhausted the resources of the Earth that I have made for you.'"

There was quiet laughter among some members of the live audience.

"Here are the facts:

"The human population on this planet currently stands at 8.3 billion people. It's probably worth putting that in perspective.

"It has been estimated that one million years ago, there were somewhere in the neighborhood of two and a half million humans on the planet; a figure roughly equal to the current population of West Virginia. By 6000 B.C., it is believed that the population had doubled to five million. Thereafter, growth accelerated, reaching 500 million in the year 1650—roughly the time during which Europeans began arriving on American shores. And in just 400 years, it has doubled over four times.

"To look at it from another angle, it took all of human history, up through the early 1800s, for the population of this planet to reach 1 billion people, yet it took only 12 years to add the most recent billion.

"Now, there is a fair amount of credible evidence that world population growth is slowing, and that we may see it stabilize at around nine billion in the second half of this century.

"However, growth is no longer the issue. If you have an enormous swarm of destructive beetles in your garden, it is hardly comforting to learn that their numbers have peaked; they will still consume your flowers and vegetables.

"Simply put, humanity is overwhelming this planet, and we are now consuming renewable resources at a rate that is significantly faster than their ability to regenerate. This is fact. Whether we are discussing trees, fresh water, or fertile soil.

"Each one of these is, of course, absolutely central to mankind's survival on Planet Earth.

"As many listening tonight know all too well, countless communities—even entire nations—have been forced to make draconian choices as they wrestle with the realities of insufficient resources. And while we have made some progress in slowing the causes of global warming, this too has created dire circumstances for many peoples; and will likely cause a massive and difficult migration from lands that soon will lie underwater or become desert.

"In ancient times, there are numerous examples of vibrant civilizations that literally collapsed and vanished because they were unable to come to terms with their over-consumption of resources. Some, like the Sumerians or the Mayans, were incredibly advanced; yet their knowledge and innovation was no match for the harsh reality of resource supply and demand.

"These examples were local phenomena; today, we are looking at a situation that is global in scope; if we do not resolve our current resource issues, then the entire human race will be at risk.

"Now, I have faith in man's ability to find solutions, and I am not among those who think Earth's demise is imminent. However, I do believe that the explosive growth and, more important, the current size of the human population is a fundamental cause of our predicament.

"Every living creature on this planet has predators which ensure that its species is kept in check. When such predators are absent, the species overpopulates and either crashes—as we've seen with animals in many of our own communities—or we will step in and manage the population issue ourselves.

"Of course, as a species, we have no predators, so we have no choice but to manage our own population growth. This does not mean mandatory limits on offspring; it simply means that Cerulean society, as it grows, will have to give the issue some thought, and find solutions sooner rather than later. These might involve resource conservation policies, or birth control awareness and availability, or economic incentives. This will be up to Cerulean lawmakers and the people who elect them.

"And while I do believe that mankind has an obligation to ensure the survival of other species and their habitats, that is in no way the impetus for Constitutional protection of the environment. It could be said that the driving factor here is nothing more than human self interest."

Cynthia looked over at Reese.

"So, let's be careful when we look at what really constitutes a 'freedom.' All countries on earth have an abundance of laws which seek to protect the well-being of their citizens. Constitutional provisions regarding the environment are no different. They do not limit our freedoms so much as they ensure that there will always be a human race around to enjoy them."

As she finished her delivery, she looked down and saw Devlin grinning ear to ear.

52.

It was estimated that over 200 million people around the world tuned in live to the Reese-Fossett debate. Within 24 hours, another 125 million had viewed all or parts of the broadcast; and after three days had elapsed, viewership had climbed to 345 million people worldwide.

Cynthia Fossett and Randall Reese became instant global celebrities. Progressives and conservatives made each the poster child of their views. It was the religious conservatives, however, who reacted with force. With the mission schedule counting down, those sharing Reese's sentiments were spurred to action. Protest rallies spontaneously erupted in 23 American cities and four more abroad. Five people had already died and countless others had been injured in clashes with police, who were trying desperately to control the unrest.

The airwaves and internet were literally awash in talking heads and diatribe, with conservatives expressing outrage that mankind's future rested with a tree-hugging atheist who had no appreciation for the U.S. Constitution.

President Belknap and Roger Tucker were now extremely concerned; the March for Mankind, a suspiciously timed protest, was scheduled to take place on the Washington Mall just three days before the President's final State of the Union speech.

The embers of the religious conservative movement, which had lain dormant for over three and a half decades, had been forcefully reignited, and the fire seemed to be just getting started.

53.

Butler was having a field day.

While the debate had not yet caused any huge swings in public opinion, it had clearly and efficiently divided the electorate. What had been an ill-defined and inconsistent line with regard to how the two camps viewed Cerulea had now opened into a clear and unmistakable fissure.

And Butler was making the most of it.

Exploiting the schism was, to Butler, like catching flies in a zoo. His campaign speeches were now drawing huge crowds. The media sensed his campaign's momentum, and—in a time-honored catch-22—began to accelerate it.

Butler was perfectly positioned. He kept Reese off to his right, and Fossett well to his left. He had the luxury of serving as the judicious centrist who could appreciate both sides of the issues. He shared Reese's view that man should not be subservient to the environment—but at the same time espoused his belief that industry, using technology as its fuel, must address the critical resource issues that threatened the planet's well-being.

He carefully spoke out in favor of separation between church and state, yet had his writers pepper his speeches with quotes from the bible, and made it a point to speak in front of at least one sizable congregation in every town he visited. It had been a long time since a presidential candidate had so blatantly chummed these waters for political benefit, and Butler was doing an excellent job of it.

In short, Derek Butler was having his cake and eating it too. And at every opportunity, he used the mission to Cerulea as the icing—artfully decorating every campaign issue with one or more references to the mission to drive home his point.

His balancing act seemed to be highly effective in attracting voters, but it made others nervous. Randall Reese and Derek Butler had become well acquainted, and seemed to have a strong mutual respect. Since the debate, Reese's star had risen substantially, and he felt he was now in a position where he could help Butler a great deal. Yet, given Butler's apparent middle-of-the-road stance on the mission, Reese was incapable of embracing him publicly as a candidate for President. So for the time being, Reese spoke out eloquently in favor of many Butler positions, but rarely supported Butler directly.

Max Caulfield also had some reservations, but kept them mostly to himself. Butler's investment firm had recently decided to proceed with an initial round of financing for Caulfield's Atlanta Station project. The contract made it clear that if all milestones were reached, they would furnish roughly half the funds required for the development—a total of over two and a half billion dollars. The deal was contingent, of course, on Caulfield getting Congress to provide the other half.

Caulfield had wanted Butler to be more aggressive in advocating for changes in the Mission Council, but Butler wouldn't be persuaded. He reasoned that such a strategy would only generate conflict between his campaign and the current administration--and with a President who had consistently held on to very high approval ratings. Butler counseled patience; first the White House, then the Council.

Caulfield sensed that there was somehow more to the topic than their conversations would indicate, and that Butler wasn't putting all his cards on the table. But one thing was clear: Butler was a master politician, and both Reese and Caulfield—and a growing majority of the United States, along with many world leaders—were increasingly under his spell.

54·

President Belknap's limousine drove swiftly along the edge of South Lake, known as Nanhai; the small island of Yingtai—in actuality a peninsula—stood out at the lake's center. As the motorcade passed through the Xinhuamen gate and took a left onto Changan Avenue, she could see Tiananmen Square up ahead.

It had been her second trip to the Zhongnanhai complex, the seat of China's government. During her first trip, she had been given a full tour, the first time a sitting U.S. President had been offered such an honor.

Up until 2025, Zhongnanhai had been strictly off-limits to the public, and the few foreign dignitaries who'd visited the compound had been whisked in for a ceremonial event through the gate on Nanchang Street, then whisked away without ever seeing the full splendor of the place. But as the Chinese economy continued to flourish, and its global influence increased accordingly, the country opened up politically. To the world's great relief, China began to embrace democracy just as it truly emerged as an economic superpower. The Zhongnanhai complex was now a showplace.

This time around, President Belknap's schedule allowed for nothing more than a day of meetings with China's new president, a brief evening ceremony to celebrate the two countries partnership in the Cerulean enterprise, then an early morning departure back to Washington.

Her objective in coming to China had been simply to ensure goodwill. She—and the Chinese president—knew all too well that the mission would require very strong financial support from both China and the United States, and the trip gave both leaders the chance to tout the progress that the Mission Council had made thus far, and to generate further popular support.

That was the public face of the visit. Behind closed doors, it was made eminently clear that the Chinese were not going to just ante up more funds and get nothing in return. They wanted export restrictions lifted on certain American technologies, and more favorable terms on an upcoming trade agreement.

Though there'd been some tense moments, in the end they reached an acceptable compromise, and the evening ceremony had been jovial. The relationship between the United States and China, so critical for the success of the mission, was perhaps stronger than it had ever been.

Nonetheless, Ginny was exhausted, and a little unsettled.

She had been incredibly proud of Cynthia Fossett's performance, and pleased that, as Roger had predicted, both Cynthia's popularity and that of the mission had increased slightly in recent polling. But those strongly disapproving of the approach being taken by the Mission Council had also increased; it worried her that the opposition was hardening.

But her fatigue extended beyond the political. With less than a year to go in her eight-year tenure as President of the United States, Ginny was suddenly in love. And while she savored the small slivers of time that she stole from her schedule to spend with Vladimir Belechenko, they were simply not enough. For the very first time, she was starting to feel somewhat imprisoned by the job.

Her new-found romance had created in her a longing to live a normal life; to spend quiet, boring evenings with Vlad. To have a predictable rhythm to her life did not seem so much to ask. Yet it was impossible—for now.

As the motorcade sped past Worker's Stadium and onto Xindong Street, the President's press secretary answered a call, spoke for a moment, then handed the President a small earpiece.

"It's Roger Tucker, Ma'am."

"Thanks." Ginny placed the device in her ear. "Roger!"

"Madame President, congratulations on a very successful trip."

"Thanks, I hope that's the way it was portrayed at home. In truth, it was more complicated."

"What did we have to give away?"

"Well, no more than we'd discussed before I left, but it was nonetheless a grueling negotiation."

"Well, get some sleep on your flight if you can. My guess is that Washington will be a little hot when you get back."

"I assume you mean the March for Mankind?"

"Yup. Turns out that the organizers sandbagged us. Their initial permit was for 200 thousand. This morning they refiled for 750."

"Ouch. Roger, can we get an updated copy of the agenda?"

"I've already got it. No surprises. Just the usual laundry list of conservative speakers."

"How do you feel about security arrangements?"

"Queasy. I've asked Joe Petrullo over at Homeland Security for recommendations on beefing it up. We're meeting this afternoon. Regardless what we come up with, I'll still be nervous; a crowd like that is tough to manage. It's too big to force everyone through Sniffers, so it will boil down to having as much manpower as possible."

"And what's your take on the latest state of the union draft?"

"Well, I think we're in good shape regarding your synopsis of the Belknap presidency, but I'm thinking that recent events may force us to do some rewrite on a few other sections."

"Why don't you put your ideas down and shoot them to me on Air Force Bravo."

"Will do."

55.

They came from all over the country. From Washington state, from Southern California, from Texas, Louisiana, Florida, North Carolina, Maine, Michigan, the Dakotas, Kansas, Iowa, and then some.

Buses poured into the city from nearly all fifty states, then followed a prearranged route to the Washington Mall. Like a chorus of centipedes, they penetrated the city from every angle, all descending on a common point on the map.

Trains, filled to the brim, released a floodwater of travelers at Union Station, generating waves of people along the five blocks between the Capitol and the Mall.

Airports were at or exceeding capacity, as Dulles, Reagan and Baltimore Washington processed thousands of travelers through their runways, gates, and jetways. People from all over the country, and from countries all across the globe crowded each and every terminal concourse as they made their way to subways, buses, taxicabs and limousines.

Security was tight for anyone getting onto a train or plane. In fact, for anyone living in a city, it was a daily ritual. Biometric scanners—usually studying fingerprints or the iris—were most common; a person might be expected to validate their identity several times in the course of an average day.

However, securing any outside area was still a complicated proposition. One of the primary tools in the fight against terrorist activity was something called the Sniffer. This machine, essentially a cylindrical pod resembling a standalone revolving door, used a number of sensors simultaneously for metal detection, bomb ingredient detection and bio weapon detection. The more advanced models included a DNA scanner and even disease detection sensors. The machines were fairly reliable and relatively fast, but they were also expensive; each Sniffer cost over $10 million to produce. Not only that, they also cost an additional eight dollars per test. For a planeload of 400 people, this was an acceptable expense; for a large event with hundreds of thousands of participants, it was a burdensome expenditure—especially when coupled with the fencing and manpower to enforce the machines as the sole means of entry to a large area.

As a result, with the exception of the backstage area, they were not in use for the March for Mankind. Instead, the city had deployed thousands of uniformed and undercover officers to manage the massive crowd.

Condon looked out at the growing ocean of faces, and shuddered. He felt goose bumps as he contemplated the magnitude of what was happening. The past 48 hours had been frantic as a crew of over 350 worked tirelessly to position the stage, sound system, video screens, concession stands, bathroom facilities and medical tents. From the stage where he stood in front of the Capitol, it appeared as if the crowd now filled the mall back to the Smithsonian, roughly the halfway point between the Capitol and the Washington Monument.

And it was only seven am.

By eleven am, the crowd was beginning to fill the lawn surrounding the Washington Monument.

Joe Condon entered the speaker's tent, grabbed a cup of coffee and walked over to Tom McKenzie, the crew chief responsible for planning and managing all ground operations for the event.

"Morning, Tom," Condon offered cheerfully.

"It may be morning for you, Joe. For me, it's late in the evening after one of the longest days of my life".

"I'll bet. How go the preparations?"

"All in all? Great."

"I'm impressed. An event of this size and no problems?"

"Oh, I didn't say that. The usual set of last minute catastrophes. Swapping out two faulty half ton speaker systems, cleaning up after an overturned concession truck, negotiating with irate police officials over permit issues. But nothing unexpected." Tom grinned.

"Well, I've got to hand it to you. Looks like we're ready to go."

"And my compliments to you for getting so many folks to attend. Looks like quite a mob out there."

Condon inwardly winced at the choice of words.

"It's quite something," he agreed. "You're a veteran of Mall events. How many you figure we've got?" Condon asked.

"Well, it's a funny thing. From any point on the ground, the mall can look filled to the brim with only 200 thousand. It's only when you get a look at the aerials that you can really get a sense of turnout."

"The aerials?"

"Shots of the crowd from the air. I'm no expert, but there are folks who've developed various formulas for calculating density and coming up with estimates of actual crowd size."

"You're not going to hazard a guess?"

Tom smiled. "Well, I was up on the stage about twenty minutes ago, and I'd say we've got well over 400 thousand—and climbing."

Joe smiled back. "The record's 650; think we'll make it?"

"Looks possible."

Out of the corner of his eye, Condon saw Randall Reese enter the tent. He waved to get his attention, then looked back at Tom.

"Well here's hoping." He held up his coffee cup in salute. "Great job, Tom. Once we're underway, be sure to let me know of any issues with logistics, okay?"

"Sure will."

Joe patted Tom on the shoulder and walked over to speak with Reese.

"Randall."

"Joe."

The two smiled at one another. They had both put in an incredible amount of work planning this thing, and their smiles confirmed their mutual excitement now that it was actually coming together.

"You ready?"

"Ready to throw up, mostly." Reese drew a deep breath. "But I'm ready."

"Good." Condon looked down at his watch. "'Cause it's showtime."

❦

Reese walked out onto the stage. The crowd in front of the Capitol quickly recognized him and began cheering furiously. The cheering spread outwards until the entire mass of the Washington mall was focused on the stage, roaring with energy.

Reese's stomach was in his throat. Yet, since the debate, his physiological reaction to speaking had changed. He was still nervous. Incredibly so. But at the same time, it was electrifying. Although he'd been a public figure for some time, it had always been with a small and select slice of the American people. He was now known worldwide, and, for the first time, he felt deep down the magnetic seduction of power.

Reese put his mouth to the microphone. "Ladies and gentlemen." He could feel the reverberation in the air, the unbelievable presence that the sound system gave his words. The crowd roared even louder. Reese paused for a moment. "Ladies and gentlemen, welcome to the March for Mankind!"

The noise was deafening, but Reese smiled and held up his hand as a symbol of thanks and welcome.

His stomach had calmed down. His skin was tingling. He was absorbing the crowd's energy directly into his brain and bloodstream.

His introductory remarks would be short, but he was looking forward to his speech later on in the day.

56.

Donny left Doug's suite at the L'Enfant Plaza scowling. They'd just had a tempestuous argument over the exact rules of engagement, and Donny disagreed strongly with the strategy, but Doug was the boss. If Donny wanted to get paid, he'd have to do as he was told.

He emerged from the elevator on the fifth floor and walked quickly down the corridor toward an alternate elevator bank. He then descended to the second floor, and entered the men's room in the back of the hotel near the function rooms. He went to a urinal and pretended to relieve himself as another man washed his hands and left the bathroom. He then entered a stall, sat down on the edge of the toilet, opened his bag, and began removing assorted elements of his costume.

His identity properly concealed, he exited the hotel through a side door and headed down 9th Street. He crossed the railroad tracks and walked into a small, tree-lined park across the street from the FAA building. He headed to the far end where he saw his sordid gang assembled.

◉◉

"You are here because of your faith, Reese bellowed. You are here because you know that the path we are on is not the path of God. It is the path of those of who have lost their faith and lost their way..."

Reese was back at the podium, and in full swing. After he'd opened the event, half a dozen speakers had taken the stage in succession, each making a cogent argument as to why the Mission to Cerulea should be altered to embrace a more faith-based approach.

The crowd's enthusiasm had not dissipated one bit.

"We must not stumble on this most important occasion," he continued. "We must not let mankind go forth from this planet without the spiritual supervision necessary to prevail on a new and unknown world. We must not allow Cynthia Fossett to sever the divine connection our Cerulean brothers and sisters will so unquestionably require. We must never let President Belknap and her nonbelieving colleagues rob this mission of its heavenly fuel."

As Reese launched into the centerpiece of his speech, he felt the audience's energy growing tangibly. The cadence of his words played on this energy, unlocking its power, celebrating its strength.

"Our society today is a cauldron of immorality and perversion. Why? Because those in positions of power have been lulled by Satan into complacence. Why? Because biblical principles, which serve as the bedrock of our country, have been forgotten by our leaders. Why? Because we, as Christians have not been sufficiently forceful in upholding our god-given responsibilities.

"Government can be a force for good, and it can be a force for evil. When its principles and laws are architected by godly men, good will prevail; but when the architects are those who reject God, when the architects seek to push Him from civil society, then evil will prevail.

"Ladies and gentlemen, the fate of Cerulea, the very goodness of this new world, depends upon us. We must rise up and insist that the social fabric of this new civilization is woven from Godly cloth. And we must not relent. We must not capitulate. We must not acquiesce or moderate our demands until they are satisfied.

"What are these demands? Let me repeat them once more so that all of you will leave today with a clear vision of our quest.

"First, the Mission Council must replace Cynthia Fossett with a scholar who embodies the traditional values so important to a healthy society.

"Second, the Cerulean Constitution must be revised to allow the Cerulean government to directly assist its fledgling colony in the pursuit of religious fulfillment.

"Third, the mission crew must be rebalanced to ensure that our faiths will remain strong and pure.

"Let us confirm today that these demands are not negotiable; they are no more and no less than simply that to which the human beings on Cerulea and Earth are entitled..."

900 thousand people roared their heartfelt agreement.

57.

M ax Caulfield looked up as an aide knocked on his door.
"Senator, we just got word that you'll be speaking in approximately
20 minutes. We should leave as soon as possible."

Caulfield nodded and stood. He looked at the clock on his desk, then turned
and pulled his suit jacket off a coat rack and put it on.

"Looks like they're pretty close to their original schedule," Caulfield muttered.

"Yes sir."

The noise from the event had been constant all day. He had watched a
number of speakers on the screen in his office, but could hear them fairly clearly
through the window as well.

So far, through the eyes of the camera, the event appeared to be a major success. The crowds had been estimated at over 700 thousand, smashing all previous
records. And the messages coming through were clear and concise.

Outside his office they were met by five Secret Service agents who would
escort the Senator to the speaker's tent, and then the stage. This was not standard
practice, but Roger Tucker had reached across the aisle and insisted on the added
security.

◌◌

Donny and his team set up shop at the edge of the Mall in front of the
Hirschorn Sculpture Garden.

The crowd was intently focused on Reese's speech when they arrived, but
after Reese left the stage, and one of the planned musical interludes began, people
started taking notice.

Donny's crew was dressed casually. Though Donny knew most of them
to be misfits and thugs, he was pleased to see that, to the unknowing eye, they
appeared to be a fairly normal bunch.

They each held signs which mocked the event taking place before them:
Keep God out of Cerulean government!; *Stop Reese's mobocracy*; *Save Cerulea from Earth's
mistakes*; *Fossett for President!*

Their instructions were to stand there with their mouths shut, and take no
action whatsoever until Caulfield had finished speaking. Donny knew this could

mean that they'd be here for 45 minutes or more, and he didn't like it one bit. He'd told this to Doug in no uncertain terms back in the suite. While Donny wanted his gang to move in quickly at the end of Caulfield's speech and get it done, Doug insisted that they should be in place before the speech to give the cameras time to pick it up. Otherwise, Doug argued, it would look suspect.

Donny felt otherwise. He felt that his crew had performed brilliantly in their prior effort in front of the White House, and the media never suspected a thing. Furthermore, he was worried. The men he'd assembled were not known for their social graces—nor were they paid to exhibit any. The more time they spent lingering, the greater the chance that the whole thing would escalate prematurely.

Donny's worries were not without merit.

After about eight minutes of holding up their signs at the edge of the crowd, a well-built young man with short-cropped hair, and "Semper Fi" tattooed on his right bicep, approached Donny's group. He stared straight into the eyes of one of Donny's compatriots who was holding the sign that read *Keep God out of Cerulean government*, and asked a simple question: "What the hell do you guys think you're doing?"

Donny's accomplice, nicknamed "Hangman" for reasons unknown to Donny, remained silent, and looked away from his confronter.

"Yo Jack! I asked you a question!" The man insisted. "Why is it so important to you jerks to mess with our event?"

Hangman again averted his eyes and remained silent. Donny noticed that several of the man's buddies had come up behind him, all of whom looked to be ex-marines as well. They were clearly interested in where their friend's line of questioning might lead. Donny stepped forward.

"Look we got a right to be heard, just like you guys. How 'bout if we all jus' leave each other alone? Huh? How 'bout it?"

The man looked up at the sign Donny was carrying, which said *Stop Reese's mobocracy*, and smirked.

"How 'bout if you guys jus' get the fuck out of here? Pronto!"

Donny raised a hand in an effort to steady the situation, but it was misinterpreted. In the blink of an eye the man thrust a quick punch to Donny's stomach. Donny dropped his sign and dropped to his knees. Immediately, Hangman ceased his strained pacifism, dropped his sign, and rushed at the man with fists flying.

He never landed a blow. One of the man's buddies intercepted and swung his hand up into Hangman's neck—a well-executed move that made it all too clear that these guys were well-trained. Hangman fell to the ground, unconscious—possibly worse.

Donny opened his mouth to make one last plea for calm, but it was too late. Another member of his squad—this one named Lippy—had tipped his sign and used the stick end to strike Hangman's attacker. The man fell back into the crowd, the side of his face ripped open and spouting blood. Several people screamed, and, within seconds Donny's entire gang was engaged in a bloody free-for all.

This was exactly what Donny had hoped to avoid, but he realized he now had no choice but to follow suit. As one of the attackers began landing blow after blow to Lippy's face, Donny jumped to his feet, swung behind the man and jammed his foot down on his calf, immediately bringing him to his knees. Donny then kicked him in the back of the head with all the force he could muster, and the man went face down in the dirt.

Lippy then finished the job with powerful kick to the side of the man's head. Blood poured from the wound, spattering Lippy's pant leg and soaking the grass where the man lay.

Donny looked up, and for a moment thought that they may have prevailed. His team was battered, but all save Hangman were still standing, while three of their attackers were on the ground, and several others seemed to have run off.

Donny knelt beside Hangman's motionless body. "Lippy! Gimme a hand here!" They each put one of Hangman's arms over their shoulders, and stood up with Hangman between them.

"Let's go!"

Another of Donny's crew grabbed his bag which he'd left on the ground and began gathering the signs they'd dropped.

"Leave the bag!" Donny yelled. "Leave it all! We're outta here now!"

They began moving quickly off the mall. Hangman's head drooped lifelessly on his chest. Donny had no idea whether he was alive or dead.

They began making their way around the Sculpture Garden toward Jefferson Drive. Donny's head was pounding; *how could this simple plan have gotten screwed up so quickly?* he asked himself. He forced the thought from his mind, and thought about the bag he'd left on the Mall. He put his hand on his thigh as he and Lippy ran as fast as they could with Hangman between them. He felt the lump in his right pocket.

No more than fifty feet ahead was the street; beyond that, they'd have some cover as they passed through the trees next to the Hirschorn Museum, and could then make a dash for their van--which was parked on Ninth Street next to the Department of Energy building. From there, they'd be on the Shirley Highway and heading out of the city on I395 in seconds.

"Donny!" Lippy barked. Donny looked over and saw Lippy looking behind them. Donny turned and saw at least a dozen men bearing down on them. He recognized two of them as the ones who had fled the earlier fight.

"Faster! We can make it!" Donny shouted.

Suddenly, he felt himself falling. Lippy had been hit in the back of the head by a rock thrown by their pursuers. As he fell, he pulled Hangman with him and, by extension, Donny as well. They hit the ground hard. Donny looked over and saw that Lippy's head was a tangled mass of blood, flesh and hair. The rock had cut his scalp badly and, though conscious, it was clear he wasn't going anywhere—let alone quickly.

Donny jumped to his feet and started to run again, but he'd banged his knee as he fell and couldn't put his full weight down on his left leg. He fell again. This time, he didn't try to get up. Instead, he jammed his right hand into his pocket and plunged his thumb into the center of the plastic fob.

58.

The group walked out of the Russell Senate Office Building and down the steps. The five Secret Service agents encircled Caulfield, each one carefully scanning their own specific quadrant of the street.

As they approached the crosswalk on Constitution Avenue, Roger Clasby, the lead agent, signaled for the group to stop. Sirens were bearing down on the intersection from their left. He put his hand to his earpiece and listened intently, barked out "Code Foxtrot!" to his team and signaled forcefully for the group to retreat back to the Russell Building. At that moment, they heard the explosion, just as three police cruisers and two ambulances raced down Constitution.

Two agents on either side of Caulfield each looped their arms under his and, as the group broke into a run, Caulfield was literally dragged up the stone steps and back into the building.

59.

The pipe bomb in Donny's bag was simple but effective. It contained six pounds of C4 explosive, surrounded by nails, wood screws and ball bearings. The blasting cap was attached to a wireless detonator. The explosion had instantly killed 17 protesters and injured at least thirty or forty others. However, the impact of the actual explosion was negligible compared to that of the panic which followed. Immediately, people began running from the blast in all directions. For many in the crowd sitting on the lawn between speeches, there had been no time to stand and join the exodus. Dozens were trampled to death immediately following the explosion; many more were killed or injured over the next several minutes.

One man, in his thirties, roughly 300 feet down the mall from the blast, had reacted quickly, grabbing his seven year old daughter and shoving her up a tree just off a side path, with himself right behind her. The crowd rushed underneath and, as he buried her head in his chest, he tried to limit both her eyes and ears from the chaos while clinging to the limb like a life ring in a deadly ocean storm.

From this perch, he was forced to witness the unfolding horror. He could see the ripple of panic spreading outwards to every corner of the Mall. The screams were constant, drowning out the feeble and futile attempts of a woman on stage trying to calm the audience. As the wave of fleeing people progressed, there were twisted mounds left in their wake, comprised of those who had not reacted in time, and had paid the price. At the Mall's boundaries, the flow of human traffic poured in between buildings and down open streets, while many were caught in between, pushed up against any and all obstacles, compressed by the powerful ground swell of humanity.

In the vicinity of where Donny's bag had sat moments earlier, there was now a crater in the lawn over ten feet wide. Surrounding the crater were bodies of the dead and dying, most missing one or more limbs, and many only vaguely recognizable as human forms.

60.

Donny opened his eyes, then squinted, the dust and activity immediately overloading his senses. He forced his brain to do a quick systems check; arms, hands, legs, feet, spine, everything seemed okay. Aside from a brutal headache and possible concussion, he had not been seriously injured. He was close enough to a large steel sculpture such that he'd avoided the crush of the fleeing crowd. He looked over at Lippy and saw that his companion had not been so fortunate. Besides the gash on his head from the rock thrown just before the explosion, Lippy appeared to have been trampled; several bodies lay nearby.

Donny crawled over and put two fingers on Lippy's neck. He was dead. Donny looked around and noted that a few of his crew were slowly rising. He thought to do the same and put his hands on the ground to push himself up. He saw the remote detonation device on the ground to his right and quickly reached over to pick it up.

A boot came smashing down on Donny's hand. He could feel the pain as the bone in his ring finger snapped. He looked up and into the barrel of a large police-issue revolver pointed directly at his head.

"Don't even think about it," the man holding the weapon said calmly. He pulled a badge from his coat pocket, flashed it, and put it back.

The plainclothes officer then reached down, picked up the plastic fob and put it in his pocket, all the while holding the gun squarely on Donny.

61.

The House Chamber was completely quiet save for the creak of several members of Congress shifting uneasily in their seats.

Ginny looked at the cabinet secretaries and justices seated closest to the podium, then looked at the throng of legislators beyond.

"America has often likened itself to a 'City upon a Hill'; we have consistently put forth the proposition that we are a chosen nation, blessed by God.

"This proposition is easily defended. The geography of our nation is endowed with abundant resources; most of our states boast of landmarks as beautiful as any on Earth; and our successful evolution as an economic, political and social power rests upon a Constitution that was drafted with extraordinary wisdom, combining many of the very best concepts in human governance, and rejecting those that fall short.

"But with regard to this proposition, we must continually ask ourselves: if we are a chosen nation, if we are indeed a City upon a Hill, has our behavior over time, not just over the centuries but day-to-day, been worthy of our supposed stature?

"Disagreements and differences of opinion in a free society are inevitable. However, it is how we deal with such conflict that determines whether our city truly lies atop the hill, in the middle—or at the very bottom. The violence witnessed this week on the Washington Mall is yet one more reminder that the path downward is as or more easily followed than that leading upwards."

Ginny's sober reflection was unexpected fare. This State of the Union speech was supposed be an enumeration of her administration's many accomplishments over the past two terms, a celebration. Instead, she had condensed the self-aggrandizement into roughly the first 15 minutes, and was now offering both Houses of Congress—and the nation—a piece of her mind.

The events on the Washington Mall just days prior had caused a national uproar. Actually, it had caused two uproars. The first was a massive outpouring of grief for the protesters, whose cause drew thousands, if not millions of new sympathizers immediately following the incident. It was not difficult for those advocating a greater role for religion in Cerulean life to portray themselves as martyrs in the wake of such a heinous attack on their otherwise peaceful gathering.

However, the second uproar, much smaller in magnitude yet in some ways more intense, erupted closely on the heels of the first, as it was learned that the perpetrators were not who they appeared to be.

Preliminary evidence was indicating that the men who had detonated a device on the Mall were not left-wing fanatics, but hired thugs whose own views, according to searches of their apartments and interviews with friends and neighbors, were more closely aligned with the protesters than anyone else. Unfortunately, exactly who hired them remained a mystery.

While this latest revelation was acknowledged by the audience that Ginny now addressed, it had not fully penetrated the American consciousness. Not because it hadn't been reported; it had. However, in the electronic shouting match that now comprised the news media, it had simply been subordinated to a detail of the larger story.

Ginny swept her eyes across those seated in the balcony, then resumed.

"The explosion that wreaked havoc on an otherwise peaceful demonstration is reprehensible—perhaps doubly so given that it was apparently perpetrated to amplify the voices of the very people killed and injured. However, it is not this event in and of itself that should be the focus of our concern. Rather, we should be wary of the growing trend to use violence and deceit as tools with which to manipulate the levers of public opinion. Clever methods for winning public support for a cause are certainly not a new phenomenon; but when our cleverness routinely involves intimidation, prevarication, or even the hint of bodily harm, then we have crossed a dangerous line.

"The cause is immaterial: whether it is opposition to the actions of a world body; whether it is opposition to the policy or behavior of an administration, elected official, or political candidate; or whether it is opposition to a form of medical research, a medical procedure, or a prescription drug; the goal of overturning what we oppose will never justify immoral actions.

"I believe this to be true for all of mankind, but it is America I address this evening. If we wish to occupy what we righteously refer to as 'the moral high ground,' then it is imperative that we behave accordingly—including not only how we engage other nations, but also how we engage each other as citizens and human beings."

The reaction within the chamber was decidedly mixed, with roughly half the audience applauding vigorously, the other applauding only politely out of political obligation.

"The conflict between those who wish to see religion play a greater role in the Mission to Cerulea, and those who do not, will be difficult to resolve. But this much should be clear to all of us: the chances that a solution will somehow emerge more quickly as the result of one side or the other engaging in immoral or violent behavior are extremely low.

"All major religions embrace some version of what is commonly called the Golden Rule. In Hindu, loosely translated, worshippers are advised to 'do naught to others which if done to thee would cause thee pain.' Buddhists teach us to 'hurt not others in ways that you yourself would find hurtful.' The Jewish religion implores that 'what is hateful to you, do not to your fellow men.' Islam teaches its followers that 'not one of you is a believer until you wish for others what you wish for yourself.' While Christianity tells the faithful to 'do unto others as you would have them do unto you.'

"The very universality of the Golden Rule is instructive. In fact, the case could easily be made that it is the very foundation of moral behavior as defined by virtually all of the world's religions.

"Why is it then, that so many people in America who put their faith in Jesus Christ continue to act in ways that directly contradict His teachings? How is it that so many people manage to convince themselves that deceit, intimidation, belligerence, and even violence are all somehow justified when used to further what they perceive as God's wishes? How is it possible that the hypocrisy of such behavior is invisible to the perpetrators?

"My objective, as I stand before you tonight, is not to lecture. It is not to admonish, but simply to ask all of us to think about how we act in the context of what we believe to be right. I, and I suspect a majority of those listening tonight, have grown very tired of the animosity that characterizes public debate in this country. The explosion on the Mall, the sabotage of a convoy carrying Mission-related equipment; these are extreme examples, but many other lesser examples abound. By all means, let us disagree, and let us voice our disagreement, and let us do so with candor and honest emotion. This is our right. But please, let us do so while adhering to what religions across the globe embrace as the central tenet of moral behavior; let us not treat each other in ways that we would not wish to be treated ourselves."

Once again, the House Chamber offered its divergent response.

Ꮺᏺ

The next morning, the shouting match was louder than ever. Editorial pages and the internet were ablaze with heated reactions to the President's speech. Many expressed the view that such use of the U.S. Presidency's bully pulpit was welcome and appropriate; many others vilified President Belknap for using the State of the Union to rebuke her opponents.

Randall Reese went even further, noting that the President's speech "personified the very hypocrisy she described, by attempting to use the power of her office to paint her political foes into a corner." He ended with a quote from the Book of Matthew, a less than subtle stab at what he perceived to be the Council's efforts to block those of faith from influencing the mission: "But woe unto you, scribes and Pharisees, hypocrites! For ye shut up the kingdom of heaven against men: for ye neither go in yourselves, neither suffer ye them that are entering to go in."

62.

"Commander, I've taken the liberty of scheduling a tour of the ship for 0900, followed by lunch with my staff. Then, starting at 1400, we'll begin the full project review."

"Thank you, Jim. Looking forward to it," said Belechenko. He continued to stare at the intercom unit groggily.

He was wiped. Though the previous day's ride from Earth to the spaceport had taken just 17 hours, his body felt terrible, and his brain felt worse—as if his neural pathways had been sucked dry of moisture. *I'm getting old* he said to himself as he unstrapped his sleep harness.

Nonetheless, he was happy to be in space once again. The past several months on Earth had been trying. His relationship with Ginny was blissful—but only in so far as they were able to spend any appreciable time together. The political mayhem that had become the status quo ever since the Washington mall tragedy left the President without much time for romance. Perhaps with Derek Butler on the verge of victory, and the launch now just months away, things would start to change; the two of them might at last get to experience the sort of mundane existence where the notion of home-life actually had a defensible position on the priority list.

After a little self-maintenance—brushing of teeth, face washing, a modest snack, he began to feel much better. And as Commander Belechenko made his way to the shuttle pod, his energy was building steadily.

He entered the small shuttle pod at 0840 to find Jim Stanton and Najid Malik progressing through a checklist before departure. "Morning Commander," Najid said cheerfully, looking up from a bank of cockpit switches and dials.

"Morning Naj, Jim," Belechenko replied, taking his seat behind the two of them and strapping himself in.

"We should be good to go in about 6 minutes," Jim noted as he floated past the Commander to a small bank of gauges and entered several readings into a tablet.

◉◉

As they pulled free of the spaceport, the shuttle pod pivoted so that its windshield filled with the massive bulk of the *Earth Spaceship Humanity*. It was larger than any craft ever built—ever. Nearly three thousand feet long, the *ESS Humanity* was the size of two Powell-class aircraft carriers placed end-to-end.

It was stunningly impressive. Though the Commander had seen early sketches, preliminary plans, hundreds of blueprints, and endless photos and video of the ship under construction, the real thing was something else entirely.

"Holy shit," he whispered, mostly to himself.

Jim turned and said with a smile: "you know, though I've been up here for over a month now, I have the exact same reaction every time I look at her from a distance. It's just hard to believe that we are actually building something this magnificent."

"Or that you're going to captain the damn thing," the Commander noted with a smile of his own.

"I try not to spend too much time dwelling on that thought," said Jim.

The spaceship looked like a giant metallic arrow shot through two giant hoops. The head of the arrow, or bow, was shaped like the nose of a submarine. The feather, or stern, was a massive cube, housing the aft SEC drive. In between these two elements was the body of the ship; a long, tubular axle housing all of the craft's main systems. Circling this axle at the mid-point were two huge donut-shaped rings. The forward ring constituted the primary living space of the *Humanity*, while the rearward ring housed all livestock and agricultural facilities. By constantly rotating around the axis of the ship, these rings provided a simulation of Earth's gravity through the use of centrifugal force. By rotating in opposite directions, they held the body of the ship stationary.

The basic design was nothing new; it had first been conceived by the father of modern rocketry, Wernher von Braun, in the early 1950s. In 1975, during a conference contemplating designs for space habitats, three specific designs for self-sustaining spacecraft emerged, and held the spotlight for several decades: the Bernal Sphere, the Stanford Torus, and the O'Neill Cylinder. These, however, were highly conceptual, and were viewed as habitats, not starships capable of FTL travel.

The design for the *ESS Humanity* was based primarily on the Stanford Torus, but borrowed features from all of them; it was the brainchild of Elizabeth Finnigan, a brilliant Australian physicist who had spent her career at the ESA's European Space Research and Technology Centre in Noordwijk, the Netherlands.

They docked at a hatch about a third of the way back from the bow. Within the arrow, or spine of the *Humanity*, there was no rotation and no centrifugal force—thus, no simulated gravity. They floated through the hatch, over to a small maglev shuttle, strapped themselves in, and began their tour of the craft, Naj at the helm. The shuttle whisked them away on a magnetic levitation rail which wound its way through tubes connecting all areas of the ship.

The first two hours were consumed by a hands-on inspection of the primary systems: water processing system, air handling system, electrical system, and monitoring system. Belechenko knew all of these intimately, since he'd worked closely with Gerhardt Schmidt and Jim Stanton on the specifications, and remained involved from prototype development through final production and test. Seeing them installed and operational, however, was immensely satisfying.

"Okay," said Jim, after they completed a demonstration of the back-up generators, "I think we're ready to move on to the fun stuff."

"Come again?" asked Belechenko, "do you mean to imply that watching all these systems work as designed doesn't bring a smile to your face?"

"Oh, it does," Jim replied. "But the rings are truly mesmerizing, Commander. I know you've seen them on screen, but just wait 'till you see 'em in person!"

The three men floated back to the maglev, and made their way to the torus access module, located mid-ship. This was a large chamber where the spokes of the outer rings, or tori, joined the spacecraft. Since the tori and spokes rotated at all times, accessing them from the axle was mechanically complex.

Naj docked the maglev into the access cradle, and the group waited. When the spoke rotated into alignment with the cradle, the maglev was shoved forward, allowing it to lock onto the spoke's levitation rail, and they began the descent down toward the outer ring. As they descended, gravity slowly increased; at the base of the spoke, they would experience precisely 1G, or gravity equivalent to the surface of the Earth.

As they emerged into the open air of the outer ring, Belechenko was dumbstruck.

"Jim, this is incredible," he said, his eyes wide as he took in the scale and beauty of it all. "You're absolutely right. Everything I've seen of the rings simply can't begin to describe... this!"

Before them stretched a small, narrow, forested valley, rich green on either side with a long, thin, crystal blue lake in the center. Within the trees, Belechenko could see the building units that would serve as the living quarters and recreational facilities for the ship's crew.

He reflected back for a moment on their early planning sessions three years earlier, when Ventine and Schmidt had referred to what lay before him as the ship's bio-oxygenation systems, or simply "greenhouse units." *One hell of a greenhouse*, he thought to himself.

"Commander: take a look" Naj pointed down and off to his right.

Belechenko looked where Naj was pointing, and saw a maglev rail winding its way through the trees. Next to the rail was a young doe, lunching on shrubbery.

Belechenko shook his head in amazement. "Unbelievable. I read the wildlife plan, but I have to admit I'm skeptical. Do you honestly think that each species can be held in check?"

"Actually, I think it's pretty straightforward," Jim replied. "All live onboard animals will be sterilized; reproduction will only occur in vitro. Besides," Jim smiled, "if the plan fails, we can always take up hunting."

Belechenko laughed; Naj turned and stared at Jim.

"Relax, Naj, it was a joke. No one's going to be firing any weapons in here."

Belechenko looked again at the doe. "What's your take on bringing other species to Cerulea, Naj?"

Naj turned his head to the side and shrugged. "I think it depends on what we find when we get there. Since the plan is not to bring any animals to the surface of the planet for at least a year after our arrival, I think we'll have plenty of time to evaluate the potential disruption. If we believe it's in any way inappropriate, these animals will simply live out their lives in orbit on the ship."

The maglev reached the floor of the torus and the three sped off through the forest toward the commissary.

63.

Georges Ventine poured himself a glass of wine and leaned back in his chair. "So Commander, many of us have been stuck up here in this astral paradise for several months. The news from terra firma looks grim; perhaps you could tell us what it's actually like down there—'on the ground'?"

Belechenko leaned forward, resting his elbows on the edge of the table. His day on the *ESS Humanity* had cleared his mind of his Earthly anxieties, and Georges question brought them back in a rush. Nonetheless, he'd expected someone to bring the subject up, and he felt obliged to offer his thoughts.

"It's not pretty," he began. "In the United States, people are quite divided. I really can't tell you how large an effect the Mall tragedy has had on daily life. Politically, it is a mess. The progressive side of the fence was outraged when it was discovered that a group of thugs with ties to the conservatives were behind the explosion. The cries of indignation have been non-stop for months on end."

"So how is it that Derek Butler seems all but a sure bet to win the general election next month?" asked Naj.

Belechenko chuckled. "Because he is a very able politician, while his opponent knows only how to whine and complain."

"You mean he doesn't have the beauty and inspirational 'je ne sais quoi' of a Virginia Belknap, yes?" Ventine interjected.

The group laughed easily, While Belechenko flushed. Although Belechenko and the President had been very discreet in their relationship, it was widely known that they were an item.

"Precisely. Well said, Monsieur Ventine," Belechenko conceded.

After a lengthy and productive review meeting, they had gone to dinner late. The group—consisting of Stanton, Ventine, Belechenko, Malik, and various members of their respective teams—were lingering over coffee and what was left of two bottles of Australian wine. They were the last people left in the dining hall, but were in no hurry.

The room was sparsely decorated, designed more for functionality than for elegance. The view, however, made up for it. The building was nestled into one side of the valley that ran around the circumference of the forward torus, and one entire wall of the dining hall was glass, providing a captivating view of the lake and the forest beyond. The light was especially alluring. A vast array of mirrors coated the outside of each ring, and were programmed to catch light from the sun—or whatever stars might be available during their journey—and simulate dawn, daylight, dusk, and nightfall. At present, the light was fading, and the view had a hypnotic glow.

Naj, stirring his coffee, pulled the conversation back to the original topic. "Well what about the conservative camp? Aren't they ashamed of the Mall incident?"

Belechenko took a drink of water before responding. "Not at all. Since the investigation into the incident never uncovered any grand chain of command, the thugs who detonated the bomb are simply seen as a few bad apples in an otherwise determined and right-minded movement."

"So the news would have us believe that it's chaos down there; protests everywhere you look, and everyone waiting for the other bomb to drop. Any truth to that, Commander? Ventine inquired.

"I'm afraid there's a lot of truth to it, Georges," Belechenko replied, sadly shaking his head. "Despite President Belknap's appeal to both sides of the divide during her State-of-the-Union speech, it's ugly, and seems to be getting uglier. On any given weekend in Washington, DC, there might be half a dozen separately organized protests. And while many are without incident, more than a few end up as yelling matches between dueling protesters, or simply between protesters and people passing by on the street. Arrests are commonplace.

"And it's nearly as bad in other areas across the country. A month ago, in Illinois, in a small town outside of Chicago, a 200 year-old church was burned to the ground after the pastor gave a sermon defending the Mission's stance on church-state separation. Fortunately, if I may use that word, the violence seems to be limited to the United States.

"Although I think I saw a report just two weeks ago, Georges, that in your beloved Paris, over a dozen people were hospitalized after a street fight broke out in La Défense—isn't that a business center?"

"Yes, it is *the* business center of the city, perhaps even of Europe. I followed this story closely. It seems that employees from Rhone-Poulenc, who happens to be a supplier to my team, got into an argument during their lunch break with a group protesting the company's involvement with the mission, and it turned quite violent."

There was silence as the group assembled around the table gave thought to all of this.

Finally, Jim Stanton broke the silence. "You know, there are times when my doubts about leaving Earth evaporate, and I look forward to life on a planet without all this political felgercarb."

"Come on, Jim," urged Ventine. "You can't honestly believe that Cerulea won't become political over time."

"No, I guess not. But I'm assuming it'll take a couple of generations before there are even enough of us to form opposing sides."

"I wish I shared your confidence, Jim" Belechenko said sternly. "I think it's quite possible that you may even see this argument follow you onto your ship."

"How so?"

"Well, Derek Butler rode the wave of this conflict brilliantly, and he is now beholden to a lot of folks within the conservative party. There's rumor that, if he wins the election, his team will quickly advance legislation to force an eleventh hour change in mission plan."

"What kind of change?" Naj asked earnestly.

"Not clear. But it's no secret that religious conservatives, most especially evangelicals, want desperately to see more of their own on the Mission Council-- and on the crew itself."

"Can he get away with that, Commander?" asked Jim.

"You know your system better than I do, but it seems to me that if the Senate changes hands, he could certainly take a good hard run at it."

Jim Stanton leaned back and rested his head on the back of his chair; for several moments, he stared at the ceiling. The group remained silent.

"Well," Jim said, looking at Belechenko and rising from the table, "whatever happens down there will not change how much work needs to be done up here." His tone was refreshed, resolute. He looked directly at several members of his team. "We've got a couple of important days ahead, folks, let's all try to get some sleep."

Belechenko rose, smiling. He said nothing, but was pleased that the leader he'd chosen to captain the *Humanity* was capable of ignoring politics and focusing on the job at hand.

The group headed for the door, sorted themselves into several maglevs, said their goodnights, and headed off to their designated living quarters.

64.

A decade earlier, there had been a determined effort by a bipartisan group of legislators to amend the Constitution so that the President would be elected not by the Electoral College, but by popular vote. They argued that the election had devolved into a circus in which candidates poured money, time & effort into the battleground states, while the rest of the country, occupying what had come to be called "spectator" states, looked on—paying substantially less attention to the process than their well-courted counterparts.

The proposed amendment failed. While it fairly easily garnered the required support of two thirds of both houses of Congress, it failed to attract the support of three quarters of state legislatures—despite overwhelming popularity among most of the voting public. The reason was quite straightforward: politicians in battleground states—including many states with questionable battleground potential—refused to relinquish what they perceived as their power to sway a national election.

However, a movement took hold which produced the desired result. By mutual agreement, a growing number of states signed on to a new process for awarding electoral votes. Instead of each state awarding their votes as soon as its own popular election was decided, the states agreed to wait—usually only eight hours or so—for the national results of the popular vote to be confirmed, then awarded all of their electoral votes to the national winner.

Once a sufficient number of states adopted this practice—comprising a majority of electoral votes—the new system presided, and the Electoral College became a quaint vestige of American governance, a procedural garnish.

Since every vote in every state now had equal importance, the behavior of candidates changed markedly, the idea of battleground and spectator states dissipated, and voter turnout began to climb steadily from a historical average of just over 50% to over 75% in the 2036 election.

❦

Derek Butler won the popular vote by four and a half million votes.

Ironically, had the Electoral College still held sway, he would have lost the election.

❦

The Montana senate race had been too close to call on election night. After a full recount, it remained dangerously close; the progressive candidate demanded another recount by hand—this time of all paper ballot receipts, which were now required by law in all 50 states. The conservative candidate, a widowed mother of four grown children, remained calm and, by most press accounts, gracious as the process unfolded.

When it was all over, Thanksgiving had come and gone, and it was early December. The conservative party had regained control of the Senate with a margin of one seat.

For the first time since 2006, one party controlled the executive branch and both houses of congress.

65.

Ginny sat at her desk, daydreaming, catching up on paperwork, and consuming various briefing papers for the coming week.

The afternoon light turned the East Wing and the White House Balcony pink; the lawn and trees, covered in a fresh blanket of snow, glistened and sparkled. Out on the Ellipse, she could clearly see the lights of the National Holiday Tree brightening as daylight waned.

She heard a knock and looked up as Roger entered the Oval Office.

"You're early."

"Yeah, well. My calendar's not quite as crowded these days."

Ginny put her briefing book down on her desk and motioned for Roger to take a seat. She'd noticed that his level of formality had dropped a bit; he no longer insisted on the "Madam President" thing every time he saw her, and didn't always have an official agenda when he entered her office. With less than thirty days until their departure from the White House, this seemed somehow fitting.

"You seem a little down. Everything all right?"

"I suppose so," Roger answered, pulling the chair out and taking a seat. "Just seems hard to believe that the treadmill is about to stop."

"Oh, I'm ready"

"Are you?" Roger asked earnestly.

"Yes, I am."

In fact, she felt oddly peaceful. She had anticipated a feeling of sadness or even depression following the election, assuming that the finality of the end of her Presidency would leave her empty. On the contrary, she was surprised to find herself feeling refreshed and strangely energetic.

A big part of it was the realization that she would be keeping what she felt to be the very best part of her job, while letting go of responsibilities that had become, over time, burdensome.

"The Mission has been far and away the most satisfying part of this job for months now, and being able to devote all of my time to that effort is a welcome change. I would think you'd feel the same way. Are you having second thoughts about taking on the Council's Executive Administrator role?"

Ginny had worked hard over the last several months first to create this position, then to get the Council to agree to Roger's appointment. As launch neared, it would be critical to have someone with Roger's talents coordinating all of the communications and high-level managerial tasks.

"No regrets whatsoever. But understand, Madame President, my job has been much more focused on domestic policy and White House Operations. This is a huge change for me."

"I see what you're saying. But are you really going to miss living in a glass house? Or coming to work everyday knowing that whatever you'd planned is inevitably going to be derailed by some other urgent priority?"

"Well, the glass house I could definitely do without, but I'm not certain that the Mission Council won't offer its own barrage of unexpected priorities."

President Belknap smiled. "Oh, perhaps. But there are too many days when the White House is just a huge open battlefield, where shots come in from any direction. I'm really tired of pivoting in place, desperately trying to manage every new skirmish."

Roger chuckled at the image. "Well said, Madame President. But I would add one small detail: the White House enjoys a pretty significant hilltop advantage. On any given day, we can usually prevail more often than not because we look down on all such battles from the pinnacle of the U.S. presidency."

"Very true Roger, but at this point in my life, I'm ready to step down from that pinnacle in favor of other interests." Ginny leaned back in her chair, and looked out once again on the fading afternoon light, now just a delicate glow, as streetlights assumed their guard positions for the night.

66.

The Gulfstream HS5 WaveRider ascended steeply out of Henry Tift Myers Airport. The jet was fairly small. It had to be. It was one of the first commercially available business jets capable of hypersonic transport, and regulations demanded that the craft be sufficiently small to prevent an overly obtrusive shock wave, or sonic boom, as the jet's speed increased beyond the speed of sound, or Mach 1.

The plane utilized what were called pulse detonation engines, and were capable of propelling the jet at just over Mach 5, or roughly 3800 miles per hour, depending on altitude. The WaveRider technology allowed the jet to essentially ride its own shock wave—like a boat that could ride its own bow wave. Although it had been in use for some time, it had only recently been FAA certified for civilian use. The HS5 WaveRider could travel from Virginia to Tokyo in under three hours—and Derek Butler simply had to have one.

It was not headed to Tokyo on this cloudless January morning; nor was it returning to Blacksburg, Virginia, where it had its own private hangar. It was currently ferrying the President-elect and the new Senate Majority Leader Max Caulfield from Tifton, Georgia to Washington, DC.

The two had spent the weekend at Caulfield's farm in South Georgia, working closely with aides on their transition plan and legislative agenda. It was the latter that consumed their current conversation.

"I spoke with Jack Wily last night," Caulfield noted, as the plane began to level off. "The usual bullshit on how we'd both like to move forward in a bipartisan fashion. I didn't get the sense that the progressives are expecting a legislative offensive. The key will be to get everyone on our side discreetly lined up in advance, so that we can bring the resolution to a vote within a day or two of its introduction."

"Max, how do you think the other members of the Mission Council will react?"

"I think they're comfortable with Belknap; some of 'em will whine like a stuck hog when you replace her as Chairman, but so be it. There's not a heck of a lot of time left to turn this thing around and put both the Constitution and the crew on the right track. It'll be noisy and bloody, but reorganizing the Council and placing the US president at the helm is the right way to play it."

Butler nodded, and turned to look out the window as the plane passed over the small city of Augusta. He felt tense; the next few weeks were going to be tumultuous, and he wanted to get on with it. Watching thunder and lightning on the horizon made him nervous, whereas finding and calmly occupying the eye of the storm was thrilling--and something at which he was exceptionally skilled.

"Besides," added Caulfield, pulling Butler back from his reverie, "the spending bills are what make this plan foolproof. The Mission Council will have an awfully hard time objecting to you as Chairman once they understand that the alternative is to lose additional US funding."

Butler nodded.

They both heard a muffled explosion, as if the report of a fireworks display had detonated within a nearby cloud. The plane accelerated rapidly; Caulfield gripped his seat and turned white with panic. Butler grinned, looking suddenly relaxed; he leaned back in his chair, and locked his hands behind his head.

"Welcome to the future, Max."

67.

Vladimir Belechenko's heart was racing as he passed through the East entrance and approached the security desk.

"Those are beautiful, Commander," the guard remarked.

Vlad smiled and looked down at the arrangement of lilies, gladiolas, and roses in his arms. "Thank you."

He walked into the Sniffer and placed his hand on a center pod; he stood quietly as all of the sensors went to work. After a moment, the unit beeped, the guard nodded, and Belechenko walked down the long hallway to the elevator which would bring him to the residence.

He and Ginny had been seeing each other for nearly eight months, but after two weeks in space, Belechenko felt like a teenager on a second date. He couldn't wait to see her.

He was 45 minutes early. He'd managed to grab an earlier transport from Canaveral, and had extra time to head home to his apartment, shower and change, and grab some flowers on his way to the White House. Earlier in his career, a post-flight de-brief might have lasted 12 to 24 hours, but thanks to a redesigned procedure—and Belechenko's position as Mission Commander—he had departed the Kennedy Space Center just six hours after stepping off the CEV.

He turned into the elevator foyer and once again offered his hand to another reader for clearance. The unit beeped, and the door to the elevator opened.

❀

Ginny stood before the mirror in her bathrobe, and quickly applied mascara. She took a hair dryer from her vanity drawer and began to dry her hair.

She was excited and invigorated. The fact that Vlad would be back in her arms in an hour or two was a huge part of it; she had missed him, and felt almost flush with excitement at the thought of him walking through the door. But another significant contributor to her mood was the impending arrival of her new life. She would be leaving the White House in just one week, and, while it was easy for her to summon plenty of nostalgic sentiment for this milestone, it was even easier for her to look forward to her departure with anticipation.

Just the day before, she had signed the final papers on a new house in Great Falls, Virginia, just outside the Beltway. It was an old colonial, built in 1873, on nearly three acres of land. Vlad had gone to look at it with her before he'd departed, and her daughters had also been out to see it.

She had also just finished outfitting her new office at Mission headquarters. It was nearly the same size as the Oval, but with a view of Oronoco Bay Park and the Potomac River beyond.

All in all, Ginny felt content. So many US presidents got bogged down in their second terms, often fighting malaise, irrelevance, or worse—scandal. Although she'd drawn criticism from some quarters for her focus on the mission, and a few members of her cabinet had drawn fire for minor indiscretions, she was leaving office virtually unscathed, and proud of her eight-year tenure.

Ginny looked closely at each of her eyes in the mirror, applied lipstick and rubbed her lips to distribute it evenly. *Now, what to wear*, she thought, putting the hairdryer back in the drawer. She turned to leave the bathroom for her dressing room, and immediately stopped short; Belechenko was leaning against the doorjamb of her bedroom.

☯

They collided in the entryway; their mouths locking. Vlad slipped one arm around Ginny's waist inside her bathrobe and lifted her off the floor; the warmth of her body next to his and the taste of her kiss was far superior to all the daydreams of the past two weeks combined. Ginny grabbed the hair on the back of his head and pulled his lips tighter against hers.

He turned to carry her into the bedroom, and Ginny wrapped her legs around his waist. As they frantically kissed each others' face and neck, the arrangement of flowers fell from Vlad's grasp onto the Persian rug.

They fell onto the bed; a tangle of arms, buttons, belts, and passion.

68.

"I ought to go away more often," Belechenko joked as they lay in bed, her head nestled on his chest as he gently caressed her back.

"That's a given, isn't it?" Ginny asked looking up into his eyes.

"Actually, no. I've got to be back on board the *Humanity* for about a week in February, then once more in April, and then in June we're both heading up for the send-off."

Ginny closed her eyes; there was silence for several moments. "You know, I think I'm ready for life after my presidency," she said, opening them again, "but I'm not sure how I'm going to feel after the launch."

"Well, assuming the launch is successful, I know I'm going to feel incredibly relieved."

"We'll then be just two middle-aged civilians."

"Is that so bad?" Vlad asked, turning them both so they were now face to face. "To me, it sounds wonderful."

Ginny smiled up at him. They stared into each other's eyes until Vlad slowly brought his head down and kissed her.

139.
140.

The new President of the United States removed his hand from the Bible, shook hands with the Chief Justice, and turned to the cheering crowd, one arm raised in salute. He wore a dark grey cashmere overcoat with a white scarf neatly bordering his collar.

It was a cold, raw day. The skies had threatened snow, and the forecast concurred. But so far, the ceremony had escaped with just a light flurry that came and went as the crowd assembled.

The past several weeks had been extremely productive. Butler's team was in place, and they were now ready for their own blizzard, although its strength would far exceed expectations. While the political clouds clearly signaled substantial change, the public at large could not yet see the magnitude of the storm.

In fact, as Butler launched into his speech, riddled with the standard platitudes promising to "bridge the divide" with a "bipartisan approach" to "addressing the issues of concern to both sides of the aisle," there was only moderate dismay among some progressives. Many pundits and much of the press—and thus a large percentage of Americans—all believed that the nation had traded a left-leaning centrist for a right-leaning one. Butler had convinced the electorate that he truly walked the line on many issues, and that, even with both houses of congress behind him, he would take a rational and level-headed path forward.

Given the tumultuous protests that had enthralled the country and the world over the past ten months, there was hope that perhaps this man could, in fact, bring the two sides together.

69.

"You can't be serious!" Jack Wily exclaimed, glaring at Randall Reese across the polished oak conference table.

"We are very serious, Senator. This legislation will be announced tomorrow morning."

One week into his Presidency, Derek Butler signed Executive Order 93191, creating the White House Office of Cerulean Affairs. It's stated purpose was "to help the Federal Government coordinate its efforts with regard to the Mission to Cerulea, and to manage a legislative effort which will ensure that the interests of the United States are properly represented therein..."

Randall Reese had been named Special Assistant to the President for Cerulean Affairs, and the Office's Deputy Director.

When Reese got the call, he was both elated and confused. On the one hand, the appointment offered him the best possible podium for his crusade. From his White House Office in the West Wing, he stood a better chance of forcing changes in the Cerulean Constitution than he'd ever dreamed.

On the other hand, he was mystified by Butler's motivation. It was unclear just how committed the man was to changing the Mission's priorities and direction. Butler had won in large part by appealing to both sides of the growing divide; now in office, it seemed crazy for him to dissociate himself from nearly one half of his constituents. Nonetheless, Reese accepted and attacked his new responsibilities with vigor.

He had been authorized to hire two deputy assistants, and had immediately asked Joe Condon to join him. Condon gladly accepted; the other slot remained vacant.

The first legislative missile that Butler and Caulfield had designed weeks prior in South Georgia was now on the launchpad, and Senate Minority Leader Jack Wily was the first member of his party to see it.

Reese and Wily were in the Roosevelt Room of the West Wing. Originally the office of Teddy Roosevelt when the West Wing was built in 1902, the windowless room was actually named for both Teddy and Franklin by Richard Nixon in 1969.

"Mr. Reese, I can assure you that, even if you manage to get these resolutions through the U.S. congress, which I certainly hope you do not, the Mission Council will never agree to install President Butler as Chairman."

"Senator Wily, these are resolutions, not laws. They simply state that it is the belief of the United States that the chairmanship, along with all other seats on the Council, should be awarded in accordance with the funding levels of all participating nations. And that, within the United States, the presiding authority with regard to all matters related to the Mission will be the President."

"Which means you want Butler to take Belknap's role?"

"It means that we believe he *should* take over Belknap's role," Reese said calmly.

"Mr. Reese, the Mission Council is not governed by this nation; it is an independent body. What do you hope to achieve—?"

Jack Wily stopped short. He glared at Reese, who said nothing.

"If the Mission Council refuses to accept your recommendation, you'll blackmail them by threatening U.S. funding, is that it?"

"Senator, these resolutions are only intended to express the heartfelt beliefs of the administration and the Senate and House majorities. What happens next is an open question."

Wily stared at Reese, incredulous. He started to speak, but thought better of it. Instead, he collected several papers off the table, including a copy of the proposed resolution, slid them into his briefcase, and fastened the clasp.

Wily stood, buttoned his suitcoat, and walked toward the door. "Good day, Mr. Reese."

"Thank you for coming, Senator."

❦

Senator Wily, his Chief of Staff, and several aides spent the rest of the afternoon calling every moderate conservative congressman on the Hill.

As of the following morning, not one of their calls had been returned.

70.

Before they'd been privately briefed several days before the vote, there were a number of conservatives in Congress who felt the resolutions were purely political, and initially refused to offer their support.

It was made clear, however, by Caulfield, the President, and the Speaker of the house that this vote was non-optional; if anyone in either the Senate or the House wanted assistance of any kind with future elections, legislation, or local projects, then there was only one way to go.

It wasn't complicated; the intimidation projected by the new dual majority was extremely powerful. As soon as the mass started moving, it was like a flash flood in a slot canyon. Choosing any direction other than downstream was simply dangerous.

So when it came time for members of both houses of congress to vote, it was over before it began. Both resolutions passed along party lines.

The Congress had made a definitive statement to the Mission Council and the World: the United States wanted their influence over the Mission to match their level of funding, and they wanted President Butler in the driver's seat.

∞

Roger Tucker turned off the screen and pounded the desk with his fist. "Son of a bitch!"

He'd been blindsided, and felt that somehow he should have seen this coming.

Jeff Wheeler, sitting in a side chair of Roger's new office, offered little reassurance. "These guys seem far better organized than we'd suspected."

"They sure do. God damn it!" Roger had a sinking feeling in his stomach, as if, after years of steadily pushing the Mission uphill toward launch, it had just this moment reversed direction and started to slip.

He closed his eyes tight and ran his fingers backwards through his hair. Then focused. "Okay, Jeff, let's get to it. Why don't you draft a statement responding to the resolutions; I'll get a hold of President Belknap and see if we can't put together an emergency meeting of the Council."

Wheeler began scribbling some notes on his tablet. "What tone do you want the statement to project? Understanding, possible cooperation, or total rejection?"

Roger spun in his chair and gave the matter some thought as he looked out the window. Wheeler stared at a photo on his boss' desk of Roger and what he assumed to be his male spouse and their two children. Wheeler glanced at Roger's back, then leaned in for a closer look.

"I would say polite rejection," Roger said, spinning around in his chair. He saw that Wheeler had been studying the photo, but was used to such scrutiny. Roger spoke slowly, forming the sentences in his brain, and delivering them verbally to Wheeler, who began scribbling and tapping rapidly on his tablet when Roger began speaking: "The Mission Council respects the interests of the United States, but remains a global body governed by carefully crafted bylaws. In accordance with these bylaws, the Council must weigh the interests of all participating nations, and cannot—especially at this late date—allow one country's politics to adversely affect its decisions or actions."

"Got it." Wheeler stood and was still writing as he walked toward the door.

"Jeff—hold it. Scratch 'especially at this late date'; that's irrelevant, and will only get us into trouble."

"Got it," Wheeler repeated. After he stopped scribbling, he turned and faced Roger from the doorway. "Roger, does this mean we're about to lose our funding?"

Roger paused for a moment, staring at Wheeler. "I don't know, Jeff. Let's just hope that these resolutions are a bluff, and that they won't have the guts to move forward with an appropriations bill."

Wheeler looked down at the floor, then back at Roger. "I'll get going on the statement."

Roger watched him leave, knowing damn well that Wheeler's question was spot on—this was *all* about funding. The only question was when the other shoe would drop.

71.

The ship's vibration had dissipated. Jim looked at the view screen. The Centaurus constellation, a glowing cluster five hours ago, was now much more distinct. He could clearly see its three distinct stars: Alpha Centauri A and B, and the smaller Proxima Centauri.

He took a deep breath. He and his crew had been testing the ESS *Humanity's* SEC drives for two days now, and still he felt as if he had just stolen his father's car.

"Nav three, bring ion propulsion engines online." Jim could feel the addition of a slight hum to the fairly complex background noise. He was beginning to get a feel for the ship, and working hard to separate all of the different sensations in his brain. Ideally, he'd soon be able to walk onto the bridge and know instantly which systems were engaged.

"Engine fifteen, what are you seeing?"

While the status of each station was indicated by a panel of large screens on the forward wall of the *Humanity's* Operations Center, where any malfunction would be visible immediately, it would be a while before Jim trusted them. Besides, he wanted to know exactly how each component of the system behaved— especially when things were going right.

"Bridge, the manifolds are experiencing a slight resonance, but well within specifications," came the reply.

The station labeled Engine fifteen was currently manned by Jia Xian Shang; she was an experienced engineer who had joined the Mission crew from the Beijing Aerospace Command and Control Center. During testing, and upon the Captain's command, all stations were tied together in what amounted to a 25-person conference call. However, to simplify ship communications, all personnel were addressed by station, not by name.

"Engine fifteen, did you sense any change as the ion engines came on-line?" Jim asked.

"Negative, bridge. Resonance has remained constant," Jia Xian said calmly.

"Excellent. Nav two, shut down forward and aft SEC drives."

This always unnerved him, but he did his best not to show it. He knew the technology well enough to know that the highest danger the ship faced was the disengagement of the SEC drives. The physics were immensely complex, but the basic gist of it was that the ship was essentially creating and occupying a wormhole as it traveled. If the forward drive malfunctioned, the ship could literally be stretched and snapped like a piece of licorice.

The background noise decreased substantially as the SEC drives disengaged.

Jim listened intently, showing no emotion but momentarily feeling his pent-up tension suppressed by a wave of awe and incredulity. *But it's real*, he thought to himself. Over the past two days, the *Humanity* had broken the FTL barrier on three separate occasions. They had traveled at over 800 million miles per hour—and that was only their break-in speed. It was mind-boggling.

At the same time, it was precisely as planned. The ship had performed pretty much as designed, while the crew had addressed all problems in exact accordance with their training. The actual experience of faster-than-light travel, while incredible to contemplate, was anti-climactic. Since the ship, within its warp bubble, was, in fact, standing still, the sense of velocity experienced under propulsion systems was absent.

Nonetheless, the feat was no less impressive.

As the ship and crew proceeded through the designated test regimen, Jim felt himself starting to move the myriad details of mission preparation into storage at the back of his brain, while unfurling the journey itself in the center of his consciousness.

He looked up at the left bank of navigation panels. "Nav three, ion engines to K-10"

"Bridge, ion engines accelerating to K-10."

Jim clapped his hands. "Good work, team. We'll hold this course for twenty minutes and then head back to L5."

Jim nodded to Naj. "Nav one, you have command." He walked to a console at the center of the bridge, placed his palm on a reader, and punched a few buttons--effectively logging off.

Naj placed his palm on a second reader, and logged in. The ship would allow only a ten-second gap in command before sounding an alarm.

"All right, I'm off to the comm for some breakfast," Jim headed for the exit.

"Captain," Naj stopped him. "With your permission, I'd like to do some further testing of low-speed acceleration."

Jim looked at Naj. "What did you have in mind?"

"Well, yesterday's test struck me as a little clumsy; the crew shouldn't be able to feel us accelerate to that degree. I'd like to try a different algorithm which may smooth the acceleration curve substantially."

"Okay, but stay within K-20. Agreed?"

"Will do."

Jim headed for the exit, then turned. "And Naj--try not to spill my orange juice."

Both men smiled. "Yes sir!" said Naj playfully.

72.

"For the most part, we are done," Cynthia said with exaggerated relief.
"So now what?" asked Devlin.

"Well, now it has to be approved by the Council. The question is whether this latest turn of events is going to have an impact on the approval process. A short time ago, I would have said that we were in pretty good shape, and that approval of the Constitution would be a rapid affair; now I'm not so sure."

The huge room was starting to fill for the meeting. Devlin McGregor and Cynthia Fossett stood at one end of a long glass wall which looked out over the frozen Potomac.

"Maybe I'm just a naïve scientist, but I never saw this coming," Devlin noted, shaking his head. He took sip of his coffee.

"Oh, I'll tell you, Devlin, I can't say I predicted it either, but it sure as hell doesn't surprise me. In a sense, what's now taking place is precisely what the new Constitution seeks to prevent. It just seems that, whenever a single party controls the presidency and both houses of Congress, sanity seems to take a vacation."

"But Cynthia, here's what I don't understand. The Council has 17 voting members, representing all nations with an established space agency; they sure as day aren't going to buckle under a couple of Congressional resolutions from the United States. So other than grabbing headlines and making a spectacle, I don't see how Butler and the conservatives could possibly prevail."

"Oh come on Devlin, now you are being naïve!" Cynthia said good-heartedly. "The resolutions are just the first volley. My guess is that, depending on how the Council responds, this will quickly devolve into a funding boycott."

The room was filling up. Members of the Council were taking their seats, and Cynthia gestured for them to do the same. As they moved to their assigned chairs, Virginia Belknap and Roger Tucker entered the room.

Not unlike the United Nations, the meeting room at Mission Council headquarters consisted of two large, concentric tables, each horseshoe-shaped. Two representatives from each voting member nation occupied the inner ring, while the outer ring held additional observers and representatives from twelve non-voting member nations.

Ginny took her seat at the top of the inner ring and, with Roger seated on her left, called the meeting to order.

Although several of the Council members had tried to make it clear in their opening statements that they were not referring either to Ginny or to all Americans, the opinions expressed all struck a similar chord: the United States was behaving like a spoiled child.

Ginny was embarrassed for her country. Yet, at the same time, she was gratified to see a definitive consensus among the Council; not a single member had expressed the slightest inclination to make any changes whatsoever in Mission strategy, policy, or leadership.

Although no one had, as yet, acknowledged the gorilla in the room.

After the last member had concluded their remarks, Ginny asked if any of the functional heads or non-voting members wished to address the Council.

Nombeko Nseki raised her hand.

"Ms. Nseki."

"Madame President, Council members. I wish only to state for the record that I have the utmost respect for this body, and that I am extremely proud to be a member of this multinational effort. However, it is no secret that your country has provided the majority of funding for the Cerulean Mission, and I fear that, while the stance we have taken today is admirable, it may not be practical if the United States chooses to withhold its support."

"Thank you Ms. Nseki. You have given voice to an issue that we obviously must address." Ginny leaned back in her chair and looked around at the Council members.

"This turn of events was unexpected, and will undoubtedly present some obstacles to the Mission. But let me be clear: all of the work performed by the Council, and by the teams which each functional head has assembled, has been driven by the beliefs, values and best interests of all member nations. True multinational cooperation is not a common occurrence on this planet, and the example we have set is extremely important—not just in ensuring the credibility of the Mission, but in providing a model that the world might follow in other endeavors, whether these involve new planets or simply the basic affairs of nations here on Earth.

"As is evident by the violent protests and heated debate we see each day on the streets and on our screens, there are many who strongly disagree with the path we have chosen. However, it is also clear that this disagreement is primarily an American phenomenon; surveys indicate that, in most countries around the globe, our efforts are supported by upwards of 60 percent of the populace.

"While it's true that approximately half of our budget comes from the United States, it's important to point out that the money was provided with the explicit understanding that U.S. influence on the Mission would be in accordance with the Council's bylaws—and not simply proportionate with America's slice of the budgetary pie chart.

"We agreed three years ago, when this group first convened, that Cerulea should reflect the essence of the human race as it exists today in the 21st century. We specifically stated our intent to endow Cerulean civilization with the full benefit of wisdom gained through mankind's progress and evolution—with regard to every facet of life. Our thinking then was not misguided; nor is it now. This is the proper path, and while our efforts have not been perfect, I believe we have lived up to our intent, and that Cerulea will be better off for it.

"In short, while an eventual decision by the US Congress to limit funding would require a Herculean effort on our part to secure alternate sources, it seems we all agree that any indication of compromise at this juncture is premature."

There was hearty applause from around both rings. As it faded, Georges Ventine signaled his desire to be heard.

"Monsieur Ventine."

"Madam Chairman, Council members," Ventine offered intently, "I move that the Council draft a statement outlining its intent to take no action in response to the US Congressional resolutions."

"Thank you, Monsieur Ventine. Do we have a second?"

Several hands were raised, but Ginny called on the representative from the People's Republic of China. *Let's get you on record*, she thought.

"I second the motion."

"All in favor?" Ginny called out.

All hands were raised.

"All those opposed?" Ginny turned to Roger: "Mr. Tucker, please let the minutes state that the motion was passed by unanimous vote."

73.

The snowmobile ripped around Linden and Laurel, the driver leaning in hard to offset the centrifugal force of the turn as he passed the two cabins. Ahead was a smooth blanket of fresh snow; behind was a billowing cloud of light, dry powder which sparkled as it fell back down to Earth in the bright, February sunshine.

A second and third snowmobile were somewhere further back, inevitably slowed by the loss of visibility created by the leader.

As the machine straightened out after the curve, the driver accelerated, his eyes tearing behind sunglasses as the quarter-ton sled raced down toward Aspen Lodge. As he approached a covered swimming pool on his right, he jammed the handlebar at the last possible second and passed the pool to his left, then skidded to a stop in front of Aspen's front steps.

He jumped off the snowmobile and tossed his helmet to one of two men standing on the porch, hopped up the steps and entered—just as the other snowmobiles pulled in and stopped next to his.

The guy on the porch put the helmet under one arm, then spoke into his wrist mic: "POTUS has entered Aspen." He turned to the man standing next to him: "A lot can change in a month, eh?"

"Boy, I'll say. Hasn't been much testosterone on White House detail in the last few years. This could be interesting."

◎◎

Derek Butler sat down on the sofa with a beer after getting out of his snowsuit. Randall Reese was seated in an armchair to his left, reading the paper.

"Nice ride, Mr. President?" Reese asked, lowering his paper.

"Very nice. Just beautiful out there." Butler took a sip of his beer, and looked around the lodge. It was his first trip to Camp David. "Did you know this place used to be called Shangri-La?"

"No I didn't."

"Eisenhower renamed it after his grandson."

"It was built for Roosevelt during the war, wasn't it?"

"Actually, it was one of three existing camps in the area, and Roosevelt picked this one. I guess he was spending a lot of time on the presidential yacht, and the Secret Service decided he needed someplace a little easier to defend. It was here that he and Churchill supposedly planned the Normandy invasion."

"And perhaps it will also be here where Butler planned the 'liberation of Cerulea'" Reese offered, regretting the silly comment the moment it left his lips. He folded his newspaper and put it on the floor next to his chair.

Butler didn't react. He took another sip of beer. "Randall, talk to me about vote count. What are your estimates of what we can expect."

"Well, the Mission Council's firm rejection of our resolutions should serve to drive a few votes our way that might otherwise have been tough to sway." Reese leaned forward and looked at Butler. "But I don't want to get anyone's hopes up, Mr. President; getting both the Senate and the House to vote for a cessation of funding will be a tough battle."

"How tough," Butler asked.

"Very tough. Sending a message that we want more influence over the Mission was a no-brainer. I think most on the Hill believe that the move was a great way to motivate and reward the base. But remember, overall the mission is very popular. Many states have lucrative contracts for research or equipment. For that matter, even those states which are just contributing a crew member or two feel very patriotic about the whole endeavor."

"Then we'll just have to figure out how to change what constitutes patriotism these days," Butler mused.

"That may prove to be a difficult task, sir."

Butler waved his hand, seemingly swatting Reese's doubts away as if they were just a few annoying insects. "In my experience, it's never that difficult to drag people into a given viewpoint. All you have to do is tell them that something they value is being attacked, and tell them that to do anything other than what you've prescribed will put that something in grave danger. Then voila! You've now redefined patriotism as the direct support of your plan. It works the same in nearly every situation—whether you're dealing with the employees of a corporation, or the citizens of a nation."

"With all due respect, sir, I think what you're suggesting is much easier said than done."

Butler pulled his head back slightly, and looked at Reese with narrowed eyes. "Randall, everything I've accomplished in my entire goddamn life was 'easier said than done.' Are you telling me you don't think it's possible to pass a bill halting funding for the Mission? Or are you telling me that it's going to be a bitch, but that you'll get it done?"

Reese was momentarily silent. He swallowed reflexively, knowing that his Adams apple would betray his nervousness. "I'll get it done, Mr. President."

74.

The Congressman from North Carolina was a portly man. He was bald, wore small, round glasses, and frequently pulled a handkerchief from the breast pocket of his disheveled light grey suit to mop his brow and upper lip. He was in his late fifties, but appeared to be a decade older. He had served in the House of Representatives for nearly twelve years.

"That land will be awfully helpful, gentlemen," the Congressman offered with his Carolinian inflection. "But there is one more thing."

Now what, thought Reese.

"Between now and the mid-terms, it'd be awfully nice if President Butler could take a few trips to North Carolina on my behalf."

Reese drew a deep breath and looked down at the notes on his tablet resting on the table. He was not looking for anything, so much as trying to divert his eyes from a man and a task he found repugnant.

Condon sensed Reese's disgust and took the lead in responding. "Congressman, if by chance that was possible, would you be willing to commit right here and now?"

"Yes, Mr. Condon, I most certainly would."

"All right, the President will pay a visit to your state, at an event for which you will receive advance notice. But only one, and the timing will be in accordance with his schedule."

"Of course, of course." The man looked back at Condon, then at Reese, who managed to steel himself for what he hoped would be final eye contact.

"Gentlemen, you got yourselves a deal." The Congressman reached his thick, moist hand across the table and Condon shook it firmly. He then offered it to Reese and the two shook hands.

As the man stood, Reese discreetly wiped his hand on his trousers under the table.

Condon rose and walked the Congressman to the door, said goodbye, and returned to the table where Reese sat, head in his hands.

"Okay, Randall, that's six out of nine. Not bad for a day's work. What do you say we head over to the Ebbitt for a drink?"

"Joe, you've forgotten that we've got Senator Wessley coming in fifteen minutes. After that, I think I may just head back to the apartment."

Condon paused, taking in Reese's defeated temperament.

"Randall, I'm not sure I get it. I'm not a big fan of this process either, but we've been remarkably successful thus far. Why are you so tormented?"

"Joe, we agreed to give that Congressman the development rights to over 10,000 acres of the Great Smoky Mountains National Park! Aside from the fact that I'm dead set against it, I find it exhausting just to contemplate fulfilling all of these promises. Don't you?"

Condon leaned on the table. "Pardon the cliché, my friend, but wake up and smell the goddamn coffee! This is how the game is played. And no, I don't get exhausted; I get energized—especially when it seems as if we're making real progress toward our goal.

"Besides, carving out a few thousand acres for development is nothing new. We just shove an earmark provision in the next bill that happens along. No one's going to object. The development of small perimeter parcels of National Park land has occurred dozens of times in the past; as I recall, that Park comprises over a half a million acres."

"Okay, fine, but what about the engineering contract we promised this morning? Or the replacement of two crew members with a couple of aging athletes from South Dakota? Are those just earmarks we shove into the next legislative shuttlecar?"

"Look. Randall. It will all come together. It always does; I've been through this literally hundreds of times. I know it sounds crass, but this is how things get done. Period."

Reese got up from his chair and walked to the window. They were in a conference room on the fifth floor of the Eisenhower Executive Office Building, just off the East Rotunda.

He looked down on Pennsylvania Avenue and the West Wing of the White House. He thought about how much he missed his family. They had decided to stay behind in Wisconsin when he accepted the position. The plan had been for him to come home most weekends, but the job just hadn't allowed it.

Reese was tired. "I'll tell you Joe. I want to win the war as much as I ever did. But maybe I'm just not cut out to fight the battles. I mean, planning strategy is one thing, but all this haggling with Senators and Representatives, and all of these give-aways. I just wish one of them would agree to vote for the bill just because they believe in it! Is that so much to ask?" He looked up at Condon, who smiled faintly.

"Probably."

Condon's wristphone began to vibrate. He answered the call, exchanged a few words, and hung up.

"Looks like Senator Wessley is going to have to reschedule. Come on, let's get out of here. I'll buy you a cranberry and seltzer."

Condon grabbed his suitcoat off a chair and put it on. Reese grabbed his tablet and stuffed it in his briefcase. He sat silently for a moment, staring blankly at the middle of the table, then shook his head and stood up briskly. "I'm sorry for my defeatism, Joe. You're right, we are making progress."

"And you know," he added, looking at Condon with renewed energy, the tone of his voice changed, "I think we're going to pull this thing off."

Condon smiled, and opened the door for Reese to exit. "That's the spirit!"

75.

Three weeks later, a bill was introduced for debate in the House of Representatives by a freshman representative from Texas. It proposed, in summary, that the United States immediately cease all financial support for the Mission to Cerulea, unless the Mission Council and the crew of the *ESS Humanity* be altered in accordance with the funding provided by participating nations, and unless the Council thereafter called for elections to decide key posts on the Mission Council, including that of Chairman.

The House Science Committee, in coordination with its Subcommittee on Space & Aeronautics, debated the bill, considered and rejected several proposed amendments, then quickly voted along party lines to give its support to the legislation.

The bill was then debated and approved by the House Appropriations Committee. The Chairman of that Committee noting, in a formal statement, that the bill "serves to protect the vital interests of the United States by ensuring that financial support is withheld from initiatives that run counter to the core values of our nation."

The Conservative majority easily passed the bill in a full House vote, and the legislation was introduced in the Senate.

The Senate Appropriations Committee debated the bill in what was clearly a well publicized but perfunctory session. It also voted along party lines to approve the measure without amendment.

There being no substantive differences between the House and Senate versions of the bill, no conference committee was required, and the full Senate vote was scheduled.

As predicted, the Progressives threatened a filibuster. Also as predicted, the Conservatives called their bluff, and forced the Progressives to take to the floor.

Day one of the filibuster, well covered by the international press, was filled with fiery speeches from half a dozen members of the Senate minority.

On day two, the cameras continued to roll, and the Progressives continued to offer eloquent orations on the egregious damage that the passage of the Conservatives' legislation would inflict on both the Mission and the relationships between America and its friends abroad.

Jack Wily took the floor as evening settled in, and launched into a long and thoughtful soliloquy on the issue, seeking wherever possible to offer lofty sound bites for the media:

"The Congressional conflict in which we now find ourselves is nothing short of a battle—a bitter war waged by those who would misdirect and restrict mankind's greatest aspiration to a set of partisan ideals, against those who wish to proceed in an open, multilateral fashion.

"Cerulea represents the perpetuation of mankind as a whole. To allow this Mission to be unduly influenced by a small minority of the human race would be a calamity of the highest order..."

76.

Derek Butler hit a button on his desk, silencing Jack Wily and causing nine other screens to transform themselves from windows on the Senate chamber and various newscasts into peaceful displays of art and nature.

He walked across the Presidential Seal and took a seat in a majestic wing-back chair upholstered in thick dark leather he had commissioned specifically for his new office. Randall Reese and Joe Condon each sat on an opposing sofa to Butler's left and right.

"Gentlemen," he began. "Let's begin. Randall, why don't you start us off with an update on how all this is being received."

"I'd be happy to, Mr. President." Reese leaned forward, picked up his tablet, and brought up the appropriate data. "So far, it looks like we've slipped by several points. Polls show that only 54 percent of the American electorate object to the obstructionist tactics of the Progressives, down from 58. However, 53 percent continue to believe that the Mission should support more traditional values."

"Whatever the hell those are," muttered Butler.

Reese looked up at the President, a little surprised at the remark. Butler seemed unapologetic; he held Reese in an even stare.

Reese retreated back to his report. "Our polling firm believes that there is a greater than 70 percent chance that those objecting to the filibuster will drop below 50 percent within 72 hours. This is based on further research into the relative strength of the opinions offered for the survey."

The door behind Condon opened and the President's secretary announced the arrival of Senator Caulfield, who entered and quickly took a seat next to Condon.

"Max, we were just reviewing the survey data. Should we bring you up to speed?"

"No need, Mr. President. I reviewed the report on my way over."

"Then let's get to it: Senator, is time to drop the bomb?"

Caulfield winced slightly at Butler's choice of words. "It may well be, sir."

"Do you see any other options at this point?" Butler asked.

Caulfield paused, leaning forward and resting his forearms on each knee. "Well, one strategy might be to simply watch and wait. Once these guys start reading cookbooks up there, the public may quickly lose patience. However, that's risky; after some discussion with the leadership, I think we're all agreed that it's time use a parliamentary maneuver to halt debate."

"You mean the nuclear option," Condon clarified.

"I do, but we better damn well find another name for it if that's our plan," the Senator countered.

"Senator Caulfield, would another alternative be to seek some sort of a compromise position? I think the progressives would probably go for it," Reese offered, hoping that perhaps a head-on confrontation might be avoided.

There was silence as the three men looked at the President.

"I must say," Butler said finally, "while my instincts tell me that public support might swing back around to our camp if we were to wait this thing out, the risks are just too high. If it didn't happen, we'd look like idiots—and we'd have squandered virtually all of our political capital.

"As for compromise, I just don't see how it might work. If our goal is to alter the Cerulean Constitution, we must get voting control over the Mission. There's not a hell of a lot of middle ground.

"Bottom line, I think we've gotta do what it takes to win this thing." Butler looked at Caulfield. "Senator, I think that means we try to halt the debate."

"Didn't this approach backfire badly in the past?" Reese asked tentatively.

"When it was last used, in 2014, did the legislation pass?" Butler asked, clearly knowing the answer to his question in advance.

"Yes, sir. But I believe the political costs were quite high."

"So be it," Butler said firmly. "The political costs of failing to get this bill through will be awfully high as well. Max, tell us how this would work."

Caulfield turned to Condon. "Joe, you probably know a thing or two about Senate procedure, so feel free to jump in if you think I'm missing any important details."

"Senator, I know a great deal about vote-counting, but very little about the minutiae of the Senate's inner workings. I think you're on your own here."

"Okay, all of this is fairly arcane, so stop me if anything's unclear. Let me start with a quick explanation of Senate procedure.

"The Senate is governed by a set of rules, but not all are written down. Many are in the form of precedents--a precedent is essentially a rule that was formulated on-the-fly when the Senate made a decision as to how it was going to handle a given situation. Once a precedent is set, it determines how the Senate will behave whenever that same situation arises.

"Now, whenever a Senator believes that established rules are not being followed, he or she may raise what's called a Point of Order. As soon as this happens, the presiding officer—usually the Majority Leader or the Vice President—rules on whether the Point of Order is valid."

"Senator, you'll have to give a new President a helping hand here," Butler said, smiling. "Can you define Point of order?"

"Sure. My apologies, Mr. President. A Point of Order is when a member of the Senate points out that a rule has been broken. However—and this is important—a Senator may also raise a point of order if he thinks that the proper procedure of the Senate is in some way different from a current precedent."

Reese was trying hard to follow. "Senator Caulfield, does the raising of a point of order halt debate on pending legislation?"

"Yes, although only temporarily; that in itself doesn't help our cause much. What is helpful is that it can be raised at any time, interrupting any ongoing business. Bear with me.

"Once the presiding officer rules to accept or reject the point of order, then any Senator can appeal. When this happens, the Senate debates the issue until a motion to table, or set aside the appeal is made. Once there's motion to table, the appeal must be voted on immediately.

"Now, this vote requires only a simple majority to prevail, and this is where the so-called nuclear option comes into play.

"Is everyone with me so far?" Caulfield asked tentatively.

Butler sat casually in his wingback chair, leaning on an elbow and supporting his chin with the thumb and fist of his right hand. "I consider myself a fairly intelligent man, Max, but I'm just barely hanging on here,"

"Let me see if I can put all of this in context." Caulfield stood, walked to the fireplace, and turned to face his audience.

"Here's how it would play out. Perhaps sometime tomorrow or the next day, on the floor of the Senate, a conservative Senator will raise a point of order, noting that the ongoing filibuster is not permitted."

"Don't they have to offer an explanation as to why it's not permitted?" Condon asked, no less confused than Reese and Butler.

"Yes, but only for appearances. Perhaps something like 'filibusters are not allowed with space-related appropriations bills.' At the end of the day, we'll never convince anyone it's anything other than a powerplay.

"Then, once the point of order is raised, I will sustain it. As soon as that happens, there'll be no shortage of progressive senators wishing to appeal. The appeal debate will begin, and someone on our side will move to table the appeal. I will call for a vote; fifty-one conservative senators will uphold the motion to table, and the point of order will be sustained, effectively changing the rules of the Senate, ending the filibuster, and clearing the way for an up or down vote on the Cerulean spending bill."

The group was silent for several moments.

"That's... that's unbelievable." Reese ventured clumsily. "How can it be that easy?"

"Well, just to make sure we understand: It may be easy to twist the rules; it's a real bitch living with the consequences."

"What do you mean by that, Senator," Condon asked.

"I mean that we're going to take a lot of heat for this. While it may invigorate the core conservative base, it's going to raise eyebrows among those in the middle—and completely piss off every progressive in the country; probably the world.

"Also, once this genie's out of the bottle, it'll be tough to get it back in. This tactic can and probably will be used against us in the future."

"I have no qualms about pulling a genie from its bottle, Senator," Butler countered firmly. "It seems to me to be a great way to get things accomplished quickly. I guarantee you there'll be many more homeless genies over the next seven years.

"Now let's get this done."

77.

Ginny emerged from the building surrounded by a phalanx of Secret Service agents. The noise was deafening.

She smiled and waved to the crowds on either side of her, but behind the smile she was a little irritated. A well-organized group of protesters across the street from the entrance were screaming and shouting with choreographed rage. Though not particularly large in number, they were unbelievably loud. Ginny knew all too well that, regardless how well-received her speech, or how much larger the group of supporters and well-wishers, this group would grab headlines.

The funding legislation and subsequent filibuster had completely re-energized both sides of the debate. The airwaves, the internet, cafes, bars; all were aflame with heated discussion. Progressives saw the filibuster as a rallying cry to protest the legislative bullying of a government under single-party rule; core conservatives regarded the funding bill as a necessary last resort in preventing the corruption of mankind's first extraterrestrial colony, and saw the filibuster as a weak, underhanded stunt to obstruct the basic principal of majority rule.

The door to the limousine opened. Ginny turned to the crowd, smiled and waved once more, and got in. The door closed behind her, and the noise level was immediately reduced by half.

"I'd say your speech was a smash hit." Roger Tucker had been waiting for her in the car, and sat across from her—his back to the front of the vehicle.

"I felt pretty good about it until I made my way out here," Ginny replied.

She had delivered a scheduled speech to the United Nations outlining the mission's progress. She had expressed disappointment about the pending legislation, and appealed to all member nations to offer additional funding, and to support the original vision and mission structure that they had helped to create.

"At this point," Roger noted, "it's a hell of lot more important that you're well-received in there than you are out here. How'd the meetings go after the speech. Any takers?"

"No, but I certainly didn't expect any UN ambassadors to write a check. The good news is that there were no flat-out rejections from the big players. The bad news is that we're going to have to pound a lot more pavement before we know what's even possible."

As the limousine pulled away from the curb, the protesters' faces were so vivid that Ginny could practically smell their breath through the bulletproof glass. They cleared the gate and took a right onto 1st Avenue, passing Dag Hammarskjold Plaza on their left.

"Well, I can't tell you that Air Force Bravo is waiting for you on the tarmac, but we have lined up a plane for your trip to Beijing. You'll be interested to know that it was provided by the Chinese government."

"Are you serious?" Ginny asked, surprised. "What do you suppose that means?"

"Frankly, Madame President, I don't have a clue. And believe me—I tried hard to find out. But the way I look at it, it can't be bad news."

"I guess not. So, when do we leave?"

"What do you mean, we?" Roger smirked. "You leave tonight at 9 pm."

"I thought you were joining me on this trip?"

"Ultimately, it's your call. But I don't think it makes sense for both of us to leave town with the filibuster in its third day, and the slightest chance that we might be able to defeat this thing."

"You're probably right, Roger. I'll go it alone."

"I've asked Jeff Wheeler to join you in my stead. Any objections?"

"No, that might be helpful."

The limo merged onto FDR Drive and headed toward the Triboro Bridge and LaGuardia Airport. Ginny looked out at the river.

"There's one other issue I wanted to discuss," Roger said tentatively. "Jeff and I were discussing how we might best approach the Chinese, and we were thinking that it might make sense if Commander Belechenko were to join you."

Ginny turned sharply and looked Roger. "What's the thinking behind that?"

"Well, if it's just you asking the Chinese government for additional funds, it's awfully easy for the discussions to dwell on the political. With Belechenko involved, there'll be an inclination to engage in a detailed operational discussion as well."

Ginny turned back to the River; several competing thoughts raced through her brain.

"Besides," Roger added, "you'd have to admit he's a fairly impressive and imposing figure."

Ginny looked at Roger and smiled. "I would have to agree to that!"

This might have been an awkward conversation with anyone but Roger. Despite any joking or comments that might indicate otherwise, he knew that she would never allow her personal feelings for Belechenko to affect her decisions.

"I guess I see your reasoning," she continued. "He's bound to be regarded as an objective expert on the technical needs of the mission. And it would be far better to spend time discussing that than the political motivations for why we're there in the first place."

"Exactly," Roger agreed.

"What about Vlad's planned trip to the *Humanity* later in the week?"

"The Commander's departure is delayed till next week due to some scheduling issues with crew training. He's free and clear."

"Well, I guess that settles it then."

78.

No expense was spared.

The black tie reception was held in the China World Tower, a giant skyscraper completed in 2022 to commemorate China's rise as the second largest economy on the planet. It looked out—and down—on the lesser buildings of Chongqing, a city of eight million people in the heart of China. The city was a modern marvel, having grown up almost entirely in the 21st century. It was roughly equidistant from Beijing and the island of Hainan—the epicenter of China's space operations.

The occasion was the 35th anniversary of China's manned space program, which began with the Shenzhou 5 mission in 2003. The guests of honor were Yang Liwei, the sole astronaut on that first mission, and Bai Lan Rui, who served as Captain of the mission marking man's return to the Moon in 2023—a joint effort between NASA, the European Space Agency and the China National Space Administration, and a tremendous feather in China's scientific cap. Two other celebrated guests were Virginia Belknap, the Chairman of the Cerulean Mission Council, and Vladimir Belechenko, the Supreme Commander of Cerulean Mission Operations.

Over a thousand people were in attendance, comprising the high society of Chinese technology and commerce. Present were high-level government officials, elite Space Administration technocrats, and numerous high-tech business leaders—many of whom had become billionaires as result of the country's sustained economic boom.

The giant hall was filled with Dragon Trees lit with miniature white lights. Hanging from the 65-foot ceilings were delicate glass chandeliers resembling ornate pagodas. Large ice sculptures depicting the space craft of CNSA missions were stationed in each corner of the hall, with a giant replica of the *ESS Humanity* in the center. Each was brilliantly lit with tightly focused halogen spotlights, causing them to appear as if they were glowing from within.

A waiter passed by the stern of the frozen *Humanity* and approached the small group, offering champagne. Belechenko took two glasses off the tray, and handed one to Ginny. They had recently arrived, and were exchanging small talk with Wu Jongmin, China's Minister of Science and Technology and his top aide.

The timing of the event was coincidental. Belechenko had been invited months earlier, but had not thought it possible to attend. His change of plans pleased the Chinese greatly. Ginny's presence doubly so; they had certainly not expected an esteemed dignitary of her stature to be present. There had been much last-minute anxiety over whether she would be properly entertained. As a result, an escort, doubling as a translator, had been assigned to her, with a specific itinerary of officials and prominent guests waiting in queue to speak with her as the evening progressed.

Minister Jongmin raised his glass. "I would like to make toast to strong relationship between United States and China," he said in passable English. "It has been honor to work closely with you both over past three years. To successful mission!"

All present took a sip of champagne. "Thank you, Minister," Ginny replied. "I certainly hope our current legislative obstacles do not result in too great a delay of that success."

"Madame President, we now understand also the difficulties of government with multiple parties," Jongmin offered. "But I am confident you and Commander Belechenko will prevail."

In truth, Ginny had no such confidence.

Just prior to touching down the day before, she had gotten word that the conservatives had put an end to the filibuster with something they called the Greater Good Provision. The vote on the spending bill was then carried by the Conservative's two vote majority. To many in Washington, this eventuality had come as no surprise, yet somehow Ginny had hoped they wouldn't risk it. But they did. And the public outcry that immediately followed didn't seem to have bothered them one bit.

Then, after spending nearly twelve hours in successive meetings with the Chinese government seeking to obtain the funding necessary to replace America's aborted commitment, she and Belechenko emerged empty-handed. The Chinese had already provided over 200 billion in funding, and had essentially reached their limit. One major constraint was that much of the country's infrastructure was in desperate need of repair, and many officials thought it would be irresponsible to divert available funds to the Cerulean initiative. Furthermore, since China was now recognized as a global superpower, its people were demanding that the country's tax revenues be applied to the care and support of its middle class and growing underclass.

Toward the end of what had been a fairly downbeat day of discussions, the idea was put forth by one government official that they might be able to get popular support for a substantial increase in funding if the mission became more of a Chinese venture. When Ginny and Belechenko pushed to understand what this might mean in practice, it was made clear that the officers and captain of the *Humanity* would have to be replaced by Chinese astronauts, the educational system and constitution would have to be revised by Chinese experts, and the percentage of Chinese within the crew—and even within the bank of frozen embryos—would have to be increased several fold.

Even then, it was not at all certain that they wouldn't encounter fierce opposition as they sought approval for the funding within their own parliament.

Ginny and Belechenko had said that they would give the Chinese idea due consideration. But they both knew it was not all that different from what the U.S. Congress had just demanded, and as such was essentially a non-starter.

Thus, they were back to square one.

As the reception picked up steam, Ginny smiled and carried on pleasant conversation. But inside she was despondent. Everything she'd worked for during the last half of her second term as President was now unraveling. She was not the type to shrink from a challenge, but if she thought she could get away with it, she would strongly consider diverting their plane home to some Caribbean island where she and Vlad could hole up and hide from the whole thing—the responsibilities, the battle with the Conservatives, the Mission itself.

Ginny's escort looked at her watch for what must have been the tenth time since they'd arrived, and looked around the hall for their next meet and greet encounter. Ginny then noted a distinguished couple approaching their ensemble from over by the Shenzou 5 space craft.

Ginny's escort whispered discreetly to her and Belechenko "Colonel Bai Lan Rui, Captain Chinese-led moon mission."

Wu Jongmin, well aware of the tight schedule, bid goodbye to both of them, and made off into the crowd with his aide.

"Madame President, it is an honor." Lan Rui bowed.

Ginny reciprocated. "Colonel, the honor is mine."

"My wife, Ying Mae."

Ginny turned and gestured to Vlad. "Permit me to introduce Commander Vladimir Belechenko, Supreme Commander of Cerulean Mission Operations."

The two men bowed. "It is very good to see you again, Colonel," Belechenko said cheerfully.

"And good to see you, Commander," Lan Rui returned.

"You've met before?"

"Yes, several years ago," Belechenko explained. "During the redesign of the International Space Station's science module, The Colonel played a key role in securing China's involvement, and lent his considerable engineering expertise to the project."

"Commander, you give too much praise." He turned to Ginny. "My involvement with moon mission many years ago has allowed me some influence as aging figurehead. I nag both ISS management and my superiors at CNSA until all parties agree."

"Perhaps you could help us convince your government to take a larger role in the Mission to Cerulea," Ginny said, tongue in cheek. Lan Rui and Belechenko laughed.

"Those decisions made well beyond my influence." Lan Rui responded.

At that moment, Jeff Wheeler approached. After the last afternoon meeting, he had stayed behind to draft a statement with his Chinese counterpart, and said he'd catch a later ride to the reception.

He asked if might borrow President Belknap for a few moments, and led her away from the conversation. Ginny's Chinese escort was distraught, but Wheeler reassured her that it would only be for a short time; Belechenko engaged his fellow astronaut in a discussion on some of the technologies that China had helped to develop for the *Humanity*.

As Ginny crossed the hall, she could feel the eyes of many upon her. Although they were simply staring at a successful and popular American President, she couldn't help but feel that somehow everyone felt sorry for her, and it made her uncomfortable.

Wheeler leaned toward her as they walked, quietly explaining his interruption.

"The gentleman represents a consortium of wealthy businessmen who've expressed an interest in the Mission."

"What kind of interest, Jeff?" While she was not particularly bothered at having been pulled away from her assigned guests, Ginny was mildly concerned that the introduction Wheeler was attempting to make was somehow inappropriate from a perspective of protocol.

"I can't offer much detail, Ma'am, but I can say that he is extremely well-respected, and seemed to believe that you'd be quite interested in making his acquaintance."

Ginny still sensed that Wheeler's escapade was improper, but to do anything other than comply would clearly embarrass Wheeler and the mystery man who was expecting to meet her. She caught the eye of an official who'd been present at one of her earlier meetings, and she smiled and nodded in silent hello as she passed by. When she looked ahead, Wheeler gestured to a gentleman in a quiet pocket of the crowd, evidently just finishing a conversation with two other guests.

He turned and faced her and Wheeler as they approached, hands patiently clasped in front of him.

He was a short man, but very handsome, with brown hair parted on the side and gelled back, revealing graying temples and a widow's peak, though not as pronounced as Ginny's. He had a look of extreme confidence—perhaps arrogance; Ginny would have to decide later which it was.

"Madame President, I'm Jodee Keeling. I am so pleased we are able to meet," he said in a strong Australian accent. He took her hand and kissed it.

It's arrogance, thought Ginny, *bordering on pomposity.*

She felt suddenly cut off from the crowd, and noticed that several men and women, seemingly in normal conversation, had created an informal wall between them and the reception. None of them looked over.

She also noticed that Wheeler had disappeared, leaving her alone with this man. "Nice to meet you, Mr. Keeling," Ginny said, taking her hand back, and now more than a little suspicious. "Jeff Wheeler seemed to believe that it was important we spoke. How may I help you?"

She was now also annoyed, mostly at Wheeler, and determined to make this a short conversation.

Keeling ignored her question. "Well, I'm grateful to Jeff Wheeler. He's a dependable young man."

Ginny furrowed her brow, *he's probably only a few years younger than you are,* she thought silently. However, she said nothing, forcing him to get to his point.

He didn't.

"This is a magnificent event, isn't it? he asked, gesturing to the hall around them and apparently not expecting an answer. "China's progress in technology has been staggering, as has its economic growth. This city alone has seen an incredible boom in new construction; I've had the privilege of helping to build a number of skyscrapers here over the past decade, including this one." He looked up to the ceiling and gestured with both hands.

She remained aloof, refusing to be drawn into idle chatter, and now losing her patience entirely. "Mr. Keeling--"

"Please, call me Jodee."

"Mr. Keeling, it was nice to meet you, but I'm afraid I should be--"

"I understand that your meetings today were not as successful as you'd have liked," he said firmly.

Ginny was taken aback. "How— did Jeff Wheeler—?"

"Jeff Wheeler told me absolutely nothing, Madame President. You have my word on that. My sources are my own. Since you won't allow any informal conversation, I'll explain why it is I wanted to speak with you." Keeling's tone had changed completely. He now spoke without emotion. All business.

"I am a very successful businessman—having built several companies and managed major projects in Australia, China, and Southeast Asia. I also represent a group of other successful businessmen who make up an investment syndicate."

Ginny started to get a vague sense of where this might be heading.

"As the situation with the U.S. Congress has taken shape, we have collectively come to the conclusion that there may be an opportunity here."

Keeling paused, yet Ginny still didn't have a full picture of what he was getting at. "Mr. Keeling, are you offering to make a private investment in the Mission to Cerulea?"

Keeling blushed slightly. It was refreshing to see even the tiniest crack in his polished exterior. "I am, Madame President."

This is crazy, Ginny thought. She looked him straight in the eye. "I want to thank you for your interest, Mr. Keeling, but I don't think it would be practical or appropriate to take on private investors—especially before we've identified an alternative source for primary funding."

For a split second, Ginny found herself feeling a modicum of sympathy for this man. His intentions seemed genuine.

"Madame President, let me make myself clear. I am offering up our investment syndicate as a sole source for the funds you seek."

For the second time in the conversation, Ginny was dumbfounded. "Mr. Keeling, perhaps you aren't aware that the Mission will require another 450 billion dollars between now and launch."

"Actually, we'd assumed cost overruns would take the total to something closer to 600 billion." He said matter-of-factly.

Ginny and Keeling stared at one another for several moments without speaking.

"And just how do you and your partners think you're going to get repaid? Let alone earn any kind of return?"

"We don't expect to be repaid; not in cash, anyway. Our interest is very straightforward: We would like intellectual property rights to the technologies that have been developed for the Mission. Nothing more."

"You want to own the technology?"

"Not own it. We would simply like immediate access to the designs of the *Humanity's* drive system, and to several of the on-board systems involved in the ship's operation. And we would require that it not be made available to other commercial entities or to the public for a period of eight years."

"And just what would you use the technology for, Mr. Keeling?"

"Tourism."

"I beg your pardon?"

"Tourism. It is our belief that there is a substantial opportunity to ferry people to the outer reaches of the solar system. Our business plan calls for the construction of a smaller-scale craft that we would use as a cruise ship in space. If our projections are correct, demand will allow us to have 3 or more ships in operation by the time eight years has elapsed. At that juncture, we would have a commanding head start on anyone who wished to launch a competitive venture."

Ginny looked at Jodee Keeling and smiled. He smiled back. She was thinking *either this is all a joke or this man is not playing with a full deck.*

"I'm not a financial expert, but it seems to me that you'd have hard time getting to breakeven in such a venture."

"Perhaps you're aware, Madame President, that people are readily paying over a million dollars apiece just to spend a week in a space hotel within barking distance of our own atmosphere. Think of how they'd value a trip that took them through the rings of Saturn, or to the moons of Jupiter.

"And you think there are enough people who'd be interested in such a journey to fill three ships?"

"Our research tells us that there's enough for a fairly large fleet of ships; three is just to start. Don't discount just how much wealth is swimming around on this planet; it's substantial."

Ginny looked into Keeling's eyes and squinted a bit, attempting to discern just who—or what—she was dealing with. On the one hand it all seemed preposterous; on the other, somewhat intriguing.

"Madame President, if you have no objections, I would like very much to send to your attention some information on our syndicate and our plan. I'm confident that, after you take a closer look—and perform some due diligence on me and my partners—you'll conclude that our offer is quite genuine."

"Well, I suppose I would not object to having my team take a closer look."

"That's all I could ask for. Madame President, I want to thank you ever so much for speaking with me this evening."

He held out his hand. She paused ever so slightly, then shook it.

"I must say, our discussion certainly added an interesting twist to the occasion. Good evening, Jodee."

Ginny turned and nearly collided with Jeff Wheeler, who had appeared seemingly out of nowhere by their side. He offered to take Ginny back to her escort, who was expecting her at their assigned table for dinner.

As they made their way across the hall, Ginny remained mildly annoyed by Wheeler's behavior, but she decided to confront him at some other time.

Meanwhile, while not in any way embracing Keeling's offer as anything other than a strange and remote possibility, Ginny still couldn't help but feel her mood improve.

It always feels good to have an offer in your pocket, even one as crazy as that she mused.

79.

36 hours later, Ginny, Belechenko and Jeff Wheeler were gaining altitude over the flat, arid wasteland that used to be the Aral Sea. They had just taken off from the Baykonur Cosmodrome, where the Commander had inspected some reworked solar panels that had failed upon their initial installation and were now being shipped back to L5 and the *Humanity*.

Although Gerhardt Schmidt's team had the situation well covered, Belechenko had wanted to make the stop as a morale booster for the Baykonur team.

They would also be stopping in Brussels for a half-day of meetings with European Union officials. While it was clear that the EU would not be in a position to compensate for the lost U.S. funding, they were willing to provide a slight increase in their contribution as a symbolic gesture. Ginny felt it was important to celebrate any and all such gestures in order to demonstrate momentum, and to get other nations thinking about increasing their own participation.

Ginny, Belechenko, and Jeff Wheeler sat in the small conference room of the CNAMC-V60 airliner. Many jokes had been made during the trip comparing their Chinese plane to Air Force Bravo, but overall it was very comfortable, and Ginny had reminded them all several times that they were lucky to have it.

They were engaged in a conference call with Roger Tucker in Washington; after covering several Mission status issues, they were just getting to the topic of the day.

"Okay," said Ginny. "The testing results are good news; we'll be sure to use it in Brussels. If you can, have someone whip up some nice visuals we can use during our meetings.

"I'll take care of it," Roger responded.

"Now, let's get to it, have you had a chance to digest the proposal?"

Within one hour of Ginny's conversation with Jodee Keeling at the reception in Chonqing, Mission Headquarters had received the proposal from his syndicate. It arrived electronically, but was followed shortly by 10 hardbound copies – each with a beautifully embossed cover, and printed on expensive, varnished stock.

It was clear that they had shipped before Ginny had even met Keeling.

"We've been over this thing backwards and forwards," Roger remarked, "and I've got 3 people doing nothing other than background research on the players involved."

"And?" Ginny prompted. "What are your first thoughts?"

"Well, it's an interesting proposal," Roger said glibly, teasing his audience.

"Roger, c'mon. Let's hear it."

"Madame President, I've got to tell you, these guys seem legitimate. Based on your description of the conversation, I was expecting something pretty flaky. But they seem to have a well-thought-out plan."

Ginny, Belechenko and Wheeler looked at one another in mild shock.

"Roger, you mean to say that you don't see any red flags or issues?"

"Oh I didn't say that. There are issues, but they're not showstoppers."

"Tell us more, Roger," requested Belechenko. "Red flags worry me."

Ginny was the only one to laugh.

"We've identified several issues that'll have to be worked," Roger stated. "The first is that they are offering the funds in four traunches, but are asking for full access to the technology up front."

"Um, Roger, could you tell me what a traunch is?" Ginny asked.

"Oh, sure. It means one installment of an investment. Often times, investors will stagger their investment in accordance with specific milestones of a project. Once a milestone's been reached, the next traunch will be made available."

"But these investors do not care about our mission, do they? They are only interested in the technology," Belechenko noted, seeking clarification.

"That's true," responded Roger. "That's why it's a red flag."

"Okay, what are the other issues?" asked Ginny.

"Issue number two is not a big deal – I think. It's the fact that approximately fifty percent of the funds will come from silent partners."

"Is this a bad thing?" asked Belechenko.

"Not necessarily," Roger replied, "but it means, in this case, that we will not know the actual source of the funds at the time we make the deal; or rather, if we make the deal."

"Doesn't it mean we would never know where the funds came from?" Wheeler asked.

"Actually Jeff, it might mean never, or it might mean that we learn some horrible truth after the fact, at exactly the wrong time, and all hell breaks loose."

"Not if there are appropriate confidentiality clauses in the contract," Wheeler responded.

"In my experience, leaks don't pay a hell of a lot of respect to confidentiality agreements," Roger said firmly. "In fact - "

"Tell you what," Ginny interrupted. "Let's get everything on the table; then we'll argue the fine points of each."

"All right. Issue number three is a stated limit on our use of the technology."

"They want to limit our use of the technology? That doesn't sound right," Ginny said cautiously.

"Well, they would require that we use the Alcubierre SEC drive for the journey to Cerulea, and on no more than three other missions, each including a single departure from Earth."

"I don't understand," said Belechenko.

"This is, in essence, a clever way of inserting what's known as a non-compete clause into the agreement. By limiting our use of the technology, but not getting highly detailed as to what we can or can't do with it, they are ensuring that we can't compete with them."

Ginny chuckled. "Hell, the odds of us getting sufficient resources for just one more mission are zero to nil; forget about three. That one doesn't bother me much. Roger, what else?"

"There's just one more." He said.

"What is it?" Ginny demanded.

"The proposal expires in thirty days."

80.

Naj gave himself a push and floated up a ladder to a small landing. He placed the sole of his right shoe into a magnetic socket to anchor himself, and offered his palm to the reader for identification. He spent a minute or two entering notes into the ship's log, then pulled his foot free, hit a button to log off, and pushed himself along another ladder to where his maglev waited.

He had come to enjoy this routine. Making rounds in each of the *Humanity's* several engine compartments was quiet, peaceful work. It allowed Naj to relax and clear his mind. As often as not, he would be accompanied by one or maybe two engineers from his team, but even then it was a far cry from the frenetic pace of the bridge.

He was becoming more comfortable at the helm, but command of something as massive and complex as the *Humanity* still made him nervous—the fear of screwing up was like a woodpecker inside his brain, constantly pecking at his confidence. But he knew it was mostly a matter of time. Besides, of the eight officers trained for bridge command, he was pretty sure that he was one of the best—next to Jim, of course. Jim took to it like a salmon to a stream; he was born to it.

He pulled himself down into the maglev and buckled in, then instructed the vehicle to take him to the next station on his route.

The *Humanity* was traveling out just beyond the Kuiper belt, a ring of some 100,000 objects on the outskirts of the solar system. Earlier in the day, Naj had gotten a close up view of Xena, a dwarf planet in our solar system, discovered in 2005. Of course, the crew knew it was officially Eris, but all had decided to use its more playful nickname instead.

Aside from such incredible views, life on the ship had assumed a rhythm that was unrelated to their location in space. It was starting to feel like home. And, although the crew compliment was large, it was beginning to feel like family.

Naj had often thought about the day when the *Humanity* would leave Earth's orbit for the last time, never to return. But he'd now been on board full time for over two months, and it seemed, to some extent, like they'd already left.

After finishing up his rounds, he made his way to the torus access module mid-ship, and headed back to the bridge.

Once he arrived, the officer on duty asked him to take the helm a few minutes early, and Naj obliged. He logged in and began scanning the panel to grab a snapshot of the ship's status. Everything appeared to be within normal operating parameters.

Jia Xian Shang approached, handed him a tablet, then waited for him to give it a look. He took the device and browsed the summarized report. It was a request from one of the on-board research scientists to move one of her experiments to a small antechamber halfway down spoke number three of the rear torus. The experiment had offered some interesting results at 1G, and she wanted to repeat it in an environment with less gravity.

Naj gave it some thought, as Jia Xian waited. *Should I wait and ask Jim?* Thought Naj. *No. He'd only ask me what I think, then support my answer.* The antechambers were rarely used access points for system modules that were controlled elsewhere, and had several small bays each where such work could be conducted. *But would Jim object?* Naj asked himself one last time. *No, damn it! He'd be annoyed if I bothered him with it.*

"This is fine, ensign." He punched into the tablet what amounted to his digital signature, and handed it back to Jia Xian. "By the way, I thought you did an excellent job on the forward drive adjustments. I was very impressed by your report."

Jia Xian gave a wide smile. "Thank you Lieutenant. I didn't know you'd seen my report."

"Of course I did. Good work." Naj said firmly. Smiling still, she bowed her head slightly and departed.

Jim had been after Naj to use positive reinforcement more often when working with his team, and he was starting to get the hang of it.

An alarm sounded on one of the panel screens. Naj looked to see the cause, and observed that the water reserve had dropped below threshold.

At that moment, Jim entered the bridge. Naj saw him out of the corner of his eye, but forced himself to remain focused.

He punched a button on the console in front of him. "Station six, confirm alarm on water reserve."

"Bridge, that's confirmed. Reserve is six percent below threshold."

Naj could feel Jim's presence behind him, and the eyes of everyone on the bridge watching Jim watch him. While the alarm was not serious or threatening in any way, handling an alarm of any kind was an event by which all bridge command officers would be judged.

"Station six, let's bring auxiliary water conduits Delta, Echo and Foxtrot online, then shut down conduits Juliet, Kilo and Lima."

There was momentary silence as his orders were carried out. "Bridge: conduits D, E and F now online; J, K and L are offline."

"Station six, check primary and secondary valves on J, K and L, clean or replace any malfunctioning units, and log a report by 2100."

"Roger that, bridge."

Naj spoke more casually: "And Yvonne, you might start with the secondary on Lima; after last week's pressure test I thought I felt a small vibration just behind the valve. My guess is that's your culprit."

"Understood, Lieutenant Malik. Station six out."

Jim came forward; "Lieutenant, I wanted to ask if you'd give her a final test at 95 percent. We held 88 last week for four hours, and after a full systems check, I think it's time we took her up to top cruising speed. Perhaps for two hours or so. Report back to me when the test is complete."

"Yes, Captain. Any special course?"

"Your choice, lieutenant," Jim said, turning to leave the bridge. "But wherever it is you take her, I'll expect you to knock the barnacles off the hull."

"Yes, sir."

As he passed by, he put his hand on Naj's shoulder and squeezed gently, a small gesture that few on the bridge noticed.

But Naj understood fully.

81.

The giant arm and hand reached skyward out of the earth. The man's bearded face, just poking out of the ground, seemed to cry out in anguish. His other hand just broke the surface, while further away, a knee of one leg and the foot of another was visible.

To a visitor unaware that the statue was called "The Awakening," it was not at all clear whether the man was straining to rise, or whether he was just about to sink into the depths.

Perhaps that's a good metaphor for this country, thought Jeff Wheeler, as he strolled down toward Haynes Point at the tip of East Potomac Park. It was a beautiful spring day; two children ran past him, trying to will a kite into the air on a day when the wind would not cooperate. Several people were washing their cars along the roadway; a common practice in the park that Jeff always found a little strange.

He walked through the statue between the head and arm. A young girl was standing on the statue's beard, staring into his open mouth. For some reason, he thought of his sister, with whom he used to play for hours on the large rocks in the woods behind their house in Windfall, Indiana. He thought of his father, the pastor of their church, who would come home from work and holler for them from the back door. They would hide behind the rocks until he would eventually come out and play with them.

The little girl turned to look at him. He looked away, and continued walking toward the railing and the river.

There was no particular reason he had come to the Park today. In fact, there were several spots far more discreet from which to conduct the meeting.

But he'd felt claustrophobic, and wanted some fresh air. He'd worked at the White House for about a year, and had now logged roughly three months at Mission Headquarters. Roger Tucker was a pretty good boss; he had to admit that he respected Roger's abilities and enjoyed their day to day interactions. He had also come to admire Virginia Belknap a great deal; she was not the dogmatic progressive that so many in the conservative camp felt her to be.

But deep down, Wheeler knew she was wrong - she might mean well, but her view of the world and what she and the Council believed to be the best course for the Mission was badly flawed. There would be no meaning or purpose to the

Mission without God at its center; it frustrated him that virtually everyone at Mission Headquarters refused to acknowledge this.

And Roger Tucker – though an intelligent, capable guy – was living a shameful lifestyle that defiled human nature. It was only by methodically blocking out Roger's unnatural choice and pretending it didn't exist that Wheeler could engage in a normal working relationship with the man.

Wheeler reached the end of the park. He rested his forearms on the railing and looked out on the river.

Two small sailboats moved lazily across the broad expanse of the Potomac; above them in the sky a large jetliner softly descended toward Reagan National Airport.

Wheeler's phone rang. Not his wristphone, but a separate unit in his coat pocket—this one without a wireless earpiece. He took it out and activated the call.

"Right on time," Wheeler said with little emotion.

"Okay, so tell me where things stand," said the man on the other end of the call. "Let's start with China."

Wheeler could hear other voices in the background. He made no assumptions, and asked no questions. "I think it's safe to say they received a firm rejection from the Chinese government. The only way the Chinese would even consider it would be if they owned it; besides, the timeline just doesn't allow it. For all practical purposes, China is seen as a dry well."

"That's good to hear. We'd gotten some intelligence that the Chinese government offered a deal and that Belknap and her Russian Romeo were giving it serious consideration."

Wheeler tried to ignore the slight on Belechenko, a man he held in high esteem. "Negative," he responded. "I can assure you the Council will not be heading down that path."

"All right then. Let's move on to the proposal. How was it received?"

"Well, I've got to tell you that your Australian partner didn't make the greatest impression. But the proposal was given immediate attention."

"And?"

"And it was well-received. In fact I'd say that it's currently seen as the only real option."

"Great. Now how about the terms; any issues?"

"After the initial review, it looks like there are four issues: payment schedule, the silent partners, limits on technology usage, and the expiration date. But I don't think any are seen as showstoppers."

"Hmmm. The only one of those that's non-negotiable is silent partners. What's their concern?"

"In a word? Scandal. They're worried that, if the silent partners were revealed at some point, it could potentially cause a major backlash."

"Ain't that the truth," the man said as much to himself as to Wheeler. "If that becomes a big issue, there's not a hell of a lot we can do. What's your overall take on their negotiating posture?"

"I think they'll make a show of pushing back on these and possibly some other issues as the proposal goes through further review," Wheeler said earnestly.

"Last question: do they have any leads for getting the funds elsewhere?"

"Not really. There's a chance they'll get a few participating nations to up their contribution, but none of it will amount to much."

"Excellent. And since we all know that these folks will never back down from this mission unless they hit an absolute dead end, I'd say we have them exactly where we want them."

Wheeler felt himself getting angry at this last remark, an emotion he found curious. *Perhaps I'm growing too attached to these people* he told himself; but he didn't allow himself to give it much thought. "What else can I tell you?"

"I think that should do it for today," came the reply. "Let's connect again in three days, same time."

"Understood." Wheeler said, and then heard the line disconnect.

He placed the phone in his pocket.

He leaned back on the railing and watched a sightseeing boat head up the river. He forced a number of thoughts out of his mind, and pretended that the empty feeling in his stomach had something to do with a light breakfast.

82.

"Mr. Victor, your guest has cleared security and is now waiting for you in the East Lobby."

"Thank you, Teresa, I'll be right there."

Mike Victor logged off his system, and headed out of the lab. Everything around him looked and smelled brand new; though it seemed a bit childish, he was kind of looking forward to showing the place off.

The new headquarters of Verintel Corporation had recently been completed on West Drive in Fairfax, Virginia. It was architecturally spectacular, a cool blue-glass pyramidal pentagon overlooking Providence Park.

The ostentatious design was a noted departure from virtually all of the company's branch offices, each of which attempted to blend in with its immediate surroundings to the greatest extent possible.

The company had quietly grown from a small firm focused on credit card verification services into one the world's largest private intelligence companies, and one of the most profitable companies on the Fortune 500. Its business focus was not unique; in fact, governments worldwide—as well as other corporations—now depended on a growing number of such agencies for their intelligence needs.

The primary business of these firms was to derive so called "open source intelligence." This was information found on the internet, in professional journals, books, video, and included credit reports, financial records, criminal records—anything relevant to their clients' informational needs. Verintel, however, had upped the ante, using a sprawling global network of human intelligence assets to evaluate threats, conduct detailed surveillance, and perform background research on anything or anyone on behalf of their numerous clients.

Mike Victor had joined the company about a month after leaving the White House, not without some trepidation. While the industry was now regulated, it was no secret that Verintel and its competitors were often accused of both minor and major ethical violations in their quest to serve client needs.

But in the end, he came to the conclusion that this was the business he was in, and of the many compelling offers he'd received—from other companies as well as the CIA, DIA and FBI, Verintel seemed no worse, though perhaps no better, than the others.

Besides, the company was known in the industry as a pioneer of new, state-of-the-art technology, and after nearly a decade in government, albeit the White House, he was eager to work in an environment with fewer budgetary constraints. It hadn't hurt that Verintel was paying him literally three times his previous salary.

Although Mike's job did not call for him to bring in new business, his bosses had been impressed when, just two weeks ago, he had been single-handedly responsible for landing an impressive new client.

It was this client who was now waiting in the lobby.

A moment later, Mike came around the corner and smiled broadly. "Roger! Great to see you!"

"Likewise, Mike." The two bowed warmly. "This place makes the White House Intelligence facility look like a high school science lab," Roger joked. "How are you enjoying it?"

"So far, so good. Some interesting projects, smart people, and amazing new toys," Mike grinned.

"I'll bet." They chatted easily for bit, mostly small talk about their new lives since leaving the White House.

Well, I burned fifteen minutes getting through your security," Roger eventually declared, "so perhaps we should dig in."

Mike led Roger through several security doors and down several hallways. At each door, Mike and Roger both had to present both palm and retina to gain entrance.

They settled in to the assigned conference room, meticulously appointed with sleek black chairs, a glass table, and array of wondrous screens and gadgets. They were joined by Rex Starden, one of Mike's colleagues from the financial intelligence group, or Fintel as it was known internally.

After introductions and some discussion of their methods, Mike zeroed in on what he knew to be Roger's primary interest. "All of our preliminary research indicates that Mr. Keeling and his two known partners are fairly clean, but we have uncovered some interesting details. Rex will take it from here."

Rex Starden cleared his throat and started to speak. As he did so, the room dimmed and a screen at the front of the room came to life, providing visuals relevant to Starden's report. No one in the room seemed to have hit a button or signaled in any way, and Roger had no idea how the technology was controlled. He decided not to ask, and simply focused on the presentation.

Starden had a chiseled face and the strong, commanding voice of a military officer. He wore a crisp, light blue oxford shirt and red silk foulard tie.

"Keeling's claim that he represents an investment fund of 600 billion dollars appears credible. We have confirmed that accounts connected to the fund currently contain roughly half that amount, and we're assuming the other half is available through capital calls—a common arrangement under which his investors, or limited partners, will make the additional funds available when they're needed.

"Two of these limited partners are identified in the proposal: both are high net worth individuals, and both are fairly well-respected businessmen with little to hide. However, in the context of the total investment being proposed, they are relatively small players. Based on our research, we are estimating their combined net worth at around 95 billion. Thus, it's doubtful that they are providing much more than fifty billion—or just over eight percent—of the total amount. And frankly, I'd be very surprised if they were putting even that much on the line for a venture with this much risk.

"Now as for Keeling," Starden continued, "The man has done very well for himself, and, like his partners, can count himself among the very rich. However, here again, our investigation indicates that Mr. Keeling's assets total at most 80 billion. Subtracting other documented financial commitments, we feel it's highly unlikely that he's contributing much more than 45 billion to the pool."

Roger looked confused.

"What Rex is saying," Mike interjected, "is that Keeling and the two partners mentioned in the proposal probably represent less than 16 percent of the total investment. The silent partners are contributing the rest."

"Got it," said Roger. "So what do we know about them?"

"Well, let me walk you through what we've learned thus far," Starden suggested. "Keeling has spent the bulk of his career transacting real estate deals in Southeast Asia. He also founded several companies to support his development projects. All of which appear to have been legitimate and profitable.

"However, one very ambitious project was a skyscraper in Brisbane that got into trouble."

"How so?" Roger asked.

"Well, the project was gigantic – he bought out roughly five city blocks, and began construction on a two million square foot tower, surrounded by a twenty-acre park, on top of a huge underground parking facility. Our sources tell us that Keeling's team badly underestimated the engineering costs, the project was severely delayed, and two anchor tenants pulled out. Here's where it gets interesting: Keeling was about to default on over 100 billion in financing; and just when it looked like he had no choice but bankruptcy, he secured a major investment from a private source, completed the building, found new tenants, then sold the property to a Japanese conglomerate at modest profit.

"On two subsequent projects, Keeling again used private financing from an undisclosed source.

"We've managed to ascertain that the private source making these investments is a holding company wholly owned by a single individual—a man named James Torgan, the grandson of Roland Torgan."

"Roland Torgan," Roger repeated the name. "The South African guy with the diamond fortune?"

"Precisely. He bought up dozens of what were believed to be exhausted mines, then employed a new technology to extract sizable deposits. He became the number two supplier, then divested just months before the market crashed in 2015. We believe his grandson James, who inherited most of Torgan's fortune when Roland died in 2026, is one of the silent partners behind Keeling's proposal to the Mission Council. We estimate that he's easily capable of providing up to 200 billion in capital."

"Interesting," Roger noted. "And should that be of concern?"

"We don't believe so, but the real answer is—we don't know yet. There's more work to do on James Torgan's past dealings, which seemed to have been conducted with extreme secrecy. We do know that he's made relatively small investments in an array of different companies and new ventures. These include several telecom companies, a toll road privatization project, and two mining companies. These transactions are all detailed in our preliminary report.

"We still haven't figured out where he's invested the bulk of his capital; and we have yet to figure out who the other partners are. We also want to better understand why these gentlemen have a sudden interest in the space tourism business."

"Didn't I read in the proposal that Keeling's connected to that space hotel?" Roger asked.

"Yes." Answered Mike. "Keeling and one of his partners have made investments in Astral Adventures, but they were made quite recently, and represent pretty small amounts."

"Then I guess you guys still have your work cut out for you."

Roger was presented with both a hardcopy of their report, along with an electronic version on an encrypted drive.

Rex thanked Roger for his business, and noted that he was looking forward to bringing him additional information at their next meeting.

Mike and Roger chatted as they made their way back to the lobby.

"Here's the problem, Mike," Roger confided. "We're on a pretty short leash here, and we may have to pull the trigger on this thing before you guys are done with your investigation."

"I wish we could move faster, but the Fintel guys say this might take six to eight weeks in total."

They reached the lobby and Roger turned to face Mike. "Right, so the question is, what can you tell me now as to whether these guys are clean?"

Mike hesitated. "Roger, I can only repeat what we just reviewed at the meeting. As of now there is no clear indication--"

"Mike!" Roger said urgently. "I know it's not your style, but I need your best guess from what you've seen so far."

Mike again hesitated, this time for several moments. "Look, in my experience, it's very dangerous to draw premature conclusions." Roger moved to interrupt again but Mike raised his hand to silence him. "But here goes: so far, there is virtually no indication that these guys are attached to any scandal, or that their proposal is anything other than sincere."

"Then why does there seem to be so much secrecy to their business transactions?"

"I'll admit it's frustrating, but in this day and age, that level of secrecy is not at all uncommon."

Roger looked him in the eye. "So you're saying that, so far, these guys look legitimate?"

Roger could see the extent to which his question pained his old White House colleague. "Let me put it this way: given the information gathered thus far, there is no reason to think they are not legitimate."

Roger smiled, and put a hand on Mike's shoulder. "Thanks. I know that wasn't easy."

"But remember, more data might lead us to a different conclusion."

Roger laughed, and Mike finally smiled. Roger told him to call him anytime day or night if more data made itself available, and Mike agreed.

They nodded their farewells, and Roger headed back down to the first floor for another exhaustive security check before leaving the building.

83.

Despite the fact that the meeting was limited to voting members, the room was abuzz with a dozen or more spontaneous conversations. Up to this point, the very existence of the proposal, let alone any specifics had been known only to a select few on the Council. Thus, the presentation just delivered by Roger Tucker to the Mission Council had come as a shock to most in attendance.

Ginny looked around the table and noted the infusion of energy into a group whose mood had, of late, been less than buoyant.

Roger returned to his chair between Ginny and Jeff Wheeler. "Well, it looks like we've certainly stirred the beehive," he noted.

"I'll say. It's good to see this team alive again," Ginny exclaimed.

"Let's just hope, Madame President, that all this energy is positive."

Roger had just presented the outlines of the proposal from Keeling's syndicate. He'd done his level best to describe the risks, the unknowns, and the possible benefits of accepting their money.

He'd also done so on precious little sleep. Negotiating the closing documents over the past couple of weeks had demanded long days and extensive travel; he'd only last night returned from Hong Kong. The two sides were close, and Roger thought that it might be possible to get the deal done very soon - provided the Mission Council gave it a thumbs-up.

After allowing several minutes of side discussions, Ginny reached forward and gaveled the meeting to silence.

"I'd like to preface our deliberation with a reminder. At the outset of his presentation, Mr. Tucker noted the sensitivity of the information discussed. I want to remind everyone that it is imperative that we keep this proposal confidential until we make our decision. Does anyone here believe that, for any reason, they will be unable to fulfill their obligation in this regard?" Ginny looked around the table, making eye contact with all members. She of course did not expect anyone to speak up, but wanted to ensure that her request had the appropriate psychological impact.

"Good. Let's proceed; the floor is now open for comments or questions."

Several hands went up.

"The Chair recognizes Ms. Eckert" Ginny said formally.

Hilde Eckert was Germany's envoy to the Council, and had been instru-
mental during their recent trip to Brussels in convincing the EU to up their funding level.

"Madame President, fellow Council members. I am concerned that the
funding would not come all at one time. It seems to me that, if there were any
disruptions, we might find ourselves here again looking for new funding partners.
Do you not share such concern, Madame President?" Hilde spoke with a strong
German accent, but her English was excellent.

"This was certainly a concern when we received the proposal," Ginny
responded, "but I believe we have successfully negotiated a solution. I would ask
Mr. Tucker to elaborate."

Roger nodded to Ginny, and turned to the group. "Ms. Eckert, Council
members. The proposal does call for the funding to be made available in stages,
but I'm pleased to report that we have identified a means for dramatically reducing the risk of not receiving it all up front.

"The agreement, as it stands today, would assess a substantial penalty on
the investors should they fail to produce funds per the schedule I outlined."

"And can you tell us what is this penalty?" Hilde Eckert inquired.

Given that they were still in active negotiations, Roger was hesitant to discuss details; he looked at Ginny for guidance, who subtly nodded. Roger looked
back at Eckert.

"Should the syndicate be unable to produce the funds, their rights to the
technology would be voided, and any monies previously delivered to the Council
would convert to a 100-year low interest loan. In short, the investors appear to
have no plans to renege on the deal once signed."

A number of other members indicated their desire to speak. Ginny recognized
Baingana Wulandari, in charge of developing the educational system for Cerulea.

"Madame President, Mr. Tucker, Council members," he began. "I do not
fully understand why there must be silent partners. Does this not present additional risk? Should we not insist on knowing who these silent partners are?"

Ginny deferred again: "Roger?"

"Mr. Wulandari, you are right in asserting that this presents additional
risk. Unfortunately, it has been made very clear that, if we demand to know the
identities of all investors, then they would not be interested in the deal. This is, to
use an American idiom, a showstopper.

"Therefore, if the Council believes that the existence of silent partners is
unacceptable, then we must decline the investment. If we allow it, then we must
accept the risk."

"And how would you characterize the risk, Mr. Tucker?" Wulandari asked.

"Well, if it's revealed at some future date that one of the investors is some-how involved in unsavory or illegal activities, I believe we'd have a scandal on our hands. But frankly, if that were to happen months or years after the *Humanity* has launched, it may not matter."

There were general murmurs of agreement with Roger's last point. Ginny recognized Suzu Nakamura, Japan's envoy to the Council. He was an engineer by training, and was actually a working member of the energy and environmental planning team, headed by his countryman, Jiro Kawamoto.

"Madame President, Council members. I am confused regarding our allowed use of the technology. There appear to be strict limits on how many times we may employ the SEC drive engine, and yet these investors may use it in an unlimited fashion for an infinite period of time. Do we think this is a fair arrange-ment?"

Ginny smiled. "No, we do not think that is a fair arrangement. We have stated our desire for any limit on our use of the technology to expire after eight years, the point at which their limited exclusivity ends. While we have not yet settled this point, the investor group has indicated its tentative acceptance of this condition."

Georges Ventine, who was in Washington for just three days before he would have to return to the *Humanity*, asked to be heard.

"Madame President, Council members. I believe you noted that the inves-tor's offer had an expiration date. When is this deadline?"

"The offer expires in three days," Ginny responded, eliciting a few expres-sions of surprise from the group. "I am confident that, given the seriousness of our negotiations, Mr. Keeling and his partners will not object if this deadline is missed by a day or two. However, I think the more important issue is how long we can continue to use all available resources as we move toward launch without ade-quate financial backing. As it now stands, we have exhausted most of our existing funding; so the deadline for us to secure a commitment is also fast approaching."

"Madame President," Ventine rejoined, "may I ask whether we have identi-fied any other alternatives?"

"Monsieur Ventine, you may indeed ask that question," Ginny said cordially. "Unfortunately, the answer is that, at this juncture, we have implied commitments for increased funding from several nations, but on their own these incremental contributions would not even begin to cover our needs." Ginny paused, and drew a deep breath. "In short, if we wish to maintain our current schedule, Mr. Keeling's offer is our only option."

The Council continued to discuss various aspects of the investment and the consequences of delaying launch to find other funding sources.

Some on the council believed that accepting private financing was inappropriate for a mission that was clearly a global effort. Others noted that what made it global was the involvement of so many nations; the fact that literally dozens of countries could be proud of their contribution to one or more elements of the Mission, while dozens more were represented on the crew. The money, it was argued, was almost inconsequential.

After several hours of deliberation, Ginny asked for an informal, non-binding vote from the Council members. Roughly 80 percent were in agreement, but she wanted greater consensus. They then spent another hour and a half listening to and discussing the specific concerns of the minority. All the while Roger took careful notes; within the member's comments were good substantive recommendations as to how certain terms and conditions of the agreement might be negotiated.

Roger and Jeff Wheeler started working up a set of conditions put forth by the council that, if agreed to by the investors, would satisfy those who'd previously been opposed.

This list was the source of much debate; but by early evening it had stabilized, and Ginny felt it was time to ask for a formal vote.

As a dramatic sunset spread across the sky, framed by the expansive glass wall of the chamber, the roll was called. One by one, each member offered their vote in favor of accepting the proposal.

It was unanimous.

The Council members erupted in applause; some shook hands, others embraced one another, while all laughed and carried on for another half hour before finally retiring for the night.

☯

As midnight came and went, Roger Tucker, alone in his office and now running on nothing but adrenaline, was on the line with Keeling's lawyers in Hong Kong, outlining the list of new conditions that had emanated from the Council's deliberations.

During the call, the lawyers had put Roger on hold several times to caucus amongst themselves as they considered these new demands. They made it clear that certain conditions might be unacceptable, and tried to negotiate some items off the list.

Roger held firm. While he was willing to allow minor modifications to several conditions, and let the lawyers alter the phrasing of a few others, he had repeatedly insisted that any substantive changes to these terms would require that the Council reconvene and conduct another vote. He had not mentioned, of course, that the Council vote had been unanimous. In fact, he implied that there were those on the Council who did not fully embrace this deal, and that a second vote might be risky.

Finally, at around 3 am in Washington—3 pm in Hong Kong—after each condition had been carefully discussed and reworded multiple times, and relevant sections of the agreement had traveled back and forth from screen to screen, the two sides seemed to reach an impasse.

Roger then played what amounted to the final card in his hand; he noted that, in light of their inability to reach an agreement on various terms, he would seek to schedule another meeting of the Council—possibly within one or two weeks. He stated clearly that the deadline would, of course, have to be pushed back.

Keeling's lawyers asked for some time for discussion, and Roger was left on hold for close to fifteen minutes. Finally, the lead attorney came back on the line.

"Mr. Tucker, if it were somehow possible for us to accept the conditions as we've structured them in our last revision, would our negotiations be complete?"

Roger swallowed hard. This had been exactly the outcome he'd desired. He felt his adrenaline surge once more, and, overcoming a sudden and predictable bout of cold feet, he answered the question.

"Yes. If you accept the most recent changes I sent you about 30 minutes ago—let's see, that would be... revision 4.3—then we would be done negotiating, and the Council would be fully prepared to execute the agreement."

"All right, then, Mr. Tucker. We have a deal."

84.

"So you're saying they're going to sew this thing up tonight?" asked the voice in Jeff Wheeler's ear.

"Unless something happens to screw it up," Wheeler explained, "the signing of the agreement is scheduled for 6 pm."

Wheeler switched the phone from one ear to the other. He was sitting alone in his living room looking out a window up at the sidewalk and the incessant rain that had been falling for two days.

He had a Georgetown address that many would envy, but it was actually a basement apartment. The townhouse above him was a stunning monument to Georgetown excess; his apartment was no such thing.

As he watched the rain, he saw someone stop outside the window. He couldn't see the man's upper half; just his legs from the waist down were visible. The man was wearing dark gray trousers and a long khaki-colored overcoat.

"So what does that mean regarding a public announcement?" asked his confederate.

"Hold on a sec," Wheeler said quietly.

The man at the window hadn't moved, and Wheeler got up to take a closer look. He approached the window from the side, and carefully peered around the curtain.

The man was holding a leash, at the end of which was a very small dog, who was relieving himself next to the tree outside Wheeler's front door. Perhaps sensing Wheeler's presence, the dog quickly finished his business, and the pair moved on.

Wheeler silently frowned. This had happened more than once, and—perhaps due to the fact that he looked up at the sidewalk from his apartment—he found it personally insulting. He walked back to his chair and sat down.

"Sorry. Where were we?" Wheeler asked.

"Everything okay?" the voice in his ear inquired, sensing Wheeler's momentary silence might imply some sort of security issue.

"Everything's fine. False alarm. Oh yeah, the announcement," Wheeler remembered. "Probably the day after tomorrow. As I mentioned on our last call, although the financing is the headliner, we'll be making a number of announcements."

The Council had been busy. Since their deliberations on the outside investment earlier in the week, they had met again just yesterday to approve the Cerulean Constitution and finalize all functional plans.

"As I recall, you're announcing the approval of the Constitution. Walk me
through the others so I can take them down."

Wheeler was baffled by this seemingly cavalier treatment of an impending
event that, frankly, depressed the hell out of him. *After all,* he thought to himself,
isn't our whole objective here to prevent that Constitution from ever being implemented?
Perhaps the strategy was to wait until the Council had fully digested the financing
hook before anyone would start putting tension on the line.

Since he knew this man was not the one making decisions, he refrained
from asking questions or engaging in any debate on the subject.

"Well, the Council has also just approved all of the major plans for life on
the new planet—including those for education, energy, and agriculture. We'll also
be releasing a revised final schedule for the launch."

"What's the date on that?"

"The launch itself is now scheduled for June 12."

"Got it. Anything else I should know?"

"I think that about covers it," Wheeler concluded.

"All right. If there are any material changes in what we've discussed, send
me a priority message with as much detail as possible. I'll then contact you on your
secure phone as soon as I can. Otherwise, we'll reconnect in three days time."

"Understood."

"And Jeff," the voice said, "get some rest. You sound wiped out."

"Thanks. I think I will."

Wheeler heard the line drop. He ended the call on his end and placed the
special phone on the coffee table in front of him.

He leaned back in his chair and stared at it, wondering what the grand plan
was. He'd been providing inside information from the Belknap administration and
now from the Mission Council in the belief that he was helping to defeat what he
truly believed to be a wrong-headed and morally bankrupt plan for the first new
human civilization since the discovery of America. Now, it seemed that, despite
their efforts, the Mission might just move forward in its horribly flawed state.

Wheeler knew that he was just a cog in a larger machine; his contact's non-
chalance was most likely the result of simply knowing the end-game. As he closed
his eyes and began drifting off to sleep, he tried to reassure himself that up the
chain, there must be smart, well-positioned players who would see to it that the
right outcome prevailed.

If that wasn't the case, he wasn't sure what he'd do.

85.

The elevator doors opened and a family with three small children entered. The doors closed again, and the car continued its downward path.

No one spoke but the littlest child, a girl roughly 3 years old. She was chatting to her self and her mother in German—apparently about all the things she might have for breakfast, as she circled her mother's legs incessantly. Her mother looked at Randall Reese and smiled. Reese knew the smile; it said *I'm sorry for my daughter's rambling—but isn't she the cutest thing you ever saw?*

Actually, thought Reese, *she's irritating and poorly disciplined.* But he said nothing and smiled back.

Reese and Condon were in Berlin. Over the past two weeks, they had also traveled to Tokyo, Beijing, and Moscow; still to come were Dubai, Paris and London. They had met with countless government officials and religious leaders in an attempt to foster support for the Butler administration's insistence that the Mission Council be re-structured to better reflect the key values so important to Reese and conservatives worldwide.

A secondary objective, but one no less important, was to ensure that every major government contemplating an increase in their contribution to the mission fully appreciate the likely repercussions. In short, if Reese and Condon couldn't bring them over to their side, they could at least try and scare them away from that of their perceived opponents.

As their trip unfolded, it was clear that the emphasis had been on the latter. While they had met with great success in generating more active and vocal support among religious leaders, conservatives, and the devout, their discussions with political and government figures all devolved quickly into veiled threats against improper actions—clearly signaling that a new and darker day had dawned in the relationships between the U.S. and other nations.

Reese watched the floor numbers illuminate as the elevator descended. About half way down, he felt his wristphone pulse. He brought his hand up, pulled back the cuff, and hit a button to see the message. His eyes narrowed. He threw a quick glance at Condon, who was staring at the ceiling. Reese then accessed an updated news summary and began to rapidly page through the top stories to find the one he was after. His fingers finally stopped, and he simply stared at the small display.

The doors opened at the lobby, and the family exited, the little girl still talking a blue streak. But Reese was oblivious. Condon had exited as well, then caught the door when he realized Reese hadn't moved.

"You coming?" Condon asked.

Randall Reese was paralyzed.

Condon heard the beep of Reese's phone at the exact moment his own wristphone began vibrating. He was still holding the elevator door as he reached into the pocket of his suit coat with his other hand to retrieve his earpiece.

"Randall!" Condon barked, entreating him to move. He activated the call, letting go of the elevator. "Condon. Yes. No, I..." His demeanor suddenly shifted; the elevator door started to close. "Are you absolutely sure this is legitimate? Okay. No, I think Reese already knows. We'll call you back."

The elevator doors reopened. Reese and Condon stood motionless, staring at one another.

"How in God's name could this have happened?" Reese asked disbelievingly, shaking his head and still staring at Condon. "And right under our noses. How could we have not known this was coming?"

Reese stepped forward and the doors closed behind him. They began walking mechanically down the hall toward the hotel's restaurant, but their previous destination was no longer relevant.

"I just got a call from Sue Hensley, one of Caulfield's aides," Condon remarked. "Apparently, they're as surprised as we are. She noted that Belknap will be holding a press conference this afternoon."

Reese was still dazed, barely listening. "I was expecting that they'd announce the approval of the Constitution any day now, but 600 billion in funding? That just doesn't seem possible! And from a private source?"

Reese sought to regain control. He turned around and began walking back toward the elevator bank, not bothering to see if Condon was following or even listening. "We've got to get back to Washington immediately. We've got to rethink our entire strategy from the ground up. Let's see if we can get a quick meeting with the President from the plane."

☾☽

Halfway over the Atlantic, Reese tried for the third time to connect with Butler—to no avail. He was told the President's schedule would make it impossible for Reese to speak with him until tomorrow morning. Reese begrudgingly accepted a half hour slot at 7:00 am on Butler's calendar.

The plane ride was excruciating. Reese and Condon fielded call after call from key conservatives, evangelicals, political leaders, and others who had trusted their strategy for combating what they all saw as the dangerously progressive plans of the Mission Council. Many of these people had expended a significant amount of their own political capital to enlist others and rally their own supporters to Reese's tactical plan.

Reese's response was a mixture of defensiveness and determination. He claimed that he'd been ambushed by poor intelligence—although it wasn't clear who, other than him and Condon, should have had a better handle on the opposition's activities—and offered confident assurances that they would find a way to undermine this new funding source.

But inside, Reese felt as if his entire world was crumbling, and there seemed to be nothing he could do about it—especially given that they were in a plane 40 thousand feet over the ocean, and unable to get the President to take their call.

As they watched the afternoon press conference from the plane, Reese endured further humiliation. It was clear that the financing was real, and the Council seemed to have all of their ducks lined up and dancing in unison. This Jodee Keeling character, whoever the hell he was, appeared to have the press in the palm of his hand. He painted grand visions of some tourism venture that this whole deal would enable, and spoke eloquently about the "synergistic benefits" of "collaboration between private enterprise" and this "most important public initiative."

"Smarmy bastard!" Reese said aloud.

Condon looked over at his boss. Condon was far less despondent, and far more accustomed to the victories and defeats of political battles. "Randall, I can't pretend that this isn't a major setback. But that's all it is; we'll figure out a way to turn this thing back around. It'll just take some time."

Reese was about to respond, when a reporter at the press conference asked Virginia Belknap a question about the schedule and launch date. Reese snapped his head back to the screen.

"Well," Ginny began with a slight smile, "I'm pleased to report that the launch schedule is now back on track. As of this moment, the ESS Humanity will leave for Cerulea on June 12th."

Reese slid down in his seat, leaned back on the headrest, and closed his eyes.

Condon thought it best to just leave him alone.

86.

There were small protests in cities across the globe. Most were limited to a few hundred people—in some cases a few thousand. It seemed that, despite Reese and Condon's efforts to incite the international conservative base, most were either too stunned or simply too defeated to respond quickly.

In America, however, the announcement caused a firestorm.

Not unlike the initial announcement three years prior regarding Cerulea's discovery, every media outlet was 100 percent devoted to the breaking story.

Evangelical leaders, hard-core conservative congressmen and senators, and all those who shared their beliefs were livid, lashing out in interviews at the under-handed nature of the Mission Council's new financial backing, and pledging to do everything in their power to reverse this turn of events.

The massive and often violent protests taking place in Chicago, Dallas, Kansas City, Phoenix, Birmingham, Atlanta and Washington clearly got substantial play. But Ginny was pleased to see that they did not overwhelm the coverage.

There were many interviews with moderate conservatives, independents, and a range of pundits and analysts with unknown political beliefs, who all expressed their support of the deal. There seemed to be a consensus within this middle camp that private funding represented a powerful compromise; since tax-payers were now off the hook for a substantial portion of the Mission, it was much less important that the Council and crew mirror the beliefs of the U.S. Congress.

It was also clear that many supported the Mission Council's new backing because America loves an underdog. In short, while the cutoff of US funding for the mission was celebrated by many in the conservative camp, it had turned many others into sympathizers.

Ginny and Belechenko lay in bed watching the coverage. This was no longer a process of surfing various news programs on the air at a given point in time. Instead, it was a conglomeration of individual news reports, specific interviews & prepared statements, and selected snippets from protests, town-hall forums, and opinionated individuals who'd injected their own home-made op-ed video into the mix.

Most citizens of this new frontier relied on an electronic agent to sort through the plethora of possibilities and assemble a menu of choices based on past viewing habits. Ginny's menu, however, was still hand-crafted by humans on her residual staff—one of the many perks of an ex-president.

Belechenko watched this stream of fact and opinion with some bewilderment. He was still somewhat of a neophyte when it came to the political wrangling of religious conservatives in America.

"Ginny, why is it that, in America, one of the most diverse countries on Earth, there is so much hostility around how other people practice their faith?" he asked. "It seems that people can be very accepting of each other's differences; but when it comes to God, such tolerance seems to evaporate."

Ginny shook her head. "It's a good question." She thought about it for a moment, then sat up and looked at Belechenko. "I think much of the hostility is not around how people practice religion. It's between those who put God at the center of their lives and those who don't."

"And in a country as modern as America, this still leads to violence?"

"Remember, Vlad—like so many religious conflicts in history—this is about power, and the desire of one group to impose their views on another. It's about whether we should be governed by reason and logic alone, or whether we should be guided by what might be called biblical values. And as soon as the pendulum swings too far in one direction, and one side starts getting the upper hand, the other side inevitably gets very angry."

"I understand that there is much argument in this country regarding the role of the church in American society. But I always thought that America's political leaders tended to keep their religion a private matter."

"That was more or less true for a long time. It was really only in the 20th century that religion began to creep into politics in an organized fashion, but it really began much, much earlier as the evangelical movement formed and first began to push back against the advancement of scientific thought."

Vlad picked up the remote and paused the screen. "Tell me more about this."

"Well, during the past 200 years, there have been three so-called Great Awakenings—periods in our history when the country experienced a tremendous upsurge in religious fervor. The first of these, beginning in the 1730s, was a response to the Age of Enlightenment in Europe. It was driven by those who felt that science and reason were threatening our relationship to God, and that mankind should govern itself more with the heart than the head."

"Interesting," Belechenko mused. "That seems ironic; many of your esteemed Universities were founded in the 18th century, correct?"

"Yes, but the forces behind their creation may surprise you. Princeton University, for instance, was originally founded by Presbyterians with the intention of training ministers. In fact, one of its early presidents was Jonathan Edwards, perhaps the best known of the evangelical preachers who inspired the first Great Awakening."

"This is true?"

"This is true." Ginny confirmed. "These movements led many to push back even harder against the advancement of science. During the third Great Awakening in the mid-1800s, various groups sought to resolve what they perceived as science's assault on the bible through the creation of several new religions, including Mary Baker Eddy's Christian Science. Her premise was that the material world, including sin, death and disease, was really an illusion, and that, through prayer and a better understanding of God, man could rise above it—thus their insistence on the use of prayer in lieu of modern medicine."

"So when in America did the religious right emerge as a political force?"

"Oh, I guess the point could be argued, but I'd say it wasn't until the 1960s. It might have been earlier, but in 1925, evangelicals suffered a serious setback. The American Civil Liberties Union was seeking a test case to reverse a growing number of state laws against the teaching of evolution--"

"The Scopes Monkey Trial."

"Yes, exactly. The event was really a disaster for the evangelical movement— even despite the fact that, technically at least, they won. It initially seemed like a golden opportunity to deliver their message on the national stage, but instead the media portrayed them—to the entire country—as an ignorant laughingstock. The Scopes trial sent evangelicals scurrying back into the woodwork for several decades.

"Then, in the 1960s and early seventies, a confluence of events—including the sexual revolution and perhaps most important, the Roe v. Wade decision, impressed upon evangelicals that, if God was to remain a central force in American life, they would have to become politically active.

"Of course, the cold war was also a major contributor. It was widely held in the United States the spread of communism threatened not only our political and economic system, but the practice of religion as well.

"Some scholars point to this period as a fourth Great Awakening. From a political standpoint, it was definitely the point at which the faithful in this country began advocating more openly for a seat at the table."

"What do you mean by 'a seat at the table'?"

"Well, groups like the Moral Majority began organizing their followers to vote as a block in order to effect change and wield influence over national laws and policy. The goal was to get people "saved, baptized and registered"; so that they could then better support candidates who might help them put a stop to abortion, homosexuality and feminism within American society."

"Who was president at this time?"

"It began with Nixon. His overt relationship with Billy Graham and the Christian right was really a first; Christians had never before come so close to endorsing a candidate. But, needless to say, the whole thing turned into an embarrassment, with Graham eventually backpedaling once Watergate and the moral indiscretions of the Nixon administration emerged.

"Then, in 1980, it looked as if Christians' prayers had been answered. America elected Jimmy Carter, a man who stated publicly that the most important thing in his life was Jesus Christ. But once again, they were disappointed; Carter's policies were quite progressive. Unlike the Moral Majority's fervent pro-life, pro-family stance, he was pro-choice, and actively pushed the equal rights amendment, which Christians felt would destroy the traditional American family by encouraging women to pursue careers outside the home."

"Then, as I recall, came the great Ronald Reagan," Belechenko interjected. "I remember when I was a boy, watching on television as he told Mikhail Sergeyevich to tear down the Berlin Wall."

Ginny smiled, thinking of Belechenko as a boy, and thought of the two of them as children, on opposites sides of such a great divide. "Vlad, how old were you then?"

"This was in the late eighties, correct?"

"Yes."

"I was 5 years old at the time, but I remember it well because the video of this was shown many times as I grew up."

"I have never seen any pictures of you as a boy."

"I don't have many photos from that time." Belechenko paused. "My brother does; perhaps I will have him send me a few and we can share a good laugh."

"You must have been very handsome."

Belechenko grinned. "Not in the least. I had what you call a crew cut. I had very large ears, bulging eyes, and I was ridiculously skinny."

"I'll bet you were adorable."

Belechenko held up a hand, blushing slightly. "Enough. You have sidetracked us, and I wish to know more. Was Reagan helpful to the Moral Majority?"

"Not particularly, although he was revered by conservatives. The next two presidents weren't very helpful either, but then came George W. Bush. He probably did more to encourage and embolden the religious right than any president in history. He was a self-described rabble rouser in his youth, but became a devout Christian at the age of 40. His born-again status made him hugely popular among evangelicals, and his campaign staff artfully parlayed this to victory. Once in office, he attempted to pass legislation—even constitutional amendments—which directly served the interests of religious conservatives.

"As a result of his presidency, or perhaps I should say his campaigns, the religious right is now a formidable and critical constituent for anyone seeking the White House."

"So how were you elected?" Belechenko asked half-jokingly.

Ginny laughed. "It's actually a fair question. In truth, I got lucky. Two of the three presidents since George Bush were fairly clever centrists, so the divide had lessened by the time my turn came."

They continued watching the coverage in silence. A number of pundits and so-called Mission experts took their turns discussing the implications of the funding announcement. As the clock struck midnight, a strange thought crossed Ginny's mind.

"You know, perhaps this whole miserable funding debacle was for the best," she suggested, turning to Belechenko. "I think it may have caused people to think about the Mission in a new light."

Belechenko stared at Ginny and smiled, but said nothing.

"What? What are you thinking?"

"You don't honestly believe that, do you?" he asked her.

"To some extent, I do." She turned back to the screen. "It's not a tidal wave, but on a small scale, there's been some movement," she explained. "It's like every election; it all comes down to those few folks in the middle, vacillating with the political winds."

They continued watching in silence; after a while Ginny put one of the pillows she was leaning against next to the bed, turned off her light, and lay down and closed her eyes. "But I've got to say; it sure has been a while since those winds blew in our direction."

Belechenko looked down at Ginny and stroked her hair as she fell asleep.

87.

Jim Stanton quickly reviewed several screens full of data within his quarters, then initiated several programs. The noise of the Level 2 alarm, which had begun several minutes ago, was like the steady, short blasts of a foghorn.

The sensor data he'd reviewed indicated a Xenon leak, suggesting a containment breach in one of the ion engine compartments.

Jim grabbed his tablet and headed for the bridge. As he passed down several corridors, he could hear the closing of steel containment doors echoing through the ship in between the incessant blasts of the alarm.

He inserted his earpiece and began monitoring the chatter between his officers and other key personnel as they executed emergency procedures and began the process of diagnosing the failure. He offered no input; just listened.

All around him, non-essential crew were moving hurriedly from their quarters to specialized emergency living shelters located throughout the forward torus. Many looked at him with worried expressions; a number of children were crying uncontrollably.

"Captain, can you tell us anything about the cause of the alarm?" one crewman asked calmly, though his expression belied his concern.

"I believe we have a Xenon leak in one of the ion engines," Jim answered truthfully. "But all safeguards appear to be operating as designed; we should have containment reestablished shortly." His response seemed to mollify the inquiring crewman.

A Xenon gas leak was probably not all that high on the danger scale; humans could withstand some exposure without injury. The question was what caused it, and whether the crew could handle it efficiently.

He entered the bridge and immediately looked up at the panel. There was, as yet, no clear indication of what caused the leak. He turned to the officer on duty, a young woman named Belinda Sergeyev, who in a previous life had worked on the ISS, several layers beneath Commander Belechenko.

Jim suddenly put the middle fingers of each hand on his temples and closed his eyes tight. He appeared to be in pain.

"Captain! Are you all right?" Lieutenant Sergeyev asked urgently.

Jim opened his eyes and put his hands on a rail in front of him to steady himself. "Just a headache, Lieutenant. Tell me what we've learned so far."

"Yes, sir. Sensor data are telling us that the leak released approximately forty-two kilograms of Xenon gas. The engine compartment has been fully sealed. It does not look as if there was any malfunction or explosion in or around the injector, but we've dispatched a team to perform a manual inspection. They are suiting up now."

"What was the status prior to the alarm."

"The ship was at K10, sir. We immediately executed a full stop and took all ion engines off-line."

"Good. Who's leading the inspection team?" Stanton asked.

"Lieutenant Malik, sir."

Jim looked back at the panel. "It looks like Lieutenant Malik was on duty when the alarm sounded."

"Yes sir. He felt it was best for him to lead the inspection given his familiarity with the ion engines, so he transferred bridge command to me, sir."

Jim shook his head. *That figures*, he mused. "Okay, I'll take it from here."

They both placed hands into side-by-side readers, but Jim pulled his back and grabbed his head again with both hands. He crouched in apparent pain.

"Captain!" Sergeyev cried. Several crew members turned to look; one rushed to the Captain's side. "Ensign, take the Captain to the infirmary immediately!" Sergeyev demanded.

Jim waved them off. "No. It's all right, Lieutenant, just a migraine." He reached into a small pack on his waistbelt, removed a vial, and took two pills without water. "Just give me a minute. Carry on; you have command." Jim retreated to the rear of the bridge, and took a seat at an unoccupied navigation station. He leaned forward in the chair, face down, both hands still holding his head.

Lieutenant Sergeyev watched him go, then, tentatively, turned and faced the panel. She activated communications with Naj's team. "Lieutenant Malik, this is the bridge. What's your status?"

"Bridge, we are just entering the engine compartment now."

At that moment, a secondary, Level 3 alarm sounded.

Christ. What now? Thought Sergeyev. She looked up at the panel, and her heart sank.

The external sensor array was warning of a massive micrometeoroid cloud headed directly at the bow of the ship.

Sergeyev reacted immediately. "Data five, how far away is that cloud?"

A young crewman responded from his station. "It looks like it'll be on us in about twelve or thirteen minutes, Lieutenant."

"Can you speculate on size or speed?"

"Velocity appears to be nearly thirty thousand kph; size is roughly one square kilometer; there do not seem to be any objects over 3 millimeters."

The cloud was larger than most, and had appeared at the worst possible point in time. Although micrometeoroids were common, and Sergeyev knew that the ship was designed to withstand a direct hit from such a cloud, she also knew it could inflict real damage. Specifically, if the cloud hit the transparent sidewall of the forward torus, it could badly pit the surface, dramatically reducing its ability to let light filter through to the ship's primary living environment.

If at all possible, they had to get away from that cloud.

"Engine fifteen, report status of ion engines."

Engine fifteen, a remote station at the stern of the ship, responded. "Primary ion engines are off-line due to the leak condition. Reserve engine is available, Lieutenant."

Sergeyev froze for several moments. She knew the reserve engine couldn't possibly move the ship in time, while activating the SEC drive would require at least half an hour—besides the fact that creating a warp bubble with foreign debris around the ship was highly ill-advised. One of the many thoughts that raced through her mind was that if they hadn't brought the ship to a full stop after the first alert, they could have used the momentum to steer around the cloud, or at least bring the ship perpendicular to limit the damage.

Finally, Sergeyev barked several orders: "Engine fifteen, bring reserve ion engine to full power. Nav three, hard to starboard ninety degrees. Torus control, close all internal louvers on both tori."

Engine fifteen once again responded. "Bringing reserve to full power. Bear in mind, lieutenant, the reserve engine does not have the power--"

"I'm well aware of that!" Sergeyev shouted. "Even if we can just cut the angle, we can limit exposure. If anyone has other suggestions, I'm listening."

Several of the bridge crew looked back at Captain Stanton, who was still crouched over in what looked like extreme pain. There were several tense moments as no one spoke.

Then a voice broke the silence. "Bridge, this is Malik. I have an idea."

"Go ahead, Lieutenant," Sergeyev urged.

"It's possible that if we manipulated the rotational speed of each torus, we might be able to create a wobble that, in conjunction with the reserve engine, might adjust the ship's position in time."

"Wouldn't that effect the gravity within each torus?" Sergeyev asked.

"It would," Naj replied, "but only temporarily. We'd have to do the math to know the full impact."

Sergeyev wasted no time. "Data five, calculate the required changes in rotation speed of the tori to turn the ship perpendicular."

"Understood, this'll take a minute," the crewman remarked.

"It better take less than a minute." Sergeyev said sternly. She looked at the panel for the external sensor array and note that the cloud was now just 9 minutes away. There was complete silence as they waited for the result.

After what seemed like an eternity, the crewman at station Data five yelled out "I have it! If the rear torus accelerates to 5.5 rpm, the forward torus slows to 2 rpm, and the reserve ion engine remains at full power, we will be perpendicular to the cloud in six minutes, and will not exceed acceptable gravitational parameters in either torus."

Sergeyev looked back at the panel: eight minutes to impact. "Okay, let's do this quickly." She gave the orders to Torus control, who immediately began the adjustments in rotational speed. She then asked station Data five to transmit all calculations to the bridge display.

Once the orders were implemented, the bridge crew waited. After less than a minute, they could all feel the gravity on the bridge dropping. Sergeyev opened all communications channels: "Attention all crew, we will be adjusting the rotation speed of each torus to reposition the ship and lessen the impact of an oncoming micrometeoroid cloud." She looked up at the data on the bridge display. "The rear torus will increase to 2G, while gravity in the forward torus will be reduced to .19G. Please prepare accordingly. We will bring both tori back to standard rotation and gravity as soon as possible."

On the main viewscreen, a computer-generated diagram of the ship relative to the approaching cloud was displayed. As the bridge crew waited in silence, the ship slowly began to wobble. As the gyration increased, the ship, imperceptibly at first, then more noticeably, began to turn clockwise.

With three minutes to impact, Naj Malik interrupted the tense silence, entering the bridge still wearing a bright yellow hazmat suit, minus the gloves and helmet.

He looked up at the display, then at Sergeyev. "Looks like it's working."

"It was a brilliant suggestion, Naj," Sergeyev said quietly.

By the tone of her voice, he became immediately aware of just how much pressure she must have been under. He immediately thought of the Captain, and turned to see Jim still crouched over. He knew from past experiences with Jim's migraines that there was nothing that could be done other than to let the pills take effect.

He turned back and watched the display as the ship slowly turned perpendicular to the cloud. There were murmurs of excitement, which grew into cheers of celebration as the display indicated that the ship had weathered the impact of the cloud directly off her starboard beam.

As the cheers subsided, Sergeyev asked for a damage report.

"The young crewman at station Data five turned to her with a perplexed expression. "Lieutenant, sensors are indicating no damage whatsoever. In fact, the cloud does not seem to be registering at all."

Naj walked over to the crewman's screen and manually called up data from several specific sensors. "He's right, it's as if the cloud never existed."

He turned to Sergeyev, and noticed the Captain, who had emerged from the back of the bridge, signaling his desire to take over bridge command from Lieutenant Sergeyev.

They both presented their hands to the readers, and Jim took command. "Torus control, return both tori to standard rotational speeds. Data five, perform a hard reset of the forward sensor array."

After he'd had heard confirmations from both stations, he addressed the bridge crew. "There was no meteoroid cloud. My apologies for the deception. This was a drill—specifically requested, I might add, by Commander Belechenko and the Mission Council."

"But Captain," noted Naj, "what about the Xenon leak?"

"That was real, Lieutenant, as I believe your inspection team discovered. It allowed us to use a low-level alarm condition as the backdrop for a more serious situation. And may I say," Jim pronounced, panning his gaze across all present, "that you all did an outstanding job." As he made direct eye contact with both Belinda and Naj, he began to applaud; the bridge crew quickly joined in.

Jim then hit a button on the command console. "Anything to add, Commander?"

Belechenko's resonant voice could be heard clearly over the bridge communications system: "I have monitored all of your activities from Mission headquarters, and I have to tell you how proud I am of your coolheaded response. Your solution to the emergency was clever, resourceful, and well-executed. As Captain Stanton noted, I'm sorry that it required that we deceive you." Belechenko paused. "This last drill has proved to me that you have all proved yourselves ready for the journey to come. Congratulations."

The atmosphere on the bridge, which only moments ago was charged with tension and suspense, was now decidedly more relaxed.

After some celebratory conversation and some shared laughter and relief, Naj headed out to remove his hazmat suit. He looked at Jim as he passed the command console. "How's the headache, Captain?" he asked facetiously.

Jim laughed. "It occurred to me that no one will ever take one of my migraines seriously again."

88.

Reese looked at his watch for what must have been the hundredth time in half as many minutes.

He'd been early for his 7:00 am meeting with the President, hoping perhaps to get a little extra time to discuss how they were going to deal with the catastrophic turn of events.

It was now 7:40—Butler had yet to show. Not only was he egregiously late for his meeting with Reese, he was now late for his next meeting. The President's secretary had assured Reese that they would be able to spend at least a few minutes together, but this was small comfort. Reese was wearing a path in the Presidential Seal as he paced back and forth in front of the President's desk.

Finally, at 7:45, Butler breezed in with two aides. He seemed engrossed in conversation, and didn't so much as acknowledge Reese until several minutes later, when the conversation concluded and the aides were dismissed.

"Randall. Good morning. Sorry for the schedule screw up."

Good morning, Mr. President." Reese did his best to be calm and civil, despite his intense frustration.

"So, I would imagine that yesterday's announcement came as quite shock to all of us," Butler offered magnanimously.

"Yes sir. It was a total surprise. My apologies; I should have been able to see this coming somehow."

The President's secretary opened the door of the Oval Office. "Mr. President, the Treasury Secretary is here."

"Thank you, Agnes; tell him I'll be with him in a few minutes."

"Yes, sir." The door closed.

Reese bit his lip. *How the hell could a meeting with the Treasury Secretary be more important than this?* he thought to himself.

The President sat on the edge of his desk. "Randall, if I was Belknap, I would have bent over backwards to keep this thing from leaking. While it certainly would have been helpful to know about this in advance, I'm not sure if anyone could have seen this coming." Butler chuckled. "I suppose it's oddly reassuring to see that at least someone can keep a secret in this town."

Reese did not find any humor in the situation, and was increasingly peeved at the President for not treating the situation with the seriousness it deserved. "Sir, I think we need to formulate a strategy for overturning this new financing deal. Joe Condon and I have come up with some options that I'd like to review--"

"Randall."

"Yes, sir?"

"I don't think there are any options. We played our hand, and they beat us. Fair and square. Short of some highly unethical undertaking, I don't believe there's a damn thing we can do at this point."

Reese felt as if he'd been punched in the stomach—for the second time in two days. "But Mr. President, Joe and I believe that there's a legal case to be made that giving away the technology may be illegal. If we can get a number of world leaders to support-"

"Randall. Let me be clear. I have spent considerable political capital on this whole affair. The Greater Good Provision was terrific for our base, but clearly set us back with regard to next year's mid-term elections. A majority of the electorate out there is cheering for Belknap and the Council. After being down by quite a few runs in the bottom of the ninth, they pulled a rabbit out of their hat and won this thing. Any effort on our part to somehow reverse or nullify their victory would, I believe, come back to bite us in the ass bigtime."

Reese stared at the President. Butler's logic was not unreasonable, but he remained completely baffled by the man's apparent change of heart. He'd always known that Butler's belief in the cause, unlike his own, was much more political than emotional; but he'd simply never expected the President to throw in the towel without more of a fight.

Reese tried to buy more time and bring in reinforcements. "Sir, do you think it would make sense for us to put our heads together with Senator Caulfield? Perhaps if we spent a couple of hours brainstorming this afternoon we could come up with some straightforward--"

Butler cut him off yet again. "I already met with Max this morning," the President said coldly. "We discussed the situation, and I believe you'll find that he shares my view that it's time to admit defeat and move on."

The two men looked at each other fixedly. Reese was incredulous that Caulfield was willing to give up that easily, but he said nothing. His emotions were a boiling cauldron of anger, frustration, disbelief, and unbelievable despair.

Finally, Butler broke off and looked at his watch. Reese knew instantly that there was no point in arguing further. Before the President could open his mouth, Reese beat him to the punch.

"Thank you, Mr. President." He walked to the door, grabbing his briefcase off the sofa as he passed, and let himself out.

Butler watched him go. He then edged himself off his desk, picked up the phone, and made a quick call on a secure line.

89.

Senator Caulfield placed a large spoonful of the renowned bean soup into his mouth. Then another.

Randall Reese followed suit and immediately wished he hadn't; the soup was extremely hot. So much so that Reese was sure he'd just done a pretty good job of burning the roof of his mouth—which only caused his mood to further deteriorate. He chose not to say anything, since the discussion with Caulfield was very important, and he wanted to remain focused.

His pain, however, must have been evident.

"Perhaps I should have warned you that the soup here can be a little on the warm side," Caulfield said in his southern twang. "I always ask the kitchen to put an ice cube in mine before bringing it out."

"Oh, no. It's delicious," Reese replied, wondering why the warning hadn't come thirty seconds earlier. "It certainly lives up to its reputation." This was essentially a lie, since Reese's singed taste buds were now completely incapable of tasting anything.

They were eating lunch in the Senate Dining Room of the Capitol Building, and had each ordered a bowl of the bean soup to start. It was a famous recipe which had been served there for over 125 years.

The room was a dark, wood-paneled and somber place, with thick navy blue curtains and dim lighting. There was not, however, a more prestigious place to eat in Washington.

Reese had dined there on two previous occasions, but today had little interest in seeing or being seen. His objective was crystal clear: it was imperative to get Max Caulfield's support in quashing the Mission Council's private funding. Although the President had been unequivocal in communicating his desire to move on, Reese was incapable of doing so; he thought that, if he could just get Caulfield back on board, together they might be able to convince the President to change his mind.

Caulfield, knowing full well what Reese was after, had no objection to addressing the topic head on. "I'll tell you Randall, when I heard the news the other day, it really jerked a knot in my tail. I thought we had 'em in a box."

"I did too, Senator. The question now is how to get them back in," Reese offered, trying to play on Caulfield's colloquialism.

"Well, it sure ain't going to be easy, I can tell you that right now."

"Joe Condon and I have been working on a possible strategy for challenging the funding in court. We think that the whole idea of selling the technology rights may be illegal. At the very least, we believe it's possible to tie this thing up in court for months—if not years."

"Well, Randall, I've worked in this town for a very, very long time. I've won quite a few, and I've lost my share. As much as I want to stop this Mission from moving forward, I'm not at all convinced it's possible."

Reese's inclination was to jump back in and argue otherwise, but thought better of it and allowed the Senator to elaborate.

"Now mind you," Caulfield continued, "your notion of a legal challenge might be a viable option. In fact, I'll grant you that it might even succeed. But my gut tells me that in the court of public opinion we'd be vilified. And at the end of the day, that would do more harm to our cause than anything else I could think of."

"But Senator," Reese pleaded, then held back as one of Caulfield's colleagues approached the table.

"Max, congratulations. I understand you've got your amendment all locked down," the gentleman remarked.

"Why thank you, Wade. Still crossing my fingers, but I think we're in good shape for the vote." Caulfield gestured to Reese. "By the way: Senator Wade Palmer, this is Randall Reese, Special Assistant to the President for Cerulean Affairs."

"Pleasure, Randall." Reese pushed his chair back to stand. "Please, don't get up."

Palmer remained on the other side of the table, so Reese pulled his chair back in and simply nodded. "Nice to meet you, Senator."

"Sorry to interrupt." Palmer patted Caulfield on the shoulder, then started away from the table. "See you on the floor, Max."

Max raised his hand in response as a farewell gesture.

Reese leaned forward, seeking to refocus their attention on the topic at hand. "Senator, if we do nothing to block this new source of funding, the *ESS Humanity* will leave for Cerulea on June 12 with a crew and constitution that both of us find abhorrent."

Caulfield pushed his now empty bowl off to the side, and leaned forward as well. "Randall, I am in violent agreement with your perspective on this Mission. During my political career, I have taken every opportunity to infuse our society with my Christian faith and the values that I believe are critical to the health of humankind. And it sickens me that a ship leaving this planet to establish a new civilization will do so with homosexuals on board and a set of laws which practically prohibit the ability of Ceruleans to get to know their God."

Reese was momentarily encouraged by the Senator's candid admissions.

"But I am also a pragmatist," Caulfield declared. "There is a time to engage the enemy, and there is a time to retreat and regroup. I assure you, if we attempted to win every battle, we would most surely lose the war."

"But Senator, don't you think the fate of Cerulea represents far more than just a battle?" Reese implored.

Caulfield lowered his voice and spoke just above a whisper. "C'mon, Randall, we don't even know if that ship has a snowball's chance in hell of ever making it to Cerulea, let alone whether anyone'll survive the first year or two. Meanwhile, this planet's got a whole host of problems that I'd like to help solve. So no, in the grand scheme of things, I don't look at the Mission to Cerulea as much more than one battle among many."

Reese found this line of argument unconvincing. And he was fairly certain Caulfield didn't buy it, either. Mankind's record in space was enviable; every single time the world had set its sights on a space-related goal, it had prevailed.

Their lunch arrived; Caulfield took time out to flirt with the waitress for several minutes, then switched their conversation to a series of innocuous topics that carried them through most of the meal.

As the dishes were bussed, Reese took one last shot. "Senator, Joe Condon and I are meeting with some attorneys from the Justice Department this afternoon. Would you at least allow me to brief you on the outcome of our discussions?"

Caulfield put his hands flat on the table and smoothed the tablecloth in front of him. "Randall, I think I made myself clear: whether there is a valid legal challenge or not is pretty much irrelevant. I just don't believe the American people are behind us on this thing. Period."

An elegant woman in a gray wool suit waved to Caulfield as she passed the table with several colleagues. He waved back. She looked at her watch, then back at Caulfield. "This bill is up for a vote in ten minutes with your amendment attached, Max. I do hope you'll be present."

"I'll be there, Maggie, don't you worry." Caulfield looked at Reese. "Thanks for coming by, Randall; I'm sorry I couldn't be more encouraging."

They nodded goodbye, and the Senator left for the Senate floor.

Twenty minutes later, Reese walked into his office. A screen nestled in the bookshelf was broadcasting 24-hour news. An on-air reporter was announcing that Senator Maxwell Caulfield, Conservative Senator from Georgia, had just

90.

The ship was practically covered with small shuttlecraft, some hovering in and around major components, others traveling from one section of the ship to another. To Keeling, who had spent some time diving in the South Pacific, the scene was reminiscent of a large coral reef inhabited by hundreds of small fish.

"Is there really that much damage to repair before launch, Lieutenant?" Keeling asked.

Naj smiled. "No. Actually, the number of necessary repairs is far less than expected. The majority of these shuttles are performing inspections and pre-launch maintenance procedures."

"What's going on over there? It looks like a whole bunch of them are in a feeding line."

"Close, but it's the reverse. Those ships are loading cargo into the main input bays. From there, maglevs—small cars running on magnetic rails—bring the supplies to various points within the ship."

Jodee Keeling and Najid Malik were in a shuttlecraft of their own, only this one was specifically designed for observation. It was called the "space limo" by many of the crew, since it was most often used for giving VIPs sightseeing tours of the ship and L5 operations. Instead of being crowded with equipment and tools like most of the craft, the space limo offered a spacious sitting area with plush chairs. On each side of the lounge area were large, reinforced windows; the chairs were designed to swivel so that guests could turn to look out either side with minimal effort.

After several months of rigorous testing, the *ESS Humanity* had returned to the L5 Spaceport, where it would remain until launch. Jodee Keeling, whose investor syndicate had just come through on schedule with the second funding installment, had requested a tour of the ship. The joke was that Naj had drawn the short straw; in truth, Jim Stanton had been asked by Commander Belechenko to "roll out the red carpet," and Jim felt that, of all his senior officers, Naj's knowledge of the SEC drive and other key systems would make him the best ambassador.

As it turned out, Naj's expertise had not yet been called upon; Keeling did not seem particularly eager to explore the ship's technology in any depth.

He was, however, fascinated with the experience of being in space. Keeling turned his back on the ship and looked out the opposite window at the moon.

"Lieutenant, tell me about the L5 spaceport. Was the intent to create a space operations center with proximity to the moon?"

"Yes and no," Naj replied. "L5 actually refers to one of the Earth-Moon Lagrange points. Each point represents an area where the gravitational pull of the Earth, moon and Sun are in balance. They were discovered—I guess I should say calculated—by a French mathematician in the 18th century, and can be applied to any moon or planet orbiting a larger body in space.

"For the purpose of this operations center, L5 allows us to remain in a stationary orbit without requiring any fuel to adjust the position of our facilities. It also ensures almost constant exposure to the sun, so that our supply of solar power is very rarely interrupted. And last, as you pointed out, the location gives us the ability to harvest resources from the Moon without requiring the tremendous amount of fuel necessary to bring them up from Earth."

"And what does the Moon provide?"

"Well, water, for one thing. The *Humanity's* water processing system holds over one and a half million gallons—all of which was mined from the Moon's ice caps. That's over twelve million pounds of water; the equivalent of roughly a hundred Earth launches of a CEV shuttle."

Keeling whistled at the figure. "And aren't you also mining Helium from the moon as well?"

"Actually, it's Helium-3, a form of Helium that is extremely rare on Earth, but relatively common on the lunar surface. It's used as the primary fuel in the *Humanity's* fusion reactors, which provide power for all of its subsystems."

Keeling continued to ask questions about the ship's operations for the better part of an hour. Naj was patient, explaining the basic workings of various systems and some of the basic technologies which drove them.

Keeling eventually asked to be taken to the far side of the spaceport. Naj complied, but let his guest know that there were a number of projects and activities at L5 with which he was not familiar. In fact, as they came around the other side of one of the large spheres that housed L5 administration and quarters for L5 personnel, they were in what was, to Naj, uncharted territory.

Through the starboard side of their shuttle, they could see the wireframe of a new project—essentially scaffolding surrounding the beginnings of some new module.

Keeling turned to Naj, smiling broadly. "I believe that one's ours."

Naj didn't understand. "I'm sorry, Mr. Keeling. You mean this new module is Australian?"

"No, Lieutenant. If I'm correct, it's the first few pieces of the *ESS Goldstar*, my syndicate's first ship."

91.

The rain was coming down in sheets.

The White House was well insulated from the sounds of the city outside—in large part due to the bulletproof glass on its windows. The incessant pounding of the rain, however, was clearly audible as Joe Condon walked down the corridor toward the Northwest entrance. It was like the muffled sound of a stampede going around and over the building.

Condon presented his briefcase to a seated guard, who placed it into a machine that generated and archived detailed images of its contents. After the process was complete, the guard handed the case back, and Condon walked out the door and stood on the portico, watching the rain. The sound was deafening.

It was late in the evening, and Condon was tired. Not just tired from another twelve-hour day, but tired of the game he'd been playing for the past three decades. The only constant in his professional life had been the steady cycle of ups and downs. Earlier in his career, on the heels of achieving a few legislative victories for his clients, he'd fool himself into believing that he was truly beating the odds, that he was becoming a more effective lobbyist, and that he had real power and the ability to shape events. Then the tide would turn, and he would once again be humbled by a string of defeats that left him wondering why he'd chosen this field of work. Over time, he'd learned to moderate his emotions, becoming a little less celebratory after a success, and a little less despondent after a failure.

But the recent turn of events had upended this equilibrium, and left him quite depressed. After lecturing his boss on numerous occasions regarding the need to stay focused and positive, Condon was falling prey to Reese's malaise. Right now, all he wanted was to go home and pour himself a stiff drink.

He looked down at the waiting car; the driver came up the steps with an umbrella. Together, they walked back down; the driver opened the door, and Condon gently tossed his briefcase into the middle of the backseat. The driving rain played a drum roll on the top of the car, creating a fine mist that penetrated his face and shoulders. He paused for a second, letting the moisture reawaken his senses, then slid in next to his briefcase, and the door closed behind him.

The noise of the rain on the roof of the car was meditative. He leaned back and closed his eyes.

As the car stopped at the gate before exiting the White House grounds, Condon briefly opened his eyes and looked across at another limousine coming in. He was about to close his eyes again when the light inside the limo was illuminated. One of two men in the back seat pulled some papers from his attaché and handed them to the driver.

Condon's brain suddenly snapped to attention. He narrowed his eyes and tried hard to get a clearer look at the two men. The limo pulled forward out of the gate and the interior light was extinguished—just as Condon's car pulled out into the street. Though the rain diminished his visibility, Condon was certain he'd seen them clearly, and was dumbfounded.

He sat frozen as his car picked up speed and headed west toward Condon's townhouse in Georgetown. He could feel chills running up his spine as his brain started to grasp the implications of what he'd just seen.

He abruptly reached forward and raised the glass shield between the front and back seats, hit a button on his wrist phone.

He heard just one ring before the call was answered. "Hey Joe. What's up?" Reese asked wearily.

"Randall, I hope you're sitting down."

92.

Roger Tucker and Commander Belechenko were down to the last few items. For the past several months, the two had tried to get together every week or so to work through Mission-related issues and strategy.

As the launch neared, there was a long list of loose ends; at the same time, the energy level at Mission Headquarters was soaring. Ever since the announcement that the Mission was back on track, the place had been electrified; and with the launch now just 60 days away, it was a beehive of activity.

"Okay, what's next?" Roger asked, rubbing his eyes and looking out the window.

They were seated at a small conference table in Roger's office at Mission Headquarters, which looked down the river toward the Woodrow Wilson Bridge. The view looked like an impressionist painting, with the steady rain softening the edges of the sharp, angular V-shaped piers of the bridge.

Belechenko worked the tablet in his hands, but was clearly not finding what he was after. "I had sent you an updated budget for pre-launch activities. Did you get it?"

"I did," Roger replied. He hit a few buttons on his tablet, found the file, then looked up.

"Would you mind sharing?" Belechenko asked sheepishly, unable to find the file on his own device.

"Not at all," Roger responded, putting the tablet between them and sliding his chair over a bit.

"Overall, the news is good," Belechenko began. "While we anticipate some extra expenses during final provisioning, it looks like we are going to come in well under budget on pre-launch maintenance. In short, the ship will require much less repair from its test runs than we'd planned."

"Good. It looks like you've added four shuttle flights in early June," Roger remarked, pointing to a cell in the spreadsheet. "Are those supply runs?"

"Three of them are; the last one is for us."

"For you, maybe. You aren't getting me up in one of those things," Roger said smiling.

"Roger! After all this time, you are not going to join Ginny and myself at the launch ceremony?"

"Sorry, Vlad. Call me what you will, but I'm one of those rare humans who has no desire whatsoever to dangle around in space."

"As you wish, but we'll miss you."

"I'll be there in spirit, I assure you. For the record, has the launch event been broken down and factored into the budget?"

Before Belechenko could respond, Roger's wristphone emitted a high-pitched beep, indicating an urgent call. He looked at the display: *Michael Victor, Verintel Corporation.*

Roger turned to Belechenko. "Vlad, would you mind if I took this? It'll probably just be a minute."

"Not at all. Go ahead."

Roger hit a button on the device. "Michael, what have you got for me?" He got up and walked to the window.

"Well, I'd love to have more than I do," Victor replied. "But we do have some data that might interest you."

"Great. Shoot."

"Well, for starters, it looks like we were right; we've now confirmed that James Torgan is indeed one of the silent partners. We've also identified two others: David Hildebrand out of Hong Kong, and Kyle Van der Hoven, a South African. All together, we are estimating that these three represent approximately 300 billion of the total investment. If we add in the investors listed in the proposal, that's 400 billion."

"And how about the rest of it; any leads?" Roger asked.

"If we're correct, the remaining third is being supplied by a single investor—a big one. However, it looks as if he—or she—has gone to great lengths to hide their tracks. I'm guessing it'll take another couple of weeks to surface a name."

"And now for the big question," Roger said cautiously, "are any of these guys going to get us in trouble?"

"I don't think so," Victor said slowly, "but there is one thread that you should know about."

"And what's that?"

"It's probably nothing, but—like Torgan—the rest of these guys seems to have made a sizable portion of their money from mining."

"Hmmm. I guess that's not too surprising; do you suppose that means the other investors are colleagues of Torgan?"

"We're not sure yet, and I wouldn't want to speculate," Victor responded.

Roger chuckled. "No, Mike, I'm sure you wouldn't."

"Anyway, we've already sent you an updated report with all of this information. After you give it a look, let me know if you have any questions."

"I will, Mike, thanks for the call."

Roger ended the call and went back to his seat next to Belechenko.

"That was Mike Victor, who's performing the due diligence on our investors," Roger reported.

"Anything new?" Belechenko asked.

"Not really," Roger offered. "So far, so good."

93.

Reese threw two shirts on top of a pair of shoes in the bottom of his travel bag. It was Saturday morning. After four days of non-stop rain, the sun was shining brightly, and he was going home for the first time in many weeks. The last time he'd been in Wisconsin, there'd been snow on the ground. He longed to see his family, and the emergence of spring in his hometown.

But, as he placed his dopp kit into the bag, he paused. He wanted so much to get away—from Washington, from politics, and most of all from the deepening quagmire that was his job and primary focus in life. But he realized that it would take more than a thousand mile plane trip.

He sat on the bed and stared at the floor.

His mind inevitably returned to Derek Butler, the source of his despair. *That duplicitous bastard*, he thought to himself, wondering just how far the deception stretched, and whether that should be singular or plural. Since the call from Condon 36 hours ago, he had been in a funk, barely able to function. Tenacity had always been his partner and ally, driving him forward under the most wrenching circumstances. And yet, at Condon's news, he'd felt his will slip away; at that moment he uncharacteristically surrendered, and allowed himself to be swallowed in a paralysis of defeat and self-pity.

The forces against him were simply too great. Fighting Virginia Belknap and her gaggle of atheists was one thing, but to encounter a whole new front—one with the power of the US presidency behind it—this was unwinnable.

Reese's shoulders slumped. His grip loosened and the toiletries case fell to the floor. He looked down at it vacantly.

The enormity of his defeat overwhelmed him. For the better part of his adult life, he had fought the forces of evil that led mankind down a dangerous and wayward path. And here was a new planet; an entirely brand new world with the potential to rise above the mess that people like Belknap and Fossett had made of this Earth. Cerulea had the chance to be a veritable Garden of Eden, a blessed civilization fully embracing the ideals espoused by Jesus Christ, and repudiating all that had led this planet astray.

Reese leaned down and grabbed the dopp kit. He looked at his packed bag, and clenched his teeth.

There is nothing so important as this Mission, he said to himself; *even if the fight is doomed to failure, it must be fought; the future of man hangs in the balance.*

The enemies of virtue may be on the march, but they have not yet won. I must do now as I've always done; put my faith in the redeeming love of Jesus Christ, and carry on.

He felt his muscles snap to attention. He looked around the bedroom of his apartment, then got up and grabbed a tablet off his desk.

He spent several minutes dictating a message, made a few edits and, with a few final keystrokes, sent the missive on its way.

He then punched a button on his wristphone, requested the desired number, and placed the call to Mission Headquarters.

94.

Outside Reese's apartment, a man behind the wheel of a plain-looking dark green sedan pressed the power button on the dashboard. He turned to someone seated next to him who was holding a screen in his lap.

"Did you get the message?"

"Yeah, but it's encrypted; it'll take a while to decipher," the other man replied. "By the way, where're we goin'?"

"He called some guy and they agreed to meet in Rock Creek Park."

Reese emerged from the building and walked to the curb to hail a cab.

"All right," the driver said. "After a whole fuckin' week of nothing, here goes something."

A taxi stopped after just a few seconds. Reese got in, and they pulled away.

The driver waited for several cars to pass, then pulled out into traffic behind them.

95.

Roger Tucker's mind was abuzz with a hundred thoughts as he walked through the parking garage to his car.

As he opened the door and got in, he returned to the first thought that had entered his brain after receiving the call: *what the hell is this all about?*

Roger—along with most of the Headquarters staff—had been working Saturdays and Sundays for several weeks, and would continue to do so up through the launch.

However, regardless how much he had on his plate, the call from Reese was just too intriguing; Roger had immediately agreed to meet.

He wormed his way out of Alexandria, jumped on the GW Parkway, and headed across the 14th Street Bridge. It was a gorgeous day; Roger opened the sunroof and turned on some music.

As he took a left on Mass. Ave and then a right on 16th Street, he accepted a call from Cynthia Fossett.

"Hey! Are you confirming our lunch date?" Roger asked, in reference to a conversation they'd had the day before.

"I am. But it sounds like you're on the road. Are we still on?" Cynthia asked.

"Oh, sorry." Roger turned down the music and closed the roof. "Yeah, let's do it, but I may be late. I can't wait to tell you why."

"Tell me!" Cynthia insisted.

"Randall Reese called me this morning and asked to meet."

"No!" she said with disbelief. "And you said yes?"

"Of course I said yes! I'm dying to know what the hell he's after."

They chatted for a few minutes. Roger offered what little else he knew, and they moved on to another topic. The financing deal with Keeling had spawned some lawsuits from several taxpayer groups, and Cynthia was pitching in to get them thrown out.

Roger was grateful for her help. She ran circles around their General Counsel, and had been a joy to work with. They'd become good friends.

Before signing off, Roger promised to call and let her know when he'd be back.

"You'd better," she teased. "I want to be the first to hear what this is all about!"

96.

The trees were exploding with delicate, bright green leaves. Up above, their limbs formed a cathedral over the trail. After four days of rain, followed by bright morning sunshine, Roger could almost feel Spring emerging. It was that time of the year in Washington when the gradual rise out of Winter hit an inflection point, and the natural world accelerated upwards rapidly toward Summer.

Moments earlier, as he'd hacked his way North through the stoplights on 16th Street, he'd wondered why it was necessary to meet in such a remote spot. Granted, it was probably a good idea to be discreet; anyone witnessing a meeting between himself and Randall Reese would surely find it newsworthy, but surely there were other more convenient locations offering just as much privacy.

But now, walking the trail to the spot where Reese had said he'd be, Roger was grateful for the rare chance to get out of the city. He inhaled deeply, filling his lungs with the lavish aroma of damp earth and flowering trees.

He came around a bend in the trail and saw Reese. He was sitting on a bench off the trail, focused intently on his tablet. Roger thought it slightly incongruous; out here, amidst the beauty of a new season, staring at a computer.

"Randall," Roger hailed, as he neared the bench, not wanting to surprise him. He held out his hand.

Reese stood and shook it. "Mr. Tucker, thank so much for agreeing to see me."

"Please, it's Roger."

Reese nodded in acknowledgement. There was an awkward silence as the two men stood facing one another. Under most circumstances, any such meeting might begin with a little small talk, but—given the great divide that separated these two men—that seemed uncomfortably superficial.

Roger gestured toward the trail with his arm, suggesting perhaps that they might walk and talk. Reese, clearly apprehensive, nodded again and began to walk.

"So, I must say, your call certainly has raised my curiosity," Roger offered. "What's on your mind, Randall?"

Again there was an awkward silence.

Reese was still intensely conflicted by what he was about to do. He was furious with Butler, and felt deceived. Furthermore, he knew this strategy held the only remaining hope of seeing Cerulean civilization follow the path of righteousness.

At the same time, he was, in no uncertain terms, squealing on the President of the United States; revealing crimes in which he was, at least to a degree, complicit. And doing so to a man whose lifestyle Reese found abhorrent.

"Roger, what I have to tell you is hard for me to say, and may be difficult for you to hear," Reese began.

This, of course, only further piqued Roger's curiosity. He patiently said nothing, not wanting in any way to divert Reese from delivering whatever message or information he'd brought Roger out here to receive.

97.

The two men in the green sedan had parked on Holly Street, a short distance away from where Reese's taxi stood waiting for him to return—the cabdriver reading a book to pass the time.

They had watched as Roger had parked just around the corner on 14th Street and walked to the trailhead and into the park. Not having been able to pull a number from Reese's call back at his apartment, and not exactly the types to recognize the previous president's chief-of-staff, they quickly ran Roger's plate number to identify him.

After reporting in with the news, they'd been instructed to follow Roger and record the conversation. The two men had immediately protested, claiming that this was not what they'd been hired to do, and that the terrain would make eavesdropping very tough to pull off. They were told to get whatever audio they could without getting spotted, and to call back in as soon as the meeting concluded. They begrudgingly agreed.

"This is bullshit," said the taller of the two, untangling some recording gear as he pulled it from the trunk.

"It's a paycheck, Kevin. Just remember that," said the other, still sitting in the driver's seat.

"Yeah, it's a fuckin' paycheck," Kevin repeated. He put on a pair of head phones and tested the directional mike by pointing it in various directions. Apparently satisfied, he closed the trunk and walked along the side of the car.

He glared at his partner. "Joey, tell me this; why in hell does it gotta be me doin' this!"

"Oh, quit whinin'. With my bum leg, I'd never get close without makin' a big scene," Joey answered. "Now get your butt in there; you're gonna hafta run to catch up."

"Thanks for the advice," Kevin deadpanned. "And fuck you, too."

Joey laughed as Kevin started in to the park.

98.

"I guess the best way to do this is just to blurt it out, and then answer your questions," Reese suggested. He turned to look at Roger, who nodded, hoping Reese would get on with it.

Reese didn't, so Roger offered some encouragement. "That sounds like the right way to proceed. Please continue."

The two men walked along the path, both looking ahead as they talked.

"Okay," Reese said with determination, "here it is: I think President Butler is tied up with your investor group."

Roger stopped in his tracks and looked at Reese. "Tied up with Keeling? How? And how do you know this?"

Reese turned and sighed deeply. "Joe Condon saw Jodee Keeling and another man entering the White House two days ago."

Roger was visibly relieved. "Randall, I admit it's a little surprising, but I'm sure there's a bunch of reasons why Keeling might--"

"Wait. Hear me out. The man who was with Keeling is apparently a long-time flunky of Butler's. His first name is Doug; I don't know his last. I guess he used to work at Diametrix. Anyway, this is where it gets crazy." Reese paused and briefly looked up at the sky, as if for guidance. "I believe Doug was behind the explosion on the Mall last year."

"What!" Roger barked, stopping again. "You *believe* this guy was behind it, or you *know* he was behind it?" Roger was having a hard time swallowing any of this.

"I know he was behind it." Reese looked away, then back at Roger. "To a certain extent, I was too."

Roger was wide-eyed; he simply couldn't comprehend what he was hearing.

"Trust me; I had no idea that they might detonate a bomb. They were only supposed to start a fight with some of the Mall protesters," Reese said this as if he were pleading his case.

Roger ignored his belated contrition. "You were behind the other incident at the White House a year earlier, weren't you? The one where some woman got hit with a bottle."

"No, but I think Doug was behind that, too. I didn't--" Reese stopped himself. His shoulders dropped. "I knew about it. Listen, Roger, I know it may make no difference in your eyes, but I had nothing to do with arranging any of this. In fact I--" He stopped himself again, realizing how pathetic he sounded, and stared at the ground in shame.

Several moments passed as Roger stared at Reese with his head hung in guilt.

"Randall," Roger said calmly. "Why in God's name are you telling me any of this?"

Reese looked up, subconsciously noting the ironic wording of Roger's question. "I—I think it's important you know all this before the *Humanity* launches."

Roger's hunch was confirmed. "Okay, I get it. You think this information will somehow give us pause in using Keeling's money."

Reese said nothing.

"By the way, aside from the fact that Keeling knows this Doug character, what's the connection between him and Butler?"

"Well, Keeling and Doug were obviously heading to the White House for a meeting with the President." Reese stated matter-of-factly, as if this said it all.

"Randall, here's the deal; if you want me to get concerned about Keeling's money, I need to know—is there a direct connection between Keeling and the President, or between Keeling and the protests?"

Reese felt very unsure of himself. Until a few minutes ago, he'd been convinced that the information he was offering Tucker would cause the Mission Council to rethink the propriety of accepting Keeling's money, and thus their launch schedule. Now he suddenly realized that it might not be enough; that there was no real smoking gun.

"Randall!" Roger persisted, "Is there a direct connection?"

"I'm not sure... there must be," he said meekly.

The two men stared at each other without speaking. Roger searched Reese's eyes for any sign of guile or deception. He found none, but couldn't shake a growing sense of unease. Although Reese knew of no direct connection, that certainly didn't mean that there wasn't one. In fact, Reese was probably right. If Keeling was entering the White House with some lackey from Butler's past, it definitely wasn't good news. But he sure as hell wasn't going to share such thoughts with Reese.

"Is there anything else you want to tell me?" Roger implored.

Reese closed his eyes for several seconds. He opened them and pleaded with Roger: "You've got to stop the Mission. You and the Mission Council have the ability to help mankind, after thousands of years in the dark, to walk hand in hand with God."

There was a pause as Reese scanned Roger's face for any sign of understanding. "Please! Please Roger, don't let the Council turn their back on the Lord. With your help, Cerulea can become a second Eden!"

Roger stared at Reese a moment longer, then shook his head in disbelief. He turned and began walking hurriedly back the way they'd come.

Reese just stood on the path, watching him go, and contemplating the repercussions of the discussion that had just taken place. An hour ago he'd been so confident that this was the only clear path forward, and the right thing for him to do. Now he was a mass of uncertainty and confusion; he had no idea whether his disclosure would have any effect on the mission, or whether it would simply land him in jail.

99.

Kevin came out of the woods and walked rapidly back to the car. He had waited until both of the men he'd been following had left the park before emerging.

He got in the car and closed the door. "Let's get the fuck outta here."

Joey didn't move. "Whadja get?" he asked his partner.

"Not much. I think this thing is either busted or I was outta range."

"Didja hear anything?" Joey asked.

"Oh, some bullshit about a guy named Keeling. One of 'em also mentioned somethin' about the Mall explosion. And get this!" Kevin hit Joey on the shoulder with the back of his hand. "As they're walkin' out, Reese dives into this whole religious thing. Like he was a preacher or somethin'."

"He is a preacher, you fuckin' idiot." Joey hit a button on his wristphone and spoke his boss' name. "We better report in."

"No, screw that! Let's just do it when we get back to town."

"Kevin, cool it! This'll just take a sec."

Joey reported what Kevin had told him. He listened for a minute, then argued for a while, and finally agreed and hung up.

He pushed the start button, and pulled out of their parking spot. As he accelerated down the street, he turned to Kevin. "Boy, this is really going to piss you off."

100.

Roger Tucker passed Walter Reed Medical Center and headed back downtown; his mind was racing.

If what Reese had told him was true, then clearly there was a whole lot more to the story than he and the Council had been led to believe.

The vague outlines of a theory were forming in the back of Roger's brain, but he would need some more information before it could be considered anything other than crazy speculation.

He hit a button on his wristphone and requested a call with Mike Victor. Victor's electronic assistant answered; Roger noted that it was extremely urgent. He waited impatiently for thirty seconds; then another thirty. Finally Victor was on the line.

"Roger, sorry for the delay. What's going on?"

"Listen, Mike, I need some information. But I've got to insist that this doesn't go beyond the two of us."

"Roger, that's our business."

"I know, but I don't want this shared with anyone else at Verintel—at least for now. Are we understood?"

"You have my word. But Roger, before we go any further, I'd recommend we scan the line."

"Okay, go ahead."

"All right. Hold on a sec." Mike was silent for a few seconds as he initiated the procedure. "Okay, it looks clear, but these scans are only about 95% accurate. The only way to be sure is to use a secure phone on both ends, and it looks like yours is not fully encrypted."

"I know. Ninety-five percent will have to do for now." There were a number of perks that Roger missed from his White House days; state-of-the-art phones and not worrying about eavesdropping was one of them. "Mike, I need you to give me a full report on any connections between any of the investors, their companies, and Diametrix. Specifically, I want to know if Derek Butler and James Torgan have ever done business together."

Victor was silent for a moment. "Um, sure. No problem, Roger, I'll take care of it."

Roger sensed that his old friend was holding something back. "Your voice tells me there *is* a problem. What's the issue here?"

"Roger, this is a pretty sensitive topic for a line we don't know to be fully secure. I think it's probably best if we spoke in person."

Roger found himself a little irritated. His world had just become complicated enough without Mike Victor's constant circumspection. Not to mention that Mike's time was costing the Council over $800 an hour.

He looked at his watch. "Can you meet me at Mission headquarters in one hour?"

"Yes, I can," Victor replied.

"Good. I'll see you there."

Roger pulled to a stop at a traffic light on the Military Road overpass. He looked out the passenger window at the road winding its way through the park.

Then it hit him.

He thought back on Mike's last report, and the disparate pieces of the puzzle suddenly formed a cohesive whole in his mind. He ran around the perimeter of this unexpected conclusion, testing it to see if there were any gaping holes. There were none that he could see at first glance.

A car honked behind him. He looked up and noted that the light was green. He accelerated through the intersection, then almost immediately began breaking for a four-way stop at the next intersection.

Roger shook his head. Was he jumping to conclusions? If he was right, then Keeling had to be stopped. He thought of the agreement, and tried to remember whether there was any language that prohibited alternative use of the technology. *Frankly*, Roger reflected, *the whole notion that tourism could generate that amount of money seemed pretty far-fetched to begin with.*

His phone rang. As he reached over to activate the call, he realized that the answers he needed were in space—specifically, at L5 and on Cerulea itself; to get to the bottom of it he'd have to talk to Commander Belechenko and Devlin McGregor.

It was Cynthia. "Hey. I don't think lunch is going to work today," Roger said quickly.

"That's Okay. But I'm dying to know how it went. Tell all," Cynthia countered lightheartedly.

Roger was now paranoid himself about line security after his call with Mike Victor, so he got to the point without offering any details. "Cynthia, are you at headquarters?"

"I am; I'm in Jeff's office." Sensing his seriousness, she responded in kind. "Would you like me to meet you somewhere?"

"No, but I want you to do me a favor. I need you to get Belechenko, President Belknap, and Devlin McGregor to headquarters as soon as possible. Just tell them I requested it, and that it's important—nothing more. Understood?"

"Yes, but Roger, I believe Devlin's at NASA's Wallops Island facility for few days."

"Where is that?"

"I think it's on the Virginia shore."

"Cynthia, it's critical that he be present. Get an aircraft to pick him up immediately."

"Understood. I'll do it."

They hung up. Roger gripped the steering wheel tightly as he came to yet another one of the seeming incessant stoplights that inhibited forward progress in the nation's capital.

101.

A few cars ahead, they watched as Roger Tucker took a left hand turn into an underground parking lot.

Joey signaled to follow.

They turned left down the ramp and saw the tail lights of Roger's car pull out of sight. They stopped at a gate.

A voice came out of the intercom unit next to Joey's open window. "This is security. How can I help you?"

Joey shot a glance at Kevin, then stuck his head out the window. "My name's Sean O'Malley; I'm here to see Jeff Wheeler."

"Hold on." Several seconds passed. "I'm sorry Mr. O'Malley, I don't see you on the list."

Joey rolled his eyes, and nervously tapped his fingers on the steering wheel. He did his best to remain calm. "Uh, are you sure? He should be expecting—"

"Oh, I'm sorry," the guard interrupted, "it looks like Mr. Wheeler called down just a couple of minutes ago. Please park and proceed to the fifth floor. Mr. Wheeler will meet you there."

The gate went up. As the sedan slipped in to the garage, Kevin reached into the glove box, removed a case containing a stainless steel dart gun, and lowered the passenger side window.

Roger parked, grabbed his coat, and hopped out. He locked the car and headed toward the elevators.

As he gave further thought to the connections between Butler, Keeling and the protests, he realized that, above all else, he was pissed off. After all their effort, it infuriated him that they should have to deal with this crap at the end of the line. Maybe they should have seen it coming; maybe they were naïve to think that Keeling and his partners would invest so much money without an ulterior motive, but regardless, it just made him unbelievably mad.

And Butler. *What the hell were they going to do about that?* It was one, gigantic mess; Roger truly wished he'd never accepted Reese's invitation. Ignorance would be a hell of a lot easier than what he now faced.

He walked through one row of cars, then another, then took a right. The garage was fairly quiet; just one car looking for a place to park. The car turned down the lane Roger was in, so he quickened his step to pass in front of it.

As he did so, the car's engine surged and its tires screeched on the coated cement.

He turned to see a dark green sedan bearing down on him, and still accelerating. Everything seem to happen in slow motion; he turned back, attempting a retreat, just as the car swerved to pass behind him. The car smashed into his left hip, and Roger was thrown up and back along the passenger's side of the speeding car. The side view mirror caught his arm, twisting his body around and forcing his elbow back until his arm snapped.

He landed on his right shoulder and rolled several times, landing in a heap no more than fifteen feet from the glass doors to the elevators.

The car screeched around the corner and out of sight.

Roger lay there just barely conscious. For a brief moment, he felt nothing, then the pain came in a rush, shooting through his abdomen, arm and shoulder. Tears involuntarily welled up in his eyes as the pain overwhelmed his senses. Blood from a head wound trickled down his forehead, and pooled in his eyebrow; a drop landed on his eyelash, mixing with the tears.

He squeezed his eyelid shut. Then, with piercing pain in his shoulder, he managed to bring the hand of his unbroken arm to his face and wiped the blood away.

He lay there for what seemed like several minutes, breathing slowly, and fading in and out of consciousness. He began to feel dreadfully cold.

His eyes closed, and his breathing became more shallow. Part of him just wanted to sleep; he was suddenly so incredibly tired. But somewhere in the back of his brain, he realized that he had one last task to perform.

With all his strength, he rolled his body off his broken arm, grabbed the useless wrist with his other hand, and rolled back. The pain was excruciating.

He lay there again for a minute or two, catching his breath. Then, slowly, he pulled back the shirt cuff of his broken arm, and painstakingly began working the small buttons on his wristphone.

102.

Cynthia Fossett stood up from the conference table, cupping her ear, and raised a hand asking others in the room to quiet down. The noise subsided, but she still was unable to hear much of anything.

Cynthia turned away from the assembled group toward the window and put a finger in her other ear to concentrate on the call. "Roger, I can't hear you. If you can, please speak up," she implored.

The faint whispers grew a bit louder, but were still unintelligible. "Roger, are you hurt?" Again, there seemed to be a response, but she was unable to make any sense out it whatsoever.

The line went dead. "Roger? Roger!" She turned around. "The line dropped. I think he's in trouble somewhere."

She stabbed at the emergency button on her wristphone, waited a brief moment, then explained the situation to the police, offering what limited information she had. They told her that they would trace Roger's location, and that they'd get back to her with any new information.

She slumped down in a chair and looked at the concerned faces of President Belknap, Commander Belechenko and Mike Victor.

103.

The inside of the military transport plane was sparse—and very loud. An array of different equipment was strapped to hooks on each side of the fuselage, and rattled noisily. The steel skeleton of the craft had only rudimentary padding to prevent injury during turbulence. The floor was bare stainless steel.

Reese sat in a fold down seat bolted to the side of the aircraft. He realized it could be worse: several prisoners, hooded and in orange one-piece suits, were fixed in place by straps which anchored them to the floor.

He, on the other hand, was anchored to the wall. Like the prisoners, his wrists and feet were secured with plastic ties, but he was, for all practical purposes, fairly comfortable. And he didn't have to wear a bag over his head; although his mouth was taped shut—a not very subtle reminder, he assumed, of why he was here in the first place.

On the way back from Rock Creek Park, he'd been crestfallen. He'd felt as if his bold plan had done nothing more than make a bad situation yet more complicated. It certainly didn't seem as if his revelation to Roger Tucker was going to have any impact on the mission; and while squealing on the President of the United States might have been the right thing to do, he had definitely not done it with any eye toward truth or justice.

The fact that someone was waiting for him when he got back home somehow didn't come as much of a surprise. And as he was forced into a windowless van, then bound and gagged, it occurred to him that, if he was going where he suspected, he'd at least be spared the humiliation of a trial and accompanying media frenzy.

How stupid he'd been to think that he could set out on some autonomous crusade to stop the launch; as if he, Randall Reese, was going to outfox Derek Butler.

Reese rocked forward and put his face in his tethered hands. He closed his eyes and tried unsuccessfully to let the noise of the plane drown out the thoughts in his head. But visions of his family permeated his brain, along with his home in Wisconsin where, if he'd had any sense, he would be right now.

He began to cry softly; then harder. Finally, he sobbed convulsively, the engines muffling his grief.

104.

The afternoon sun illuminated the faces of the meticulously placed head stones. Behind them, long shadows created dark rectangles in the manicured lawn, as if each stone was placed before fresh earth.

The land on which Arlington National Cemetery stood was once the property of George Washington Parke Custis, the adopted grandson of the nation's first President, who built a large mansion on the property in the early 1800s. By a strange twist of fate, it eventually became the home of Robert E. Lee, who was married to Custis' daughter.

Toward the end of the Civil War, military graveyards in Washington were overflowing with fallen soldiers, so a Union General recommended using the land surrounding the Mansion for gravesites. It is said that this recommendation was motivated, at least in part, by a desire to lessen the prominence of a mansion belonging to the leader of the Confederate army.

Initially, soldiers buried at Arlington were from families too poor to have their bodies shipped home. Eventually, it became a distinguished honor to be buried within the cemetery.

Ginny looked on as two uniformed soldiers took the U.S. flag off of the coffin and folded it tightly into a triangle, while another played Taps. She heard sobs from Cynthia and several other onlookers. A few tears of her own worked their way out of her eyes and down her cheeks, as they had countless times over the past several days.

Although the launch of the *ESS Humanity*—one of the greatest achievements of her career—was now just a few weeks away, she felt completely empty. Roger's death had robbed her not only of an extremely close friend and confidant, but of her ability to care about the mission, her legacy, or even the fate of Cerulea.

She felt Belechenko squeeze her hand, and she leaned her head on his shoulder as the flag was presented to Seth Newben, Roger's spouse. She began to cry openly; Belechenko let go of her hand and put his arms around her shoulders.

As the graveside service came to a close, the group slowly dispersed and made their way toward a row of waiting cars.

Ginny approached Seth, and they embraced. They did not know each other well, having only chatted briefly on a few occasions. But as the two people who Roger spent more time with than anyone else, they shared an unspoken bond.

She then placed a hand on the shoulder of each of Roger and Seth's two children—both of whom were at that awkward age when a hug from an adult, regardless of the circumstances, was not particularly welcome.

She took Belechenko's hand and they headed for their car. Just as the driver opened the door and she was about to slide in, a Secret Service agent informed her that a police officer had requested a moment of her time.

The young woman, standing next to the agent, pulled a badge out of her pocket and presented it to Ginny. "President Belknap, I'm Detective Jackson. I'm very sorry to bother you at a time like this."

"That's quite all right, Detective, what can I do for you," Ginny replied, wiping tears from her cheeks and attempting to regain some composure.

"Well, Ma'am, we believe we've discovered some new evidence, and we wanted to follow it up as soon as we could. Would it be possible for me to ride with you just to the front gate?"

Ginny really wanted nothing more than to be left alone, but had no intention of obstructing the investigation into Roger's possible murder. "That would be fine."

The detective signaled to her partner as Ginny got into the car. Belechenko gestured for the detective to get in behind Ginny, then climbed in himself.

As the car began moving forward, the young woman wasted no time. "In studying the pictures of the crime scene, we noticed something that may be significant."

She pulled some photos from her pocket. "By the time Mr. Tucker was brought back to our lab, the display on his phone was blank—it must have timed out. But when our photographer took pictures at the scene, there appears to have been some characters still visible. They went unnoticed until just this morning."

Detective Jackson handed the photos to Ginny. "If we understand the timeline correctly, it appears that, after calling Cynthia Fossett, Mr. Tucker may have entered what looks like some type of equation on his phone."

Ginny stared at the photographs. The crime lab had cropped the image to include just the screen of Roger's phone and a portion of his wrist, but she could see blood stains on the small keypad. She shuddered, thinking of Roger's last moments in the garage, alone & dying, while they scrambled to find him from their conference room five floors up.

"President Belknap, does the character string mean anything to you?"

"Oh, I'm sorry," Ginny replied. She had temporarily forgotten the reason she'd been handed the photos in the first place. She looked back down and concentrated on the letters and symbols, then flipped to the next photo, which was essentially the same view from a different angle.

She stared, parsing the strange equation several different ways. All at once, it became clear that certain letters within the string were initials, and for a second she froze, as at least one possible meaning of several characters became clear. However, if she was right, it was not a theory she was willing to share with the detective. Not yet, anyway. Besides, the rest of it didn't seem to make any sense, and she wanted to be careful before she incriminated anyone.

"I apologize, detective, but I'm afraid this doesn't mean anything to me just yet, but I'd like to take these photos back and show them to some other people at Mission Headquarters who were working with Roger. Would that be all right?"

"That would be fine, Madam President. Please have someone call me immediately if anyone has any ideas." Detective Jackson handed Ginny her card.

"I will, Detective. Thank you."

105.

Ginny, Belechenko and Cynthia walked down the corridor toward a small meeting room at the far end of the Mission Headquarters building. All of them were still dressed in black from the graveside service.

They passed an office which had police tape across its locked door. Cynthia shook her head. "Boy, I'd like to know where the hell he is."

Ginny responded in an even voice. "Me too. But let's be careful not to condemn him before we know the facts."

"You're right, but the fact that the guy suddenly disappeared sure seems suspect."

They continued walking down the hall in silence.

Jeff Wheeler's office had been sealed by the police the day after Roger was hit. Security had confirmed that a car had entered the garage shortly after Roger's, and that the two men in the car were Wheeler's guests. However, that was all anybody knew. It wasn't clear whether that had been the car that ran Roger down; because it was Saturday, there was no one on duty in the fifth floor lounge, so it wasn't even clear whether Wheeler's guests ever made it up to see him.

Of course, the garage and all common areas of the facility, like just about every building in every major city, had an abundance of security cameras to record the comings and goings of personnel and—more important—persons unknown. Some building security systems used removable storage media, wherein storage modules were swapped out every few days, and the recorded video was then taken and archived at an alternate site. This was extremely expensive. Other systems simply used a looping algorithm; such that a rolling time interval of recorded video from each camera was always available for review, but the system would simply record over all footage beyond a designated point in time.

The system at Mission Headquarters used such a system, but somehow the time interval had been set futilely short; it had been programmed to loop every six minutes. Whether this had been done by accident or by malicious design was not yet clear, but the end result was that, by the time authorities got to the system, it had already recorded over every view of the incident many times over.

Thus, any evidence pointing to Wheeler's involvement was purely circumstantial. What kept him in the glare of suspicion, however, was that he had vanished. He was not answering his phone, and apparently had not even been back to his apartment since the incident.

The fact that Randall Reese had also been unreachable lent a conspiratorial air to the investigation, but the police had gone out of their way to emphasize to the media and others that such coincidences were common, and that no one should get too worked up until they'd made further progress.

☽☾

They reached the small room and found Devlin McGregor and Mike Victor waiting for them. After some introductions—Belechenko and Cynthia had never met Victor—everyone took a seat.

The room had been chosen precisely because it was a cramped, non-descript conference room that was rarely, if ever, used by high level Council staff. As such, it was far less likely to have been bugged. Nonetheless, it had been fully swept for listening devices just before their arrival. Like a number of meeting rooms within the facility, the walls here hung with a series of stunning photographs of space, taken over the past several decades by ever more powerful telescopes. Several of these were now askew, no doubt from their recent inspection.

As a result of Roger's death, security within the facility was undergoing a major overhaul; but until it was complete, Ginny wasn't taking any chances. As she began the discussion, she first impressed upon everyone present that if Roger was, in fact, murdered, the reason may well have been something he knew. Therefore, they must all be extremely cautious from here on out with regard to their own personal security and—in particular—with regard to what they said to whom.

She opened a folder that she'd brought with her, and grabbed the two photographs that she'd been given by Detective Jackson. She passed one to Cynthia on her left, and one to Belechenko on her right.

"What I'm passing around are two photographs taken of Roger's phone by the police shortly after his death." She explained what the detective had told her and Belechenko in the car as they left the cemetery.

"I think it's possible that the string of characters in the photos means absolutely nothing. But knowing Roger, I'm guessing that's not the case. At some point between heading out for the meeting with Randall Reese and returning to Headquarters, I think Roger got his hands on some information; information that he wanted to communicate to us before he died. Mike, would you do me a favor and write the characters from his wristphone on the board for us?"

Mike Victor had placed one of the photographs on the table in front of him. He was leaning on both elbows with his thumbs on his temples, clearly in deep concentration. He looked up after Ginny addressed him. "Oh, of course, Madam President." He got up from his chair and approached the board; with the photograph in one hand and a stylus in the other, he wrote out the character string. As he wrote, the characters automatically converted from Victor's handwriting into printed text.

1/3jk$=db-es
sgs=auptonc?
-m4mx=db

There was silence as the group studied the characters on the whiteboard.

Cynthia finally spoke up. "I've got to say, I've always been miserable at word puzzles. If Roger was trying to tell us something, I'm afraid it's totally lost on me."

Mike Victor stood at the board, arms crossed, his head at a slight angle as he contemplated the string. He turned to the group.

"I think," he began, "that there are three different messages here, each one separated by a dash."

He turned back around and, using the stylus copied the text string and pasted it on the other half of the board. He then began reformatting this new version. "As we can see in the photograph, the phone is using a typeface that allows twelve characters on a line, and is wrapping the lines accordingly. If we were to rewrite it as three distinct messages," he said, with a few final strokes of the stylus, "and removed the dashes, we would have… this."

He took a step back, revealing what looked like three different equations.

1/3jk$=db
essgs=auptonc?
m4mx=db

As everyone fixated on Victor's new arrangement, he looked directly at Ginny. "And I believe I know precisely what the first of these equations means."

All eyes immediately swung to Victor.

"Madam President, I believe I need your permission to discuss this with the group; the Council's contract with Verintel clearly states that all of our findings are to be reviewed only with Roger Tucker or yourself."

Ginny understood immediately. "Of course, Mike, please proceed."

"As I think some of you know, my company was working with Roger to investigate the identities and backgrounds of the investors comprising Jodee Keeling's syndicate. We had made substantial progress, but had yet to nail down the name of one last investor—an investor who was providing approximately one third of the $600 billion.

106.

It took a while for this revelation to sink in. Ginny had suspected as much when she'd first seen the photograph, and had shared her suspicions with Belechenko on the way back from the funeral. But to hear Mike Victor essentially confirm it was unsettling.

Cynthia and Devlin were flabbergasted. Partly because the President of the United States had anonymously invested in a mission he had publicly been dead set against; and partly because neither of them could contemplate that one individual had the money to make a 200 billion-dollar investment.

When they finally refocused their attention on the remaining two equations, Cynthia posed an obvious question. "If 'db' is Derek Butler in the top message, can we assume that 'db' refers to him in the third as well?"

"I think we have to make that assumption; at least until we prove otherwise," replied Victor, writing the name on the board next to the second "db."

For the next twenty minutes, the assembly alternated between discussion and silent study, jumping from one piece of the puzzle to another, without any real breakthroughs. All the while, Victor remained at the whiteboard, writing down bits of words and best guesses from the others. Given his career and expertise, it seemed only natural that he should serve as the facilitator of the group.

After a particularly long silence, Victor walked up and circled the third equation:

m4mx=db

"Let's take another look at 'm4m.' Has anyone come up with anything? We noted earlier that '4' in this case probably means 'for'; so what we've got is: blank for blank is somehow tied to President Butler."

The room was quiet save for the scratching of pens on paper; Cynthia and Ginny had both begun using a pad to play with different word combinations. Devlin had borrowed a sheet of paper and began doing the same.

Belechenko, who'd been staring intently at the board, either ignored Victor's last comment or had simply been too absorbed to hear it. He leaned forward and pointed. "Mike, it's possible that 'ess' in the second equation stands for Earth Space Ship, but I'm not sure about the--" His face suddenly lit up. "Of course!" He raised both hands above his head. "Keeling's ship! 'essgs' must stand for the ESS Goldstar."

Mike immediately began writing 'ESS Goldstar' next to the equation on the board.

"That's great, Commander. How about the rest of it? Anything?" Mike asked.

"March for Mankind!" Cynthia blurted out, looking up from her pad. "Is that a possibility?"

Victor laughed at the haphazard nature of the team's breakthroughs. "This is great; keep it coming," he encouraged, writing the phrase next to the last equation. There was quiet as everyone pondered the newly placed pieces of the puzzle.

"Oh, I don't know," Cynthia added, doubt creeping into her voice. "Maybe that's wrong. Maybe 'mx' means something differently entirely."

"Unless," Ginny said slowly. "Unless the 'x' stands for explosion."

Cynthia gasped. "Holy cow! That's not possible!"

"No?" Ginny asked rhetorically, as Victor wrote out the possible meaning in full on the board: 'March for Mankind explosion = Derek Butler.'

Cynthia, Devlin and Belechenko all stared at Ginny, amazed that she didn't seem to have any problem believing that this translation was even a possibility.

It was Belechenko who challenged her. "Do you honestly think it's possible that Derek Butler was behind the Mall incident?"

Ginny put her pen down and leaned back in her chair. "I'm not sure. But I'll tell you this. If Butler is the third investor, then it's pretty clear that the man is not who he appears to be. It's also worth noting that he surged ahead in the polls in the days that followed. The March itself was significant; but that explosion did more to galvanize religious conservatives than any other single campaign event. Even after we learned that the perpetrators had ties to the right, Butler still walked away with a pretty substantial net gain in popularity.

"So yes, I think it's possible." She turned to Mike Victor. "What about you, Mike? As I recall, you and Roger spent a fair amount of effort looking into various protests, and found some fairly underhanded tactics at work. Do you think it's possible that it somehow went all the way up to Butler?"

"Boy, I don't know, Madam President. I certainly don't believe that it's *im*possible. But I also don't think we have a shred of evidence one way or the other, so I'm not inclined to lean toward any specific conclusion at this point."

Ginny smiled. She distinctly remembered Roger's frustration when he would come back from his meetings with Mike Victor in the White House Intelligence Lab. He had great respect for Mike, but always felt that he was unwilling to take a stand until the evidence was overwhelming.

In this case, Ginny had to admit that he was right, and said so. "I agree with you, Mike. I don't think we have a clue what the actual truth is here, and I think it awfully unwise to jump to any conclusions. But we also have to remember that we're not trying to find the truth right now—we're trying to figure out what Roger thought was the truth, and what you just wrote up there is the best fit we've looked at thus far."

A thought occurred to Ginny; she crossed her arms pensively. "Let's think about this," she began, "Roger was returning from a meeting with Reese, so it's only logical to assume that Reese gave him some or all of this information—or at least hinted at it. Whether it's true or not, the question we might ask ourselves is why Reese would want Roger to know any of this--"

As soon as Ginny had given voice to the question, several others at the table arrived at the same conclusion.

"Of course!" Cynthia exclaimed.

Devlin and Mike Victor looked at her with slightly confused expressions; they clearly hadn't gotten there yet. Cynthia explained: "Randall Reese had watched as President Butler effectively gave up on actively opposing the *Humanity's* launch. With just two and a half weeks to go, he had to be beside himself. Giving Roger some of this information was probably a last ditch effort to throw a wrench into the launch schedule."

Ginny jumped back in. "He obviously reasoned that if we were to become aware of Butler's involvement, we'd inevitably have second thoughts about the launch; we'd hesitate to use what we would consider tainted money. Telling Roger that Butler was behind the tragedy on the Mall may have been a ploy to ensure that Roger had no choice; to proceed as planned would, in effect, make the Council an accessory to the crime."

There was a long silence, as everyone in the room realized that, if this was indeed Reese's plan, it was a damn good one.

Belechenko finally spoke up. "So now what?"

Ginny let out an audible sigh. She stared at one of the photographs on the wall, a gorgeous image of a nebula in which several stars were being born. She thought of the incredible journey that awaited the *Humanity*, and reflected on the notion of leaving this twisted and conflicted world and starting over on another. It was actually the first time she'd ever sincerely been attracted to the idea of leaving Earth for good.

At the root of her anxiety was a painful yearning to have Roger back at her side. She missed him terribly; not only as a friend, but also as a critical partner in situations like this. Without him next to her, problems seemed larger and more formidable, while she felt smaller and less capable. She realized—not for the first time—the extent to which their collaboration had been the foundation of her success over the past decade.

"Well," she said at last, noting that everyone in the room was looking at her for an answer to Belechenko's question. "I don't think we're going to resolve that here. Ultimately, the Mission Council is going to have to weigh in and make some very tough decisions."

She sat up in her chair, clasped her hands in front of her, and changed the subject back to the matter at hand. "Mike, why don't we see if we can't decipher the last piece of this puzzle."

The group refocused their attention on the middle equation: $essgs=auptonc$? However, their momentum had stalled. Another twenty minutes elapsed, during which they methodically documented the initials of everyone involved in the Mission, and eventually every member of the Butler administration. But nothing clicked. The fact that Roger had appended the equation with a question mark was a further source of discussion. Did this mean he wasn't sure? Or was the question mark part of the puzzle?

In the end, the meeting broke without a solution. Ginny thanked everyone for their efforts and retreated to her office, carrying on her shoulders the boulder-sized burden of figuring out where to go from here.

107.

The V-90 Dragonfly tiltrotor aircraft streamed through the sky five thousand feet above Chesapeake Bay. Devlin had ridden on helicopters in the past, but this was something else. An offshoot of the V-22 Osprey, this was the next generation; with a top speed of 425 mph, it was 30% faster than its sibling and two and half times faster than its fixed blade ancestors. While the technology had encountered some pretty heavily turbulence as it moved from testing ground to commercial use, it was now the U.S. Military's primary short-flight workhorse—and had already replaced more than half of all commercial helicopters.

Devlin was not used to traveling in such style, but at the moment, as he surveyed the dark blue waters and familiar shoreline, his mind was elsewhere. He was thinking of the unsolved equation, trying to make sense of it.

Cynthia told him that Roger had insisted he be retrieved from Wallops Island, yet it wasn't at all clear to Devlin as to why. He wasn't an official member of the Council; he certainly had nothing to do with the financing effort, and had never even met President Butler.

Yet for some reason, Roger wanted him there. Devlin's inherent sense of order and logic dictated that there must be a specific reason. All he could think of was that the unsolved equation was somehow relevant to his expertise.

He reached into his shirt pocket and removed a piece of paper on which he'd written the message.

essgs=auptonc?

He stared at it for the fifth or sixth time since leaving D.C. What Devlin knew about the ESS Goldstar was minimal; it was essentially a smaller version of the *Humanity*. So what was the meaning of "auptonc?"

He started repeating the first two letters over and over. A strange idea entered his brain, and a chill ran down his spine. He had to be wrong. In fact, he wanted desperately to be wrong.

As he gave it further thought, he gained some comfort in that it seemed somewhat forced. Although it offered one very frightening solution to the puzzle, it was only one possibility—and, he hoped, a long shot at best.

Nonetheless, he felt compelled to call it in. He grabbed the sat phone from its cradle on the bulkhead in front of him, and was about to call Cynthia, but thought better of it. *She'd go berserk at the mere suggestion*, he thought. Instead he called Commander Belechenko.

"Commander, this is Devlin," he yelled over the drone of the rotors.

"Yes, Devlin. What can I do for you?"

"Well, I was thinking about this last unsolved equation, and I had a silly thought."

"I'm sure it is not silly. What've you got?"

"The elemental symbols for gold and platinum are au and pt. Do you suppose it's possible that Roger was raising the possibility that the ESS Goldstar was going to try and find precious metals on Cerulea?"

"'essg=auptonc'," Belechenko repeated the clue out loud. "Boy, I hope you're way off on this one, but I don't think we can rule it out. Let me discuss it with a few other members of the group, and see what they think. I'll give a call tonight if we think it bears further discussion."

"I sure hope it doesn't," Devlin noted. They hung up.

Devlin stared out the window of the aircraft and thought back to a technology briefing he and Commander Belechenko had delivered to Roger Tucker in the Cabinet Room of the White House, shortly before the discovery of Cerulea was announced. They'd discussed the presence of magnetite in the atmosphere, and Roger had been intrigued that it might be an indication of gold and platinum in the crust of the planet.

Devlin shook his head and tried to put the whole idea out of his mind. He reached down and grabbed a binder out of his bag. He was on loan to a team at NASA's Wallops Flight Center as part of a consulting engagement on a new telescope design; the team had recently had their budget cut, and they wanted Devlin's help in evaluating how best to trim back the operational scope of the project, while sacrificing as little of the telescope's functionality as possible.

Devlin had taken on a number of such assignments over the past several years. His instant celebrity following the initial discovery of Cerulea, coupled with the distinction of winning the National Medal of Science had changed the trajectory of his career.

He had not been placed on a management track – nor had he wished to be. Instead, he became a full time NASA fellow, a tribal elder of sorts, who was expected to lend his expertise and wisdom to projects of his choosing. At first it seemed awkward; but it quickly became clear that, as an outsider, he could add a lot of value by helping teams to think in new directions. By coming at issues from a new angle, he was quite successful in helping them overcome stubborn obstacles with innovative solutions.

Devlin was deep in thought regarding the proposed redesign of the telescope's gyroscopes, when he felt the aircraft bank hard to the left.

He looked up from the binder on his lap and heard the captain in his headphones: "Mr. McGregor, we just received orders to return you to Washington. There's a Commander Belechenko holding for you on the sat phone; just punch 76 to access the call."

Devlin followed the captain's instructions. "Commander? What's going on?"

"Well, Devlin, apparently Mike Victor thinks your crazy idea isn't so crazy. And we're going to need someone with knowledge of planetary geology."

108.

As the team began exploring Devlin's hypothesis, several discoveries seemed to offer some corroboration.

The first of these was the design of the *Goldstar*. After Belechenko's efforts to get access to the new ship's blueprints were unsuccessful, he confidentially briefed Jim Stanton on their situation, and asked him to casually invite a few of the *Goldstar's* low-level engineers on a tour of the *Humanity* as a friendly gesture.

Stanton understood immediately. Once the engineers came aboard, the conversation was enlightening; Stanton learned that the *Goldstar*, although one third the size of the *Humanity*, would have roughly four times the cargo space; a design feature that seemed to make no sense for a space-based cruise ship intended for relatively short expeditions. This also meant that there wouldn't be much room left for the type of luxurious living quarters that Keeling had described in his proposal.

Furthermore, Mike Victor discovered a fair amount of conjecture on the internet regarding large deposits of gold, platinum and other precious metals on Cerulea, along with some rather frightening proposals involving the use of nuclear devices for extraction. This in itself didn't mean much; the internet was a veritable treasure trove of bizarre theories on all things Cerulean—including the existence of dinosaurs and how they might be brought back to Earth. However, what gave Victor pause was that two scientists who'd written fairly well-supported papers on mining the planet appeared to have since taken jobs with one of James Torgan's companies.

Once this evidence was in hand, the next question was what to do about it.

Devlin and Cynthia, both incensed, advocated that they should immediately go to the FBI and the press and release everything they had, so that Keeling, Butler and Torgan would be stopped in their tracks. Cynthia was beside herself that, after she and her team had carefully crafted environmental protections into the Cerulean Constitution, Butler had quite deliberately forged a plan to defy the document and harvest resources from the planet without even informing its eventual inhabitants.

To Devlin, the news of the *Goldstar's* design was an absolute nightmare. Ever since his discovery had been made public, he'd worried that, as a result of his efforts, a pristine, unsuspecting planet would be abused by an invasive species.

The idea of someone mining Cerulea using nuclear devices, and bringing its minerals back to an overpopulated Earth, made him physically ill.

Commander Belechenko was actually more intrigued than perturbed. He had spent several years earlier in his ISS career helping to build the Lunar extraction facility. While he was decidedly suspect regarding Butler and Torgan's ultimate motives, he was more comfortable with the notion of mining other planets, and professionally curious as to how they actually planned on making the whole venture work logistically—let alone economically, since it would take close to thirty years to send a ship to Cerulea and back.

Ginny was single-minded; the only question in her mind was how to handle all of these revelations ethically and in such a way that the *Humanity* launched on schedule. Clearly, the public would be outraged—and rightly so—if they waited until post-launch to disclose that members of the Mission Council knew in advance that their new investors were planning to mine the planet. As for Butler's involvement as an investor, and his possible connection to the Mall tragedy, she'd need a lawyer's advice.

Meanwhile, the media intrigue surrounding Roger's death had started to dissipate.

The police had come up empty in their investigation, and the FBI had refused to get involved in the case. The disappearance of Randall Reese, which had kept the story alive, ceased to be a mystery when he made two calls—one to a detective, and one to a reporter, telling them both that he knew nothing about Roger's murder, and that he was taking a long, well deserved vacation, and would provide the police with everything he knew in due course.

Although the police had questioned the taxi driver who drove Reese home on the day of Roger's death—providing Reese with an irrefutable alibi—the detective was nonetheless insistent that Reese immediately report for further questioning. He refused, and they had no legal means to back their request with force.

After discreetly sharing details of the situation with the voting members of the Mission Council, speaking with the Council's attorneys, and engaging in several long conversations with Belechenko, Ginny at last came to a decision as to how she wanted to proceed.

109.

Over 12,000 miles away, on the other side of the globe, Jodee Keeling stepped off the elevator on the 98th floor of the Torgan Tower in Kuala Lumpur, Malaysia, and was greeted by Asmida Farah, Torgan's appointed research director for the project. She led him through a set of double glass doors into the laboratory.

The project team had been assembled rapidly once Keeling's proposal had been formally accepted by the Mission Council. They had immediately gotten to work, and already had something to show for their efforts.

The lab was exquisite; though focused primarily on computer-based research, every piece of equipment was state-of-the-art. Along with the exorbitant salaries offered to everyone on staff, the facility itself had been a huge draw in recruiting top talent.

Asmida gave Keeling a tour, after which they ended up at the workstation of a young engineer who was making final, last-minute changes to his presentation, which was next on the agenda. He was seated in front of three oversized screens.

He nervously began with a brief history of space-based mining:

"For decades, scientists have dreamed of mining asteroids within our solar system. The riches embedded in these rocks are estimated to be in the thousands of trillions of dollars. In fact, it's believed that just one of the roughly one million large asteroids in the belt between Mars and Jupiter could produce close to 7,500 tons of platinum, valued at over $510 billion at today's prices."

As he spoke, different images appeared on different screens, relevant to his key points.

"The problem, of course, is economics. Even though an asteroid might have an extremely high concentration of platinum, it's often evenly distributed throughout what is essentially a giant block of stainless steel. So the refining process would be very expensive, not to mention the fact that you've got to bring all of the unwieldy ore to the refining location.

"And, of course, the secondary issue is zero gravity. While a zero G environment may facilitate the transportation of heavy loads, it makes just about everything else infinitely more difficult; that's one reason why something as simple as a toilet sells for a few hundred bucks on Earth, but costs millions of dollars on a spaceship.

"So, despite years and years of effort, the whole idea of mining asteroids was eventually abandoned as cost-prohibitive."

Keeling was mildly intrigued by the lesson on asteroids, but he was also impatient.

"I very much appreciate the history lesson, young man, but what's it got to do with mining Cerulea?"

Asmida Farah, worried that her esteemed guest was not being well served, took control. "Well, Mr. Keeling, the point here is simply that, without access to the Alcubierre FTL technology, the mining of nearby space is simply not practical. Cerulea—along with the other distant planetary bodies under consideration—does not present such problems, and thus offers a much better return on investment."

"Well, I'm awfully glad to hear that," Keeling replied, remaining more or less cheerful. "But I'd love to know how exactly how we'll be getting gold and platinum off the planet's surface."

"Of course." Asmida said, relaxing a bit. "Although we still have some work to do on the details, a conceptual plan is in place."

She gestured to the one of the screens, and the engineer resumed his presentation. "The *Goldstar* will perform an initial scan of the planet and identify target mining sites. It will then assume a stationary orbit above a selected site." On screen, Keeling witnessed a simulation of what he'd described.

"Next, the *Goldstar* will launch a series of planet penetrating weapons, or PPWs, which will open the surface of the planet for mining." The middle screen displayed another simulation.

"Once a crater is created, robotic collectors will be sent down to the planet's surface to search for rocks with high concentrations of target minerals, sending only high grade ore back to the ship. Equipment on the Goldstar will refine this material and dump the waste into space." He pointed to the third screen.

"While further refinement will be required, we are estimating that the materials making the return trip will be of a very high concentration—in the neighborhood of 85%-90%."

"And how do we plan on bringing this ore back to the ship?" Keeling asked.

"All of the collected material will be delivered back to the ship via space lift."

"And what is that, exactly," Keeling asked the young engineer.

The engineer pointed to a screen showing an animation of the concept. "It's essentially an elevator. The Goldstar would lower a solar powered base station and climbing car down through Cerulea's atmosphere to the planet's surface using cable made from carbon nanotube fiber. This would then serve as the means for hoisting the high-purity ore back up to the ship."

"Wouldn't the weight of the ore pull the ship down with it?"

"A good question, sir." The engineer did his best to suppress a smile. "The short answer is no, it would not. The ship would assume a position just beyond geosynchronous orbit. As the planet and ship rotated in tandem, the centrifugal force would actually counterbalance the weight of the cable along with even the largest of loads."

"Fascinating." Keeling was quiet for a moment as he studied the repeating simulations on each screen. Finally he looked up at Asmida. "These PPWs; they're similar to what we used to call 'bunker busters' here on Earth?" Keeling asked.

"They are," Asmida confirmed, "Only more powerful."

"And these are nuclear devices?"

"They are, but we believe any fallout would be localized."

"Hmmm." Keeling crossed his arms and gave this some thought. "So the Cerulean colony would not be affected?"

Keeling had addressed Asmida, but threw a sideward glance at the engineer to see if the question elicited a reaction; it did not.

"No, not at all," Asmida assured him. "The mining sites would be chosen specifically such that fallout would dissipate well away from any human inhabitants."

"Okay," Keeling said, seemingly satisfied. He turned to the young engineer; "I must say, very impressive." He patted the young engineer on the shoulder, who nodded his acknowledgement, blushing slightly.

"Now, Mr. Keeling, if you have time," Asmida declared, "I'd like to review some schedules and budgetary figures."

They started walking down a long corridor between rows of workstations toward her office.

"So how goes the search for secondary targets?" Keeling asked as they walked.

"As per your instructions, we've contracted with a private observatory in New Mexico," Asmida replied, "they're analyzing all known exoplanets in an effort to identify their mining potential--"

"Asmida, I'm still learning your language. Is that the same as an extrasolar planet?"

"Oh. I'm sorry, Mr. Keeling. Yes, they're essentially the same thing; any planet which orbits a star other than our own sun. Anyway, the observatory will be providing us with a report of their findings within a month or two, but their preliminary data is promising."

"Well, that's good news. I'll look forward to getting my hands on the report."

"I should warn you, however; it may take some time before we identify additional planets with Cerulea's gold and platinum concentrations."

"Understood," Keeling replied. They continued down the corridor to Asmida's office.

110.

Ginny sat patiently outside the Oval Office waiting for Butler to finish up a meeting with his chief of staff.

This was the first time that she'd been back to the White House since her departure four months ago. It was a surreal experience; virtually everything was new; new furniture, new carpets, new drapes, even the wallpaper was new—leaving absolutely no doubt in anyone's mind that there was a new captain at the helm of the U.S. ship of state.

Agnes Murphy, the President's secretary, saw the light flash on her console. "Madam President, President Butler will see you now."

Agnes got up from her desk and escorted Ginny into the Oval Office.

"Madam President!" Butler exclaimed, smiling broadly and striding toward her with hand outstretched. "Welcome."

Ginny allowed his bold charm to evoke a smile and shook his hand. "Thank you for seeing me, Mr. President."

The whole Madam/Mister President thing seemed overwrought, but it occurred to Ginny that, on this occasion, it would be helpful to have some level of parity with this man.

"Would you like some coffee? Water?"

"Coffee would be great. Black."

"Agnes?" He caught his secretary as she was closing the door behind her. "I'll have some as well."

"Yes, sir." Agnes closed the door, leaving them alone.

"Please," Butler gestured to the sofas, inviting Ginny to take a seat.

She sat where Roger used to sit, although the furniture was so different from when this was her office, any nostalgic flashback was muted. Butler sat down next to her in his leather wingback chair.

The two of them chatted casually for several minutes. Ginny congratulated him on the recent passage of a major deregulation bill, the fulfillment of a major campaign promise; Butler asked her about the final preparations for the launch of the *Humanity*—now less than two weeks away. They talked about life in the White House, and eventually ran out of pleasantries.

Ginny then wasted no time.

"Mr. President, I came here today to discuss a few issues surrounding Cerulea."

"Well, given my attempt to take over your job at the Mission Council a while back, I must say I wasn't expecting to be consulted."

Ginny smiled warily. Butler's candor was disarming, but she had no intention of laying down her ammunition. "Actually, it concerns the activities of the investor syndicate who's funding our launch."

"That's a clever way of phrasing it; I believe the American taxpayers are still funding close to 55% of the Mission overall. I believe your new investors are well below that mark."

Ginny looked at Butler. She had a momentary flash of doubt. *Either this guy's very sharp, or my ammunition is all wet* she thought to herself. She quickly settled on the former; Mike Victor had been certain of Butler's involvement in the syndicate.

"We've discovered," Ginny said carefully, "that our new investors are not exactly who or what they appeared to be."

The two executives held each other's gaze. Butler offered no indication whatsoever that her comment had rattled him in any way.

At that moment, Agnes knocked and entered the office carrying a small tray. "Excuse me, Mr. President." She placed the tray on an end table next to the sofa across from Ginny, then handed each of them a cup and saucer. Both Ginny and Butler thanked her, and she left, closing the door behind her.

Butler dove right back into the line of fire. "Not what they appeared to be. How so?" he asked naturally.

"Let me put it this way," she replied. "We've learned that the identities of the silent partners, if revealed to the general public, would cause quite a stir."

"I see." He took a sip of coffee, and held the cup and saucer in his lap. "Wouldn't revealing their identities be a breach or your agreement?"

Just as the Mission Council attorneys had predicted, the dance had begun. Ginny would have far preferred a much more straightforward approach, but she was also very well-versed in the intricacies of plausibility of denial—as was the man sitting next to her. The lawyers had insisted that she make no direct accusations, and if possible, make no definitive statements regarding what she did or did not know.

"Yes, as a matter of fact it would violate the agreement—that is, if it was the Mission Council who did the revealing."

Butler nodded his acknowledgement of her point, but remained silent. She suspected that her first shot had found its mark.

"We have also come to believe that the business plan attached to the investment proposal might not have fully represented the syndicate's intended use of the technology." She let the statement hang in the air for a few seconds before continuing. "And we are extremely concerned that some of their future activities may directly interfere with the well-being of the Cerulean colony."

Butler raised an eyebrow slightly, then downed the remainder of his coffee. Ginny wasn't sure, but he seemed to have been angered by her last remark.

He turned in his chair, placed the cup and saucer on the table. "Let me ask you: does your agreement with your investors limit their use of the technology to space tourism? Or are they free to use it for other profit-making ventures as they see fit?"

He asked these questions with the sharp, cold tone of a defense attorney seeking to establish that the DA hasn't got a case.

Ginny hesitated, then answered his question. "I believe the agreement is somewhat vague on the subject, so I would presume that, legally, the investors are free to use the technology for other purposes. However—"

"Then I think we're about through here, Ms. Belknap." He stood up from his chair.

His comment was biting; completely absent the cordiality that had characterized their conversation just moments earlier.

Ginny rose from the sofa, and they stared at each other for what seemed like half a minute. Ginny had an involuntary urge to swallow, but suppressed it.

Butler was an intimidating bastard, but she hadn't held this office successfully for eight years without a well-developed ability to stand up to such men.

Tired of all this obfuscation, she abandoned the script she'd been given, and responded to Butler with the same cold tone. "May I ask if this conversation is being recorded?"

She knew full well that the Oval Office had a sophisticated system for capturing every word spoken during a meeting—but only if the President chose to activate it.

Butler glared at Ginny. "No. This conversation is not being recorded."

Something told her he was telling the truth. But it really didn't matter; he stood to suffer far worse than she if their words were ever to find their way into anyone else's hands.

Ginny took a step toward Butler, and spoke firmly and directly. "Then I'll cut to the chase. You can ask all the questions you like regarding the agreement, but let's be clear here. This isn't about what is and isn't legal. This is not about what may or may not happen in a court of law; it's about what will happen in the court of public opinion. So let me tell you what I want, Mr. Butler."

She paused, drawing a breath. "I want you to agree that none of your syndicate's ships will ever come within one light year of Cerulea."

Ginny had clearly pushed the right buttons; Butler was incensed. He responded with venomous hostility. "Those ships will go wherever they damn well please. Go ahead, tell the press and the public about my involvement. In fact, why don't you hold a press conference this afternoon? Then see if your precious *Humanity* ever makes it out of spacedock.

"Frankly, I'm not sure you know who you're dealing with. I think you'll find that I'm well prepared to fend off a few grenades from the press—and equally prepared to throw a few of my own."

Ginny jumped on his last comment: "Oh, I'm well aware of that!" She strolled over and looked out the window behind Butler's desk, "In fact, I'll bet if you threw one from here, you might even be able to hit the Mall."

She turned and looked back at Derek Butler. For the first time since she'd ever laid eyes on him, he was speechless.

III.

The two men walked slowly down the tree-lined path meticulously layered with crushed shells. The lake was visible ahead of them to the right. The elaborate mansion rose majestically from a small hill just beyond. The woods surrounding Butler's Virginia estate were rich with the sights, sounds and smells of approaching summer. A pilated woodpecker hammered an oak tree not far way, while the scent of lilac permeated the warm, mild breeze.

Derek Butler was oblivious to all of it.

"I don't give a shit," he barked. "This thing is too far along for us to back out of it now," Butler insisted to his old associate. "Besides, Torgan would have my head if we reneged on the deal."

"But sir, you're the President of the United States; what can he—"

"Oh, screw that!" Butler interjected. "Torgan wouldn't care if I was emperor. The guy has never exactly shown much deference to those in power."

Butler paused and thought for several moments. "If we take Cerulea off the target list, the odds of a decent return on investment go right out the window." He turned to his old colleague. "Listen Doug, you simply have to find a way to neutralize the threat of disclosure. I don't care what it takes, or how much it'll cost."

Doug responded to the President's command carefully. "I'm not sure that's possible, sir. They've got enough information to sink our entire venture—and your presidency along with it. There is no way to neutralize this without taking Cerulea out of the equation. Period. We've got to start thinking about alternative strategies."

They walked along in silence. Butler angrily kicked a pine cone off the path and into the woods.

"God damn it!" he shouted, clearly frustrated by the turn of events. "All right, let's suppose we did rule out Cerulea. What do you see as our options?"

"Well, for starters," Doug said calmly, "I would suggest we scale up the contract with the observatory in New Mexico, and redouble our efforts to find new targets."

"And if we come up dry?"

"We won't come up dry, sir. The resources are out there; it's simply a question of how much longer it will take us to reach breakeven. Keeling told me just last night that they've already begun evaluating a number of other planets."

Butler stared down at the path, shaking his head. "All right. Let's do it. Buy the damn observatory if you have to—buy several; just make sure we find the targets we need, and fast."

"I will take care of it," Doug replied, as he had so many times before.

They had come around a bend in the path. Off to their left, Doug could see the endless maze of paddocks, each with several beautifully groomed horses lazily grazing in the early afternoon sun. Up by the stables and indoor ring, a young girl appeared to be training a colt. He watched as she led him in a circle at the end of a long rope.

"Now, what's to prevent Belknap from coming at me again?" Butler inquired, pulling Doug back to the conversation.

Doug let his eyes drift back to lake up ahead. "That's easy. I'll have an addendum to the Mission Council contract drafted, which clearly states that if your investment in the venture—or your involvement in the Mall tragedy—ever becomes public, for any reason, then Cerulea will once again be a target of our mining efforts."

"Doug, how the hell are you going to contractualize that without admitting guilt in the process?"

"We'll find a way; that's what good lawyers are for."

"Okay, but I want to see the language before it goes. Understood?"

"Yes, sir."

"Now, what about our other loose ends? Let's start with Wheeler."

"Well, he did exactly as he was told: after calling security, he got the hell out of there and made himself scarce."

"Have you found him yet?"

"No, not yet, but we're working it. I'm not particularly worried; the guy's a speechwriter, not a trained operative; my guess is he's just scared and hiding somewhere. He'll turn up."

Doug was more worried than he let on. Wheeler had never failed to check in before. In addition, he was clearly rattled when Doug had called him that day to let his boys into the garage. He'd agreed to do it, but had then asked Doug point blank whether there was a definitive plan in place to halt the Mission.

"And what about Reese?" Butler asked.

"We'll be releasing him shortly. He's been apprised that his continued cooperation and his family's well being are directly linked. The same with Joe Condon."

"Doug," Butler said, his eyes almost pleading. "I need you to come through for me on all of this. Everything depends upon your success."

Doug looked over at his boss. He had served this man for the better part of three decades. Once upon a time, in the early days of Diametrix, the tasks he had been called on to perform had all seemed to be for a good cause—and well within the bounds of the law. But over the last ten years, he felt himself sliding down a slippery slope into activities that increasingly placed him on the wrong side of a line he'd never wanted to cross. At first, he thought it temporary; the questionable assignments were just anomalies within a continuum of good hard work for a man with exceptional drive and talent.

Now, he realized that this man's ambition had turned a corner, and that he had followed. Perhaps there had once been a time when he might have cleanly extricated himself—but now it seemed that time was passed. He had crossed the Rubicon, and the fate of this man was now his own.

Doug looked into Butler's eyes. "I'll take care of it, sir. You can count on it."

112.

The addendum to the agreement arrived at Mission Headquarters by courier at just past 10 am. Ginny read it through briefly, then had it sent to their general counsel for a full legal review.

As far as she could see, it was exactly what she'd requested. The *Goldstar* and any subsequent spacecraft built by Keeling's syndicate were prohibited from traveling to Cerulea under any and all circumstances. At the same time, as expected, the confidentiality section of the original agreement was expanded considerably; Ginny noted not without some admiration the artful language employed to prevent her from ever mentioning what she knew about Butler. While his name was never mentioned, the meaning was clear.

So Derek Butler's role as a silent partner in the syndicate would now remain silent. His involvement broke no laws, nor did her discretion. With regards to the Mall tragedy, the idea that she was withholding evidence might have been a bigger issue—if, in fact, she had any. To date, despite numerous attempts by her team to corroborate their suspicions, the only piece of evidence linking Butler to the incident was the equation on Roger's wristphone—which could barely even be characterized as hearsay.

She spent some time reviewing her speech and making several modest changes, then tidied up her office and prepared to head off to the big event.

113.

The parade route, running along Constitution Avenue from 7th street up to 17th, had been blocked off for 48 hours to allow for a full security sweep and subsequent containment of the area.

Spectators had begun gathering along the road at dawn; there were now over 250,000 people lining the route. Except for those with proper credentials, every single one of them had passed through one of several dozen Sniffers placed around the perimeter on their way in.

A platform had been built in front of the Washington Monument, where Ginny, along with the Secretary General of the UN and several other World leaders, would deliver their speeches. In the center of the platform was a podium, with a dais on either side; here would be seated all voting members of the Mission Council, as well as Jim Stanton, who had traveled back to Earth specifically for the event.

Although he'd done so under protest.

He had pleaded with Belechenko to allow him to stay on board the *Humanity*, claiming that there were numerous issues to resolve before the launch. The Commander was unmoved. This event was the world's send-off to the crew, and it was imperative that the leader of that crew be present.

There had been another reason Jim had wanted to stay in space. In the months leading up to his departure, the strain on his relationship with Stacy had proved unbearable. They had fought often, always about little things, but it was clear that she had built up a tremendous amount of resentment over the fact that the *Humanity* would soon remove him from her life.

So they had said their goodbyes early, effectively ending a relationship that had been doomed for nearly two years—ever since Stacy had failed her health qualification for a position on the crew.

It was wrenching for both of them; when Jim left to return to space, he felt completely drained—almost unable to function. Ironically, it was only by immersing himself in the needs of his ship that he eventually began to heal. Even though they had no plans to see one another during this visit—he would only be on Earth for a total of 36 hours—the mere fact that they could made his chest ache.

They all took their positions within their assigned vehicles, which were parked in a garage beneath the National Gallery.

Stanton was in the lead car with President Belknap and Commander Belechenko. The car was essentially a stretch limousine, but instead of a conventional roof, it had a bulletproof, plexiglass bubble that allowed the crowd to clearly see the vehicle's occupants.

Ostensibly, this security shield was for Ginny; but given that the fate of what she'd worked for over the past several years was now firmly in the hands of Jim Stanton, it was her belief that he was a far more important figure than she.

Behind them were a number of open cars: one carrying Devlin McGregor, Georges Ventine, Cynthia Fossett, and Gerhardt Schmidt; then three more holding Jiro Kawamoto, Nombeko Nseki, Baingana Wulandari and representatives from all of the Council's member nations.

At exactly 1:59 PM they pulled out of the garage and took a left onto Constitution Avenue, inserting themselves between a university marching band from Japan and a troupe of ribbon dancers from Brazil.

It was quite a spectacle.

The parade had attracted people from all over the world, many waving signs, flowers, and any number of space-related souvenirs which street merchants had been only too happy to provide.

As they began moving slowly down Constitution Avenue, passing the National Archives on their right, the crowd erupted in cheers and applause. Multi-colored confetti rained down on their heads, launched by truck-mounted confetti cannons parked along the route on either side of the road.

In the second car back, Cynthia, Devlin, Georges Ventine and Gerhard Schmidt all waved vigorously to the crowd. All of them had seen their lives change considerably since their appointments to various Mission posts, and each had experienced their share of publicity as the Mission evolved—especially Cynthia, who was now quite used to being recognized. To the rest of them, however, the immediacy, the adulation, and the emotion of this event was unlike anything that had gone before.

It was gratifying, as they'd all worked extremely hard to prepare the *Humanity* and its crew for life on Cerulea; but it was more than that. Ventine leaned back against the seat and surveyed the scene, as sunshine and confetti showered their car. He thought to himself how much he was looking forward to slowing down once it was all over.

Ventine's schedule for the past three and a half years had been exhausting. It seemed as if a decade or more had passed since the day he'd received that first call from Roger Tucker as he navigated the streets of Paris on his way to meet Martine. Nonetheless, despite the hours, the challenge had been incredibly rewarding. Initially, Ventine found himself concerned that, as the leader of the agricultural effort, his responsibilities would be overburdened by bureaucratic chores. But Tucker and Commander Belechenko had been true to their promises; they had sheltered Ventine from much of the politics and paperwork, permitting him to focus on building a great team and conducting the science necessary to finish the job.

Unfortunately, Ventine had to pay a very high price for his new position; after he'd accepted, his fiancé decided they should postpone their wedding. Over the next year their relationship atrophied badly, then ended as the time they spent together dwindled to practically nothing. The separation had been painful but tolerable; Martine understood the importance of Ventine's appointment, and acknowledged that circumstances had conspired to pull them apart.

For two years thereafter, Ventine had been busier than at anytime in his career, and allowed himself little time to dwell on the sacrifice he'd been forced to make. Then, as the launch neared, he—along with other functional leaders on the Council—was flooded with offers from organizations vying to recruit him once the *Humanity* departed. One offer was from Syngenta, his old sponsor. It was more or less a blank check; they were asking him to build and operate a research facility in the location of his choosing, with a small team of his choosing. Pure research; no pressure to produce products.

He started to think back to his dream of living on a farm with Martine, raising a family, and tinkering in his lab. This sparked in him an overwhelming desire to reconnect with Martine; he deliberated anxiously over whether to give her a call. He finally decided it was a bad idea, then, a day later, threw aside his hesitations. After a few awkward moments, they lapsed into comfortable conversation; he sensed that she was happy to hear from him. They talked for two hours, and then several more times over the last few weeks. Just yesterday, he'd finally asked if she might like to get together after the launch, and she had agreed.

Ventine hadn't a clue what might come of it, but it was wonderful to hear her voice again and to feel his emotions coming back to life. Since they'd planned their date, he'd had a difficult time thinking of anything else.

He looked up at the flurry of swirling confetti above them, and felt more relaxed than he had in years.

As the parade passed between the Department of Justice and the Museum of Natural History, the marching band in front of them began playing Strauss' *Voices of Spring*, a composition that had had become an unofficial anthem for the Cerulean adventure. Cynthia briefly closed her eyes and let the music and the noise of the crowd wash over her. She happened to love this particular piece of music—ever since she'd first heard it as a child. She reopened her eyes and turned to the crowd in front of the Museum. She waved as she looked into the faces of dozens of well wishers waving back. A very old man tipped his hat. A small girl, no older than four or five, clapped her hands and grinned while seated atop her father's shoulders, a stain of chocolate ice cream ringing her mouth. A man with a mustache and beard, wearing a hat and glasses stood motionless, staring at her as her car rolled by.

Cynthia's eyes swept passed the man, then stopped. That face, those eyes were somehow familiar, but she couldn't quite place them. She turned and looked back at where he'd been but couldn't find him again in the crowd. Her eyes scanned the mass of people while her mind sought to put a name on the face she'd just seen. After half a minute, Devlin tapped her on the shoulder, and pointed. She gave up on her search and looked in the direction he'd indicated. A group of college-age kids, dressed in judges' robes were holding aloft a large banner that read "We the people salute Judge Fossett for creating a more perfect planet!" Cynthia laughed; she and Devlin waved to the group, which elicited wild cheers in response.

As their cars approached the next intersection, Ginny could see the signs and hear the chants of the protesters above the otherwise supportive crowd. The permit for their demonstration confined them to roughly 200 feet of 12th Street north of Constitution Avenue. On the one hand, this was an excellent location; it was in the middle of the parade route, making it difficult for a news camera to pan the event and miss the protesters signs. On the other hand, it was completely invisible from the base of the Washington Monument where she would soon be giving her speech, perfectly blocked by the Museum of American History.

As the car passed, the protesters chants grew louder. Ginny noted one sign equating her with the Antichrist; another offered what she hoped was meant as prophesy and not as a threat: *Repent, or ye shall all perish!* Clearly, by reading their signs and offering her attention, Ginny was giving these people exactly what they wanted, so she turned to face the opposite side of the street, and waved to those who waved back with smiling faces.

◌

Finally, after one mile and 20 minutes, the head of the parade reached 17th Street, and all three cars turned left. They headed down 17th and took another left onto the grounds of the Washington Monument, traveling a small access road which brought them to the base of the white stone obelisk.

114.

The Washington Monument soared above the stage, guarding the members of the Mission Council as they took their seats on their assigned dais. The afternoon light amplified the disparity in tone between the top of the monument and its base.

At 555 feet, it remained the tallest stone structure in the world. The plan to build it was launched in 1833, at the 100th anniversary of George Washington's birth, but the construction effort was plagued by political machinations. When the civil war halted construction in 1860, only 152 feet of the monument had been erected.

After construction finally resumed in 1879, it took just 4 years to finish the remaining 403 feet. However, the stones used in the final construction effort were mined from a different quarry than those that form the base; as a result, there was a distinct difference in color between the lighter stones at the bottom, and the darker stones which form the top two thirds of the tower.

Against this backdrop, the first speaker rose to deliver her address. Ekta Pratesh was the 11th Secretary General of the United Nations, serving her third term. If success in this role equated to the lessening or halting of armed conflict across the globe, then Ekta Pratesh had been extremely effective—or extremely lucky. During her twelve years in office, the United Nations had successfully quelled or resolved over 19 separate wars and insurgencies.

But she was also getting old. At 82, she no longer had the stamina to serve as diplomat, cheerleader, and traveling salesmen for what was still a somewhat contentious organization.

As she made her way to the podium, the audience of seated VIPs applauded heartily. Those seated onstage applauded as well. Cynthia Fossett was sitting almost at the end of the row; Devlin on her right, Ventine on her left.

As the applause subsided, the Secretary General began her remarks.

"Members of the United Nations, members of the Mission Council, ladies and Gentleman. The road that has brought us here has been long, fraught with stubborn obstacles and unforeseen setbacks. However, the Mission Council has ably navigated our way forward, and we now stand on the threshold of one of mankind's greatest endeavors.

"The Mission to Cerulea has involved the direct efforts of over 29 nations. People from radically different cultures have overcome their differences, and achieved what many thought impossible. This coming together, this melding of personalities and perspectives, has ultimately made every aspect of this mission—its crew, its plans for Cerulean society, its very goals and dreams—infinitely stronger.

"Might the effort to mount this journey have been a good deal easier if just one nation had governed all aspects of its planning and execution? I dare say it would have. But if that had been the case, would the mission truly represent the people of Earth? I believe that it most certainly would not.

"There has been much concern expressed by many in America—and others across the globe—that the Cerulean colony will lack religious faith and that Cerulean society will be overly secular in nature. There is a fear that the populace will fail to appreciate the higher powers at work in our universe, and that it will fail to instill in future generations a deep appreciation for the almighty.

"I would beg to differ.

"As many of you know, I am a deeply religious person. But as a Hindu, I fully accept—and even embrace—the notion that different people will practice their faith in very different ways.

"When the Earth Spaceship *Humanity* sets out on its journey, it will carry with it people from over 100 different nations. This diversity of race, culture and ethnicity is accompanied by an equal diversity of thought. Among the crew, there is a great and wonderful disparity of beliefs with regard to many different facets of life. These are as simple as differing tastes in diet and dress, and are as complex as cultural and personal values, and religious beliefs.

"Provided that these differences do not cause harm to others, they are to be exalted and cherished. Diversity is healthy. It encourages and nourishes freedom of thought. It will serve to make the Cerulean experience richer and more interesting. It is, as the old saying goes, the spice of life.

"As I contemplate the future of the Cerulean colony, my greatest fear is that this diversity may be imperiled by those who wish to impose their views on the greater society. The only defense against such homogenization is a government that is structured specifically to support and defend the beliefs of all citizens—especially those whose religious, political or sexual predilections sit apart from an emerging majority.

"This does not mean that Cerulea must be a bastion of secular humanism; surely there is an inherent danger in any pure technocracy—just as there is also danger in any theocracy. It simply means that if one wishes to pursue self-realization through science and reason, they should be entirely welcome to do so. Just as

Cerulea's laws and institutions should reinforce the individual's right to worship their chosen deity, they must also respect the idea that the scientific method—and the truths it reveals—also deserve protection.

"Let us not forget that our ability to travel the immense distance between Earth and Cerulea is a direct result of man's intense pursuit of scientific truth. Without this pursuit, mankind's ability to prevent and overcome disease, our ability to successfully feed the majority of the world's populace, our ability to understand the complexity of our planet's ecosystems—would never have evolved."

"So as we gather today to celebrate the imminent departure of the Humanity, let us also celebrate the wisdom of the many nations that make up the Mission Council; for they have created a governmental framework that strives to protect the diversity of the Cerulean citizenry..."

As the Secretary General neared the end of her remarks, Cynthia shuddered slightly, reflecting on the magnanimity of the moment. They had indeed traveled a very long road; despite all of the controversy, the mission was at last culminating in a successful conclusion. She looked out at the audience as she listened, starstruck by the impressive collection of dignitaries sitting in the front row.

She scanned the line of faces, seeing how many she could name. As she reached the far end of the row, her eyes rested on an unknown but yet somehow familiar face. Then she realized why it was familiar, and she froze.

Her heart started racing; the man she'd seen during the parade was seated at the far end of the front row. Only he'd removed his hat, and it was suddenly evident who he was. Despite the glasses, mustache and beard, the man sitting before her was clearly Jeff Wheeler.

115.

Doug continued scanning the rows of filled seats. *The son of a bitch has got be here somewhere*, he said to himself, inwardly panicking but doing his best to remain outwardly focused.

He had entered the area using credentials that Butler had arranged for him. As far as the security detail was concerned, he was just another VIP suffering through a few boring speeches.

His initial instincts when he'd arrived were to inform the agent in charge of the pending threat; but he knew all too well that, in order to make the warning credible, he would have to explain way too much. Besides, if he could just get his hands on the guy and get him out of there before anything happened, no one would have to be the wiser.

It had been a hell of a day. At around 9 am Doug had found Wheeler's hotel room; earlier that morning, Wheeler had used the secure phone he'd been given, and Doug had been able to track its location. But when Doug got there, Wheeler had already left. There was an open newspaper on the desk, and a handwritten note on top of it:

To President Belknap, the Mission Council, and the world at large:

I offer no apologies for my actions.

The Mission to Cerulea, as currently structured, is deeply flawed. While I had hoped that the actions of others might successfully halt the mission or at least repair its rejection of God, I realize now that it may be unstoppable, and will most likely depart as planned in less than a week's time.

This is a travesty of God's will. He has given us life, given us reason with which to explore His eternal truths, and taught us the path to His Kingdom through his son, Jesus Christ. That we could reach beyond our planet to another, extending ourselves as God's greatest creation, without giving unto Him the respect and devotion He so very much deserves, is an insult of the highest order.

Any death or injury I may have caused should be seen as a message; a warning to all of the evolutionists, the abortionists, the pagans, the feminists, and the homosexuals who have sought to secularize human civilization—and by extension, Cerulean society.

As the Apostle Paul wrote to Jesus in Romans 1:24: "They are fully aware of God's death penalty for those who do these things, yet they go right ahead and do them anyway. And, worse yet, they encourage others to do them, too."

Let my actions point the finger at you, for it is you that bear ultimate responsibility—not just for the violence surrounding this mission, but for the corruption of what might have been a blessed planet, free of the blasphemous behavior that plagues Earth in our time.

For everything there is a season, and a time for every purpose under heaven: A time to be born, and a time to die; A time to kill, and a time to heal; a time to keep silence, and a time to speak; a time for war, and a time for peace.

I pray for Cerulea; I pray that the righteous among its inhabitants shall find the strength and power to rise up and lead its people toward the light of God's love.

Jeffrey A. Wheeler

June 7, 2038

After reading the note, Doug saw that the newspaper underneath was displaying an agenda of the day's activities. Between that and the note's not-so-subtle quote from Ecclesiastes, it was quite clear what Wheeler had in mind. Doug arrived at the parade route 20 minutes later, but had so far come up empty-handed. No sign of Wheeler anywhere.

He turned to look back at the stage before starting another scan of the audience, and saw Cynthia Fossett, white as a sheet, slowly get up from her chair and walk down the steps at the back of the stage.

He sensed that whatever had caused her to leave that stage was somehow related to his reason for being there.

He watched as Cynthia approached a security agent and spoke in his ear while subtly pointing to the opposite end of Doug's row. His eyes darted over to where she was pointing, and landed on the disguised Wheeler.

Doug noted that Wheeler was holding something tightly in his hand, with his thumb capping his fist. *Holy shit*, he said to himself, instinctively charging in front of the stage toward Wheeler.

One of the security agents turned to face him, but Doug had too much momentum, and simply barreled the man into the crowd as he passed. The other agents had all been alerted to Wheeler's presence through their earpieces, and were converging.

But they were too late; Wheeler had scrambled up onto a corner of the stage, with several agents right behind him. Doug raced along the front of the stage, leapt up a small set of narrow steps, and put himself on a collision course with Wheeler, who was heading straight for President Belknap and Jim Stanton.

Doug slammed into Wheeler's hip with his shoulder and grabbed him around the waist. Inside Wheeler's shirt, Doug could feel the compartmentalized belt, and knew straight way that this would not end happily.

The force of the tackle sent both men off the side of the stage. As they flew through the air, Doug's last thought was of Derek Butler; once again, he had come through for his old boss.

116.

Devlin McGregor, along with Nombeko Nseki, four representatives of the Mission Council, seven dignitaries, and three security agents, lay on the grass. Each was enclosed in a dark green, polyethylene, heat sealed body bag. All of them were dead.

Wheeler and Doug would have been in body bags as well—had there been anything left of them.

President Belknap, Ekta Pratesh and 34 others had already been taken to George Washington University Hospital, with injuries ranging from minor to critical. Ginny and Pratesh each had a separate security detail; when Wheeler mounted the stage, the two of them and Belechenko had been pulled off the back of the platform and shielded by agents, one of whom had lost his life in the explosion. Pratesh was badly hurt, but stable. Ginny had gone on to the hospital mostly as a precaution; Belechenko had stayed behind.

Georges Ventine and Jim Stanton were still trapped in what was left of the stage; both were presumed dead. But Belechenko, more than a little distraught, wasn't going anywhere until Stanton's body had been retrieved.

Cynthia, in large part a result of her having left the stage just before the blast, was virtually unscathed.

She sat in a folding chair with a blanket over her shoulders, drinking some hot mixture she'd been given by an EMT, and watching the emergency workers cut through the mangled aluminum carcass. Her eyes were red and puffy, but the explosion of tears had played itself out.

One of the workers successfully cut through a stubborn, fused mass of metal that had inhibited their progress; the hulk creaked as its own weight pulled open a crevice down the center. The worker called for help as several other men and women came and began pulling the two sides further apart. Belechenko joined in.

Another emergency worker yelled for the group to hold up; he disappeared inside the mass, and then, slowly, emerged with the body of Jim Stanton. As the worker was laying him on the ground, Stanton began blinking and coughed several times. The group cheered.

Moments later, Stanton was on his feet, one arm around an EMT, the other around Belechenko. All three got into an ambulance, and sped off to the hospital.

After 35 minutes of agonizingly slow but steady progress in dissecting the wreckage, they located Ventine; critically injured, but still alive. He was carefully placed on a stretcher and taken immediately to the hospital. Cynthia rode along with him.

117.

Stanton, as it turned out, had miraculously escaped with just a mild concussion and a sprained wrist. As he prepared to leave the hospital and return to the *Humanity*, he joked with Belechenko to let him know when his next all-expense paid trip to Earth might be. Belechenko replied firmly that this would be his last.

Ventine was not as lucky. He'd suffered a broken collarbone, a punctured lung, a broken ankle, a broken nose, and various cuts and lacerations. Nonetheless, he would heal. On the plus side, Martine flew in from France, determined to remain at his side and help him convalesce.

The story dominated the press for several days. Wheeler was described as a Christian fundamentalist fanatic who had lived what appeared to be a double life, although details were frustratingly murky. He had somehow managed to obtain White House credentials for the event, and had thus escaped closer scrutiny by security personnel.

There was an open question as to whether he had used his biometric identity pass dating back to the Belknap administration; if so, it would have been a breach of security with regard to both White House transition protocol and on-site security procedures. The agent who had apparently checked Wheeler in was quite certain that he'd presented valid and current White House credentials. This was immediately ruled impossible by the White House and the agent was dismissed from his job.

The story faded in priority, however, as the imminent launch of the *Humanity* took center stage. All over the world, different nations and cities had organized ceremonies and send-offs ranging from fireworks over Hong Kong and Sydney Harbor to candle-lit prayer vigils in Rome and Sao Paulo to colorful festivals in New Delhi and Beijing.

The ship's departure was as big an event as Earth had ever experienced. Though there would be no dramatic blast-off, there were few humans on the planet who did not plan on watching at least some portion of the launch proceedings.

In New York City, the harbor had filled with tall ships, now ancient reminders of civilized man's humble but adventurous beginnings. Ginny and Belechenko had been invited aboard the France II, a replica of the famed five-masted barque originally constructed in 1911.

It was a beautiful warm, starlit night.

Following various speeches and ceremonies, they and what seemed like a good portion of the city's residents were treated to a tremendous pyrotechnic extravaganza, a 2-hour, choreographed fireworks display that had delighted the huge crowd.

Ginny and Belechenko were, at long last, heading back to their hotel on Central park. Ginny leaned her head on Belechenko's shoulder as the limousine crawled forward in downtown traffic.

They were both very tired. Their schedule had been filled with back-to-back events beginning with last week's parade in Washington. As a result, neither had really fully digested the horrific events of that day.

Belechenko was thinking about the tremendous anger and hostility that Jeff Wheeler, Randall Reese and others had directed toward the Mission, when Ginny broke into his thoughts.

"Vlad, do you ever wish you were going on the expedition to Cerulea?"

Belechenko put his arm around Ginny. "Oh, I suppose so. There've been a few times when I've found myself envious of Jim Stanton. It is the ultimate adventure for an astronaut."

Ginny looked up at Belechenko; he bent his head down gently and kissed her softly on the lips. "But those thoughts are fleeting." He smiled and took her hand in his. "I have a hard time imagining us growing old together on board a spaceship." He kissed her again.

The limousine passed Bryant park, and the traffic lessened. Their car accelerated up 6th Avenue. "How about you?" he asked finally.

"To tell the truth, the whole thing seems rather exhausting," Ginny said with a sigh. "But part of me wishes my daughters were going. Not for the adventure, only so that they—and their children—could live their lives somewhere other than Earth."

Belechenko looked back down at Ginny. "What makes you say that?"

"I'm just not that big a fan of what we've done to this place," Ginny answered. "There was a time when I had tremendous hope for what might still be accomplished, and tons of energy for solving the problems we face."

"But now, I sometimes think that mankind's future on Earth is more about survival than it is about really living—let alone thriving."

"Wow. That's a pretty depressing thought."

Ginny sat up and looked into Belechenko's eyes, their faces just inches apart. "I guess it is a depressing thought, isn't it?"

118.

Ginny looked at the faces of the crew, seated in a crescent before her. The event was being held in the forward torus of the *Humanity*, in an outdoor garden near the main administrative facility. The view beyond the audience was of the rich, green valley below, and the silver-blue lake that ran down its center.

"Your responsibility, as emissaries of Earth, is to take with you to Cerulea all that is good about the human race, and to leave behind all that is bad. Sometimes, what is good and what is bad will not be obvious; all of you will have to make choices, and judge for yourselves. As you do, remember that every positive action you take sets an example; every negative action establishes precedent."

The journey from Earth the day before, with Belechenko by her side, had been exhilarating. While she'd seen the ship many times on one screen or another, it was something entirely different to approach it by shuttlecraft, then tour its vast interior in person. It was, by anyone's estimation, magnificent. Since her arrival, she had felt continuously in awe—and at the same time very proud to have helped bring this enterprise to life.

"Life on Earth is full of negative actions that we all accept as inevitable, as unavoidable foibles or flaws in our species. Do not accept them on Cerulea; there is no reason that the ugliness and pettiness of human history must follow you to a new world.

"Conflict will undoubtedly occur, as it occurs among most living species. I dare say this is part of the human condition. The question is how that conflict will be addressed and resolved. Is it possible that humans on Cerulea will never see war? Yes, it is possible; but it will never happen unless you make it happen, unless all of you are determined to consistently settle differences by some means other than force and weaponry, and to teach your children to do the same."

Ginny had written her speech herself over the past several weeks. She'd thrown away several earlier drafts, wrestling with whether this should be a pep talk for the journey through space, a celebration of the expedition as the ultimate human achievement, or thoughtful advice for a new civilization.

In the end, she'd decided on the latter. It seemed a bit presumptuous, but she was, after all, the U.S. President who had guided and architected this venture. To a large degree, she felt responsible for the fate of this crew. If at all possible, she wanted to light a spark within each of them so that, collectively, they might take it upon themselves to help steer their new democracy in the right direction, and not fall prey to behavioral maladies that still plagued the people of Earth in the year 2038.

"As the U.N. Secretary General noted in her speech last week, before it was so violently interrupted, this crew's diversity should be cherished and vigorously protected. It will no doubt prove to be one of Cerulea's most valuable assets.

"However, it may also prove to be the cause of most conflict. As we've seen throughout the course of history, those with one set of beliefs often seek to influence those with another; who more often than not, resist. Both the desire to influence and the resistance is natural; it has gone on since sentient man first walked the Earth. The problem occurs when, instead of engaging each other in dialogue, and attempting to use reason as a means for altering one another's viewpoint, we resort to force or intimidation.

"Force and intimidation are two very different things; force typically involves the threat of punishment such as physical harm or imprisonment. This is the tool used by tyrannies; I certainly hope it never manifests itself on Cerulean soil. Intimidation, on the other hand, is often seen in a democracy. Though it is usually more subtle, it can be equally or even more powerful. If I can convince you that any belief other than my own somehow threatens the safety of all, I may well succeed in altering your viewpoint. If I can get a majority behind me, my chance of success increases several fold.

"In short, by painting dissent as treason, it is possible for one person to effectively rob another of their freedom of thought. And nothing, absolutely nothing, is more vital to the health of a civilization than freedom of thought."

Ginny paused, and looked around at various members of the crew. She wondered whether they found her speech thought-provoking, or if they found it too preachy—or if any of them were even listening. *Maybe I'm way off base here*, she thought to herself.

Wary that the event was being televised, she nonetheless decided to go out on a limb, looking out at the crew and gesturing with her hands. "Does anyone know why I'm dwelling on all of this?"

Slowly, one or two hands tentatively went up, then perhaps five more. She called on a young woman halfway back on the right, who stood up. She was probably in her late teens or early twenties. "I think you're trying to warn us that a small group can easily go astray if it lets its leaders convince them that disagreement with their views is somehow wrong."

Ginny smiled. "That's exactly what I'm saying," she said softly, nodding at the young woman. "Thomas Jefferson, addressing the dangers of tyranny, is believed to have said 'The price of freedom is eternal vigilance.' This is a price that all of you, as Ceruleans, must be willing to pay.

"Many people believe that freedom is a god-given right. Perhaps it is, but it is not necessarily our natural state. Over the course of history, many more have lived under despotism than democracy. Freedom is and always has been earned through effort. It is a privilege that you must work very hard to achieve and maintain.

"I know that most of you are well aware of the bloodshed that led up to today's launch. Last week's incident in Washington was tragic; we all mourn the death of Devlin McGregor, whose efforts serve as the foundation of this Mission.

"I will miss Devlin terribly, and I mourn all of the others whose lives were lost as a result of this Mission." She thought of Roger, but chose not to single him out. "Last week's horrific explosion, the incident on the Washington Mall, the sabotage of a Mission convoy in Louisiana—these will collectively take their place among innumerable such events witnessed during the last several decades.

"All of them have something in common: they are all the direct result of one bloc of individuals seeking to impose its views on another. Is there ever a time when such violence is justified? The answer, I offer cautiously, is yes—but only under very specific conditions: only when one party is oppressed; only when one party lacks the recourse to effect change through other, non-violent means.

"The Constitution that will govern Cerulean civilization offers such recourse. Use it. Argue vigorously, debate artfully, engage each other and your elected representatives in forceful discussion on whatever issue you deem important to Cerulea's health and future. And to those of you who will serve in positions of leadership, I say this: use all of the methods, procedures and tactics that your Constitution offers; but do not break the laws of your new world to impose your will.

"As soon as you decide that the end justifies the means, you have taken the first step down a path that will inevitably weaken your democracy, weaken the rule of law, and lower yourself and your entire civilization in the eyes of your citizenry and those who would observe your progress as a people."

As she moved to conclude her speech, Ginny switched gears and spoke about the personal challenges that each of them would face, and sought to lessen their inevitable fears and anxiety over leaving Earth forever.

"To date mankind's exploration of space and other planets has been the purview of astronomers and scientists. Your journey marks a turning point, after which the presence of ordinary humans in space and on other planets will become commonplace. As you depart for Cerulea, rest assured that, just as we have transformed the crossing of oceans from months to minutes, so too will we transform the passage to Cerulea from years to days.

"I do not doubt that my great-grandchildren will one day greet yours face to face; whether on Cerulea, on Earth, or on some new world we have yet to discover.

"In the meantime, best of luck *Humanity*, and Godspeed."

After applause and handshakes between Ginny and the ship's officers, she briefly returned to the podium to introduce Supreme Mission Commander Vladimir Belechenko.

Belechenko acknowledged those in attendance, and noted that his comments would be brief.

"Throughout my career I have given much thought to what might one day be possible in space," he told the audience. "But I never dared dream that travel to, and colonization of, a remote, habitable planet would occur in my lifetime. I feel very fortunate to have helped guide this effort.

"Perhaps the most fortunate, however, are all of you. Everything you are about to experience will represent a first in human history. While I have enjoyed several such firsts in my many years in space, none of them compare to what all of you will see and do in a single day of the voyage to come.

"I salute each and every one of you for your courage and hard work; I'm confident that, as a team, you will make your home planet very proud."

After Belechenko embraced each officer, all rose for the playing of an abridged version of Strauss' *Voices of Spring*. This had been Cynthia's idea, and it seemed a fitting conclusion to the ceremony.

Once the piece had ended, Belechenko and Ginny were escorted by Stanton to a maglev.

"By the way, Jim," Belechenko noted softly, "I've had a small gift placed in everyone's living quarters to make sure they will not forget us; it's a crystal replica of planet Earth."

"Commander, I can't speak for the entire crew," Stanton replied, "but I need no such reminder. I will remember you always, and think of you often."

Belechenko put a hand on Stanton's shoulder, and glanced at the brace on his forearm. "Per Aspera Ad Astra."

Jim smiled. "Nothing truly worth doing is ever easy."

Belechenko held Ginny's hand as she climbed into the maglev, followed her in, and they were off.

☯

Through the expansive windows of the space limo, Ginny and Belechenko watched and listened, as the *Humanity* went through its final pre-launch check list with Mission Control. At long last, they were ready to go.

"Nav three, ion engines to K-1," Stanton commanded.

"Bridge, ion engines moving to K-1"

The *Humanity* began moving away from the L5 spaceport. Although the ship had logged many millions of miles in her test runs, this was her first actual step toward Cerulea.

"Mission control, we are away and clear," Stanton offered.

"Roger that, *Humanity*, we have you clear. Godspeed."

The ship began to accelerate toward the outer reaches of Earth orbit. Several thousand people at L5, along with over five billion more down on the planet, watched as the ship carried one thousand human beings to their new life on a brand new world.

As the ship turned slightly, setting the first course of the long journey, Captain Jim Stanton offered one last thought to all those listening.

"From the new citizens of Cerulea to those of Earth: although the distance between us shall be great, we shall always be one. May the stars shine more brightly with us among them."

Ginny and Belechenko smiled, and watched as the *Humanity* became ever smaller, then vanished into the great expanse of space.

The space limo was now quiet. Ginny felt exhilarated yet also tremendously sad as she stared at the blackness that was now the new headquarters of the Mission to Cerulea.

She turned to Belechenko. "Vlad, what was it you said to Jim as we left the ship? It was in Latin."

"Oh, it's an old expression between astronauts. It means 'through adversity to the stars.'"

Epilogue

R andall Reese climbed out of the maglev and walked slowly down the path to an octagonal structure featuring eight doors, one on each side. Behind him, the vehicle powered up and returned itself to its assigned hub.

He looked down the valley, and saw several children playing at the edge of the lake. The light had assumed a dusk-like quality, spreading a gold tint across the forested floor of the giant torus.

Reese walked halfway around the right side of the structure and opened one of the doors, entering one of the two rooms that made up his living quarters, this one a small sitting room, the other a bedroom. His wife, Sylvia, was reading with her feet up on a reclining chair made of aluminum and fabric mesh, and ergonomically designed such that it held her tablet at an appropriate distance from her eyes, letting her arms rest at her sides.

"Good evening, dear," she said, looking up from her reading, and swiveling the tablet off to the side. "How was your Bible class?"

Reese walked over and gave her a kiss on the forehead, then took a seat in a chair next to hers. "Oh, it was chaotic, as usual. The age difference in the children makes it difficult at times. Some of the older ones are clearly ready for more disciplined study, while the little ones demand so much effort just to keep them in their seats."

Sylvia laughed. "Sounds pretty normal. And how's that pretty young assistant of yours working out?" She looked over at him with a smile to make sure he knew she was only teasing him.

He smiled, but answered the question seriously. "I must say, she's a godsend. I certainly could never handle the group on my own."

Reese leaned back against the headrest and took his wife's hand in his. He closed his eyes briefly as his body began to relax.

The two of them would be celebrating their 50th wedding anniversary next month. Convincing her that the two of them should embark on this journey had not been easy; his central argument was that life aboard the *ESS Genesis* would be much more rewarding than growing old in some assisted living center in Wisconsin.

But in the end, it was not his powers of persuasion that convinced her. It was the decision of their son Jake, now in his 40s with a wife and two boys of his own, to join the crew of the *Genesis* and accompany his parents. To Sylvia, this was a gift from heaven; while she fully understood that her final days might be spent in space, they would at least be spent in the company of her family. Nothing, to her, was more important.

Another factor had, of course, been the increasingly difficult situation on Earth.

☯

When the *Genesis* departed L5 for the planet Cirque in the year 2055, world population had just passed nine billion. As predicted, growth had stabilized, but this was of little help to both developed and developing nations scrambling for resources to serve their needs. The United States, still one of the "Big Three" along with China and India, had begun rationing electrical power. The build-up of nuclear power plants begun early in the century had come to a screeching halt following the Yucca Mountain disaster in 2052, and U.S. households were forced to conserve in ways that seemed draconian to a populace completely unaccustomed to sacrifice. Solar, wind, biofuels and geothermal were all racing to fill the shortage, but it would take time.

Global warming had also wreaked havoc in so many ways. Major cities in the American southwest which had boomed up through the 2030s, including Phoenix and Las Vegas, were now experiencing an accelerated decline in population as average temperatures climbed precipitously and air conditioning was no longer a given. The same was true of desert regions on other continents. Coastal cities on the Atlantic seaboard were also witnessing massive demographic shifts as summer storms and rising waters made waterfront real estate virtually impossible to maintain, let alone insure. The forearm of Cape Cod had been breached in two different places, so that the Cape itself was now really just a stump protruding from southern Massachusetts. Likewise, the Hamptons, Cape Hatteras, and the Florida Keys were all but inhabitable except for those willing to spend vast amounts of money on structures capable of withstanding a Cat 5. The phenomenon's global impact was more dire: refugees from island nations around the globe had become a critical issue.

Technology had steadily marched onward, and had been of considerable assistance in dealing with the impact of these global changes. For starters, using ever more powerful models running on ever more powerful computers, mankind's ability to predict storm behavior had improved several fold, while smart highway systems and gigantic hydrogen fueled air transports could efficiently manage the evacuation of a threatened region in a matter of hours.

However, for a period of time, severe shortages of copper, silver, gold and platinum jeopardized Earth's ability to manufacture all of the required electronics necessary for highways, vehicles, and pollution control equipment. The solution ultimately came from space.

Although Derek Butler left office after only one term, losing in 2040 to a more conservative challenger, the mining venture he'd covertly launched with James Torgan, Jodee Keeling and others in the late 30s proved prescient. By the time the *Goldstar* was launched, the price of platinum, a key ingredient in catalytic converters and a range of other emissions control technologies, had been driven to stratospheric highs as a result of rapidly dwindling supply. After its first two-year mission, the *Goldstar* returned with a payload valued at over $565 billion. The syndicate, which had assumed the unimaginative moniker "Astral Mining Corporation," and which was now openly led by Butler himself, completed three more ships, which were immediately put into service, and began contracting for more.

The company had, by necessity, become a pioneer in extrasolar planetary discovery and analysis. They owned and operated several of the most advanced space telescopes ever built. It was Astral Mining who had discovered Cirque, a planet roughly twice the size of Earth with an atmosphere that, like Cerulea, could fully support a human colony.

By the time the journey to Cirque began, the company's fleet had grown to over 23 ships; Astral Mining had become the single largest supplier of platinum to the planet, and a major supplier of copper and gold. Derek Butler had also become the wealthiest man in human history, with a net worth of just over six trillion dollars. James Torgan was a close second. In fact, it was their wealth that had ultimately financed a sizable portion of this new mission.

Initially, Cirque's discovery had been kept under wraps, as it wasn't clear how best to proceed. At this point in time, the idea of another Mission, financed by governments, was beyond impractical; even the Big Three were in no position to offer the necessary funds when so many of their citizens and geography required critical attention. So Astral Mining quietly formed a private consortium, and assembled a governing body with substantially different views from the Mission Council that had so inflamed religious conservatives 15 years prior.

Different corporations invested in the mission in return for temporary market exclusivity within the new colony, while a number of renowned conservatives, including Randall Reese, had assumed a prominent role in shaping how the new society would function. The project proceeded with intentionally little fanfare. Astral Mining built a magnificent new ship, the *ESS Genesis*, assembled the crew, and began its countdown without ever dominating what was now an all-electronic and highly fractured news cycle.

Ironically, it was during the countdown for the launch of the *Genesis* that the first close-up images of Cerulea were at last received on Earth. As far as was known, the crew of the *Humanity* had now been on the planet for over 15 years; these images, taken as the ship was entering the Cerulea's solar system, had taken that much time to make their way back to Earth.

They were spectacular. The topography of Cerulea was richly diverse; with what appeared to be 19 separate continents, two of which featured mountain ranges that dwarfed the Himalayas. Devlin's team had been correct—judging by the images, the planet's seasons were less pronounced than those on Earth. Weather patterns also appeared to be less severe—although few on Earth could even remember what normal weather patterns were like any more. All in all, Cerulea was remarkably similar to Earth, but it was pristine; clearly there were no indications that any intelligent species had developed the planet's surface in any way. While the ship—at the time the photos were taken--was still too distant to understand what other life forms might exist, it was plainly evident that much of the land mass was covered in vegetation. This had been expected, but its confirmation was, of course, a cause for some celebration to its approaching inhabitants.

The images, along with an accompanying report on the ship's successful journey, sparked a last-minute fervor around the impending departure of the *Genesis*; suddenly, everyone wanted a say in a mission that had nearly snuck out of orbit like a mouse tiptoeing past a sleeping cat.

Although the cat woke from its slumber, the mouse was already beyond reach. The ship was fully tested, the crew was fully trained, the cargo bays fully loaded. Any opportunity for the general public to have an influence on the mission—if such an opportunity had ever existed given the mission's private funding—had come and gone.

As a result, the ESS Genesis slipped out of spacedock with much public commentary but very little public celebration. If nothing else, it was clear to all that the human colony it foretold would be radically different from the one now taking shape on Cerulea. Virtually all aspects of the new civilization would reflect the conservative values of its benefactors; the crew was almost entirely Christian, save for a number of scientists and engineers recruited to manage the ship's systems. The new planet's constitution ensured that religion would play a central role in how its citizens would be governed; Bible study would be inherent in both elementary and secondary school curriculum.

In short, as mankind witnessed the passing of the mid-point of the 21st century, it appeared on the verge of successfully extending itself to not one but two new planets elsewhere in the universe. Those remaining behind on Earth could now only look to the stars and wonder how each of these two new worlds would fare.

☯

Afterword & Acknowledgements

This book was a pretty interesting journey.

A long time ago, in a galaxy far, far away, I graduated from college with a degree in English Literature. I then launched my career in the technology industry. Two decades later, an idea entered my brain for a novel, and circumstances allowed me to pause, take time out, and write the novel.

Circumstances include, of course, the encouragement and patience of my wonderful wife Jill, who was unbelievably supportive, and insisted that I stay on course and finish what I'd started. And my incredible children, Zach and Tracy, who each read earlier drafts of the book and offered terrific ideas and suggestions.

Way up there on the list of those to whom I owe many thanks is Cynthia Fox, an old friend from boarding school. She was the one who convinced me that the original idea and first several chapters showed sufficient promise that—well, I should actually quit my day job (temporarily) to see where the idea took me.

And there are countless others, including Congressman Lamar Smith, venture capitalist Bill Frezza, my sister Mindy, author Christina Baker-Kline, and author/dear friend Rosemary Graham. I suppose, however, that the ultimate helper behind the scenes was, simply, the internet. It boggles my mind to think about those who, not long ago, wrote novels like this without a world of knowledge at their fingertips. Without the web, I would never have had the patience.

I have no idea whether I'll ever try this again. If I'd known in advance that the effort to get a first book published is nearly equal to what it takes to write it—I don't think I ever would have taken the plunge. In fact, shortly after finishing the final draft, I took on a new role in the clean energy space, and only sporadically sought to get the book published. In the end, I published it myself.

So, if you liked the novel, and know of a great agent or publishing house (or Hollywood screenwriter or filmmaker) who might like to take a look, please let me know.

About the Author

In his everyday life, Nick d'Arbeloff works as an agent in the clean energy revolution, working to transform our energy infrastructure in the face of climate change and finite fossil fuel supply. He lives in Carlisle, Massachusetts.

⚭

Made in the USA
Charleston, SC
27 June 2013